57

Applause for Catherine Friend's Fiction

The Spanish Pearl

"Friend tackles both science fiction and romance in this adventurous tale...Is it really cheating if you have an affair nine hundred years before your partner is born, or does love and commitment span centuries and confound the linear nature of time? A most entertaining read, with a sequel already in the works. Hot, hot, hot!" — *Minnesota Literature*

"1085 AD is a perfect backdrop for this wild romp. The observations Kate Vincent, our plucky heroine, makes about eleventh century Spain through her contemporary eyes are priceless. This is a rollicking good tale, full of adventure, humor, romance, and high stakes suspense, for Kate's friends and foes are not always who or what they seem...The author does a terrific job with characterization, lush setting, action scenes, and droll commentary. This is one of those well-paced, exciting books that you just can't quite put down." — *Midwest Book Review*

"A fresh new author...has penned an exciting story...Exciting, thoughtful, and told with the right amount of humor and romance. Friend has done a wonderful job...*The Spanish Pearl is a hit.*" — *Lambda Book Review*

The Crown of Valencia

"...brilliant descriptions of people, time, and place. Her storytelling talent is superb and her plot twists continually keep the reader in suspense..." — *JustAboutWrite*

By the Author

The Spanish Pearl (Bold Strokes)

The Crown of Valencia (Bold Strokes)

A Pirate's Heart (Bold Strokes)

The Compassionate Carnivore: Or, How to Keep Animals Happy, Save Old MacDonald's Farm, Reduce Your Hoofprint, and Still Eat Meat (DaCapo)

Hit By a Farm: How I Learned to Stop Worrying and Love the Barn (DaCapo)

The Perfect Nest (Candlewick)

A PIRATE'S HEART

by

Catherine Friend

2008

ISBN 10: 1-60282-040-6
ISBN 13: 978-1-60282-040-1

This Trade Paperback Original Is Published By
Bold Strokes Books, Inc.
P.O. Box 249
Valley Falls, NY 12185

First Edition: December 2008

Credits
Editors: Cindy Cresap and Stacia Seaman
Production Design: Stacia Seaman
Cover Design By Sheri (graphicartist2020@hotmail.com)

Dedication

For Melissa

Acknowledgments

Many thanks to my publisher, Len Barot, for being patient as I juggled deadlines on different books and missed them all. I appreciate her flexibility.

My editor Cindy Cresap makes me feel brilliant, even when I'm not. My writing buddies Pat, Phyllis, and Lori bravely read a rough draft and gave me very helpful comments. And Phyllis proved to be a great source for pirate jokes, such as: What kind of socks do pirates wear? Arrrghyl socks.

Pirate stories are full of adventure, excitement, and romance, and I've tried to follow in the footsteps of the authors and screenwriters who've given us so many wonderful pirate stories over the years. It seems a pirate story should have a pirate, a ship, a treasure, a map, and if it's *really* good, it'll have a lovely wench as well…I decided that if one lovely wench was good, four would be even better.

PART ONE

THE PIRATE, 1715

Pirate captains were often vicious and sadistic villains whose careers rarely lasted more than two or three years. They were more likely to drown in a storm or suffer death by hanging than they were to live out their days in luxury on the riches they had plundered.

—David Cordingly, *Under the Black Flag*

Chapter One

1715, somewhere in the West Indies

Captain Thomasina Farris stood on the quarterdeck of the *Moon Shadow*, widening her stance as the ship rolled beneath her. While a pirate's life was short and dangerous and Tommy longed to escape it, when the *Moon Shadow*'s taut lines hummed, her sails snapped, and the waves beat pleasantly against the hull, Tommy didn't care, easily putting aside her burdens.

The *Moon Shadow* was a three-masted merchant ship Tommy'd stolen from a drunken captain, and it could handle both storm and battle surprisingly well for such a large ship. Tommy lifted her face to the sun, soaking up the moist, salty air, the gulls wheeling and calling overhead, the smell of tar and working men, the feel of the wind against her skin. When the tip of her braid whipped behind her like a tail, she draped it forward over her shoulder. Tommy's thigh-length hair, jet black save one shocking streak of pure white, terrified more sailors in the West Indies than the skull and crossbones.

Perched up in *Moon Shadow*'s crow's nest, fourteen-year-old Billy Flood had his arms wrapped around the mast, singing some bawdy tune as he watched for sails. The poor pup was madly in love with Tommy, which was why she refused to let him be her cabin boy. After her cabin boy had been killed by a cannonball last year, she'd struggled alone with her hair but refused to cut it since it was as powerful a weapon as her pistol or cutlass. Billy had begged for the job, but since he already dogged her heels all over the ship, she didn't need his moony eyes in her cabin as well.

Tommy's quartermaster and oldest friend, Ezekiel Sawkins, stood next to a gunner's mate on the forecastle and bawled him out for not doing a proper job of tying down a gun. Pirate ships not only kept guns below deck, with ports cut in the hull for running out the guns, but had guns mounted all along the upper deck to give them every advantage in a battle. Sawkins's already tanned skin glowed hot with anger as he cuffed the boy and showed him the proper way to tie down a gun so it didn't roll around deck and kill someone.

One deck down in the galley, Cookie banged pots and pans, and from the forward hatch beyond him came lighthearted insults from the crew's quarters as two men argued over a bet. She'd get involved only if it came to blows. Three men pounded oakum into gaps in the deck planking, their heavy mallets a chorus of reassuring thuds. Hatley stood mid-deck with the log line measuring their speed, counting the knots as they slipped over the rail. "Six knots," he called. These were the sounds of her world, and God help her, she loved them. She loved the ship, she loved the men, she loved the sea. It was the killing that'd begun wearing her down. That, and this blasted sadness hanging over her like a tropical thundercloud.

Below Tommy, the mid-deck hand pump squeaked as two men worked it. The *Moon Shadow* took on too much water without those damned pumps. Tommy lived day and night knowing the sea was reaching its fingers through the cracks in the hull, seeking to drown the ship and all one hundred souls aboard. Two other ships sailed in her fleet, so one strong storm and a heavy dose of bad luck could claim three ships and three hundred lives.

Sawkins appeared at her side, a compact man nearly thirty years old, and together they soaked up the sounds of their ship. "Noisy ship, ain't she?" Sawkins said.

"Noisy as a Newcastle whore," Tommy replied, and Sawkins laughed so hard he choked. He was a good man, and had been with Tommy since the beginning. When she'd formed up her first band of men, she'd been relieved when they'd voted Sawkins as quartermaster. You needed a fair man to be in charge of dividing up the spoils and running the ship, and there was none fairer or more honest than Sawkins.

Tommy's job on the pirate ship was navigation—without her they'd be lost since none of the crew could do the mathematics required. Her role as captain included inspiring her men, scaring them if necessary, and leading them in battle. Sawkins did the rest.

"Crikey, it's a sail!" Billy cried from fifty feet above the deck. Young Billy was almost always the first to sight a sail skimming the horizon. For pirates, a new sail was either a potential victim or a potential threat.

At his shout, Tommy's heart sped up a knot or two. "All hands make sail!" she cried. The men sprang into action, scrambling up rigging to unfurl the highest sails. Tommy raised the signal flags to her other two ships, letting them know she'd sighted a prize. The *Tiger Eye* and the *Windy Queen* followed to help as needed, but the plunder was shared three ways.

"Mr. Sawkins, let's be doing this quiet-like, shall we? No use giving the poor labbernecks a fright until we be right on their arses."

"Aye, Captain." Sawkins barked a command, and although excitement pulsed through the men, the pounding and singing and arguing stopped as they squared the ship for battle.

They followed the ship at a safe distance until Tommy could see that the small French sloop was cut for only six guns, hardly a match for the *Moon Shadow*'s twenty-four nine-pounders. Tommy moved quietly to mid-deck. Captains on pirate ships were elected, and all the men shared in the decisions about where to go and which prizes to pursue. "Listen here, you unhung rascals, there be a sloop ahead. It's floating low in the water, so it be loaded with goods, and an easy prize. What say you?"

The men raised fists in assent but kept silent.

Tommy grinned. "Well, then, methinks you'd better let the French dunderheads know we're here."

The war whoops began, and men streamed up from below to line the decks, pumped for a fight. Tommy ordered more sails raised, and soon the *Moon Shadow* had closed the distance to her prey to a mere one hundred yards. Gun ports slammed open and the deck rumbled as the *Shadow*'s guns were run out on the lower deck. Men began loading the guns, and the closer they drew to the sloop, the louder Tommy's crew yelled bloodcurdling promises of horrid tortures. Cookie stood near the hatchway banging two pans together. Hatley stood on the forecastle blowing on that infernal bagpipe. He couldn't play a note, which made him all the more effective.

Wincing at the shrill sound, Tommy moved past Hatley to the bow and rested one foot on the gunwale, two loaded pistols jammed into her sash. A sailor undid Tommy's braid so the black hair billowed out behind her like a velvety sail. Captured sailors often said that when they looked back at the *Moon Shadow* pursuing them and saw Tommy standing in the bow, it was as if the Devil's own shadow bore down upon them.

Even in the heat of the chase, Tommy registered that her ship was responding with the sluggishness she dreaded. After months at sea, the *Moon Shadow's* hull had once again become encrusted with speed-killing barnacles and other marine life, not to mention the planks that had pulled away from each other to let the seawater in. After this chase, there was naught to be done but find a quiet cove and careen the ship for maintenance.

The captain of the French sloop couldn't have missed their black-and-white flag, which declared Tommy'd give quarter if her prey yielded, but the fool took flight. The French crew yelled in fright as their captain shouted orders.

Sawkins handed Tommy her spying glass, a long monstrosity they had taken from a prize three years earlier. Through it she could see the French crew pointing toward the *Moon Shadow*, waving their hands to mimic her hair. Fear creased their sunburned faces, but the French captain sadly thought he could outrun them.

Sighing, Tommy returned the spyglass. "Sawkins, my musket."

"Aye, Captain. By my blood, these sacks of entrails'll be regretting they've run."

Tommy nodded. Nine times out of ten, captains chased by pirates surrendered in fear of the black pirate flag, the decks of pirate ships packed with bloodthirsty men howling like animals, and pirates' reputation for torture. One out of ten, however, thought he could outrun Tommy. He quickly learned how difficult it was to stay upright on a deck slick with his own blood.

The *Moon Shadow* drew up close behind the sloop but stayed out of her line of fire. Tommy didn't want to injure the ship with her cannon; some pirates believed in blasting holes in the ships they pursued, but

Tommy didn't unless necessary. While her men were hungry for a fight, she wasn't, so she took aim, noting the rhythm of the ship as it rose and fell under her feet, then she shot the poor helmsman of the French sloop.

The helmsman's death brought shouts and confusion on the sloop. The French captain ordered another man to the helm, but all hands refused, knowing Tommy would continue to shoot whoever stood at the wheel. Finally, the captain marched another poor devil there only by pressing a pistol to his back.

Shaking her head, Tommy accepted the reloaded musket from Sawkins and once again took aim. She considered shooting the new helmsman, then realized there was a better way to end this ridiculous flight. She shifted her aim slightly and shot a goodly-sized hole in the captain's back. The helmsman dropped as well and crawled behind the mizzenmast.

Within thirty seconds, the French crew struck its colors, lowered its sails, and came about. Sawkins brought the *Moon Shadow* alongside the sloop and put out the longboat so they could row over and board their new prize.

The French ship's first mate bowed deeply as Tommy stepped onto the deck, apologizing in halting English for his captain's folly. Sawkins shouted orders, as it was his job to record what they took so it could be split among the crew later. The gunner Coxon and his men collected weapons and discussed how to best pass the captured ship's six cannons over to the *Moon Shadow*, bringing her total guns to thirty. Sawkins reminded Coxon that Billy had earned the best pistol they found.

"That drooling puppy has more pistols than the Royal Navy," the gunner growled, but he would comply since the punishment for cheating another pirate was death. Ten of the French sailors decided to join the pirates, so Hatley took them back to the *Moon Shadow* to hear and sign the Articles.

As her men worked, the thrill of the chase still pounded through Tommy, an energy that didn't cease with the capture, so she climbed five feet into the rigging and looked out over the French crew, huddled around the mainmast.

Upon boarding a new prize, while Tommy's crew took stock of the provisions and booty on board, she took stock of the men and chose among them the most handsome, or at least the one with the most teeth, and took that man back into the captain's cabin. She'd learned, through unhappy experience, that intimacies with her own crew only led to jealousies, discipline problems, and lovesick sailors.

This prize was no different than others, so to the amused and lewd shouts of her men, Tommy chose a tall, slender Frenchie with freckles who blushed violently, obviously in possession of enough English to know her intent. She pulled the man into the captain's cabin and put her pistol down on the bunk, motioning for the man to do the same. "Don't be trying anything sudden, or I'll be blasting your head off." He nodded, and she reached for him. None of the men she'd chosen had ever resisted, and the Frenchie was no different.

A few minutes later, Tommy rearranged her clothing and returned on deck, wondering why the act held less pleasure each time she performed it.

"Here be the plunder, Captain," Sawkins said, waving his arms toward the material her men had begun moving to the *Moon Shadow*: two mizzenmasts, a mainsail, extra rigging, two canoes, about a hundred bags of flour, beans, and peas, five barrels of sweetmeats, a goodly amount of marmalade, dried beef, and a barrel of seal oil. That was it. No gold or silver or medicines. Or books. Tommy loved books. "Sorry, Captain," Sawkins said. "The sloop's riding so low because its holds are fillin' with water, not because it carries cargo."

Tommy nodded, but said nothing. She knew what her men would say. After a string of three highly prosperous years, Tommy and her crew had gone months without taking a decent prize. Few large ships had blown across their path, and as Hatley was fond of remarking, "no prey, no pay."

"Strip the ship and leave her," Tommy said. "Last thing we be needing is another ship to keep afloat." Inside an hour, they left the French crew with enough water and provisions to safely reach land, provided the sloop didn't sink first.

Tommy returned to the *Moon Shadow* and informed her men of the booty, attempting to make the marmalade seem as worthy as silver. Coxon scowled when she finished. "We ain't seen a decent prize for months. We're doing naught but chasing worm-ridden scum. Mebbe we be needing a new captain of this here ship."

Tommy, heart pounding, sauntered as close as she dared to the man's fetid breath, then rested her hand on her sword hilt. In her five years as pirate, it'd been necessary now and then to bash on a man's skull with her sword hilt to remind the crew she was captain not only by their choice, but because she could keep the crew in line.

Coxon was of ordinary stature, rawboned, very pale with dark hair. He was deaf in his left ear from cannon blast and was missing most of his right ear, also from a cannon mishap. He and Tommy were of the same height, but he outweighed her by a great deal.

"Who be captain of this ship now?" She tipped her sword back and ran the scabbard tip all the way up the inside of Coxon's thigh, stopping just shy of the Coxon family's disappointment. His jaw twitched, but he didn't jump back as she'd hoped.

"Ye," he muttered.

"And I'll still be captain when your rottin' corpse washes ashore. So quit the mutinous rumblings, keep that tongue behind your teeth, and stand off." Tommy kept her hand on her sword. Coxon was new, but surely even he realized if Captain Tommy unsheathed her sword, she wouldn't return it to its scabbard until she'd used it.

Coxon stomped away, and Tommy and Sawkins exchanged a cool glance. Sod it all to hell. There were bloody few benefits to being captain, yet she'd managed to cling to the job this long. She got two shares of the plunder, the quartermaster one and a half shares, and the rest of the men one share apiece. She ate the same weevil-infested hardtack they did, and had she been a man, she would have slept in the crews' quarters with them. The only allowance for her sex was that she could use the captain's cabin for privacy.

Being captain was all she knew. It was her only way to remain on ship and at sea. Were she voted out as captain, she'd lose the respect and fear that kept the men at bay. Her life would deteriorate faster than a dead fish in the sun until the men grew so bold that neither her bunk nor her body would be her own. No, being captain of a ragged horde of pirates was the only way she could continue to live free. She hated London, hated cities, and would die if she couldn't stand on the deck of a ship and see the horizon in every direction. She'd be a pirate until her death, which was coming soon enough.

"Great guns, Captain! Another sail!" Billy scampered down from the nearest yardarm.

Relieved to be done with Coxon, at least for now, Tommy climbed up into the rigging and shielded her eyes. Damn it. Avery Shaw's ship, the *Sharktooth*. Bloody bastard. For every man Tommy threatened to kill, Shaw killed ten. For every man Tommy tortured, Shaw tortured twenty. Tommy lived to feel the sea beneath her feet and Shaw lived to cause others pain.

She still cursed herself over Shaw because it'd been her fault he'd gone pirate. Three years ago she'd caught a small British sloop and had chosen Shaw for the visit to the captain's cabin. Most disappointing five minutes of her life, yet in his little mind he became the Chosen One. Tommy'd stripped the ship as usual and sailed away, since the last thing she needed aboard the *Moon Shadow* was a lover, especially such a clumsy one. But she'd ignited Shaw's interest in piracy, and within a few months he'd taken up the sweet trade as well. Tommy did her best to avoid him but heard of his exploits through the gossip.

As a pirate, Shaw was a total cock-up. The man couldn't navigate his way out of a barrel. He made stupid choices that got his men killed. Only his habit of letting his men rape any woman they came across kept his men from flaying him. That, and his dumb luck at taking rich prizes.

"He be raising a flag to talk," Billy said, opening the worn wooden chest storing the *Moon Shadow*'s flags.

"By thunder," Tommy snapped. "I'll do no such thing. Raise the flag that says 'Kiss my arse, you mealy-mouthed maggot.'"

Billy looked up, bewildered, then down at the assortment of colored flags in his hands. "Which one—"

"That would be no flag at all, ye little whelp," Sawkins said. "Helmsman, easy as she goes."

If she just ignored Shaw, he'd go away. Tommy stood on the quarterdeck as the *Shadow*'s sails snapped overhead. She disliked killing the captain of the French sloop. She took no joy from her snog with the Frenchie. She worried about being voted out as captain, and she was avoiding Shaw.

Bloody hell. Was she losing her nerve? How the hell would she hold her men together if she did? And if she lost her role as captain, what work could she do? Once she was off the water, she'd either be stuck working some hellhole of a pub or spreading her legs for a few coins. Only a blooming idiot would give up the sea for that. But God's blood, she was tired. What was the matter with her?

Chapter Two

Tommy stood on the broad, white beach, her boots sunk up to the ankles in warm sand. She gazed up at the *Moon Shadow* and *Tiger Eye*, both beached at low tide and tipped in the clear turquoise cove as if drunk. Crew worked in the waist-high water scraping and burning barnacles and seaweed from the hulls and stuffing oakum into the planking gaps. In a few days they'd heat up tar and recoat the boats' hulls. The *Windy Queen* lay in anchor farther out in the bay, rocking gently, sails furled.

Tommy disliked careening her ships. Not only were her men vulnerable with two out of their three ships lying useless in shallower water, but it also meant a week of walking on solid ground, which always made her queasy after months at sea. Some of the men preferred solid ground, but not Tommy.

To careen her ships, Tommy chose Sombrero Island, part of a string of small islands in the northeast corner of the West Indies. Sombrero had a sheltered cove to the north, and because the prevailing winds and currents ensured that few ships passed to the north of the island, Tommy and her men could work without being bothered. Since it'd been months since the *Moon Shadow* had put in at Tortuga, a pirate stronghold, or any other port friendly to pirates, careening was the men's rare chance to get off the ship.

Some of her crew hiked inland, seeking fresh water to fill water casks, while others combed the beach for clams, crabs, and turtles. Her only complaint with turtles was that Cookie couldn't bear to keep them on their backs, alive, until he needed them for soup, so they either wandered the mid or lower decks, tripping Tommy, or found their way into the galley and consumed the greens Tommy was growing in three boxes of soil. Tommy felt murderous when something ate her greens.

Beside Tommy stood the other two captains in her fleet, McLeod and Stratton. Four years ago she'd captured a Dutch brigantine, named it the *Windy Queen*, and her men had elected the most popular man among them, McLeod, to be the captain. The pirate band grew as Tommy took on more sailors from captured ships or men who'd fled the brutal life in the Royal Navy, and soon the two ships grew crowded. Two years ago Tommy captured a British sloop, and the men elected Stratton as captain of the *Tiger Eye*. Tommy, McLeod, and Stratton made fleet decisions together, but the younger men always agreed with her. Both men loved to tell her that when all three crews were drinking and whoring in Tortuga, the men made sure everyone knew they were "Tommy's boys."

"My men be restless," McLeod said, voice gravelly from months of shouting at sea. McLeod was of ordinary stature, squint-eyed, with thin brown hair.

Stratton nodded. "As are mine. Mark me, if we don't come across some silver soon, we'll be tossed off our own ships." Stratton's bony face and twisted nose gave him the appearance of always being unhappy, yet his broad smile always ruined that impression. Both men had proved steady in battle, fearless in storms, and welcome brothers to Tommy in all other times.

"Tommy." Stratton nodded up the beach. "Your whelp shadow comes for you."

She didn't need to turn around to know Billy must be approaching their stern. "Captain," Billy gasped, eyes even wider than normal. "I been up to the top o' the cliff, and I seen sails to the west."

"This better not be Shaw," Tommy growled. "That bilge-sucking jackass has been sniffing around us for weeks."

"Damn my buttons, but you do smell nice," Stratton said, eyes twinkling.

Tommy smiled smugly. "It's called soap. What did you two chuckleheads do with the bars I gave you?"

McLeod shrugged. "Used it to swab down the quarterdeck."

Stratton pulled a carved pelican from his coat pocket. "Made me a little bird."

"No, Captain," Billy said, tugging on her sleeve. "It ain't Shaw. The ships are too big."

"Bugger it," Tommy muttered. She sent Billy to the ship for her spying glass, shouted to Sawkins to cease all noise until she returned, then she and her captains sprinted across the beach and began thrashing through the underbrush. It took them fifteen minutes to climb the peak and find a worn pathway to the western edge of the island.

The boy had been right. Four ships sailed straight for Sombrero Island.

Stratton cursed under his breath. "Friggin' Spaniards."

Tommy took in the sight of the Caribbean stretching out before them, blue as a robin's egg in places, green as jade in others. When she died, Tommy was certain Heaven would look just like the West Indies. Too bad she was going to Hell for all the killing she'd done. She'd be doing more killing if those Spaniards discovered her fleet tucked into the curve of this island.

"If they sail north of this island, they'll see the cove," McLeod said.

"Maybe they'll head south down the passage between this island and the next. But what's a fleet of Spanish ships doing over here? This isn't the route down to Puerto Bello."

They discussed the possibilities while they waited in the bushes, then Billy finally joined them, panting and sweaty, with the spyglass. "Billy, sorry to send you back again, but we be needing Calabria up here. He might know these ships." Beaming to be asked, Billy whirled and flew back down the path.

Tommy held the glass to her eye and focused. "Spanish galleons they be. One big galleon, two smaller, and a fourth, very small." She focused on the largest ship with faded wood, sails gray with age, and masts pocked with cannon blast. She whistled at the activity on deck. "They be painting the deck, the gunwale, the masts."

"While they's under sail?"

Tommy squinted through the glass again. "Stupid bastards. They got men hanging by ropes off the sides painting the hull above the water line. What the devil are they at?" The ship itself looked old and worn where it hadn't yet been painted. "Oh, this be rich. They's whitewashing the sails." Men had scrambled up the rigging to paint the unfurled sails, and men on deck were running brushes over smaller sails laid out on deck.

"Sounds like a right spruce-up," Stratton said.

"Spain always be short of silver," McLeod added. "Could they be sending another fleet down to Puerto Bello?"

The ships quickly closed on the island, and Tommy once again considered them through her glass. The largest galleon reminded of her an old woman worn down by her life. The ships had most certainly come from the Bahamas, where the ships sailing from Spain stopped for provisions.

"Maybe they don't want anyone to know another treasure fleet be in the making," Stratton offered.

"But why sail this way?" Tommy asked. "No, they be hiding something they don't wish the likes of us to see. Smart rogues, too, since nothing spreads more quickly among pirates than gossip. I'm guessing it's the condition of that big galleon. Something about it smells fishier than a seaside pub."

Calabria joined them, muttering about having to climb to such great heights, but he fell silent at the sight of the four ships bearing down upon them. Tommy handed him the spying glass. "Calabria, do you be recognizing these ships?"

The short, swarthy sailor put the piece to his eye, squinting to focus. "*Santo mío!* That first one, the largest, she be the *Barcelona*. I didn't know the maggot-ridden hulk still sailed." He pursed his lips. "The second be the *Santa Maria*, the third would then be her sister. The fourth ship, she is—" Calabria gave a short, dry laugh. "Madre de Dios, can it be?" He laughed again. "*Sí, sí, es la Maravillosa.*" He handed Tommy the glass with a sad grin. "Anyone who has seen her sail calls her the Little Walnut because she bobs on the water like a toy."

McLeod snorted. "Only a dull-witted numbskull wants a ship like that."

The first ship had reached the mouth of the passage between the islands. Tommy and her men fell silent, watching through the leaves and holding their breath. Should the ships continue sailing in a straight line, the pirates were doomed.

But the captain of the galleon began shouting commands, and the ship turned south into the passageway. In minutes, the four ships would pass right below the cliff where Tommy and her men hid.

She peered through the glass again. The *Barcelona* was cut for forty guns, the *Santa Maria* and her sister ship looked to be smaller, cut for twenty guns but with room on deck for ten more. Tommy scanned the sea for the last ship, the *Maravillosa,* finally finding it bobbing along behind like a child's toy, cut for ten guns only, with room on deck for ten more. She slowly moved the eyeglass forward along the ship's deck. The small galleon carried a lofty quarterdeck, poop deck, and a double forecastle. Her hull was painted white with a cheery yellow and red. Spanish crests hung from the rail, and she looked like a lady dressed for a carnival. Tommy scanned forward to the bow, out the bowsprit, then began to survey its hull. That was when the figurehead came into view through her glass, and she gasped.

The figurehead was a woman, rising above the splashing waves, arms flung back, hair flowing behind her. Water and wind had darkened her to a warm brown. Her more intimate regions were discreetly draped, but the rest was revealed to the sea, the carver being most generous in his design of her. All the air left Tommy's body as surely as if God had reached down and pressed his heavy palm against her.

With difficulty, she tore her gaze away from the generous bosom and settled upon the figurehead's face. The woman's eyes were not raised in supplication nor lowered in submission, but bore straight ahead, fearless, as if she possessed the courage to take on whatever the sea, or man, might fling in her path.

Bloody hell. Tommy lowered the glass to hide her shaking hands. She'd been at sea long enough to know it could make you a little mad at times. Men saw ghostly ships, or mermaids, or fire aloft. Last year Sawkins and Billy had insisted they'd seen an island when there was nothing there. But Tommy wasn't at sea, so she wasn't being bewitched by the water, waves, or the wind. She was standing on solid ground, yet she felt as if she were tipping.

"What ye think, Captain?" Stratton whispered, his eyes narrowed at the galleons passing below them.

Tommy'd seen hundreds of female figureheads, and naked women had been hard to miss at the Tortuga pubs, but this figurehead shone with independence and strength and appeared so real Tommy expected her to move. The figurehead reminded Tommy of how she'd once felt.

"Captain?"

Tommy held up her hand. The *Barcelona* was a ghost ship, the two sister ships its pallbearers. But the *Maravillosa*, despite her squat, lumbering resemblance to half a walnut shell, incited in Tommy unfamiliar happiness and unexplained desire. She must possess that ship. Tommy licked her lips and kept her voice low. "Boys, let's put the matter to the crews for a vote. If the answer be aye, we'll shadow this Spanish fleet as closely as young Billy shadows me."

"Great guns," McLeod said softly. "We be getting us some Spanish booty." The two captains and Calabria headed back to the beach while Billy waited patiently by her side. Tommy looked through the glass again, watching until the last moment when the *Maravillosa* slid past and the figurehead disappeared from view.

McLeod could call her a dull-witted numbskull, but damn her for a fool if she didn't want that ship.

Chapter Three

Tommy's men finished their repairs and tarring in half the usual time, every man among them eager to follow those Spanish galleons. When the next high tide slid in, the ships righted, lifted off the sand, and sailed from the cove.

The ship rolled beneath Tommy as she inhaled the sharp sea air, mixed with smoke from the galley chimney protruding out the forecastle deck. She hoped Cookie was making something edible. Sawkins stood at her side, steady as an island.

Tommy had gone to sea at age nine disguised as a boy, worked as cabin boy for many merchant captains, including the first captain whose kind wife taught Tommy to read. From that same captain Tommy soaked up everything she could about navigation—reading charts, compasses, using the quadrant, the astrolabe—and then made sure she learned something from every captain after him.

But when Tommy turned seventeen, she could no longer disguise her sex, and her latest captain would no longer keep her on board. She tried seven times to find a ship on which she could remain, but all too soon the captain or quartermaster or one of the mates would be crying that a female on board would curse the ship. If the captain was a decent man, he would put her in a boat and send her to shore, not caring if that shore was peopled by England's friends or foes. If not a decent man, he would first take his pleasure of her, allow his first mate to do the same, *then* he would send her ashore.

By eighteen, she'd had enough and took a job working in a pub in Newcastle where she learned to reward unwelcome pinches with punches. Any man who groped at her bosom found her knee in his privates. The work was fifteen hours a day, and her sleeping room was cramped and musty and full of snoring women and fat beetles. She was trapped in a friggin' box without fresh air. No horizon. No ship breathing in and out beneath her feet. No sharp snap when the breeze came up and filled the sails.

By the age of twenty, Tommy wanted to jump off a Devon cliff. If she didn't get back to the sea, she'd die. So she stowed away on a ship bound for Jamaica and ended up without friend or silver in a strange land. She stole a small boat, but she needed a crew. She'd taken a liking to an older man in the pub, but he was always drunk. So one night she loaded him into the boat, hoisted the one sail, and they set off. She kept the man out for five days. He begged and pleaded for ale or rum, sweated off some weight, but in the end, dried out. That was how Sawkins came to be her first crewmate.

From there, they raided the pubs and found two more men. Tommy and Sawkins took them out to sea to dry out, then Hatley became her sailmaker and Bishop—God rest his soul—her carpenter. The men were so grateful to be doing something other than staring at their reflection in a mug of brew that they had no problems sailing under a woman. They stole the *Moon Shadow* from its drunken captain, and their life as pirates began.

And here she was, with the sea once again beneath her, and the Spanish galleons before her. She was a damned good sailor, and a passable pirate, but she couldn't stop gnawing on her unease like a soup bone. All she needed was one large prize, then maybe she could buy herself a solid ship, give up pirating, and earn her keep transporting goods between islands.

Tommy shook off that dream. She was a pirate, and there was naught to be done about it. She knew of only one man who'd escaped the life. Danny McLurin was a clever Scot who'd sailed with her for a while, then last year slipped away one night while they were anchored off Tortuga.

Tommy's three ships sailed close together as they sped after the Spanish galleons, the brisk wind filling their sails with speed and hope. Tommy found both wind and sun tonics for the soul. Hatley shared her love of motion, for he sat most of the morning on deck repairing sails, singing bawdy songs in a rich baritone. Tommy'd long since learned to ignore the words, but hummed along with the catchy tunes as she paced the quarterdeck. She finally felt free of the spell cast by the figurehead. Its face was nearly gone from Tommy's memory, entirely gone. No more thoughts of brown smoothness or swollen breasts.

Two days out of Sombrero, there was still no sight of the Spanish fleet. Tommy wasn't concerned, since those galleons had to be sailing to Puerto Bello or Cartagena. Tommy'd sail down the eastern edge of the West Indies, then ride the prevailing winds along the northern coast of South America until she reached Puerto Bello.

Billy's goat had taken a liking to Tommy and followed her around, nibbling her coattails when she absentmindedly stopped to scratch the knobby bone between his ears. Below, chickens cackled and Cookie banged away in the galley. The sturdy Negro hardly spoke a word, but he kept her men fed, and he always touched his forehead when she passed, a sign of respect not often seen on a pirate ship.

A loose rope slapped against the deck, needing a quick slice to trim off the end, but Tommy let it flap. She liked the sound. Billy was aloft in the main mast, arms once again wrapped comfortably around the mast as he straddled the main yard. While some hands grumbled that Billy did little work on deck, others felt safer knowing his sharp eye would sight danger before they themselves were sighted.

This time, however, Sawkins was the first to sight the sail, and he did so merely by pointing. Tommy nodded. "Time to go adventuring, you sodden sacks of crap. Make all sail." The men laughed with delight and did as she commanded. An insult from Captain Tommy was a friendly slap on the back, not a sharp sting.

A wispy fog descended upon them as they picked up speed, as if God had stretched out a sheep's fleece low to the water but left the sky above still bright blue. Once they regained sight of their prey's masts, Tommy tacked to bring them closer. The *Tiger Eye* and the *Windy Queen* sailed joyfully beside them.

"There be a second sail!" Billy shrieked.

From west of their prey a ship shot out from what remained of the thin fog. Tommy didn't need her eyepiece to know the ship, and the three behind it, were Shaw's.

"Curse it," she yelled. "That dung-faced bastard be stealing our prize." She itched to give the order to fire the cannons, but it was against code to attack another pirate. She shouted the order to unfurl the royals and jibs, and the *Moon Shadow* leapt over the water.

Shaw reached the prize first, firing cannon and musket so violently that the captured ship's mizzenmast toppled onto the deck. Shaw quickly boarded the prize and raised his own colors.

Tommy stood down, calling to furl all tops'ls. Men gathered on the deck, grumbling and shouting insults at Shaw's men, too far away to hear. But there was naught they could do, because Shaw had reached the prize first. Heavy with disappointment, Tommy and her crew made ready to continue on their course.

"Shaw raises a flag again, requesting permission to approach," Hatley called.

"And he can be kissing me arse a second time," Tommy muttered. What the blazes did that scoundrel want? In just a few minutes the *Moon Shadow* showed Shaw her stern.

Sharp-eyed Billy shouted. "They's dumping Negroes overboard!"

Tommy raised her glass and cursed violently. The prize's bounty obviously included several dozen slaves, which Shaw's men shoved and tossed overboard. Shaw waved to Tommy, then began moving his ships away. The slaves were a good three leagues from land, too far for anyone to swim.

"By my blood," Sawkins muttered. "The murderous bastard means to leave them there."

"Bring us around," Tommy said quietly. "We'll be too late for most of them." By the time the *Moon Shadow* reached the area thirty minutes later, those who couldn't swim had drowned, and only a dozen unfortunate slaves remained alive to be plucked from the sea. Shaw's ships hovered a short distance away, the *Sharktooth* flying the flag requesting permission to board.

Hatley and another sailor brought up blankets for the dripping, trembling souls while Sawkins and Tommy discussed their options. It was written in their Articles that no man had the power of liberty over another. Tommy and her men, all from poor families, had not lifted the galling yoke of slavery off their necks just to lower it onto the necks of others. Just the sight of the Negroes silenced the entire ship.

But when the last of the slaves, three women, were brought on board, men hooted and hollered, and a few dropped their trousers and thrust their members lewdly toward the Negro women.

"Bloody hell," Tommy snapped to Sawkins.

"They've gone weeks without seeing a wench," he said, smiling weakly at her scowl. Except for her monthly courses, she often forgot she was a woman herself.

As two lewd sailors approached the women, Tommy slowly slid her sword from its scabbard. Few heard the sound, but the sun glinted off the blade well enough that her crew suddenly realized Captain Tommy held a naked blade. All the ribald comments ceased as she descended from the quarterdeck ladder to the mid-deck and approached the two men, who quickly tugged their trousers back up. With a swift chop, Tommy sliced off the end of the loose rope that had been flapping earlier.

Slowly, ever so slowly, she replaced the blade, making sure everyone heard the metal scrape against metal, a most unfriendly sound. "Sawkins, take the wenches to my cabin. Hatley, offer the Articles to these slaves. If they accept, they remain. If not, we put them ashore with provisions and water."

The minute Tommy had realized three of the slaves were female, an idea took root. If she could convince one of these women to stay aboard, she'd have her cabin boy.

To get to her cabin, Tommy passed through the wardroom which held a table, a bench, and the meager collection of charts she'd gathered from ships she'd taken. The wardroom was usually packed with booty they'd taken off ships, but the hollow sound of her footsteps reminded her of their lean months. Her cabin was wide, reaching nearly the entire width of the ship, but only about eight feet deep. She had a hammock, a trunk full of books about life at sea, and a table for eating. The rest of the space was used to store spare sails and barrels of rum. The men figured her cabin was the safest place since she didn't drink much of the stuff. Grimy windows stretched across the stern, and she again rued the lack of a cabin boy.

Once inside her cabin, she didn't look directly at the women but gazed out the stern windows, hands behind her back. "I be in need of a personal servant," she said. "I be willing to pay. The duties would be light: washing clothes, arranging meals, cleaning these windows, and braiding my hair. Your chances of surviving be better on this ship than if you're put ashore, where you'll likely be captured and sold as slaves again."

None of the women responded. "Do they speak English?" she asked Sawkins.

"Don't believe so, Captain. But, Tommy, are you sure about keepin' a woman on board? The men mostly forget you're a woman, begging your pardon, but some think a woman's bad luck."

Tommy turned to face the women. The first, short and plump, fixed her eyes on the floorboards beneath them and clutched the blanket tightly around her neck. The second, thin as a rail, raised her eyes and moved her mouth in silent prayer, having not heard or understood a word Tommy had said. When Tommy gazed upon the third woman, she nearly swallowed her tongue. The woman didn't hide her eyes, but gazed straight at Tommy, fearless, challenging. Her face wet from the sea, her ample bosom straining against the thin, wet dress, her long hair of tight black ropes—Good God Almighty, the figurehead from the *Maravillosa* stood before Tommy as a living, breathing woman. Her skin was the same dark coffee of the figurehead. Her black eyes snapped with anger. Her full mouth was set in a firm line.

"Captain," Sawkins whispered near her ear. "You'll not be wanting that one. She'll be too saucy, mark my words. Take one of the other two. Either a them'll shape up nicely, doing what you want without complaint."

Tommy didn't want a slave. She wanted a woman—that woman—to agree of her own volition to stay on board and earn her keep in Tommy's service. But apparently none of the women spoke English. She tried again to explain their slim chances of remaining free once put ashore. She tried a little French, called Calabria in for Spanish, but there was no change in the women's faces or demeanor.

The bold woman and Tommy locked eyes. She was the only woman of this bunch who would do. "Sawkins, put the other two ashore. Give'em a bell's head start before you release the men, in case the men be thinking of something besides freedom." She nodded toward the woman boring her gaze into Tommy's skull. "She remains on board." She didn't want to keep her as a prisoner, but without a common language, she had no choice.

Sawkins took the other women away, and Tommy indicated to

the woman she was to sit on the chair. Without a change in expression, she did so. "You'll be sleeping over there," Tommy said. "I'll have Hatley sling another hammock." Her heart pounded a little faster to realize she would be sharing her cabin with another person. She hadn't done that since becoming captain, but she couldn't put the woman in the crew's quarters. "Come. I'll show you the ship." Reluctantly, the woman followed. Tommy took her forward to the galley, where the big Negro cook glared at them both as he dressed a chicken. "This is Cookie. Be nice to him or he'll do something nasty to your food." Tommy pointed down a companionway and shook her finger at the woman. "Gun room, pump room, and crew's quarters—you stay out." Then she took the woman up to the forecastle, the small, high deck at the fore of the ship, meeting with scowls. Tommy scowled back, making sure her eyebrow arched in the way that so alarmed her crew. The muttering stopped as the men cleared the deck of ropes, buckets, and other unwanted material.

They sailed closer to the nearest of the Leeward Islands, where a longboat took the freed slaves ashore. Shaw still followed the *Moon Shadow*, still flying the flag requesting permission to come aboard and speak with the captain. When Tommy took the woman down the forecastle ladder, crossed the mid-deck, and tried to take the woman up onto the quarterdeck, Sawkins met her there. "Are you sure, Captain?" he said quietly enough none else could hear. She gazed into his face and knew he was thinking of her. Keeping command of three ships filled with over three hundred men was hard enough as it was. The quarterdeck was her place of power and authority and should be kept as such.

Tommy instead made her sit near a pile of torn sails, then standing next to her, Tommy watched the island until the slaves were put ashore and her longboat was safely back on deck. Then she nodded to Sawkins and they headed back out to sea, Shaw in their wake.

"How long is that scurvy weevil needing to shadow us?" Sawkins asked.

Tommy shrugged but climbed back onto the quarterdeck, aware that her men watched Shaw's ships as they worked, then shot glances first at Tommy, then for some reason, toward her gunner Coxon.

"Captain," Coxon finally called. "What be the harm in letting Shaw come aboard?" The men around him echoed his question.

Before Tommy could respond, the Negro woman moved to the side of the ship and gripped the rail. They were now far enough out to sea that land was nothing more than a thin blue wafer on the horizon, which was why Tommy was totally thrown off her guard when the woman hiked up her skirt, threw one leg up onto the railing, and leapt overboard. Tommy raced to the railing in time to watch her splash into the water, rise to the surface, and begin swimming. "Bloody hell!" she bellowed. "What's she at? We're leagues from shore."

Billy was at her elbow. "Shall I fetch her back, Captain?" She nodded wearily. It took Billy and two other men to drag her up into the longboat and get her back aboard the *Moon Shadow*. She met Tommy's glare with her own stone-cold fury, and Tommy pushed her through the wardroom and into her cabin.

What could she say to a woman who spoke no English? Tommy was left with nothing but the bare truth. "You be safe here, so don't be jumping overboard. I'm sorry I didn't let you go, but I can't help it. I don't understand it, but that's the way of it." Tommy pointed to the second hammock now swinging in the far corner. "This be yours."

Why was she so drawn to this woman? As she'd shown her around the ship, Tommy'd felt an odd tug in her gut whenever the woman looked at her. She had something Tommy wanted, but damned if Tommy knew what that was. Tommy strode to the rear of the cabin, wiped a windowpane with her sleeve, and watched the wake flare out behind the ship. Few men had the courage to stand up to Tommy Farris, yet this woman was ablaze with courage.

She turned to stare at her, then took a deep breath. "I'm not understanding this at all, but I need you on my ship. It doesn't hurt that you're one of the most beautiful women I've ever laid eyes on. I can't be thinking why I say that to you, but it's the God's truth." The woman's eyes dropped as if accepting the compliment. "Your skin is reminding me of melted toffee. When you gaze at me, I can't look away. I'm sore in need of female company. Why, I can't say, for I've never had a female friend or sought one out." Tommy shook her head. "I be wasting my breath here, for you understand nothing. I'm going back on deck. Stay here," Tommy commanded. She pointed toward the cabin door, then wagged her finger at the woman. "Stay here." Slamming the thin door behind her for effect, Tommy returned to the mid-deck.

By now the *Moon Shadow* was close enough to Shaw's *Sharktooth* that the two crews could shout insults at one another. Tommy's heart sank. She would have to let Shaw come aboard. She nodded to Billy, who hoisted the orange flag. A shout of triumph rose from the *Sharktooth*, and Tommy refused to look over at Shaw. Damn his poxy arse. She hated rats aboard her ship.

CHAPTER FOUR

Avery Shaw climbed aboard the mid-deck with a gleam in his black eyes and a smirk on his sardonic mouth that marked him as a man well pleased with himself. His eyebrows made two half-moons over a broad forehead. The man thought himself a dandy and dressed the part, in purple velvet coat with lace ruffles at throat, chest, and wrists. Gold dripped from the man like seaweed. Despite his finery and awkward attempts at manners, the man was insanely violent, even for a pirate.

In contrast, Tommy knew what others saw when they looked at her. She made no effort to hide her sex. She had a plain face with sad blue eyes, a narrow nose, and an average mouth. Her skin was sun-baked nearly to the color of the Negro woman currently sitting in Tommy's cabin. Tommy was tall and lean, but chose not to wear the usual garish clothing of a captain that Shaw wore. In her white shirt, long brown coat, and simple trousers wrapped at the waist with a brilliant blue sash, she was barely distinguishable from her crew. Her sex was obvious when she stood into the wind, but that wasn't to be helped. The heavy black braid draped over her shoulder was her only adornment.

"Captain Farris, you're lookin' fine, even fully garbed." Still grinning, Shaw offered his massive hand, but Tommy ignored it. Each time they met, the man expected her to drop into a grateful curtsey and worship his prick. Shaw shrugged and withdrew his hand. "Well, now, I'm here to discuss a proposition. Sure and certain, the least ye could do is hear me out."

Her crew began to gather around, so she jerked her head at Sawkins, and he barked orders to keep the men busy.

"Let's go back into my wardroom," Tommy said.

"I lay odds your men'll be wanting to hear what I got to say," Shaw practically shouted, bringing the attention on deck right back to him.

Billy rang the ship's bell three times to signal the ship was one and a half hours into the afternoon watch. Tommy contemplated the odious creature before her. "You've got until four bells. Talk." One half hour was more time than she wanted to spend with this baboon.

Shaw leaned against the rigging and dug at his dirty fingernails with an even grimier knife. "You hear about the Spanish fleet?"

Tommy shook her head.

"Last month the entire fleet sank in a sudden hurricane off the coast of Florida. We managed to salvage one chest, and the sight of all that silver has hungered me and my men for more. Scuttlebutt is that Spain, desperate for coin since her loss, is dispatching another treasure fleet down to Puerto Bello. One of those galleons is the *Barcelona*, the biggest damned ship on the sea."

Tommy felt an odd fluttering in her chest. Now she fathomed Shaw's intent in approaching her.

"The *Barcelona* be three hundred tons, carries forty guns, and holds three hundred men," Shaw said, "but if we be unifying our fleets, we have seven ships, six hundred men, and plenty of guns between us. We sail south, then shadow the Spaniards, watch and wait until the *Barcelona* be vulnerable, then take her, and every piece of silver aboard her. We'll be wealthy beyond any pirate's drunken dream."

Tommy's crew shouted their assent, banging on the deck and hooting. Sawkins caught Tommy's eye and she understood. She and Sawkins could be replaced at any time.

"Flog off, Shaw. I be working with you when your mother turns an honest woman."

Shaw slapped his chest. "Deeply wounded, Captain. But perhaps it would help to know that the fleet, if it sails, will probably carry over two hundred thousand pounds in silver *alone*. It'll have enough that each of us scoundrels will be well fixed and free to give up the sweet trade."

"I'll be hanged if I'll pass this up," cried Coxon. "Let's do it!"

"We'll send those Spanish curs to the bottom," shouted another, and the clamor grew even louder.

By now Stratton and McLeod had joined them on the *Moon Shadow* and had heard the whole of Shaw's proposal. Tommy motioned for Stratton and McLeod to follow her into the wardroom.

"What do you boys think? The fleet'll be heavily guarded. There be more than just the four ships we saw the other day."

Stratton nodded. "I know, but damn it, Tommy, listen." He jerked his head toward the racket the crew was raising. "Don't seem we have any choice now, does it?"

Tommy clenched her jaw, then sighed as McLeod agreed. She followed them back out even though something about this felt wrong. They would do much better on their own by silently following the *Maravillosa* until she was vulnerable to attack. Tommy knew Shaw's approach—rush in before you knew what in blazes was going on. Shaw's plans often ended up killing more of his men than his enemy's, but his crew fed off his violence and didn't care.

A foreboding as heavy as a London fog settled over her. She knew she'd die a pirate, and that each day the sun rose could be her last. She'd either end up fish food in Davy Jones's locker, a bloody decoration on someone's cutlass, or strung up on the docks of Port Royal wearing a hemp collar.

Tommy shook off the darkness, then climbed up onto the rigging to be seen by the men on the *Tiger Eye* and *Windy Queen*, anchored nearby. "Stratton and McLeod and I agree, and now put it to a vote. Be we cringing dogs or wild sea wolves?" A deafening roar rose from all three ships. "Do we chase down those brainless buggers and take what we be wanting?" The answering roar was even louder than the first, and Tommy let herself smile.

She climbed back down, then reached out her hand to Shaw. "You be the blackest sea dog there is, and I despise your guts, but my men say we're to work together."

Shaw's ugly grin turned her stomach as he shook her hand. What had ever possessed her to pick him out from the crew that day? The sun must have been in her eyes.

"I command the most men and ships," Shaw said, "so I be in charge."

Tommy shrugged. Shaw in charge was a foul idea, but he was right. "What be your plan?" she asked.

Shaw's grin widened. "Don't have one yet. First I had to get ye aboard the idea. So let's our ships be sailing south together while I work it up."

No plan. Brilliant. "So be it. Now clear your poxy mug from my deck," she growled. "The longer you tarry, the more likely I'll blow your ship up into bits even smaller than your useless pecker."

Shaw's face darkened as Tommy's men hooted, but he recovered, then donned that wolfish grin. "Ye may be sure, Captain Tommy, that ye and me be fitting together just fine."

Tommy cursed harshly, but he just smiled. Tommy had survived this long by following her instincts, and her instincts said working with Shaw was a bad, bad idea.

❖

After setting course with Sawkins, Tommy showed her new "cabin boy" what she expected of her. She began with laundry, for unlike her men, Tommy liked changing shirt and trousers at least once a month. She showed the woman where they collected rainwater on the forecastle and how to wash the clothes in half a barrel, then use the water to swab down the deck. The woman watched as Tommy wrung out her breeches, then helped Tommy dump out the barrel of wash water. Tommy was surprised at her strength, for she was not a large woman.

Once they completed the laundry, Tommy handed the woman a piece of eight from her stash. When she didn't take it, Tommy reached for her hand and placed it in her palm. "You're in my employ now, so you'll earn silver for helping me. I know you can't comprehend my words, but you no longer be a slave. You work for wages."

Those bottomless eyes considered the coin, then she tucked it into a pocket concealed in the waist of her ragged skirt.

The woman's first lessons would have been more satisfying if Tommy hadn't turned her back and the woman once again leapt overboard. The splash brought Tommy and nearby sailors to the rail. Land was still only a dark gash on the horizon. The woman was insane.

The men hooted and offered advice. Coxon leaned out with an ugly leer on his face. "Look, boys! Captain Tommy's lost her new pet." His laugh was unfriendly. "Just like she lost the last prize. Shaw'd have been able to keep that slave on board."

The bully was a magnet for the less desirable of her crew, and she'd have to deal with that soon. The crew's tittering took on a nervous note, and Tommy's attentions were torn between the woman pulling herself farther from the ship with strong, sure strokes, and the troublesome Coxon. Tommy cast a quick glance out to starboard. The woman now swam more slowly but had made considerable progress.

One of Coxon's cronies punched the air with a grimy finger. "Shaw's men wear rings on every finger. We be tired of prizes that got nothin' on 'em but wood and water." Choruses of "hear, hear," and "Bully for Shaw" rose from the group.

Billy touched Tommy's arm and silently pointed off port side, where a dark gray shark fin sliced the sea. "Wooly bollocks," Tommy muttered. "Send the boat for the woman." She barked out more orders that sent the men back to work. Coxon hesitated, but finally obeyed.

When the soggy, exhausted woman was back on board, Tommy took her firmly by the arm and marched her back to the cabin. As she did she whispered, "This be the second time I've pulled you from the sea. If there's a third, I'll not lift a finger to help." How could she make her understand?

At the start of afternoon watch, Tommy returned to the cabin. The woman was standing by the stern windows and whirled around to face her, eyes blazing, nostrils flared. When the woman's chest heaved in anger under the loose cotton dress, Tommy's privates clenched so tightly she stood there too shocked to move. How could a woman do that to her?

Tommy cleared her throat. "I know you're angry, but you can't be swimming to shore. You'll drown leagues from any island."

The woman folded her arms across her chest, her face still defiant.

Bollocks. The woman reminded Tommy of herself.

"Cookie has grub ready." She showed the woman where the few dishes were stowed, but when Tommy reached for a plate, the woman pushed her hand away and gathered up plates and mugs. She set the table for Tommy, complete with a large linen napkin Tommy'd never used, preferring her trousers or shirt.

"Thank you," Tommy said, feeling awkward. She handed the woman another coin. Tommy felt immensely stupid talking to a woman who didn't understand a word she said, but there was a certain amount of freedom in this.

Cookie showed up, ladled soup into their bowls, then disappeared. The woman sat on her hammock, her own soup bowl on her knees. Had she been a man, she'd be eating with the others, but Tommy felt a need to protect her from the coarse sailors. The woman knew her place, however, and didn't attempt to sit at the table with Tommy.

Tommy sat back and watched her eat. She ate delicately, like she'd been brought up in a fine house, not as a slave. Suddenly, words welled up inside Tommy, surprising as a spring hurricane. "I haven't spent time with another woman since my mother, and all she wanted to do was box my ears or yell at me." Tommy stirred her soup. "I've lived among men since I was ten, so I often forget my own sex." Tommy appreciated that even though the woman could not speak the language, she watched Tommy as if she understood.

"I know you've gone from being a slave to being stuck on this ship with me, but there're worse fates for our sex. You be safe on this ship, though I'd watch out for Coxon." She covered her ear. "He's the bloke missing an ear."

The woman nodded, the first actual communicating she'd done besides glaring, and Tommy relaxed.

"Coxon's a prick, and even though the other boys are better, some days I can't bear the sound of a man's voice, can't tolerate stubble or a bearded jaw, and lose patience with them all. I don't know why, because many of these men are my friends."

Tommy sighed as she sopped up the last of her soup with hardtack laced with weevils. Her meal completed, she dropped into her hammock, and it was suddenly high tide, her words racing to shore.

"I be tiring of this way of life, but I know no other. The killing's getting harder and harder. Some days my sword's so heavy I can barely draw it. I'm sick of the killing. And blast my bones, what would a woman like me do on land? Wait tables in a pub again? Marry some wealthy gent and breed? I wake up at night with bloomin' tears on my cheeks. I've no one to talk to. I never keep anyone on this ship against his will, but I couldn't let you leave. You're not like other women, and appear stronger than I often feel. Sometimes I'm thinking I'm the bravest woman on the ocean and the best pirate captain the West

Indies has ever seen. Then the next day I'm just wanting to be held in someone's arms. It's disgusting."

She closed her eyes and swung gently while the woman cleaned up, a small act but one that filled Tommy with gratitude. All she had to worry about now was whether the woman would try slitting Tommy's throat while she slept.

❖

Later that evening two men petitioned Tommy for permission to fight one another, one believing the other had cheated at dice. Tommy sighed, knowing that one man would likely mortally wound the other. She couldn't spare either of them but gave her permission to fight on deck. "But I be setting the terms and the weapons."

The two men hopped in place with the need to beat at each other and nodded their agreement. The rest of the crew gathered to watch the show. Tommy decided the men were to be tied at their waists from the lowest mizzenmast yardarm, about eight feet off the ground, and their only weapons would be two turtle shells left over from a recent meal.

Instead of a bloody battle, the dangling men swung wildly at each other with the shells, which banged hollowly as the crew shouted encouragement and insults. After five minutes, both men's anger had turned into jolly guffaws as they performed their ridiculous midair ballet and both men began mugging for the crew until Tommy could barely keep a straight face. The men's faces glowed with the fun of it, and the two men, when cut down, were probably relieved they were both still alive. Tommy returned to her cabin, hoping moments like tonight wouldn't weaken her reputation.

Before she lay down in her hammock, Tommy began showing the woman how to braid her hair using three scraps of rope, but the woman waved the rope away and reached for Tommy's hair and the brush on the small stand near Tommy's hammock. Tugging none too gently, the woman expertly brushed out the long locks as Tommy stood bracing herself against the mast, which passed down through her cabin on the way to the ship's hull. The woman then braided Tommy's hair into one thick rope. When she was done, Tommy thanked her and handed her another coin, which she deposited into her waistband.

Tommy stood close enough to notice for the first time that the woman's own hair, fascinating long ropes of tight black curls, contained burrs which stuck the locks together. Before Tommy knew her own mind, she reached for the tangles. The woman started, but Tommy clucked softly. "I won't be hurting you." Patiently, she worked the burrs out from the ropes, then held them out in her hand.

The woman nodded, eyes sparkling, then did the most incredible thing. She reached into her secret pocket and held out a coin. Tommy gaped at it but did nothing, so the woman took Tommy's hand, causing her to nearly jump from her skin. The woman's hand was much warmer than her own, and strength flowed from each finger as she opened Tommy's palm and placed the coin into it.

"No…but…" Tommy performed an admirable imitation of a fish gulping for air. "No, you misunderstand. You perform tasks for me, so I pay you. You need not…that is…"

"If you pay me, I should pay you. It's only fair." The woman's voice was low and liquid.

If Tommy's jaw had not been firmly attached to her skull, it would've bounced against the floor. The woman didn't blink as she witnessed Tommy's great confusion.

"You…speak…" Tommy suddenly felt a great need to sit down and lean back against the bulkhead. "Why didn't you tell…?"

For the first time a smile appeared on that lovely face, revealing a dimple in each cheek and straight white teeth. "Why didn't I tell you I speak English?" She spoke with a heavy Jamaican accent. She then sat down at the table as if she were in a pub, not in the captain's cabin. "Don't know. First I was a slave, and now I'm your 'servant,' and neither give me any say in my own life. Speaking's about all that I can choose to do, or not."

A hot flush began at Tommy's chest and spread faster than fire through dry straw until her entire face burned. What had she said to her? Bloody hell, she had spoken words to her she'd said to no other person. This woman had seen inside the heart of Captain Thomasina Farris. Tommy closed her eyes, shame searing her skin as she recalled her babblings during the day. Finally, she had no choice but to once again open her eyes and gaze upon the woman who had so cruelly tricked her.

Her face and body were still tight with caution, but her eyes had softened. Then she stood and offered Tommy her hand, as if she had never been a slave or a servant. "My name is Rebekah Brown."

Tommy frantically grabbed the blanket off her hammock, then fled to the quarterdeck where the sailor on watch jumped when she appeared. "Look alive, sailor! I'll have your balls for dinner if you're sleeping on watch." She proceeded to stomp around so angrily that any man not required to be there fled.

God rot that woman's bones. Tommy had always thought she'd die by the ocean or by hanging. Yet it was now clear her end was soon coming, and it was to be death by embarrassment. Bloody hell.

PART TWO

THE LIBRARIAN

The ancients saw librarians not as feeble sorters and shelvers but as heroic guardians…Most librarians, especially rare book librarians, still secretly view themselves this way.

—Miles Harvey, *The Island of Lost Maps*

Chapter Five

Minneapolis, Minnesota, present day

I had never intended to fall for a pirate, but looking back now, it made perfect sense. After I read a novel in the tenth grade about the totally hot pirate Grace O'Malley, I'd become hooked on everything from real pirates like O'Malley, Blackbeard, Captain Kidd, Anne Bonney, Mary Read, Henry Morgan, and Woodes Rogers, to fake pirates like Errol Flynn, Douglas Fairbanks Senior and Junior, Dustin Hoffman, Geena Davis, Johnny Depp, and Cary Elwes, the Dread Pirate Roberts. But my favorite pirate was a woman who'd never make it into the movies because so little was known about her. Maybe that was why she fascinated me—her life was both a puzzle and a mystery. While I was researching Captain Thomasina Farris for my *Library Journal* article, I found myself waking up in the middle of the night, hot and flushed with the comforter tossed off the bed. I couldn't remember my exact dreams, but judging by my warmth, I'm guessing Ms. Farris had surely been in them.

Tommy Farris was long since dead, of course, having lived nearly three hundred years ago, but that didn't weaken my fascination. What had she been like as a person? Bloodthirsty as the few accounts written of her claimed? Had she ever fallen in love? And how had she really died? Unsatisfied with the one account I'd found, I strove to answer this, but the pirate's death had been obscured by centuries of myth. This, of course, had been the point of my article, that while library research could solve some puzzles, others were actually mysteries that could never be solved.

Unfortunately, my brilliant article probably led to the awful disaster that took place yesterday in my place of employment, the Conrad Kline Rare Book Collection, the University of Minnesota's antiquities library. Thanks to my brilliant article, the next morning I sat in my boss's office perched on the edge of an incredibly uncomfortable leather chair. Marcus Getty, a man I respected and enjoyed working with but who was much too young for a comb-over, sat quietly, my rapt audience. As assistant director, I was in charge of the circulation desk, and the theft had happened on my watch.

I opened a heavy, leather-bound book, one of the gems in the collection. "This is DeBray's *Grand Voyages*, published in 1594. The maps are all hand tinted, miniature works of art." I skipped to the page, or rather, the missing page, that had brought me to Getty's office, then ran my finger along the half-inch stub, all that remained of that page. "This is what Michelle and I pieced together. Late yesterday afternoon a man named Edward Drummond showed his credentials from Iowa State University and requested this and two other books. Michelle checked the books to make sure they were in good condition, then took the books and Drummond to the reading room. Our best guess is that after she left him, he removed a length of dental floss from his mouth.

"He laid the wet floss against the inside edge of the paper, closed the book and waited for the floss to weaken the paper, then he—" I stopped and took a calming breath so I wouldn't break into the same nonstop cursing I'd used when Michelle had shown me the books. "All Drummond had to do was give a little tug and the four-hundred-year-old map of the Caribbean came loose. He either rolled or folded it to hide it in his clothes, then left." I tapped my finger against the other two books. "He did the same to these books, taking three more maps of the Caribbean. Michelle noticed a bit of dental floss sticking out of one of the books when she reshelved them. Otherwise it might have been weeks before we discovered the theft."

Getty leaned back in his chair, fuzzy brows pulled together. "Mr. Drummond stole maps of the West Indies. This wouldn't have anything to do with your article, would it?"

I winced. "I'm afraid it might. My article said I believe the Farris treasure map exists, so Drummond has likely begun searching for it. I should have chosen my words more carefully, but I just didn't imagine someone would start vandalizing libraries. I've sent out notices to all the discussion lists, and so far I've heard from five libraries who found missing maps. Their logs show they've all had visits from Drummond in the last six weeks. They're all west of Minnesota."

Getty tapped his chin. "The guy's heading east?"

"That's my theory. The only library I haven't heard from is the Patterson in Chicago. I've never met her, but Charlotte Brandt is known for disliking technology. She refuses to use e-mail, and rarely returns phone calls."

"Old school."

"You think?"

Getty winked at me. He was a good boss, but both our nerves had been stretched thinner than Drummond's dental floss by threatened funding cut-offs. "So let me get this straight. You write an article showing the Farris map exists, but no one knows where it is, so Drummond starts systematically going through library collections looking for maps of the West Indies. Wouldn't this Farris map, if it existed, be some handwritten, *X*-marks-the-spot sort of deal?"

"Normally, yes, but last year someone at Brown University suggested Farris might have used an *existing* map, one already published, and altered it subtly to mark the location of her treasure."

Getty stood and began pacing his narrow office. "The other libraries that have been hit, and any future ones, will likely blame us for the thefts, thanks to your article."

I nodded. I'd been so distraught over my breakup with Julia eight months ago that I hadn't even considered the implications of proclaiming the map existed but had never been found.

"Maybe you should fly down to Chicago and give Brandt a hand. Look through her collection for any books with missing West Indies maps."

"You're kidding."

"No, I'm not. We've got to stop this guy's rampage across the country. I know cops don't care about these things, so you and I must."

"How could we possibly afford a trip?"

My boss held a finger to his lips. "I inflated the contingency account this budget cycle because we'd had so many computer disasters last year, but since we've barely touched it we can afford a quick trip to Chicago. Besides, we'd be doing the library community a great service if we stopped Drummond."

"Marcus, does this have anything to do with the latest office gossip? The one that says you're bucking to become president of the American Rarities Collections Association?"

Getty pretended shock. "I'm a librarian, not a politician, Emma." He flipped through the old-fashioned Rolodex on his desk. "I'm not sure we want to run to the FBI. That's just a bit too public now that we're on the verge of getting two hundred fifty thousand dollars from the Abbotts, and maybe three hundred thousand from the Jacobsen Foundation. We can't afford to look like a library that can't keep track of its property. My college roommate runs a private investigation firm. John Lewis Investigations. I'll give him a call. Meanwhile, you think about Chicago."

I opened my Day-Timer and dropped it onto his desk, which may be why my friend Maggie calls me a Drama Queen, something I totally resent. "Tell me when there's room in here for a trip."

Getty leaned forward then shook his head. "You're very neat, I'll give you that, but Emma, when are you going to go digital?"

"Bought a PDA. Lost it. Bought another one. Lost it." That was the explanation people could accept and that one didn't make me look like some anti-tech goofball. The truth was I couldn't stand squeezing my life onto the little screen. I needed to see entire weeks or months, and everything in it. I needed to touch the pages. Turning the page to a new month in my Day-Timer was infinitely more satisfying than tapping the PDA with a stylus. I owned an off-brand PDA, but only used it for e-mail.

"Still, Emma, seeing that calendar so full just makes me tired."

"Imagine my life." I smiled at Getty, then gathered together the books as he began dialing John Lewis.

"Stay close to your office. I'll ask John to send someone over right away."

Nodding, I backed out with my arms full, trying not to bump over the floor globe or trip over the extension cords for the lamp. Getty spent the library's money on books and salaries, not on office remodeling.

My phone trilled halfway down the stairs, so I gently rested the books on the railing and answered it.

"Emma, dear, are you joining the Lunch Bunch today?"

It was Maggie. Jason from the bookstore, Cameron from the Law Library, Maggie from the Kerlan Collection, and I ate lunch together at the Student Union. We'd started out strangers, each sitting at separate tables, then somehow two of us ended up sharing a table, then three of us, then four. We became the Lunch Bunch.

"I'll try, but I might be late." I explained about the theft and needing to wait for a private investigator.

"I'm sorry you got ripped off, but you gotta eat, girl. I swear your damn calendar is going to up and kill you one day."

I couldn't be the only woman who lived a life where nearly every square was filled with appointments, meetings, car repair, haircuts, and now and then a drink with a friend. Whenever my parents wanted to drive the seven hours down to visit me, we needed to schedule it months in advance. My dad rarely swore, but one day while he watched me copy over a particularly chaotic month so I could read it better, he said, "I hate your fucking calendar."

Whoa. Dad.

At the end of every month I'd step back and marvel at the total lack of white space on the page, wondering how I'd gotten everything done. Yeah, it was a crazy schedule, but that was everyone's life, so why bitch about it? None of us, including Maggie, could shorten our seventy-hour workweeks. It wasn't like I could just quit and sail away to some tropical island and live happily ever after. I liked to eat food and wear clothes, and that took money. Last year I'd gone on a cost-savings kick and tried to knit myself a sweater. Two weeks later I decided I'd rather stab myself in the knee with a knitting needle than try that again.

I tuned back into Maggie's ongoing lecture about balance. Whenever Maggie ragged on me about balance, I imagined myself standing on one foot, arms pinwheeling wildly but still upright. I mean, really. Who has *time* to create balance in their lives?

"Emma, at thirty-seven, don't you think you should make time in your life for a relationship?"

"When, Maggie? You've seen my calendar. I challenge you to find one day last month when I could have gone on a date, let alone even *met* someone."

"Maybe you should date someone at work, then."

I laughed so hard I might have snorted. "Yeah, like those

relationships work out so well." Julia had worked at the library as an intern, which was how I'd met her. "No, falling in love, building trust, finding your soulmate? Takes time I don't have." I didn't add that relationships were a waste of time because after investing years or months in the thing, the person ended up leaving anyway. Mari and I had been together for five years, then she left me for a man. A few years later I met Julia, fell deeply in love, then seven years later Julia left me for a man. This can be surprisingly hard on one's self-esteem. I figured the right-wing conservatives should start paying me some sort of prize for each woman I converted to heterosexuality, sort of a reverse toaster oven. I'm thinking a Caribbean cruise would be nice. As a reward for each woman I drive into a man's arms, the Republican National Committee will plunk my cute ass down onto the deck of a big, honking cruise ship, hopefully an Olivia cruise full of women.

"You're a sad one, girl," Maggie said, "but you gotta keep your mind alert and your heart open. You do that, and one day some woman is gonna come along and climb right in without so much as an invitation."

For a second I felt that might be precisely what I wanted, but then I closed my eyes and saw my calendar again. Yeah, right. Adding one more thing would totally push me over the edge. "Gotta go, Maggie."

An hour later I was still waiting for the private investigator. I stood at the window in my office trying to rub away a headache. Between the stupid Drummond and his thieving, and my insomnia, my head was pounding. I'd gotten little sleep, having lain awake yet again thinking about Tommy Farris, fantasizing about sailing with her on the *Moon Shadow*. Now there would have been a Caribbean cruise worth taking.

I paced my office feeling like a caged panther. Where was that investigator? With every passing minute, the asshole thief who'd stolen the maps was getting farther away and harder to catch.

I paused and looked out my office window, then rested my forehead against the cool glass. Traffic noise from Nineteenth Avenue always grew louder this time of day as buses and delivery vans belched their way past the West Bank campus. Below, students swarmed across the small plaza as they headed for the bridge over the Mississippi taking them to their East Bank classes. The pink and burgundy petunias shone brilliantly in the sun baking the plaza. A few students turned west toward our building, but not many. Rare book collections didn't draw as much foot traffic as other University of Minnesota buildings; we tended to attract mostly researchers from other universities, curious retirees, and now, apparently, map thieves.

I pushed the intercom buzzer. "Michelle, is that private dick here yet?"

A brief pause, then my assistant buzzed back, still giggling. "No. I'll bring him back when he gets here."

I looked around my office, not sure why I was so nervous. Private investigators weren't the FBI, but they were close enough to law enforcement I didn't like them. Maybe it was because I hated how the FBI could invade privacy by demanding patron records. I didn't like watching cop or private eye shows on TV. But at this point I needed help because I had no idea how to track down a map thief, stop him from vandalizing other libraries, and recover the maps he'd stolen from my library.

I reminded myself to shake the investigator's hand firmly, since I'd recently read an article about how your handshake communicated your personality and helped people form snap opinions of you. While I think I've always had a good shake, as the fairly new assistant director of the Conrad Kline Rare Books Collection, I needed to project confidence. Nine days out of ten, I felt that confidence. Today wasn't one of those days, possibly because I'd have to tell the private investigator about Captain Farris and the treasure map and the Spanish fleet and the storm and the missing treasure. The whole thing was all too romantic to be believable.

Michelle tapped on my open door and stepped aside. "Your investigator's here."

In strode a slender woman, about my height, wearing a dark gray suit and a crisp white shirt, open at the neck. "Ms. Boyd, I'm Randi Marx. I work for John Lewis Investigations." The woman flipped open some sort of badge, pointed it in my direction, then snapped it shut so loudly I jumped. Without offering her hand, she sat down in the chair across from my desk.

Well, no handshake, then. I sat as well.

"Randi with a *Y* or an *I*?"

"What difference does it make?"

"I'm a librarian. I like to know things."

"Randi with an *I*."

"I'm guessing you don't dot that *I* with a little heart."

Randi-With-An-I raised her eyebrows in alarm, and I almost smiled. "Certainly not. Now let's get started. You've been the victim of a map thief. Could I see the affected books?"

Basically I reviewed what I'd shown Getty. As I talked, Marx took out a small notebook and began writing in it. Her thick auburn hair was pulled back into a French braid that curled sweetly around her shoulder, a confusing contrast to her emotionless, unremarkable face. She didn't look as if she smiled much.

She finally looked up from her book. "Did you check to see if Drummond requested other books?"

I opened up two more books and showed her the missing pages. "I've called Iowa State for information on Drummond, but they don't know him."

"It's unlikely Drummond is connected to Iowa State. These guys have multiple identities, switching when one gets too hot. Do you have security footage from Friday? I'd like to get a look at this man."

My palms started to sweat. "Well, that's a problem. Our security officer has had, like, zero money in his security budget. Plus he's also the head cataloguer, so he can't devote all his time to security."

Marx scowled. "Don't tell me you don't have security cameras."

"Oh, we have cameras." I took a deep breath. "The one in the Reading Room stopped working a few weeks ago and we haven't fixed it yet."

Marx frowned and scribbled something in her notebook. "Why not stick a toilet paper roll into the end of a shoe box and paint the whole thing black?"

"Our security budget is tight," I said. The private investigators on TV were sarcastic, too. Must come with the license.

When Marx sat back, silent, and scanned my office, I suddenly felt naked. These people were trained to draw conclusions about the person inhabiting a room. What conclusions would the PI draw from the perfectly groomed African violets in my window well? Or the Melissa Etheridge "Read" poster? Or the sixteen librarian action figures, gifts from friends, lined up on my bookshelf in four precise rows of four, stalwart guardians against illiteracy and ignorance? Would she notice every book on my shelves was alphabetized, that my desk was clear of debris, with my work in three tidy stacks? I liked tidy stacks. My long brown hair, much mousier than Marx's lustrous braid, swung neatly to my shoulders. My suit contained just enough synthetic fiber that it didn't wrinkle. I didn't like wrinkles.

I cleared my throat. "What do we do next? How do we get our maps back?"

The investigator's gaze focused on the action figures a second longer, then turned back to me. I found the light brown eyes impossible to read, but intriguing. "We'll check with the other libraries affected. Perhaps one of *them* will have video footage." Marx paused long enough for me to flush with embarrassment. "I've worked these cases before, Ms. Boyd. They take time, but we'll find him."

I closed the book in front of me. Here went nothing. "There's something else. My boss thinks these thefts might be connected to an article I wrote for the *Library Journal* several months ago."

"The one about the Tommy Farris treasure map."

I could feel my eyebrows doing the Surprise Dance. "How did you know about that?"

Marx nodded. "I'm a rare maps expert. It's my job. I'd heard of female pirates Anne Bonney and Mary Read before, but not Thomasina Farris. Why does Getty think they're connected?"

"Because all the missing maps, both here and at the other five libraries, are of the Caribbean, and are taken from books published before 1715. Farris sailed that area from about 1710 to 1715 and is believed to have stolen a Spanish treasure and made a map marking the location of that treasure. Mr. Getty thinks Drummond read the article and is trying to find the map."

Marx wrote more in her notebook. "You don't really believe the map exists, do you?" Her face was unreadable.

"Yes, I do. One of her contemporaries, a Captain Fletcher, insisted that she made a map before she died."

Marx shook her head. "Sounds like a romantic fairy tale someone started. Where are the other five libraries located?"

I fought the urge to argue with the woman. I believed in pirates. I believed the map existed. It had to. I opened the top file on my desk and consulted my list. "Seattle, Salt Lake City, Phoenix, Denver, and Iowa City."

Just then Marx's jacket began ringing like an old-fashioned phone. She reached into her pocket, checked the number, then stood. "Excuse me, but I need to take this." She stepped out of my office.

I took advantage of the moment to call Getty. "Okay, I'll go to Chicago."

"Excellent. Who knows? The two of you might have some luck."

"The two of us?"

"John and I just talked it over and we thought if you go to Chicago it would be good to have his investigator with you in case you encounter Drummond."

"But—"

"Relax, John says the woman doesn't bite. I'll have Michelle get you tickets for Thursday. And let's say no more about this on the discussion groups, shall we? If our potential donors get wind of this, they may back out."

Damn it. I hung up, then poked my head out into the hallway, but couldn't see the private investigator. When I moved around the corner and heard Marx talking in a low voice, I sneaked closer, feeling a bit like a private eye myself.

"John, please don't make me do this. Let me help track down Drummond instead…I know that, but looking for a map that doesn't exist is a waste of time…She's gorgeous, but what's that got to do with it?…Blond, doe-eyed femmes aren't my type, so quit matchmaking… John, I told you, I'm not dying of loneliness…Yes, but—" Marx sighed loudly. "John, you should see this woman's office. Tidy alarms go off if a hair drops onto the carpeting. Working with this anal retentive librarian will be hell…"

I stormed back to my office. Anal retentive? How dare she. I paced, trying to calm down. Anal retentive? That was such a librarian stereotype. The woman didn't even know me and she was already making snap judgments. The badge-snapping investigator was making snap judgments. How original.

I forced myself back to my desk, brought up the Patterson catalog online, and in two minutes had made a list of books to look through and even found another library in Chicago we should check while we were there. Marx thought I was anal retentive? She hadn't seen *nothing* yet.

Marx returned, face pale, mouth grim. "Change of plans. I won't be tracking Drummond down. Instead, you and I—"

"Chicago. Yes, I know. Thursday. Here are the libraries and books we need to check." I handed Marx the list, and when she sagged for a split second, then straightened, I felt the tiniest flash of sympathy. Of all the jobs to which Marx could be assigned, this might be the most boring for non-librarians. "I'll have my assistant book our flights," I said.

"I'll make my own travel arrangements, thank you." Marx checked her notebook. "I'll meet you at the first library, the Antiquities Collection in Chicago, Thursday morning at nine a.m." We exchanged cell numbers and e-mail addresses, then she snapped her notebook shut and stood. I flexed my hand, ready for that handshake, but Marx just nodded once, then left.

Exhausted, I laid my head down on my desk and sighed. Marx had been brisk and businesslike, exactly what you'd want in a private investigator, but the anal retentive comment stung a bit. Still, she was going to help us catch Drummond and perhaps recover our maps.

What would I do when I got my hands on Edward Drummond? When eighteenth-century pirates were captured, they were tried, then hanged by their necks until dead. The dead bodies of a select few, usually the pirate leaders, were tarred and put in iron cages called "gibbets," and hung for months in the harbor to warn off other pirates.

I wouldn't kill Drummond, of course, but I'd tar him up a bit, stick him in a gibbet, then hang him by the library's front entrance, between the dogwood bushes and the spirea, as a warning to any library patron contemplating theft.

I pulled out the research I'd gathered on Tommy Farris for my article and stared at the thin stack. The woman had commanded her own fleet of ships, sailed the open seas, answered to no one but her men, and lived a life of terrible adventure.

Why was I so obsessed with Tommy Farris?

Easy. She was a pirate.

CHAPTER SIX

I dashed through the cafeteria in the Student Union, banged into a man's chair and apologized, then stopped at the next table, late and out of breath. "Sorry, I was with a private investigator. She just left." My three Lunch Bunch friends nodded, their mouths already stuffed with burritos, tuna sandwiches, and salad.

Cameron Girard, librarian at the Law Library, looked up, eyes twinkling. "She? Was she cute?"

"If you like women in suits who don't smile." I told them Marx was professional but a bit on the chilly side, and that I was to meet her in Chicago. Then I peered at Maggie's T-shirt. "What's the billboard say today?"

Maggie, dressed in a gorgeous bright blue suit, stuck out her chest. "Malcolm X, baby." Maggie loved wearing 1970s message T-shirts under her sharp suits. She said that if people were going to be staring at her chest, they might as well be learning something.

Cam smelled overwhelmingly like a tropical drink—pineapple-scented hair fixative and coconut oil skin lotion, and he wasn't shy about the amount he splashed on. "If your investigator is the woman in a sharp gray suit I saw coming out of your library about fifteen minutes ago, she's totally gay. Play your cards right and she'll be wrapped around your little finger in no time."

"Shut up," I said sweetly, catching the look Maggie shot me: *Balance, balance, balance. Keep your heart open.*

"I'm just saying," Cam said. "Really, though, your private investigator sounds like a drag," he said. "You want some company?"

I stopped chewing. "She's just doing her job, but are you serious? That would be so fun."

"I have a few days' comp time, and work is really slow. I even have miles I could use. I could come with you. It'll be you and me against her, babe, so no worries."

Jason, the manager of the university bookstore, dumped more dressing on his salad. "If the PI's not gay, could you introduce us? I think private eyes are hot."

"Don't be a jerk," I said. "Cam, if you could come along, that'd be great."

"Excellent," said Cam. "We'll eat junk food, take in a play, and just have a good time."

I took a bite of my sandwich, then said, as casually as I could, "So, Cam, if there's time, maybe we could check out a few antique stores."

At that Maggie and Jason hooted and Cam groaned, covering his face. "Please, please don't put me through that again." Last summer we'd driven down along the Mississippi, then back up the Wisconsin side, checking out the antique stores for my latest passion—antique jigsaw puzzles.

"Okay, no antique stores."

Jason turned his newspaper to the last page. "Time for some News of the Weird." He smoothed out the page. "The eastern Caribbean has become the new mystical hot spot, with reports of islands that some people can see and others can't. The disappearing island phenomenon is located in what is being called the Grenada Triangle. At the same time as odd sightings have increased, annual sales of rum in Grenada have also increased." He put his paper down. "Pop quiz: do mystical events lead people to drink rum, or does rum lead to mystical events?"

We laughed, and before Jason could read the next item, I just had to ask. "Do you guys think I'm anal retentive?" The silence lasted a beat too long, which brought from my lips an un-librarian-like shriek. "You do! You think I'm uptight and controlling."

"C'mon, Emma," Cam said, "we're librarians. We like detail and order, and some people think that's a little anal."

Maggie's broad grin brought out her deep dimples. If Maggie weren't straight, I would have fallen madly in love with her since I was, sad to say, powerless before a woman with dimples. None of my previous lovers had dimples, so I didn't know why they made my knees go all wobbly. "Honey, look at your food tray," Maggie said. "You eat the same thing every day. The tray's all neatly arranged, like it's gonna be photographed for one of those food magazines. You fold up your used napkin when you're done with it. There's nothing wrong with knowing what you're gonna eat every day, or having it all laid out nice like you do, but don't you ever want a little variety?"

Jason snorted. "Like Maggie's boyfriends?" She swatted at him but missed.

I told them about the one-sided conversation I'd heard Marx have on the phone. Maggie chuckled. "I love it, spying on the private eye. But at least she said you were gorgeous and doe-eyed."

"Deer have freakishly large eyes and always look startled or nervous, not the image I'm looking to project." My PDA chirped. "Maybe this is Randi Marx, e-mailing me to remind me how anal retentive I am." I froze when I read the e-mail address: mappirate@ yahoo.com. I opened the e-mail and swore softly. "Holy crap, listen to this: *Dear Madame Librarian: You were right. The Farris map does exist, and I've found it. So don't waste your time on your little trip. Stay home and stay safe. Edward Drummond.*"

Cam sat up. "That's ballsy."

"No shit. He must be on one of the discussion lists I posted to this morning." While Maggie explained more about the theft to the others, I forwarded the e-mail to Marx, then hit reply. *Dear Asshole Thief: If you really have Tommy Farris's map, what does it look like?* I sent off the e-mail, hands shaking. This was freakin' weird, e-mailing the thief as if he were a business acquaintance.

"Damn," Jason said. "This rocks. Nothing exciting happens in the bookstore except catching a shoplifter now and then. You have such a cool job."

My PDA beeped. "It's him again. *Dear Madame Librarian: Wouldn't you like to know. Love and kisses, Edward.*"

Growling in my throat, I hit Reply. *Dear Asshole Thief: Clever retort. What are you, nine years old?* I sent the e-mail, Cam hovering over my shoulder, and we only had to wait a minute for Drummond's reply: *Wouldn't you like to know?*

"What a jerk," I said.

One more e-mail arrived, this one from Marx: *I have forwarded*

Drummond's message to the investigators in charge of finding him. That was it. No "nice meeting you this morning" or "see you on Thursday." I watched my friends laughing and talking, relieved that while I didn't have a lover because I'd sent each one off toward Planet Straight, I still had really great friends, and they were a hell of a lot warmer than PI Randi Marx.

❖

Wednesday evening I packed a carry-on bag, watched a rerun of *Buffy*, then realphabetized my CDs, struggling as usual with the Christmas CDs. Did I put them in C for Christmas? Or by individual artist? Or in a special holiday section filed under H, or should it go at the end of the alphabet? If only the world knew that librarians struggled to organize their lives like everyone else, they wouldn't think us so retentive. But then again, if the world knew how I obsessed over organizing my CDs, I'd have to kill myself.

After I'd resolved the major CD filing issue, I sat down to review all that I knew about Thomasina Farris and the map. From what I, and others, had been able to piece together, she'd led a hard life, one of violence, conflict, and very little love or affection. Unlike Bonney and Read, very little had been recorded about Tommy Farris's life. I'd found a fragment of a 1714 log book for the *Moon Shadow*, but otherwise the only portrait of the pirate I'd been able to piece together had come from other sea captains—and a handful of pirates—who'd written of their journeys. In 1725 a sea captain named Jeremiah Fletcher had grown wealthy on his book, *Pirates I Have Known*, a sensational account of all the pirates he'd met. However, the author included so many vivid details that I suspected he either had actually *been* a pirate, or that the book was more fiction than fact. He was the author who insisted Tommy Farris had made a map of where she'd buried the Spanish treasure.

Fletcher gave a fairly even treatment of all the pirates he profiled except for Thomasina Farris. With Tommy, the man actually ranted. "People said she was brave, but she was yellow. They said she was smart, but she had maggots for brains. They said she was a beauty but I could never see it. They said she had a way with men, but she wouldn't know a fine man if he were dancing naked in front of her." The guy sounded more like a jilted lover than a keen observer of pirates. I should know, since I'd had plenty of experience shopping in the Jilted Department.

When my cell rang, I almost let it go, not recognizing the number, but I answered it.

"Emma, this is Karen Girard, Cam's mother."

"Oh, yes, how—"

"Cam was badly beaten late this evening and is in the hospital."

"Oh my God." My heart leapt into my throat and cut off all breathing.

"I'm here with him now. He wanted me to call you."

"What happened? Is he okay?"

"Barely. Broken wrist, bruised ribs, and his face—" When she choked back a sob, my eyes teared up. Cam was a decent guy. How could anyone do this to him? "He's sleeping now, but he wanted you to know he won't be able to fly out with you tomorrow."

"I don't care about that. I'll come right now."

"No, the doctor said Cam needs to sleep. But perhaps tomorrow morning."

My heart beat faster. "Cam...Cam was always worried someone would beat him up for being gay."

"I know, dear, that's been my fear too. But the cops aren't sure that was the motivation. He was attacked in his condo parking lot coming home from work. The man stole his wallet, cell, BlackBerry, then left him bleeding on the sidewalk. The police think it might be a regular robbery." Cam's mother sighed. "I just want my boy to heal without scars, and I don't mean the physical ones."

"Give him a hug from me," I said. "Tell him I love him."

"I will, dear."

I hung up, frustrated there was nothing I could do. I'm not the best at comforting sick people, since I dislike hospitals, but I wanted to hold Cam's hand. I wanted to bring some coconut oil and pineapple air freshener and make the room smell like him, not like disinfectant. Instead, I found an online florist and sent a bouquet of irises, Cam's favorite flower.

I was so distraught I couldn't sit still, so I took a walk around my neighborhood, watching the kids play on the swings in Powderhorn Park, wishing Cam were as safe and healthy as they were. Damn. First

Julia dumps me, then Drummond steals the maps, and now Cam. I prayed nothing else would go wrong, not only because I cared about my friends, but because I just didn't have time in my life for any more disasters.

CHAPTER SEVEN

Before I left for the airport, I stopped by Hennepin County Medical Center, easily finding a place to park on Seventh Street so early in the morning. I hated the sounds of hospitals—the beeping monitors, the IV stands rolling down the hallways with the swish-swish of a sick person walking in hospital booties, and the morning TV news shows, but I had to see Cam.

Just inside the room I hugged Cam's boyfriend Kyle. "Are you okay?" I whispered.

Kyle got so choked up he couldn't speak, and stepped back to blow his nose. Cam's mother Karen, a trim, athletic woman with graying brown hair and weary eyes, was sitting in the room beside the bed. I gasped at the sight of Cam all bandaged up, his face purple and yellow, one eye swollen shut, his wrist immobilized. He opened his good eye and tried to smile through battered lips. "Hey, Em."

"Don't talk. Christ, I hate the person who did this to you." I don't usually cry, but my throat tightened and I struggled to hold back the tears for Cam's sake. Emotions embarrassed him.

Cam closed his eyes. "Didn't even see him."

I stood by his bed for a few minutes, babbling on about nothing as he lay there, eyes still closed. I checked my watch. Shit. "Cam, I have to leave for Chicago, but I'll call you, okay?"

"Yeah, let me know how it goes," he said weakly. His voice faded and just like that, he was asleep. I talked with Karen and Kyle for a few minutes, then excused myself.

I raced to the airport, parked, then dashed inside and joined the security line snaking toward the metal detectors, where all I could do was hurry up and wait. I scanned my mental checklist to make sure I wasn't carrying any AK-47s or liquid explosives in my bags, then shifted from foot to foot as the line barely moved. Finally the guy behind me laughed softly and I looked over my shoulder.

"If the security people had your energy, this line would move a lot faster."

I smiled at the middle-aged man dressed in an expensive gray suit, his reddish blond crew cut looking more military than businessman. He looked vaguely familiar. "Sorry," I said. "I'm probably driving you crazy."

He shrugged, then dragged his suitcase as the line moved forward. "Maybe it's because I'm older, but waiting doesn't bother me. If you're patient, you'll eventually get what you want."

"Good advice," I said. Crap. I'd have to pencil in "patience" on my calendar sometime next month. I pulled out my driver's license so I'd be ready. What did I want? And once I figured that out, would I have the patience to get it? Even worse, would I have the time? At the conveyor belt, Mr. Patience helped me pull apart two bins stuck together, and I waved politely to him once I was through security, then hurried for the last gate on the stupidly long Gold Concourse, practically jogging on the moving walkway. Thank God the gate attendants were still seating passengers. As one of them checked my ticket, someone ran up behind me out of breath. It was the man with a reddish blond crew cut. He smiled. "I'm not following you, really!"

Remarking on what a close call we'd had, we both boarded the plane, and I scanned the faces, wondering if Marx would be on this flight or if she'd left earlier. But she wasn't on board.

During the flight I couldn't stop thinking about Cam. He had no enemies that I knew of, so it had to be a random robbery. It just wasn't fair. I also remembered where I'd seen the crew cut guy before—he'd been sitting in the chair at the Student Union yesterday that I'd bumped into on my way to the Lunch Bunch table. Wild coincidence.

I checked my bag at the airport Hilton, then took the train into downtown Chicago. I loved that train because it went so fast. No pokey buses, no taxis stuck in belching traffic, but just constant movement and the city speeding by. I loved the bridges arching over nearly every block along the Chicago River, and wished I'd left time to visit the Art Museum. After I got off the train and walked five blocks, I reached the Antiquities Collection, housed in a squat, two-story building, five minutes before I was supposed to meet Marx.

The PI stood in the library's lobby wearing a black suit, white shirt, and dark sunglasses, à la Men in Black. Sharp footsteps from Marx's sensible black shoes echoed off the high ceiling as she approached me. Normally I adored women in sensible clothing, but Ms. Marx was just a bit too haughty for me. Perhaps I could take her down a notch or two today.

"Good morning, Ms. Marx." I tried to sound cheerful.

"Ms. Boyd. I hope you had a pleasant flight." It looked as if it pained her to be nice.

"Lovely."

Marx approached the circulation desk, flipped her badge open, then snapped it shut. The woman had to ID herself, but the whole badge-flipping thing was going to get on my nerves.

The librarian was ready, and escorted us back to a tiny work room where she'd pulled all the pre-1715 books that might have West Indies maps. I gaped at the two wooden tables piled high with books. The room smelled of mold, and the books bore evidence of foxing, shelf wear, and damage from mishandling before they'd been rescued by the library.

The librarian gave us each a pair of white gloves, then swept her hand toward the pile. "I'll leave you two here then. Good luck."

We sat down and each opened a book. That's when it hit me. We were here to see if Drummond had stolen any maps. But what if he hadn't yet hit Chicago? And what if, in our search for missing maps, we also kept our eyes open for the Farris map itself?

"We're looking for two things," I said. Randi raised an eyebrow. "We're looking for signs that Drummond has stolen a map." A tiny thrill zipped through me. "And while we're here, we should look for the Farris map as well."

"You're kidding."

"No, we just examine every West Indies map for an alteration of any kind—pencil, ink, scribbled notes."

Marx muttered something under her breath as she began skimming her book.

"What did you say?"

Marx shook her head. "Nothing."

"Tell me."

"I have a hard time believing in a map's existence when no one has ever seen it. I believe what I can see, hear, smell, and taste. I don't believe in tales of buried treasure."

My jaw clamped tighter than a dog trying to hang on to a bone. "Every good research librarian knows it's best to act as if what you're seeking does exist. This increases the chances you'll actually find it."

Marx shot me a look with those light brown eyes. "So if I believe there's a map, I'll find it."

"Better chance of that happening than if you *don't* believe."

Marx said nothing but began looking through the first book. I watched carefully, but Marx treated the books with the care and caution they needed. I wished the room were larger so we wouldn't have to sit so closely together that our elbows knocked against each other. She smelled clean and fresh, kind of lemony.

We barely spoke as we pored through book after book. I loved holding the three-hundred-year-old books and wished I had more time to slow down and read them. In fact, when was the last time I'd actually read a book, any book?

While we worked, my phone rang a few times—Michelle asking questions, other librarians wanting to know about Drummond, and a friend wanting to go out for a drink. Each time Marx stopped and stared pointedly at me. Finally I got in the habit of hopping up and leaving the room whenever my phone rang.

Two hours after we started, Marx put down a book and sighed, the first human thing she'd done. "Ms. Boyd, I suggest we take a break."

"Call me Emma."

"I don't—"

"Call me Emma. And I'd like to call you Randi. Truthfully, I'm not the biggest fan of investigators or the FBI, and all that formal stuff bugs me." I waited, ready to pounce on her for being uncooperative so I could suggest that perhaps Marx return to Minneapolis.

"Randi would be fine."

"I'll make sure it's Randi-With-An-I." No smile. "I don't expect we'll become friends today, but at least we can be a little less formal." I stood and walked out into the stacks to stretch my back and shoulders, then in five minutes we were back at work.

We looked at every West Indies map. Finally, we reached the

bottom of the stacks. No tragic stubs, no bits of forgotten dental floss, and no Farris map. If Farris had marked clues on any of them, she'd done it so subtly no one would notice. "What if we've missed it?" Randi asked. "Maybe we need a magnifying glass."

"The clues on the map will be visible." I noted with relief that Randi had begun to speak as if the map existed.

After we'd thanked the librarian, I turned toward Randi Marx. "Shall we get lunch, then take a cab to the Patterson Library?"

Randi nodded toward the rest rooms. "I'll meet you outside."

As I stepped out into the warm spring sunshine, blinking at the brightness, a man in a brown suit approached me. "Excuse me, are you Emma Boyd?" Behind him was a stunning blond woman in a tight-fitting kelly green suit.

"Yes, I am." Did I mention the woman was stunning?

The man, tall and lanky with muttonchop sideburns and a battered briefcase, handed me his business card. "Ricardo Benton. Your library said I could find you here. I'm a map dealer, a reputable one, I might add, and I would like to be the first to make you an offer on the Farris map. I am the first, right?" He licked his dry lips and nervously passed his briefcase from hand to hand, but didn't introduce the woman behind him.

My brain couldn't work fast enough. How did he even know I was looking for it? And why did he think I'd found it? I examined the business card. "First, Mr. Benton, we're here to look for stolen maps. And if we were, by some miracle, to find the Farris map, it wouldn't be for sale, since it will belong to the institution in which we find it."

The wooden door behind us swung open and Randi emerged into the sunlight, squinted, then hurried down the stairs.

An odd look passed across Benton's face, and he smiled without really meaning it. "Ms. Marx, what a pleasure."

"Not really. You're like a vulture sniffing around for dead meat." Randi took my elbow and began urging me down the sidewalk, but not before I caught the visual daggers the woman in the kelly green suit shot in Randi's direction.

Randi hurried me across the busy street and toward the Art Museum, which was when I noticed the hand holding my elbow trembled. I pulled my arm back, a little freaked I'd let her take charge of my body like that.

"He's just a greedy dealer, Randi. No reason to get upset. But how did he know we were here?"

She shot me an angry look. "Benton will go to any lengths, *any* lengths, to get a map he wants."

Really, c'mon. How scary could a map collector be? But the woman, that was a different matter. She'd sent tsunamis of hate straight toward Randi. "Who was that woman?" Randi didn't respond, so I stopped walking. "Who was that woman?"

We'd reached the Art Museum, where a line of cabs waited. "Lauren Gilmore, Benton's assistant."

Randi opened the back door of the nearest cab. "Patterson Library, please." She held the door open for me, but once I was inside, Randi slammed the door shut.

"What are you doing?" I asked.

"I have some errands to run, so I'll meet you at the Patterson," Randi replied. "There should be restaurants around there where you can eat." She checked her watch. "I'll meet you there in two hours."

"What?"

Randi smacked the cab's roof and the driver pulled away from the curb.

I looked back at her as the cab entered traffic. Just because I was "doe-eyed" didn't mean I could be pushed around like this. As I faced the front, I thought I saw the man with the reddish-blond crew cut slip into the crowd waiting to cross the street. I shook my head, pissed at being bundled into the damn cab and feeling just a touch paranoid.

CHAPTER EIGHT

I ate at a nearby Chinese buffet, then sat on the edge of a concrete planter outside the Patterson Library, soaking up the sun and enjoying the spring breeze that toyed with my hair. God, it felt good to just sit there doing nothing. Of course my phone rang three times, but they were matters easily dealt with. I was incredibly lucky to have Michelle as my assistant because she could do my job well enough no one would even know I was gone today.

The Patterson Library was an imposing gray granite building set back from the sidewalk with wide steps stretching up to the double oak doors. Perhaps Getty had been right—a few days out of the office might be good for me, although I'd spent my lunch on the phone with Michelle as she looked up Benton. He sold maps on eBay, through his Web site, and through a few rare online map stores. I couldn't find any obvious reason for Randi to be so alarmed.

On time, Randi-With-An-I showed up as promised.

I stood, edging my voice with steel. Maggie called it my "librarian voice." "I don't appreciate being crammed into a cab like that."

Randi shrugged. "Sorry. I consider Benton a risk, and it's my job to keep you safe."

We climbed the steps to the Patterson Library. "I thought your job was to find Drummond or evidence of his theft. Since when is keeping me safe part of the package?" Still irked, I did feel a funny flash of something I couldn't quite identify. Was I flattered she was watching out for me? Could I be that easily charmed?

"Since Benton showed up."

I made a face. "Since we're on the topic of security, if I've seen the same guy at the Minneapolis airport and here in Chicago outside the Antiquities Collection, should I be concerned?"

"Do you think he's following you?" Randi's voice was even.

"I'm not sure. I just think it's weird."

"What does he look like?"

I gave her a description, and mentioned I'd also seen him at school.

"You've seen the same man three times in two days and in two cities?"

It did sound crazy. "I'm not sure."

"Tell me if you see him again."

Randi introduced herself to the circulation librarian, flipping that freaking badge again, and the woman sent us to another librarian, who sent us to a man in a small office on the second floor, who sent us back to the first floor and the Rare Map Desk. The head librarian there, Charlotte Brandt, looked as if she hadn't slept in weeks, and barely took thirty seconds to hear my explanation of our visit.

"I didn't get your e-mails, and there's nothing to worry about. We haven't had any thefts," the round woman snapped. "We would certainly know if someone sliced maps from our books." She pointed to the cameras scattered throughout the high, arching ceiling.

"Yes, I understand you have security," I said, "but Edward Drummond has been operating in the area for months. He could have already been here."

"If you want to worry about a library, that woman at the Chapman in St. Louis is totally incompetent. Their idea of security is to put up nonworking cameras and hope that frightens people." I refused to look at Randi. "But she has even more reason for security because her collection of rare books from the late fifteenth–early sixteenth century is quite extensive."

"We'd like to help you with your collection, if we may," I said, now curious about the St. Louis collection. "We need to know if Drummond has been here."

The woman glared at her watch, then at me. "Oh, for heaven's sakes." She pulled two security wristbands from a drawer, then ran them over a scanner. "But you can't be in the stacks unaccompanied." Her pager beeped softly and she pawed at her waistband until she shut it off. "Look, if you could just have a seat over there, I'll put this fire out. You'll have to wait until I'm through. You should have made an appointment." We were directed to two low-slung chairs across from the desk and Brandt disappeared.

We watched the activity at the Rare Book desk. Patrons checked in, filled out book requests, provided ID, then a librarian disappeared into the stack room. She'd reappear and escort the patron to a quiet, brightly-lit room. It would be hard to steal a map in such a visible spot.

Twenty minutes later she still hadn't come back. Randi tapped her foot impatiently. "This is ridiculous. She expects us to wait while she takes her coffee break? Since when has that been standard procedure?"

"Relax. We're here." Personally, I enjoyed the quiet activity of the library and the low voices muted by the gray and blue geometric carpeting. But like Randi, I did itch to get back into the rare book stacks and start searching.

"How did your pirate die?" Randi suddenly asked. "You never really addressed that in the article."

"Her death is one of those mysteries that may never be solved."

"How do people think she died?"

I opened my briefcase and dug through a file until I found the photocopy. "Here's the notice posted in the *Port Royal Gazette* on July 19, 1715. It says that Thomasina Farris had been captured a week earlier, tried for piracy, and sentenced to hang. She was supposedly hanged on July 18, 1715."

"Sounds like proof enough. Why 'supposedly'?"

"Because the description of her hanging sounds like some detailed costume description: 'The bloodthirsty Mistress Farris wore a long-sleeved brown and white gingham dress, black boots, white gloves, and a black hood as she shuffled, bent over with the weight of her sins, to her well-deserved end. Her long black-and-white braid hung down her back.'"

Randi's brow furrowed. "So?"

"So was it really Tommy Farris who was hanged? No one saw her face because she was wearing a hood. In fact, given the long sleeves, long dress, gloves, and hood, no one even saw her skin. It could have been any woman, white or black, who'd been hanged. And the word *shuffled* bothers me. Tommy wasn't the sort of woman to shuffle. I realize her feet might have been shackled, but I still think she'd have been too proud to be 'bent over with the weight of her sins.'"

"Very interesting, but I'm going crazy waiting." Randi stood, paced back and forth, then dropped back into the chair. For the first time, her professional exterior cracked a bit. Suddenly she turned to me. "Remember in your article how you talked about the difference between a puzzle and a mystery?"

"A puzzle is something that can be solved, like a jigsaw puzzle or sudoku or a math problem." I loved fitting oddly shaped puzzle pieces together. That was one of the reasons I loved research so much.

"And you wrote that a mystery is something that cannot be totally resolved or explained. Some piece or step remains unexplainable, a mystery. I have the perfect example of a mystery. It's a mystery to me why I do some of the things I do, even though I know they might be wrong."

"What things?" I asked, suddenly intrigued.

"This, for one." Randi leapt up, grasped my hand, and pulled me to my feet. She led me past the counter—and this was the amazing thing—I *let* her. She retrieved the two security wristbands, and then ducked out of sight around the corner from the desk.

"What are you—"

"I'm not very good at waiting." She snapped one band onto her wrist, the other onto mine.

I finally figured out what she was up to. "I don't think—"

"Follow me." Randi steered me down the narrow white hallway and passed our wrists over the reader attached to the wall. When the door clicked, Randi opened it and pulled me through.

My pulse raced as I leaned back against the closed door. "We just broke into the rare book stacks of the Patterson Library. How does that make us any different than Drummond?"

"Got any dental floss tucked into your cheek?"

"No."

"That's how we're different. Now, where do we start?"

"This is wrong," I hissed.

"Tough," Randi whispered. "Get over it and help me find the section that might have Caribbean maps."

"You can't just break rules because you don't like them."

She moved so close the fine hairs on my neck tingled. "If we find the map, we might be closer to catching Drummond. Besides, rules are for people who need them."

The woman's arrogance was stunning. Still angry, I couldn't help but reach out and touch the nearest book. Good God, it was Mills's *Atlas of the State of South Carolina*. I'd been trying to acquire a copy of this gem for the Kline library for months. The narrow, climate-controlled room was filled with two rows of gray metal shelves reaching almost to the fluorescent light fixtures. Even with the air circulation and humidity regulated, a faint smell of old book drifted toward me. I loved the smell. "Brandt wasn't ready for our visit, so we're going to have to pull the books ourselves." I checked the classification labels at the ends of the shelves. "Let's start here with these four shelves. Scan them for titles that indicate voyages or travel or atlas. Those are the most likely to have maps that Drummond would be interested in, or that Tommy Farris might have altered."

We got to work. I cocked my head slightly as I walked, the pose enabling me to better read the spines. Unfortunately, too many hours of that would give me librarian neck and require a chiropractic adjustment and three visits to the massage therapist. I had walked both sides of one row when Randi appeared. "I found them."

I followed Randi a few rows ahead and scanned the shelf of old travel books. "Perfect. You start on the left, I'll start on the right. Any book published before 1715 means Farris could have owned the book. Between his hateful rants, Fletcher wrote that Tommy loved to read about sea journeys."

For an hour we moved through the stacks, pulling large books down, flipping through them slowly, shutting them and moving to the next. But nothing—no stolen maps with sad ridges of paper left behind from Drummond and his floss, and no maps altered with "X marks the spot." I was fascinated by the seafaring memoirs, however, and skimmed a few. I spent some time reading the journal of a sea captain from the 1800s who'd sailed whaling ships off the coast of Newfoundland.

"What are you doing?" Randi asked, suddenly right beside me.

Startled, my heart thumped hard. "I'm skimming the book. Never know when an author might mention Farris."

Randi shook her head. "We need to stay focused on stolen maps."

How dared Ms. Super Investigator tell me how to research a

topic? "The more we can use original sources, the better. We may never find the map the way we're approaching it, but instead it may take piecing together clues from other sources. That's what it means to put a puzzle together." It'd taken months of painstaking research to piece together what little I knew about Tommy Farris. Original sources were the only way I'd learn more. Who knew where I might stumble across an offhand reference to Tommy's death?

"We need to stay focused on stolen maps." The woman was like a terrier latched on to a mail carrier, unwilling to let go.

Luckily, Charlotte Brandt seemed to have forgotten us, since after a short break, we were able to spend another hour in fruitless searching. The only interesting thing we found was a stack of six seafaring books owned by a Captain R. Brown, each signed by Brown on the inside front cover. Randi tapped the signature on one of the books. "Does the name ring a bell? Was he a British naval officer? A merchant ship captain? A pirate?" Caught up in her own questions, she seemed to have forgotten her lecture about maps and only maps.

I stared at the name. "I don't know of any Captain R. Brown. I'll ask Michelle to see what she can find, since just Googling the name won't access the databases we need." As Randi reshelved the books, something struck me. I opened my mouth to point it out, but then shut it again. Randi thought I was a bit wacko anyway, and the little pattern recognition thing I'd just done could be considered anal. The six books were by Arbogast, Rothschilde, Ringrose, Franklin, Innisfree, and Samuels. Rearrange the books and their initials were F-A-R-R-I-S. That had to be a coincidence. I wanted to find this map so badly I'd begun seeing connections that weren't really there.

I lost track of time as I happily skimmed book after book. It felt just like when I cruised through antique stores looking for old jigsaw puzzles. The most amazing treasures from the past were sometimes right before my eyes, waiting to be found.

I stopped when I realized Randi was standing so close to me I could see dark flecks in her light brown eyes. "What are you staring at?" I asked.

"You're enjoying this, aren't you?"

"The search?"

"That, and being in the stacks without permission."

I chuckled. "Well, don't get all excited and think you've brought me over to the Dark Side." Randi's gaze was hard to decipher, but I thought I detected a spark of amusement.

"It's a shame you think I'm so devious."

"Well, you're right about one thing. I am kind of excited. I love treasure hunts."

Randi's eyes widened just a sliver. "Me too."

We stared at the bookshelf next to us, both suddenly uncomfortable. What had just happened? A moment of connection between the badge snapper and the anal librarian? I cleared my throat. "What do you think the treasure might be?"

"If it exists, it'll be silver. The Spanish mined the silver and gold in the mountains of Peru using the natives as slaves, then carted the silver by donkey train down to Puerto Bello and loaded up a fleet for Spain. Somewhere northwest of Puerto Bello the fleet was attacked by pirates. Your article left no doubt in my mind about that."

I jammed a hand into my back pocket. "I've been thinking more about it. The treasure could be a place. A place can be a treasure."

Randi rolled her eyes, a sight so uncharacteristic I bit back a laugh. "That's a bit romantic, don't you think?"

"It could be a person. A person could be a treasure."

Randi shook her head and actually chuckled softly. "A map to a person wouldn't work unless that person was no longer moving, which meant he or she was dead. And why would anyone make a map like that?"

I replaced the book on the shelf, then leaned against the bookcase. "Ready to give up yet?"

There was that flash again, a spark of amusement in her eyes that she obviously tamped down before it could reach the rest of her face. "No, but there's something intoxicating about a hunt. You were right. Just in the act of looking for something you come to believe it's real and that you'll find it."

Something leapt between us that I couldn't explain. Thrill of the hunt? Recognizing we might have something in common after all?

My cell trilled. "Emma, Getty here. How's it going? Found anything yet?"

I explained what we'd learned so far.

"Well, just think of the prestige of the library if we help stop

Drummond and find a treasure map at the same time. Remember, I'm behind you a hundred percent." I hung up, thinking that Getty was like a little kid who'd watched *Pirates of the Caribbean* too many times. He was no different than most people—thrilled by the idea of buried treasure somewhere.

By the time we left the stacks, Charlotte Brandt was working behind the Rare Map circulation desk. I thought she was going to burst a blood vessel when she saw us emerging from her stack room. The muscles along her jaw twitched as if getting a repeated electric shock. "I thought you'd gotten tired of waiting and left. Yet it appears you entered the stacks without my permission."

Randi whipped out her badge and flipped it open again, and I wondered if she was showing off for me. "PI, remember? You didn't return when you said you would, so we proceeded with our investigation."

"Without my permission, and without supervision. Ms. Boyd, you of all people should know how inappropriate this is."

I suddenly felt seven years old. "I'm sorry, but we're pressed for time." By now all the staff and fifteen patrons had stopped to watch, and the blush burning my neck skipped happily all the way up to my cheeks. What had I been thinking to let Randi lead me into the stacks like that?

"Should you ever request admission to our materials again, you'll be denied entrance." She snapped off our wristbands. "I'll be reporting this incursion to both your supervisors. Follow me."

Heels clicking angrily on the marble, Charlotte Brandt led us down the stairs and across the wide lobby, only stopping when we pushed open the doors and slunk from the building.

I whirled on Randi. "Well, Ms. Rules-Aren't-For-Me, I hope you're happy. Why did I let you talk me into this?"

Randi jammed on her shades. "In my line of work, some things are necessary."

My blood pressure rose. "Well, in my line of work, we follow the rules. So I think it would be a good idea if you returned to Minneapolis."

"And you?" Marx was totally unfazed by my anger. She was in some sort of ethical bubble, untouched by right and wrong.

I shifted my briefcase and checked my watch. "I'm intrigued by Brandt's suggestion of St. Louis, and since I'm halfway there I might see if Getty will let me go to St. Louis."

The look of horror on Randi's face almost made me laugh. "You can't be serious."

I smiled. "Perfectly serious, so you may go home. I'm going to catch a train back to the Hilton O'Hare. Where are you staying?"

"Not there." Then she whirled on her heel and walked away.

"It's been nice working with you," I said to her retreating back.

By the time I reached my hotel using the train and a short taxi hop, I'd reached both Getty and Jennifer Binder, the librarian at the Chapman in St. Louis. Getty had grown even more excited that I might find the map, so agreed to another day, and the librarian sounded frazzled and grateful for my help. I left a message on Randi's cell. "I'm going to the Chapman in St. Louis tomorrow, but you might as well fly back to Minneapolis. I can take care of myself."

I had a phone message from the Gates Library in Seattle, offering to share its security DVD of Drummond with me, so I asked them to overnight it to the Chapman in St. Louis.

For the fifth time that day I called Cam's cell, and this time his mother answered. "He's slept all day, but he's going to be fine. He remembers more now, though, and said he'd passed a man in the parking lot before he was struck."

"What did the man look like?" Between Benton and the crew cut guy, I was feeling just a touch paranoid.

"Cam couldn't remember much, but the doctor says each day more memory will return."

I tried to read the latest Janet Evanovich but kept closing the book, unable to shake the image of Randi walking away from me. She seemed almost haunted by something. She wouldn't discuss her travel plans. She'd been shaken to run into the map dealer. She mysteriously refused to share cabs or reveal her hotel. I'd never really been drawn to lost souls, but I was torn between two emotions: embarrassed that I'd followed Randi into the stacks to be publicly humiliated by the librarian, and curiosity over a new puzzle: Was private investigator Randi-With-An-I Marx hiding something behind that flipping badge?

PART THREE

The Wench, 1715

Pirate's Article 9. If at any time we meet with a prudent woman, any man that offers to meddle with her, without her consent, shall suffer death.

—from the Articles of Captain John Phillips, Charles Johnson, *General History of the Pyrates*

CHAPTER NINE

Tommy Farris woke in one of the *Moon Shadow*'s longboats, stiff and sore and embarrassed beyond all reason. She'd fled her own cabin and spent the night under a tarp in the wooden boat. This woman Rebekah had tricked them all. With her silence, she'd made a safe place for Tommy to speak thoughts she'd never shared with anyone. And now Tommy felt more exposed than if she'd undressed before the entire crew. She considered slitting the woman's throat and tossing her overboard, but that seemed extreme even for a pirate of Tommy's reputation.

Tommy threw off the tarp, then peeked over the longboat's gunwale. The sky over the West Indies had already lightened, and the bell had just rung for watch change. She was alone, so she hopped from the boat and straightened her coat as if she had just paused for a moment near the boat instead of slept in it. Bugger it all. There might be something to the banning of women on ships. Tommy had brought one aboard, and only a day later was skulking around her own ship, sleeping in the bleeding boat.

Tommy raided the galley for hardtack and a mug of ale, then returned to the quarterdeck. Since the woman wasn't allowed on this part of the deck, it seemed the best place to avoid her.

The morning passed uneventfully. The weather was favorable for sailing, though a heavy bank of clouds lumbered behind them, as if just waiting for the chance to attack. Tommy disliked the summer weather in the West Indies because the region's great storms could lift her ships and dash them against the shore or bury them in towering waves. But the English colonies had begun capturing and hanging pirates along their coast, so it was safer to remain down in the tropics where only four Royal Navy ships and two fast sloops patrolled an area over seven hundred leagues long and nearly five hundred leagues wide, with over two hundred islands providing places to hide, or take on food and water.

For most of the day Tommy avoided her English-speaking servant, but it seemed everywhere she turned Rebekah was there, washing something or helping the crew with the rigging or just looking out at the horizon. While a smile never crossed those lips, Tommy suspected Rebekah was greatly amused by this whole situation. Tommy reviewed what she had said to her these last two days, and shuddered, wishing she'd never rescued the woman.

Midday Tommy unpacked her quadrant and took a sighting. They were running down the long string of islands in the eastern West Indies that ended in Grenada. It was slow going thanks to a southern wind, but it couldn't be helped. While these islands tolerated pirates, it was best to be staying sharp so Billy was stationed up in the crow's nest full time now, with volunteers bringing him food and water. If the boy had to piss, he did so against the nearest sail so it wouldn't rain down upon the deck.

Tommy's navigation tasks were interrupted by the appearance on the quarterdeck of Coxon and his band of followers. Coxon looked no more pleasant than at their last encounter. "Captain, sir."

If he'd had more teeth, perhaps his grin would not have been so hideous. Tommy maintained a constant supply of fruit on board, believing it to be beneficial to health, but not every captain in Coxon's past had done that, judging by his mouth. She waited.

"The men and me are thinking we have a battle ahead of us, and…" He hesitated, gazing over the crowd of men who had formed around them. Sailors had an inbred sense of when something interesting was about to happen aboard ship and came from all corners to watch.

Tommy suspected what Coxon had in mind but said nothing.

"No disrespect intended, o' course, but I'll fry in hell before a bunter like you takes us into such a battle. That's why we're calling for a vote to elect a new captain."

Tommy didn't answer, but leveled her gaze at Coxon. She rested a hand on her sword hilt, tipping her head back just a bit to look at the man with all the disdain she could muster. "Coxon, you be more trouble than you're worth. You're so ugly Hell'd never have you. You've got but one ear, one eye, and no good sense. Shut your fucking gob or you can eat what falls from my tail."

Coxon's men glowered, and those who supported Tommy chuckled, but it was unclear which group was in the majority at this point. Coxon widened his stance to intimidate her, but it didn't work. "Don't them Articles give us a say in who our captain be?"

Her ship's Articles did say that. Tommy felt backed up against the mast. The men were certainly within their rights as ship's company to elect a new captain. She'd just never thought they would. But if this pirate fleet captured the Spanish silver, each captain would get two shares of the take and regular crew one share each. Coxon was fixing to put himself up as captain and double his booty.

Tommy glared at Coxon, her mind searching for a solution. Did she have the votes? Had Coxon turned more of the crew against her? Reluctant to let the vote go forward but powerless to stop it, Tommy caught Sawkin's subtle nod toward the northeast. Sweet Jesus. Another sail. Could the Fates have delivered a prize just when she needed one to build the men's confidence?

"We could be voting now, or—" Tommy stopped. She undid her braid and shook it out across her shoulders. "Or we could be chasing down that ship to the northeast." One hundred heads turned in unison. Hope, and Tommy's billowing hair, ignited the men.

All hands shouted and ran for their stations. Tommy sent a silent thank-you to Sawkins. "Signal Shaw we're taking a little detour." From the bow, hair whipping like a silk flag, Tommy fired command after command until her small fleet had nearly overtaken its prey.

"'Tis a merchant ship," Hatley crowed happily. The *Moon Shadow* herself nearly shivered in anticipation, since merchants carried goods, silver, medicine, and very rich passengers.

When the *Moon Shadow* and the *Tiger Eye* moved up on either side of the merchant's stern, the pirate crews made the racket that was music to Tommy's ears. The panicked captain of the large, lumbering vessel fired off all sixteen guns in an impressive display of smoke and booms, a thoughtless action because the pirate ships were too far astern to actually be targets for the long guns protruding out the merchant's sides. Tommy shook her head at the waste of sixteen perfectly good cannonballs.

"All hands fire as you bear, boys. Sweep her deck!" Tommy yelled, and any gun in a pirate's hand fired with a deafening bang and puff of gray smoke. Men on the merchant ship screamed and ran, and within seconds they'd lowered their flag in surrender. The *Moon Shadow* was now close enough to bump the other's hull.

"Grapplin' hooks to larboard." The lines flew through the air and hooks clattered onto the prize. Led by Tommy, the pirates swarmed onto the merchant ship, daggers in their mouths, eyes wild. But before the killing began, Tommy raised her cutlass. "Stand down, men. We be guests on this grand ship. We should behave politely. Let me speak with these fine gentlemen." Her men stopped, pulsing with energy, but they grinned, having seen this act before. They herded the merchant crew up to the forecastle where Hatley and the others would explain why they should give up honest sailing and join the sweet trade. The remaining prisoners were the captain and first mate, a priest in heavy black robes, and a wealthy passenger.

Surrounded by her men, Tommy sauntered past the captain, a rotund man in a grimy, discarded naval uniform, to the wealthy gent wearing a silk waistcoat with a gold pocket watch, clean white breeches, and shiny black boots. She looked down at the boots. "Sawkins, you think these boots would fit me?"

"Aye, Captain. Them boots be fitting ye just fine."

Tommy smiled at the man as her crew guffawed. The passenger wordlessly pulled off both boots and handed them to her.

"Ah, thank you, sir." Leaning against the rail, she yanked off her old, scuffed boots and slid the new ones on. "Perfect." She returned to the wealthy man. "My first mate lacks a timepiece." The man handed over the gold watch, which Tommy tossed to Sawkins.

Enough playing. Tommy returned to the captain. "My name's Thomasina Farris. Ever heard of me?"

The man nodded, sweat soaking the tight collar of his shirt.

"Good. Then you know it'd be best for all involved if you tell me where you've stashed the valuable cargo, including the coin of this fine, bootless gentleman here."

The captain cleared his throat. "We carry no coin. We carry cloth and spices bound for Jamaica. Nothing more."

"And your rich passenger?"

"Also bound for Jamaica."

"Sawkins, what time is it?"

Her first mate snapped open his new pocket watch. "About two bells into the afternoon watch, Captain." The crew was spellbound, as if watching a play. Even Coxon stood silent, unsure of what would happen next.

Tommy shook her head. "I be very late for an appointment and don't have time for this. Be you both good Catholics?" When the captain and the merchant nodded, Tommy strode over to the priest and grabbed him by the collar, dragging him forward. "Then surely you'll be telling me what I want to know so I won't have to torture this poor man of the cloth."

Neither man volunteered any information, so Tommy shook her head sadly. "I'm going to torture this priest until he begs Satan to take possession of his soul. I'll be jamming sticks up his fingernails and gouging out his eyes, cutting off his ears, then pulling out one end of his intestines and forcing him at swordpoint to walk the length of the ship, unraveling his own guts."

The merchant paled and the captain swallowed hard.

"Still nothing? Come with me, Father, and prepare to enter my version of Hell." The priest struggled, pleading with the captain, but Tommy dragged him single-handedly across the mid-deck, through the crowded wardroom, and into the captain's cabin, where she threw him inside and slammed the door behind them. Not a sound was heard on deck as all waited to hear the screams.

The priest stood, straightening his cassock, then turned to face her. "God, Tommy, but you're a beautiful sight." Laughing, they embraced, then stepped back, grinning widely at each other.

"Danny McLurin, you stupid scug, what the devil are you doing parading around as a priest?"

The lean man laughed, his eyes bright and hair still unruly even as a holy man. "Thank you, by the way, for not giving me away. My flock may not accept a pirate as a priest."

Tommy shook her head, delighted to see her old friend, one of the few she actually had. "Don't be telling me this is for truth, that you really be playing at priest?"

"Heading to Port Royal to start up a mission."

Tommy winked. "You need a donation to that mission? I'm sure the two gentlemen aboard would be happy to share. All you need do is a little bit of acting."

In reply, the ex-pirate threw back his head and howled pitifully with pain. Tommy banged the cabin wall as if throwing the poor priest around like a sack of flour. Then she pulled out her cutlass. "Watch your timing, man," she said, then slammed the cutlass into the table. Danny screamed so realistically even Tommy's hair stood on end. They repeated this a few more times, but still nothing. She held up her hand, then strolled back out on deck, where the captain and gentleman were trembling in horror. "Still can't remember where you put those darned little coins?" she asked. No reply, so she returned to the cabin. "It's not working. We need something more drastic."

McLurin snapped his fingers. "The poor bosun took the fever and died this morning. His body's in the wardroom waiting burial." Together they dragged the dead man into the cabin and Tommy stretched out one arm. "Okay, big finale," she murmured, and hacked off the dead man's hand. McLurin outdid all his other screams. Tommy returned to the rich men, tossing the hand at their feet. "You gentlemen be next." Just then, moaning pitifully, Danny staggered onto the deck, his "stump" jammed under one arm, wrapped in cloth dripping with "blood." Tommy raised her eyebrow at her friend. Nice touch.

Both the merchant and the captain babbled at the same time, listing all their hiding places. Sawkins sent men off to retrieve the goods. Once they had three small chests of coin and a box full of jewelry in hand, the men tore the ship apart for anything they might be able to use or sell in the next pirate-friendly port.

Two hours later Tommy hesitated as she prepared to leave the ship. The captain had tried to flee her fleet, and her men expected her to punish him for that. She kept emotion from her face, but inside cursed a blue streak for what she must now do. She could cut off the man's hand, but she'd already appeared to do that to McLurin, and her men valued originality. She could spend time torturing the captain, but she totally lacked the stomach for that and her men would notice.

A sigh escaped before she could stop it, so she approached the captain, sighing dramatically this time as if she were quite put out. "It hurts me mighty to have to do this. I'm sure you're a decent enough bloke, but it's best not to run from Tommy Farris." She dared not glance over at the *Moon Shadow* to see if Rebekah watched. What would she think of her? No matter. Tommy'd made her decision.

The man clasped his hands together. "Please, spare me. I—"

The kill was quick and clean. The captain crumpled to the deck and two of Tommy's men dragged him to the railing and tossed him overboard. Tommy wiped off her sword, resheathed it, then swept her gaze across the merchant ship to meet the eye of every sailor brave enough to lift his head. By the time she finished, she knew none of them would forget her. They'd spread the word that running from Tommy Farris and refusing to give up the gold were stupid acts. Yet Tommy left them enough water and sail to reach land, and enough coin hidden beneath Danny McLurin's cassock to start his mission. How he'd explain he still possessed his hand would be his problem.

As the *Moon Shadow* and *Tiger Eye* made sail, Tommy called the crew up onto the mid-deck while she stood above them on the quarterdeck. Rebekah was not among the men. Tommy nodded to Sawkins, who stepped up.

"Several hours ago Coxon called for a vote," he said. "Captain Tommy just showed us why she be the best captain sailing the West Indies. I imagine Coxon would like to be your captain. So let's put it to a vote. How many say aye for Captain Tommy?"

The chorus of male voices was deafening, and Tommy let herself smile.

"How many for our good man Coxon here?"

A handful of cries responded, but the result of the vote was clear.

Tommy raised her fist. "To celebrate, this be a wash day, with a double ration of ale. In fact, Cookie, mix us up some bumbo."

Cookie made bumbo, a mixture of rum, water, sugar, and nutmeg, only on her orders, and it was the crew's favorite. Wash day only happened once or twice a year, but the men seemed to enjoy it.

The majority of the hands returned to their stations, leaving Coxon and his men standing there with red faces. "Ye think you're damned smart, don't ye?" Coxon said.

"I think I be captain of this ship, nothing more. You'd do well to remember that."

After he stomped away, Tommy gave the orders to bring the *Moon Shadow* around to rejoin Shaw's ships. Billy sent the information to the other two ships via flags, then Tommy asked Sawkins to get the pumps going to bring seawater on deck for the men to strip and wash. She watched Coxon help drag out the hose. The last thing she needed on her ship was trouble from that man, but he'd signed the Articles and was an equal member of the crew. If he did something wrong and broke the Articles, only then could she banish him from her ship. She would watch, and wait. She'd had a bully on her ship once before, and he'd nearly killed her.

Chapter Ten

Tommy returned to her cabin, as was her habit during wash day. Blast it all, but Rebekah was there with the noon meal. Flushed, Tommy sat at the table without a word, and Rebekah perched primly on her hammock, those black locks framing her dark face as if it were a painting.

"How did it fare for you on the captured ship?"

"Fine. You didn't observe the events?"

"No, I remained here in the cabin."

Tommy was relieved Rebekah hadn't witnessed the death of the merchant captain. "Why are you not eating?" Tommy asked.

"I feel unwell. My stomach is bothered."

Tommy bent over her bowl, suddenly shy. Rebekah did look ashen, as if taken ill with some complaint. Thin beads of perspiration clung to the figurehead's amazing face.

"I'm glad you remain captain," Rebekah said.

"For the sake of your safety, of course," Tommy muttered between sips of hot soup.

"Why, Captain, you think me that selfish? Couldn't I be happy for your sake?" Tommy looked up and the she-devil was actually smiling; a deep dimple appeared and Tommy nearly choked as her groin tightened again. What was it about this woman?

"You're angry with me for not telling you earlier I speak English."

Tommy put down her spoon, taking great comfort from the roll of the ship beneath her. "I made a fool of my—"

"You didn't. You're very brave, and I admire what you've done with your life, even though you're a pirate. My life has been…"

She stopped, gripping her hands together, and Tommy's own selfishness suddenly became clear to her. "I'm thinking your life hasn't been easy as well."

"No, it hasn't."

"How long have you been a slave?"

Rebekah raised her head, her gaze now the defiant look of the figurehead on the *Maravillosa*. "I was born into it. My mama and I lived in the big house on a cane plantation west of Port Royal. Four months ago…" She stopped, her throat working, and Tommy was seized with panic. Was she going to cry? What did one do with a crying woman? "Four months ago Mama and I were sent out into the field to work the cane. And now, when you…when you plucked me from the water, I was bound for the plantations on Trinidad."

Tommy wanted more, so she gently coaxed the story from her. Because Rebekah's mama cooked for the Quiring family on their plantation on Jamaica's southern coast, Rebekah grew up with, then waited on, young Mistress Lily. She'd been tutored alongside Lily, taught to play the pianoforte, and trained to draw.

"Sounds like a fine life," Tommy said, thinking of her childhood spent roaming muddy streets in search of food. But at least she'd been free.

"It wasn't unbearable, although Mistress Lily was selfish and often treated me poorly. But when I turned eighteen, young Master Quiring came home from years at a London boarding school, and everything fell to pieces." Rebekah stared down at her clasped hands.

"Did Quiring meddle with you?"

Rebekah looked up through long lashes. "He tried, but my knee cooled his ardor, at least for a few days."

"Had I been there, I should have sliced off his balls, fried them up with some butter and salt, and served them to you for supper." When Rebekah smiled gratefully, Tommy wished desperately she'd been there to help.

"One day Madam noticed her son pursued me and proclaimed that no slave, no matter how beloved, would weaken their lineage with a bastard mulatto child."

Rebekah sighed, but Tommy lightly touched her hand. "Please, go on."

"The next day Mama and I became field hands, living in a filthy hut with two other families and working cane for hours in the hot sun. Mama passed out from the heat at least once a day. After four weeks, I knew Mama would not survive much longer, so when she collapsed that day, I picked her up and marched toward the Big House. The overseer was at the far end of the field so did nothing to stop me.

"Feeling faint myself, I kicked open the door to the kitchen and laid Mama down on the cool tile floor. Madam Quiring was there, and threatened to call the overseer if I didn't leave. I'd lived in that house for years, but she looked at me as if I were filth, and I wanted to die of shame. But I convinced her that Mama wasn't the problem—I was, and if she sold me and brought Mama back into the house, all would be well."

"So she did."

"Yes, but only because she missed Mama's cooking. Within two days I was in chains on an auction block in Port Royal and sold off to another sugar plantation.

"I've done my best to blot from my memory the next two months, but then once again I was on the auction block, sold, then loaded onto the boat bound for Trinidad. That evil Shaw captured our ship and threw us overboard, then you rescued me."

Tommy was horrified to hear of a slave's life firsthand. Cookie had been a slave, but he wasn't much for talking. "Why did you jump overboard my ship, not once but twice? You spoke English so you knew I meant you no harm."

Rebekah considered her hands, resting in her lap. "I feared you would sell me to the next ship that passed. I let myself lose hope." She brushed away a tear so smoothly Tommy almost missed it. "I forgot what Mama always told me."

"Which was?"

"*Dum spiro, spero.*"

Tommy swallowed, then pushed ahead. "My Latin's a bit rusty," she said, having none at all.

"While I breathe, I hope."

"While I breathe, I hope," Tommy repeated. "I like that."

"I was still breathing, but I'd lost hope. The second time I jumped I realized I didn't want to drown. I was still breathing, so I would not lose hope. What do you hope for?" Rebekah asked suddenly.

Tommy looked into Rebekah's deep brown eyes. "To keep on living, simple as that." She was done admitting she wanted a way out of pirating but couldn't find one. Instead, Tommy told Rebekah tales from her life as a pirate, leaving out, of course, the killing and torture.

After Tommy's story of how she'd accidentally left Billy behind on an island and had to elude a Royal Navy ship to recover him, Rebekah leaned forward suddenly. "Was it difficult for you to kill that captain?"

Tommy's heart sank. Rebekah had heard what Tommy'd done. Somehow she steered the conversation to a safer topic, and Rebekah didn't bring it up again. Both women relaxed and carried on a conversation about life for another hour. Outside came the sounds of water on deck, men shrieking at the cool water, and hoots of laughter. With her door open, Tommy smelled the pungent bumbo now being drunk on deck.

At one point the hoots on deck grew louder, and something, or someone, thundered through the wardroom. Rebekah and Tommy both looked up to see Billy's goat scamper into the captain's cabin with a pair of trousers clamped in his teeth, followed closely by a loudly cursing Hatley, buck naked and mad as a wet hen. Both crashed around in Tommy's cabin, then went back out the way they entered, bleating and cursing.

Tommy looked at Rebekah, and something passed between them. It was not unusual, of course, to see a naked man aboard a ship, but this particular sight touched a funny bone, and they began to laugh. Tommy didn't know why, but the more Rebekah laughed, the more Tommy did. Soon Rebekah lay on her side and Tommy clutched at her stomach. She could not remember the last time she had done this. Had it really been so long? Finally they both regained their senses and wiped their eyes. Rebekah joined Tommy at the table while she finished her meal and they talked about nothing in particular.

❖

That afternoon Tommy decided to give Rebekah another job. Since Tommy's cabin boy had been killed last year, the men had been taking turns on the bell, but if Rebekah took the forenoon and afternoon watches, that freed up two men to repair sails or man the pumps. Tommy brought Rebekah to the small navigation stand inside the wardroom.

"You be needing two things for this task. This half-hour sandglass, and that ship's bell just outside this door. On your watches, you must mind the sandglass. When it runs out, ring the bell so the man on watch will know to drop the log line and be reading our speed. Then just turn the glass over, and be back in time to see it run out again. You be on the forenoon watch, from eight in the morning to noon, then afternoon from noon to four p.m."

Rebekah repeated the instructions. "That's it? Just ringing the bell and flipping the glass over?"

"Yes. But you ring the bell more than once accordin' to time. One bell is the first half hour of the watch. Two bells is the first hour, three bells is one and half hours, four—"

Rebekah held up her hand. "So a four-hour watch will have eight bells."

Tommy grinned. Beautiful *and* smart. "That be right."

The men hated working the bell, so all seemed glad of Rebekah's help. She didn't stop asking questions, though, which drove Tommy a bit barmy. All day she was explaining the log line, how she took their latitude readings with her quadrant, how the man on watch would record the ship's speed on the traverse board, then how Tommy would record all the ship's movements in her log book every night. The ship's log book was like a Bible to a captain, she told Rebekah. Anything important that happened on a ship was recorded in its log book. Rebekah soaked up the ideas like a sponge, and Tommy was happy to spend her day with her.

❖

Tommy was in the wardroom working on their course and Rebekah had just rung eight bells on the afternoon watch when Billy called down that Shaw had raised a flag. All captains were to meet on board the *Sharktooth*.

As Tommy and her officers prepared to climb down into the longboat, Coxon tried to join them but Tommy stepped into his path. "Stay here and square away the gun room."

He shook his head, black eyes blazing. "No, Captain, I'm coming along."

Out of patience, she reached for her cutlass, but one of the older crew stepped up, voice shaking but determined. "Beggin' yer pardon, Captain, but some of us boys think Coxon should go along. The more men with ye on Shaw's boat, the safer ye are, right?"

"We're not in battle," Coxon said, "which means we all have a say in what goes on. And scuttle me if some of the men don't think it might be a good idea to have me there."

No one spoke the words hanging in the air—that some of her own men didn't trust her. Jaws clenched, Tommy descended to the bobbing boat. When she arrived at Shaw's towering frigate, she struggled not to feel as if she were a defeated captain forced to kneel at Shaw's feet.

The day was overcast, the wind brisk as she climbed aboard, then walked along the gangboard to the forecastle. Hot stares and low whistles dogged Tommy as she followed Shaw toward the ladder down to the wardroom. Apparently Shaw's men were moved to see Captain Farris up close, so she stopped before a group of ogling men and gazed at each one, letting her eyes rest overlong at each crotch, after which she smiled sadly. She found this worked well to disarm lewd sailors. Each man quieted down as he considered he might be inadequate for the job he had in mind. Feeling oddly light, Tommy laughed heartily then descended to the mid-deck and crossed to Shaw's wardroom.

The room quickly filled with smoke as the officers of each ship crowded in and chewed on stubby cigars. Shaw stood in the center of the room, as puffed out as if someone had blown wind up his arse.

"Gentlemen and gentle lady." He guffawed. "No, that doesn't work. Gentlemen and Captain Farris, we have before us a great opportunity. Our fleet now be big enough we can easily cut the *Barcelona* from the fleet, take her and her booty."

His officers cheered heartily, and both Stratton and McLeod beamed. Tommy's unease grew as Shaw presented his plan, which was to hide behind St. Andrew's off the eastern coast of the Nicaraguan area of New Spain, like every other pirate had done, and wait for the fleet to pass.

When he finished, Tommy stood and pointed to the map. "Captain Shaw, if I may. By waiting at St. Andrew's Island, we be doing the same thing many a pirate's done before us. The Spaniards'll be knowing we be there. Why don't we wait up here, at the Dolphin Islands? First we send a ship down to Puerto Bello to report back when the galleons set sail. Then we send a ship to the west of the Dolphins to spy on the fleet if it passes between the coast and the Dolphins. We could also send another ship to the east in case the fleet cuts right up the middle of the sea."

Shaw considered his charts, slid a thick finger from their position at the eastern edge of the West Indies over to the Dolphins, then squinted at her. "Not a bad idea, Captain Farris. Wetherly, ready the *Black Widow*. You and a small crew'll sail to Puerto Bello, then report back to us here at this cove on the eastern side of the largest island in the Dolphins. The Spaniards will pass St. Andrews, think they're safe, and get sloppy and drunk, and when faced with our fleet they'll practically hand over the silver."

"One of my men be a Spaniard," Tommy said. "He and a handful of the *Moon Shadow* crew could go with the *Black Widow*." Unspoken, of course, was her clear statement that she didn't trust either Shaw or his men.

"As you wish, m'lady," Shaw said with a condescending bow. "Now for our course. We'll be turning west soon and heading straight for the Dolphins. We'll wait there for the Spanish to pass by then we'll surprise the buggers and be rich."

The men responded with lusty cries.

"The *Barcelona* will be ours," Shaw added.

Tommy waited until the cheering died down. "My ships be sailing a bit farther south before we turn west." The last thing she wanted was to sail clear across the West Indies with Shaw on the horizon. She'd grind her teeth down to stubs. Instead, she would sail a parallel course so Shaw would have to rely on his own navigation rather than following her. If she was lucky, Shaw's poor navigation skills would send him and his men up to Jamaica and the whole stupid scheme would fail. She took a deep breath. "Also, why not take the *Maravillosa* instead of the *Barcelona*? She be just as worthy of a prize, and not likely to be as heavily guarded as the larger galleon." She told Shaw and the men what they'd seen back up on Sombrero Island while careening. "Something isn't right with that big ship. It be too old and pocked full of holes to be bringing treasure all the way back across the Atlantic to Spain. She'll never survive the voyage."

Shaw gave an unpleasant hoot and shook his shaggy head. "Are ye a pirate, Captain Farris, or a woman?"

"I'm both, you son of a—"

"Yellow ain't a pirate's color, especially not one who sails with me. Who here wants to take the *Barcelona*?" All hands shot into the air, even those of Tommy's own captains. At least they were unable to meet her eye after doing so.

"Do ye want your men thinking you're a shivering petticoat lacking the nerve to take the biggest ship in the West Indies?" Shaw scolded.

"Flog off, you slab-faced prick." Tommy's hand twitched but she kept it well away from her sword hilt.

Shaw laughed, then began pacing, expounding on "his" plan as he walked. The faces of the men in the room followed his every move, and Tommy saw the future. Shaw possessed the passion she once had for taking prizes, for killing men, for fearlessly leading men to their deaths, and this enthusiasm was taking hold, not just of his own crew, but of hers as well.

The rendezvous point was chosen, the men on the *Black Widow* given their instructions, and the rest of the details worked out. The plan would succeed only if the Spanish fleet was stretched out far enough that the *Barcelona* was vulnerable. The chances of that happening were slim unless Mother Nature intervened with a storm.

As the pirates left the room and climbed down the rope ladders into their waiting boats, Tommy noticed that Shaw pulled Coxon aside for just a second, long enough for Coxon to nod several times, then sprint across the deck. Just as she'd suspected. Coxon was Shaw's man. No wonder he felt like a damned thorn in her paw.

As Tommy returned to her ship, she admired the *Moon Shadow*'s clean lines, sparkling white hull, trim forecastle, and ramrod straight masts. But then a shudder passed through her, as if she were examining her own coffin.

Chapter Eleven

Later that day Tommy stood on the quarterdeck discussing their course with Sawkins. They would sail another few leagues until they were directly across from Carriacou, the small island to the north of Grenada, then they'd turn west and sail straight for the Dolphins. It was a route she'd taken many times and could do in her sleep. She took another quadrant reading, then stood at the stern with the man on watch to record their speed. They were making good time. Shaw's ships were fading into the western horizon. Rebekah dutifully rang the bell as needed, and the ship ran as smoothly as one could expect from a band of sailors.

Two bells into the first dog watch, Tommy realized she hadn't seen Rebekah since she had ended her afternoon watch, so Tommy slipped into her cabin. Rebekah was curled up on her hammock, clutching her stomach, moaning softly. Tommy stood next to her, unsure of what to do. "You be ill."

Rebekah shivered, pulling the thin blanket more tightly around her shoulders. "I'll be fine. Perhaps I'm seasick."

"No, you've been on the water too many days for it to suddenly lay you up." Tommy frowned.

"The last four months have been difficult. Now that…" She closed her eyes.

"Don't worry," Tommy said roughly. "I'll be taking care of you."

Rebekah shook her head weakly. "No, I can take care of myself. I've always taken care of myself. And since I turned twelve, I took care of Mama and Mistress Lily and anyone else in the Big House who needed caring for." Tommy suspected Rebekah couldn't *need* to be cared for because she'd never had anyone who could do so. With that thought, Tommy's focus shifted from the ship to Rebekah. Sawkins could run things just fine, and for the moment, Coxon seemed tamed.

Tommy spent hours pacing her cabin, moving to Rebekah's side at the slightest sigh or moan. Many times during the day she held a mug of ale to Rebekah's lips, encouraging her to drink. She fed Rebekah onion soup in small spoonfuls.

Now and then Tommy touched Rebekah's forehead, then clucked her tongue with worry. Rebekah's skin burned hot as the deck on a windless July day. The next day she was even hotter, so Tommy brought Sawkins into the cabin.

"She's sick as a dog, burnin' up with fever," he said.

"You old cow, I know that. But what must I do?"

"Cool the wench down with water and a rag, all o' her. Might help." And he left. Cool the wench down. Tommy filled a bucket with water from a barrel in the wardroom, then stood next to the hammock, unsure. All over her?

Finally she began, dipping the cloth in the cool water, then dabbing it along Rebekah's forehead, cheeks, neck, and throat. The feverish woman stirred, moving toward the cloth, so Tommy repeated her actions. Then she moved to Rebekah's feet and ankles. Swallowing, she slid the wet cloth up Rebekah's calf to her knees, did the same to the other leg, then stepped back, aware she was sweating like a sailor in the sun.

"Bloody hell," Tommy said. "All over her? How?" She knew she had to cool Rebekah's trunk down. She put the bucket on the floor, took a deep breath, then reached for the front of her dress. "God's blood," she muttered, and ripped the dress down the front.

Tommy froze at the sight of Rebekah's smooth skin. Dazed, she reached out and cupped one of Rebekah's breasts, then jerked back as if burned. "Jesus, I'm gonna burn in hell," she murmured. "Sweet Lord, I can't bear how beautiful you be."

Hands trembling now, Tommy ran the cloth over Rebekah's breasts, down her rib cage, and across her belly. When Rebekah shuddered, Tommy froze. Rebekah's eyes opened slightly and she mumbled words Tommy couldn't understand. Then Rebekah's gaze fixed on Tommy's braid and she reached for it. "Moonlight," she whispered, then fell back to sleep with Tommy's braid clutched in her hand. Tommy stood in that spot for nearly an hour dabbing the cloth on Rebekah's skin until her back ached and she was due on second dog watch, so she had no choice but to undo Rebekah's grasp and free her braid.

That evening after her watch ended, Tommy moved her own hammock so close to Rebekah's they might as well have been sleeping in the same one. When Rebekah woke up long enough to spy the braid and reach for it once again, Tommy lay in her hammock while she served as Rebekah's anchor. Now and then she felt a tug as Rebekah stirred in her sleep.

Tommy, however, couldn't sleep. The ship dipped softly, creaking and popping. The bell rang quietly every half hour. Squares of moonlight flickered on the far wall, as it always did at this phase of the moon. Despite the familiarity of her world, Tommy felt lost at sea. Nothing inside her felt the same. What if Rebekah didn't recover? How could God plunk the woman down in Tommy's path, then take her away again so soon? Unfamiliar panic washed through her.

Late that night, four bells into the midwatch, Tommy gave up on sleep and went out onto the mid-deck, fully awake when most landlubbers slept. Despite her fears for Rebekah, this was her favorite time of the night. Even though the moon was waning, it still lit up the ocean, as if a flickering blue-white candle rode each wave rolling alongside the *Moon Shadow*. As she'd ordered earlier, her ship had turned west and sailed to the Dolphins.

Below deck, the off-watch crew enjoyed its double rations of grog with much dancing, or rather, much stomping around to a sailor's attempt to play the pipe. That the ill Rebekah could sleep through the noise amazed Tommy.

Two figures appeared up the companionway, then slowly wove their way up to Tommy. Sawkins and Billy each lifted a mug, bleary-eyed and red-cheeked. They perched on the railing beside her.

"Evening, Captain," Sawkins said, voice slurred.

Tommy wished she had a mug of her own. "Boys."

"Lovely night, ain't it?"

Tommy bit back a smile. Fill Sawkins with grog, and he put on the most charming airs.

"That it is, Mr. Sawkins."

"The black wench doing any better?"

"No."

Sawkins leaned closer. "You know some o' the men are saying having her aboard when we go after the Spaniards will bring us bad luck."

"I'm not surprised. And what do *you* say, Mr. Sawkins?"

He raised his mug again. "I say you're the best damned captain I ever sailed with."

"Prettiest, too," Billy whispered, then belched.

"Boys, you need to head for your hammocks."

Sawkins took another swig and wiped his mouth. "I just thought ye oughta be warned." As he turned, he peered into the darkness off starboard. "Now there's that big floggin' island again. By fire and flame, didn't me and the pup here see that same one last year? Is that Carriacou?"

"No, Carriacou's to our stern." Tommy followed Sawkins's nod but saw nothing, save silver-tipped waves and a low-hanging mist. "What island?"

Billy whistled. "Cricky, it's a big'un. Good thing we didn't run ourselves right into it. In fact, we're sailing right around it." The boy giggled.

Tommy grasped each man by the collar and hoisted them to their feet. "You boys be truly in your cups. We be three leagues from Carriacou. Off to bed with you." A gentle shove sent them back the direction they came. She chuckled when they staggered away, but no matter what Tommy did or who she spoke with, she wanted to be back down in that cabin, worrying if Rebekah was too cold or too hot.

During the two days Rebekah was ill, Tommy's fleet sailed west, riding the prevailing winds and making good time. On the third day, Rebekah felt well enough to sit up. When she did, she clutched her ripped dress and glared at Tommy.

"I...it be necessary...you had the fever..." Finally Tommy threw up her hands and dug shirt and trousers out of her trunk and handed them to Rebekah. "Here," she said, then fled.

Eventually Rebekah appeared on deck for short spells in her baggy sailor's clothing, but then she'd return to the cabin, drink and eat, then sleep. Tommy had tried to continue caring for her, but Rebekah had waved her away, claiming she was perfectly capable of feeding herself. Tommy suddenly missed being responsible for keeping her alive.

Soon Rebekah was back to her watch duties, ringing the bell and turning the sandglass. As Tommy worked, she swore she still felt a slight pressure at the back of her head, as if Rebekah were still clinging to her braid for all she was worth. At one point Tommy leaned against the railing, arms folded, knowing it was wrong to wish Rebekah were still ill enough to need her, but doing it anyway.

Tommy was hard-pressed to remain focused on navigation, but instead was aware of Rebekah forward in the galley helping Cookie, teaching him some sort of song. Then she was up and down from the stores room helping Sawkins, then later standing high up in the rat lines, her dress flapping like a sail.

As Tommy stood on deck, berating a sailor for smoking below, she realized something felt different. She felt different. She couldn't explain why, or what that meant, but something within her had shifted. She and the ship and the hands and the water all appeared the same, but Tommy knew better. The change in her was like after a storm pounded an island. Everything on the surface of the water looked the same, but underneath the sand along the shore shifted and reshaped itself. That's how she felt—like sand reshaped by a storm. She couldn't stop thinking of Rebekah, grew shy when they spoke, and dreamed, even while awake and on deck, of the smooth, round breasts she'd seen. God help her, but so many times while cooling Rebekah down she'd wanted to touch her again, lightly brushing that smooth chestnut skin, those deep brown—Tommy stopped, shaking her head. Bloody hell. What was she thinking? Tommy closed her eyes and swayed in dismay, queasy at her thoughts.

CHAPTER TWELVE

They had about five more days of sailing before they reached the Dolphins. Tommy spent the time walking with Rebekah up and down the deck, asking more about her life and telling her more about her own. As ever, Tommy was painfully sensitive to Rebekah's presence. Whenever they accidentally bumped knees under the table or passed each other in the narrow passageways, Tommy's body hummed like a taut rope. She didn't know which was more disturbing, that she couldn't stop thinking about a member of her crew, or that the person was a woman. Tommy knew her thoughts crossed into the unnatural, but when Rebekah was near, she didn't care.

Late one afternoon, as Tommy leaned out so spray from the bow could refresh her face, Sawkins stood close, using the low voice he saved only for Tommy. "Captain, might I be so bold as to say you're lookin' different?"

"Different? How so?"

He either smiled, or squinted into the sun; with Sawkins it was often hard to tell the difference. "If I didn't know better, I'd be saying ye look happier than ye've looked in months. I'm thinking it's good for ye to have another lass on board."

"Don't be daft, you old sea cow."

Then he did grin, and set back on his heels, steadying himself as they rode the waves.

That night as Tommy lay awake, her belly full from a satisfying meal shared with Rebekah, who slept in the nearby hammock, Tommy realized that her quartermaster, blast him, might be right. Rebekah

Brown filled a hole in her hull she didn't even know was there. It must be happiness which added the spring to her step, lightened her heart, and found the laughter long since buried within her.

Now if she could only get herself and Rebekah, and her ship and her mates through the dangers of the next few days, then she would have the time to think about what it meant when one person—and a woman at that—could make her so happy.

❖

Tommy's fixation on Rebekah only increased the next morning when Rebekah suddenly dashed up from a lower deck, face flushed and mouth grim, to be followed minutes later by Coxon, who ambled smugly across the mid-deck. When Tommy caught his eye, the cur tugged his forelock in a mock salute and smiled.

After dusk Tommy took a minute to wolf down a piece of salted meat and two hardtacks in her cabin. When Rebekah entered Tommy leapt to her feet and choked on the bread in her mouth. Tommy bent over and coughed until she could breathe again.

"I'm sorry my presence upsets you," Rebekah said softly.

Tommy wiped her eyes, moist from her coughing fit. "What happened with Coxon?"

Rebekah stepped back and looked out the stern windows. "Nothing."

"I'm not sure I'm believing that. Did the bastard touch you or hurt you? God's blood, I'll kill—"

Rebekah held up a hand. "You don't need to harm him on my account. I can take care of myself."

"I know." Then why did Tommy feel this desperate need to make sure no harm ever befell her? "If Coxon touches you, I'll kill him."

"No." Her gaze softened and Tommy's heart thumped.

"Why not?"

"Because of what you said that first day I came aboard. You said you hated the killing. I know you abhorred killing that captain, even though you wouldn't say. I don't want you to kill someone because of me."

Tommy clenched her jaw. Damn the woman for reminding her.

"The Articles clearly spell out the fate of a man who meddles with a woman without her consent. If I kill Coxon, I be doing it for the ship. No use having Articles if they aren't enforced."

She stomped from the cabin and sought out Coxon, finding him below on the gun deck repairing the fuse on one of the guns. Tommy glared at the other men in the room and they fled under her fierce scowl.

"Coxon."

The man stood lazily and stretched. "Captain, what be on yer mind?"

"You signed the Articles six months ago."

"That I did."

"What be Article Nine?"

Coxon stroked his grimy chin with hands filthy with cannon grease. "Let me see. Article Nine. Oh yeah, somethin' about us being able to meddle with cunts without their consent."

"Try again."

Now Coxon glowered as darkly as Tommy. "That's the way Shaw's Articles read."

"Then maybe you be on the wrong ship. Our Articles say should you be meddlin' with a woman without her consent, punishment is death, and that'll be death by my hand."

Coxon's glare turned defiant. "Assuming ye still be captain when it happens."

The man's lack of fear worked in Tommy's head like a rat gnawing on the hull. A rat was a small rodent, but if a ship had enough hungry ones aboard, they'd be powerful enough to destroy the vessel. She rested her hand on her sword hilt. "I'm not needing to be captain to kill you. I can do that anytime." She whirled on her heel and strode away before she drew her sword and did just that.

❖

Seven bells into the night watch, Tommy quietly gathered Sawkins, Billy, and Hatley in her cabin. Calabria was on Shaw's *Black Widow* down Puerto Bello way, spying on the Spaniards, or she'd have had him there as well. She hoped the man was managing. Rebekah sat quietly in the corner mending her dress.

"In a few days we be reaching the Dolphins," Tommy said. "Then we wait until the fleet comes by. Shaw's wanting to go after the *Barcelona*. I say we need to avoid that old hag and instead take the *Maravillosa*."

"Why ye so barmy about that ship?" Hatley asked. "It's like ye been possessed or something. It's just a bloomin' ship." Tommy considered Hatley's comments. Had the *Maravillosa* and Rebekah become so entwined in her mind that she felt compelled to free them both? Surely Rebekah's appearance in Tommy's life meant the *Maravillosa* was somehow important.

"Hatley, you believe in signs."

"Ye know I do. We never should have started this voyage on a Friday."

Tommy looked around the room. "Any of you remember the figurehead on the *Maravillosa*?"

Sawkins shook his head. "Billy was the only one of us to get a good look at the ships."

Tommy turned to the boy. "Billy, seen anyone since who looks like that figurehead?"

Billy blushed. "She weren't wearing any clothes, and I ain't seen a naked woman for a while. But her face be very pretty. She—" Billy faced Rebekah. "Wait one durned minute. She be looking something like you." Rebekah's jaw dropped.

As the men considered the news, Tommy could feel the wheels turning inside their heads. The *Maravillosa* had sailed by the island where they were careened. A few days later a woman looking like the *Maravillosa's* figurehead was saved from sure death when the *Moon Shadow* plucked her from the sea. And now they must decide whether to take the *Maravillosa*.

"It be a sign," Sawkins said softly, and the men murmured their agreement.

No more discussion was needed. Tommy had to find a way the *Moon Shadow* could take the *Maravillosa*, and she had to do it without tipping off Coxon and his mates. If they learned what Tommy wanted to do, they would take over the ship not with a vote, but with violence.

❖

That night a storm descended on them with the speed of a cannonball. The sky roiled with twisting clouds that strangled and squeezed each other into horrible shapes. Tommy couldn't take any readings in the storm, and the men knew their jobs, so she wasn't needed on deck. Instead, in her cabin Tommy watched Rebekah grow ashen as the ship pitched violently. Soon the seas stood at ten feet, which the *Moon Shadow* could easily handle but apparently Rebekah couldn't. While she didn't vomit, her knuckles were white with fear as she sat at the table whimpering softly.

"It's just a squall," Tommy said, patting her shoulder awkwardly. "By thunder, woman, you're shaking like leaf. C'mon, in the hammock with you." After she'd gotten Rebekah settled, Tommy lay down on her own hammock and closed her eyes. The ship plunged and slammed into the next wave. Tommy's heart swelled with pride, for she knew the sturdy ship could easily take this beating and be none the worse come dawn.

After the next wave, Tommy's eyes flew open when Rebekah climbed into Tommy's hammock and wrapped her arms and legs around her.

Tommy didn't say anything more, but held the trembling Rebekah as she once again clung to Tommy's braid. Eventually Rebekah's breath evened out and she slept, which was more than Tommy could do. She gently stroked Rebekah's arm with her thumb and with great effort forced herself to not explore farther.

She must have slept, for when she woke Rebekah had extricated herself from Tommy's arms and stood by the stern windows watching the ship's wake in the faint moonlight. The storm had blown itself out, so beyond the wake the water would be as smooth as glass, but the air was hot with moisture.

Sighing heavily, Rebekah turned toward the bucket of water and used the moist cloth to wash her arms and face, likely sticky with sweat. When she turned around, Tommy slammed her eyes shut, holding her breath as Rebekah walked toward her, then stopped at her hammock. Tommy nearly moaned as Rebekah pressed the moist cloth against her forehead, then slid the cloth down her cheek and across her neck. Tommy's muscles tensed. She needed to open her eyes and leave, right now. She needed to get as far from this cabin as she could.

The pulse in Tommy's throat begin to pound as Rebekah sighed, then put down the bucket. Warm, firm breasts brushed Tommy's arm as Rebekah leaned in and kissed her neck. Tommy's eyes flew open in shock, but she shut them again as her heart raced. What was Rebekah playing at?

Tommy didn't move, but felt Rebekah tremble as she kissed Tommy's neck again. Then Rebekah moved her lips higher and kissed Tommy beneath her ear. Then on her cheek. Then one small kiss at the very corner of Tommy's mouth.

Tommy held her breath. Rebekah's bosom now rested on hers, and she thought she might faint. Then Rebekah Brown kissed Tommy Farris directly on the lips.

For a second neither woman moved, but as Rebekah started drawing back, Tommy slid her hand behind Rebekah's neck and pulled her into an even deeper kiss.

PART FOUR

THE LOG BOOK

The hard part isn't the actual stealing. It's the getting in and getting out.

—Miles Harvey, *The Island of Lost Maps*

Chapter Thirteen

R andi Marx and I had found nothing at either Chicago library, so I flew to St. Louis. Ms. Marx would be meeting me there, but she'd volunteered no information about her travel arrangements, so for all I knew, she'd be arriving by dogsled.

I'd never seen the Gateway Arch near the Mississippi in St. Louis, so I pressed my face against the airplane window and glimpsed it in the distance. The lovely arch soared toward the sky then returned to earth. Too bad this trip would be too quick for any sort of sightseeing, since I'd not been on a vacation in four years. My more-than-full-time job and small savings account made vacations rarer than a first-run printing of the Bible.

Once we landed, I checked my e-mail but there was nothing more from my archenemy, Mr. Drummond. Randi said that her company hadn't been able to trace his e-mail address yet. There was an e-mail from my newest friend, Ricardo Benton, the map collector who had confronted me outside the Patterson in Chicago: *Lovely to meet you. I regret we were unable to finish our conversation. Willing to pay you $50,000 for the Farris map. This is one of those offers you shouldn't refuse. Believe me.*

I stared at the e-mail. First of all, what part of "Not for Sale" didn't Benton understand? And second, $50,000? Who on earth would pay such a ridiculous price for the map? Only a handful of maps brought that price or higher. And third, was that last sentence a threat?

I clicked Reply. *Dear Mr. Benton, Thanks for your interest in the Farris map, but the map has not been found. Sincerely, Emma Boyd.*

I rode the St. Louis Metrolink downtown, then took a five-minute cab ride to Merrick Park, which wasn't far from the Mississippi. When the cab drove down Cherokee Street, I pressed my face up against a window yet again. Good God, look at the antique stores. It was like an antique orgy. Maybe I'd have time to stop on my way back to the hotel that evening.

I arrived at the Chapman Library before it opened and before Randi arrived, so I sat on a cold concrete bench tucked in some massive pines along the sidewalk and watched Randi emerge from the five-level parking garage across the street and walk toward the library. The private eye had obviously rented a car. Hmm. I wished I had my own little notebook for jotting down the clues about Randi Marx.

Today Randi wore another suit—navy—with a pale pink shirt and no jewelry. Her loose hair fell past her shoulders in enviable waves, and seemed to change colors with the light. Yesterday in the library it'd turned dark brown under the fluorescents, but this morning in the sun it was burnished copper. I hadn't noticed it before, but she walked with incredible confidence and grace, a feline smoothness to her gait. One of the pirate biographies I'd read had described Tommy Farris as "the sort of lass who strode across the deck, fearing no one, able to take stock of a man with a mere glance." Farris must have moved like Randi, and leveled the same steely glare at the rest of the world.

I felt self-confident most of the time, but I'm not sure that came through in my walk, which I'd never paid much attention to until now. What type of person did Randi Marx see when she watched me walk?

I laughed at myself. Why would Randi even be paying attention to the way I walked?

The library was opening just as I stood and greeted Randi. We exchanged pleasantries about the weather, which I considered an improvement over yesterday's awkwardness.

Jennifer Binder was a breathless woman with bangs in her eyes and a crooked nametag. Before Randi could flash her badge, Binder bent over her desk and shuffled piles. Randi put her badge away, possibly disappointed.

"I'm so glad you're doing this," Jennifer said. "We just don't have the staff for this kind of search. I received a FedEx package for you this morning from the Gates Library in Seattle." The piles at the edge of the desk threatened to slide off onto the floor, so Randi moved closer and steadied them.

I nodded. "That would be the DVD of Edward Drummond from their security camera. I asked them to send it here."

Jennifer brushed back her bangs. "I'll find it. Meanwhile, just step outside my office, take a left and go straight. You'll run right into the stack room. Spend all the time in there you need."

Randi cleared her throat. "We'll need access to your security system to get inside."

The woman waved her hand. "No security system yet. Maybe in next year's budget. Now where did I put that?" The librarian stopped them with a yelp. "Oh, I almost forgot. Eleanor Levinson, a friend of mine who works at the Freeport Library in Cincinnati, has a thing for pirates and has been collecting and compiling a database with information on individual pirates. I'll have her check Farris, of course, but who were some of Farris's contemporaries?"

That was easy. "William 'Salty' Griffith, Tee Wetherly, Avery Shaw. Branded Ann," I said.

She smiled. "No Blackbeard?"

"I think he was a few years after Farris, but it wouldn't hurt to check. His real name was Edward Teach. Also, Farris's ship was the *Moon Shadow*, so your friend could search for that as well."

Randi motioned toward the door, then we followed Jennifer's directions. Inside the stack room, I gasped at the chaos. Books were piled on the shelves, on the floor, stacked on tables. "Well, this is going to be fun," I muttered. My library didn't have the best security system, but at least things were filed and in order. My fingers fairly itched to set things right, but this wasn't my library, and I didn't want Randi to see me being "anal."

The shelves weren't labeled, so Randi grimly headed for the first shelf, and I headed for the second. The only thing of interest I'd found after two hours of looking was a map of the West Indies from 1700 that had been scribbled on with red, blue, and green crayons. Randi stared intently at the map. "Are you sure this is crayon? What if it's Farris's map?" The scribbles were of flowers, dogs, and houses. When I pointed to a pink airplane in the lower corner, Randi groaned. "Damn kids." She replaced the book. "Good thing I forgot to have them."

I laughed, which Randi rewarded with a slight twitch of her lips. Now if I could just get her to smile, it'd be a real coup. "Good thing someone rescued the book and donated it before more damage was done."

The scattered librarian finally interrupted us, waving the FedEx envelope. "Found the DVD. Let's watch it on the staff computer in the break room." We followed her into a small room with a laptop and digital projector. A few curious librarians eating lunch gathered around the computer. Luckily, the quality of the security DVD was excellent. Part of me was relieved; part was pissed that my library hadn't done as well. I leaned forward, anxious for my first look at my nemesis. Surely he would look as evil as I imagined him to be.

Instead, Edward Drummond was just an average guy. He wore a white shirt buttoned up to the neck, no tie, a baggy dark jacket, and matching pants. His face was pale and nearly obscured by his massive mustache. His hair, probably brown given its shade in the black-and-white video, was medium length, brushing the top of his collar, the tips of his ears.

"Oooh, what a cutie," crooned one of the librarians. At first I thought they were joking, but additional comments made it clear they weren't.

We watched as Drummond entered the reading room, sat down facing the camera, then paged through the book quickly, as if he knew just what he sought.

"He is totally hot, don't you think?" Jennifer Binder nudged my shoulder, and I was once again faced with that stupid choice. Did I go along and pretend he was hot, or just explain he'd need a sex change operation to even be in the ballpark for me?

"Hmm, well, if you say so," I finally said. "But he's not my type."

"No? I think he's adorable, even if he is a thief. How about you, Randi?"

A muscle twitched along Randi's jaw, a sign I was learning meant she was pissed. "Not my type either." Our gaze met and my stomach did this odd little somersault. Not her type either? Hmm.

At one point Drummond looked directly into the camera, as if he knew he was being filmed. It gave me the creeps to have those unemotional black eyes staring right at me.

Then Drummond dipped his head and spat something out into his hand, and I moved closer to the screen. "There it is. The dental floss." The man stretched the floss out along a page, then closed the book and opened another.

A few minutes later he returned to the first book, opened it slightly, found his page, tugged gently, and before I could blink the stolen map was hidden under the book. Then Drummond coughed, dropped the book, and fumbled for it under the table.

Randi snorted. "This guy is good. Right now he's folding the map and jamming it up his pant leg." All the librarians behind me groaned, and one cursed colorfully.

Randi replayed the DVD over and over again, but I didn't glean anything new from it, just that sick feeling in my gut every time Drummond tugged the map from the book. The other librarians eventually drifted away, leaving Randi and me alone.

"Was it just me, or did something seem off about him?" I asked.

Randi ran a hand along the smart crease in her slacks. "What do you mean?"

I frowned at the computer screen. "I don't know. Something seems not right, but I can't put my finger on it."

Randi checked her watch. "We've watched it twenty times. We won't gain anything by watching it again."

"Yeah, I suppose you're right."

"There's a cafeteria in the building, basement level. I have some errands to run, but I'll be back in thirty minutes so we can finish up." And with that, she was gone.

Not so fast, I thought, and I leapt to my feet. Hanging back, I stealthily followed Randi from the library, then hid behind the bushes as Randi looked both ways, crossed the street, and entered the parking ramp on foot. I considered my options. Following her into the ramp wouldn't help because Randi might see me as she drove out. And once Randi drove out, I wouldn't be able to follow her on foot.

I paced near the bushes, checking every ten seconds or so for an exiting car, if only to find out what vehicle Randi drove. I waited nearly twenty minutes in the shade, but the only drivers who left the ramp were men, or women with big hair or long blond hair. When Randi emerged from the parking ramp on foot, I squeaked like a little girl and ran back into the library. I grabbed a candy bar from a vending machine in the cafeteria, wolfed it down with a Diet Coke, then returned to the stack room, where Randi was back looking through the books. Questions for the this woman burned on my tongue—were you napping in your car? Did you have lunch in there? Were you on the phone? Did you have some mysterious meeting in the ramp with an informant? What type *is* your type?

But instead, I finished my shelf and moved to the next. I took a few phone calls from Michelle, one from Getty asking for circulation data, two from our computer techs, and one from Cam.

"How are you?"

"They sent me home this morning, and Mom's here, cooking up enough to feed all of Minneapolis. I'm going to get fat."

"Hardly. Have you remembered anything more about the attack?"

"Yeah, the guy I passed must have come up behind me. I remember him saying something like, 'it's mine,' and then something about keeping me away from the hunt."

"Is it just me, or does that make no sense?"

"The cops weren't all that impressed either. But that's all I can remember. The doc said my brain swelled a little from getting hit, and it'll take a while for my brain to return to normal."

"And how will you know what normal is?"

"Ha, funny."

I hung up and went back to scanning the shelves, but every book I pulled off the shelf held nothing.

"Does your phone ever stop ringing?" Randi's voice came from the next aisle over.

"No, actually, it doesn't."

"How can you ever get away from your job?"

Good question. I ran my hand along the books in front of me, letting my finger bump from book to book. "I don't. But that's okay. The job's the thing, right?"

We didn't speak for a while, then Randi said, "Are you getting discouraged?"

"How did you know?"

"You've been sighing every two minutes."

"Sorry."

Jennifer Binder showed up brandishing a piece of paper. "I might have something for you from my friend's database. She didn't get that many hits, but she did find a letter Avery Shaw sent to his mother. She just faxed me a copy." Her phone rang. "Oh, gotta go."

I took the letter eagerly and squinted at the rough, impatient handwriting.

July 6, 1715

Dearest Mother, Though seas be choppy and my life hard, I'm as well as can be expected under these difficult times. I send no money with this letter. Our silver's escaped, but I'll find it, Mother, I will.

This letter does bring the news that on July 6th the Moon Shadow *went down, and its "fair ass" captain with her.*

I looked up from the paper. "Fair ass is in quotes."

"Fair ass...Farris," Randi said, eyes bright. "Our captain wasn't hanged after all?"

Pulse racing, I returned to the letter.

She deserves to die for not following my plan. I had everything worked out and she ruined it. Oh, Mother, how I hate that woman. Damn the bitch clear to hell and back. By drowning, she stole from me the chance to torture the location of my silver out of her. I'd have tied her to the yardarm and used her as target practice, aiming for her eyes first. I'd have wrapped rope around her head and tightened it with a stick, woolding her head until her eyes popped from their sockets. I'd have hanged her by her thumbs and toes, dropped a stone on her gut and lit her face on fire. My only consolation is that she's dead. She's fish food, her flesh gnawed down to brittle bone.

Affectionately yours, Avery

Randi whistled. "This is news. Captain Tommy Farris went down with her ship."

I sat down, silent, trying to absorb this new information. Which should I believe—the newspaper notice of her death, or this letter from a fellow pirate? He sounded so sure of her death. If there'd been any doubt, wouldn't he have tracked her down and gotten the silver back? Shaw must be referring to the attack on the Spanish fleet, the one where the ship with the treasure disappeared in the storm, and no one—not even the Spanish—knew if the ship had slipped away, been captured, or sank in the storm.

Had she drowned or been hanged? Despite the description in the *Port Royal Gazette* article about a hooded woman shuffling to the noose, I preferred to imagine Tommy as strong and fearless as she marched up the steps of the scaffolding, her long black hair billowing behind her like a sail, ready to take her soul on the next leg of its journey.

When I reread the letter, a strange fear gripped my heart. How had Tommy drowned? In the middle of a Caribbean storm, trapped inside her ship as the water rushed in? Adrift in the open sea clinging to a broken mast, finally losing consciousness and slipping below the surface? Or had she been rendered unconscious during a battle, becoming a helpless passenger on the *Moon Shadow's* one-way journey to the bottom of the sea?

"Neither hanging nor drowning would have been pleasant ways to die," Randi said, breaking into my thoughts.

I didn't know whether to be irritated that Randi had read my mind or irritated that I enjoyed it. "I don't like either option," I said softly, wishing the world awarded more happy endings than it did.

As we walked toward the exit, thanking the librarian, Jennifer hit herself gently on the head. "I almost forgot. Eleanor from the Freeport was a font of information. Turns out Edward Teach wasn't Blackbeard's real name. Not that it makes any difference in your search, but the pirate's real name was Edward Drummond."

Crap. I was no longer surprised by much. "While our map thief is a bastard, at least he has a sense of history…and a sense of humor."

"Eleanor says she has lots of pre–1715 books, but she doesn't know if they're the sort you're looking for. She'd be happy to show you around if you're interested."

"Cincinnati?"

"The Freeport, right downtown."

We thanked Jennifer, shook her hand, then Randi and I stopped outside the front door. "Well, I guess it's back to the hotel," I said, hoping Randi would suggest we get a bite to eat and discuss the case. God, I really was a workaholic, thinking only about work even though a string of antique stores waited a few blocks away.

But I walked over to the marble bench and sat down, suddenly unsure of what I wanted to do next. I'd found out something amazing about Tommy and hungered for more, either as proof of Avery Shaw's claim or as proof he'd been wrong. This woman in Cincinnati—what if she had more materials like the Shaw letter? I couldn't keep flying on the library's dollar, since I doubted Getty's contingency pockets were that deep, but I could drive. What if I was only a few hours' drive from more information on Tommy, or the map itself?

I pulled out my pocket US atlas.

Randi guffawed, sitting down next to me. "I don't believe this. You carry an atlas with you?"

"It's small, and you never know when it will come in handy." I refused to feel stupid just because I carried an atlas, and turned to the mileage guide. Cincinnati was 311 miles from St. Louis. Work was piling up on my desk. Michelle was doing her best, but there were many things I had to deal with. I should consider the Shaw letter a lucky find and fly home tomorrow.

I sat there in the shade, watching the cars whiz by, feeling the warmth from Randi's shoulder next to me, and I realized I didn't want to stop. I didn't want to go back yet. Two days wasn't enough. I opened the atlas to the main map. "Look how close we are to Cincinnati."

"You're not serious."

"The librarian collects pirate stuff. She probably has a huge collection of journals and books from the time period we need. How could I not go to Cincinnati?"

Randi jammed on her sunglasses even though we sat in the shade. "You're scary."

"I know." Clearly I was growing on her.

"This one-day trip to Chicago is turning into a damned treasure hunt."

"You don't have to keep going. We haven't seen Benton here, so we've lost him, and I haven't seen the crew cut guy, so that was probably just my imagination. I think people get a little spooky when they spend too much time with private dicks. Oops, I mean private eyes."

Randi's shoulders shook gently as I stared straight ahead, triumphant. I'd made her laugh. She was now putty in my hands. I returned the atlas to my case. "I'm going to book a flight to Cincinnati for this evening or tomorrow morning. I have enough points to keep it cheap. I'll go through the Freeport Library tomorrow, then fly home the next day. Tell your boss I'm grateful for JLI protection and help, but I just don't think anyone's going to jump out of the rare book stacks and threaten me. So, Randi-with-an-I, you can go home now."

"Why are you so focused on the spelling of my name?"

"Because it bugs you."

"I appreciate your honesty. But I can't return to Minneapolis if you're going to Cincinnati."

"So fly there with me." Oddly, the idea of spending a few more days with Randi wasn't unpleasant. In fact, while my calendar held no room for a relationship, I could certainly squeeze in a little flirting, especially if Cam was right and Randi was gay.

"I can't fly."

An interesting bit of news. "Afraid, huh?"

"No, I have my car here."

"You've been driving this whole trip?"

"Yes."

"To Chicago and then down here to St. Louis?"

"Yes."

"Well, then let's use your car to drive to Cincinnati. It'll be cheaper." I waited as Randi tried to figure out how to avoid riding with an anal retentive librarian. I detected a sigh.

"Okay."

I jumped to my feet, more excited than if I'd scored a first edition of Esquemeling's *Buccaneers of America* for the library. A road trip. Bags of red Twizzlers. Too much Mountain Dew. Hostess Twinkies. And more opportunities to see if I could make the Ice Investigator laugh. I followed Randi toward the parking ramp, at the same time calling Getty and leaving a message on his machine assuring him that the rest of the trip would be on my dollar, not the library's. I also talked to Michelle about a few fires that needed putting out. She wasn't happy I'd be gone another day, but the woman was a trouper.

Inside the dark, cool ramp, we took the damp stairwell to the third level, where Randi stopped behind a massive black SUV with tinted windows, a shiny grill, and a vanity plate that said "Marley." Already I was learning more about Ms. Randi Marx. "Is that Jacob Marley from *A Christmas Carol*, or Bob Marley?"

"We'll drive to your hotel and pick up your bag," Randi said, ignoring my question.

"What does this vehicle get," I asked, "five miles to the gallon?"

"On a good day," Randi said, clicking the doors open. "I need to warn you there will be three of us traveling to Cincinnati." My eyebrows shot up. No wonder she couldn't wait to get away from me at every meal and every night. She'd brought someone with her. I followed Randi as she walked around toward the passenger door.

Randi sighed heavily as she reached for the door handle. "Meet Marley," she said. When she opened the door, out hopped the biggest, blackest, curliest poodle I'd ever seen. The dog threw his paws up onto my shoulders, slammed me back against another car, and began licking my ear enthusiastically.

I laughed at the warm tongue tickling me and tried to push the dog off as Randi yanked the poodle down with his collar. "I'm sorry. He gets excited when he meets someone new." She dragged him away and opened the door to the backseat. "C'mon, Marley, up." The dog bounded into the car and I climbed into the passenger seat, wiping my wet ear and chuckling. A dog. The woman brought her dog along on the trip. Luckily he didn't have the big poofy poodle cut but was clipped close all over, save his long curly ears and a pom-pom at the tip of his tail.

I tried not to laugh, but failed. "A poodle? You?"

Randi actually smiled. When she did, I nearly fainted. The smile lit up her eyes and revealed a dimple in one cheek. A dimple. I went all light-headed and had to touch the armrest for stability. Gone was the uptight, stern private investigator. In her place was a beautiful woman embarrassed she'd been caught caring about something. Marley stuck his long muzzle between us and leaned toward Randi, who scratched his chin and murmured something in the dog's ear, then kissed the side of his face. I stared, transfixed, at the warm, glowing woman across from me and felt my stomach lurch down four floors, then up two, then down again.

I looked away, fastening my seat belt. Yes, yes, yes. Now all I had to do was determine her sexual preference, and I could freely flirt. How long had it been since I'd done that? I hadn't even flirted with Julia.

Randi drove us out the ramp then down Cherokee Street. We passed the long stretch of antique stores, and I leaned close to my window to peer at the storefronts, but wasn't going to ask Randi to stop three minutes after she'd started driving. How irritating would that be? Sighing, I watched as the last shop slipped past me. Then I sneaked a peek at Randi and hid my smile by looking out the window yet again. Amazing how adorable Randi had become with a dog at her side.

Chapter Fourteen

An hour out of St. Louis on I-70 we exhausted all work-related topics and speculations about Drummond and Captain Farris, so fell silent. Southern Illinois stretched out on either side of the highway, cornfields reaching practically to the horizon.

I'd now spent enough time in the car to realize it needed a good, thorough cleaning. The floor of the backseat was littered with Gatorade bottles, wadded-up fast food bags, various dog toys and leashes, magazines, and clothes. The litter had crawled its way forward under my seat and was threatening to bury my feet. I tried to ignore it but found it hard. Would Randi be insulted if I straightened up around my feet? I needed a distraction. "So, any family?"

There went that arching eyebrow again as Randi probably wondered why I was so damned chatty. "Mother, two older brothers, all on the East Coast. Father died when I was fifteen."

I waited, but she didn't offer anything more, or ask me a question. Well, that was a short conversation. "What do your brothers do?"

"Investment banker and doctor."

"Cool."

"The banker never gets outside and the doctor looks at people's feet all day long."

"Oh." Now a napkin seemed to be stuck to my shoe. "My parents live up by Warroad, and come to visit me four times a year. No siblings, in case you're wondering." Okay, now I was babbling. "My favorite color is green. What's yours?"

"Color?"

"I find it hard just sitting here doing nothing while you drive. Asking questions is something I can do."

"Bright yellow."

"From what I've seen, not much of that color in your wardrobe."

"No."

"My GeeGeeBee loved yellow. She had her whole house painted bright yellow once."

"GGB?"

"Great-grandma Boyd. GeeGeeBee. Very cool lady. Died when I was fifteen." Still babbling. God, this was going to be a long drive for both of us, and I'd be lucky if Randi didn't pull out a gun and shoot me in the next hour. "Do you carry a gun?"

"No."

I gave up and stared out the front window. Suddenly Randi reached back and patted Marley, resting on the backseat. "This guy is my family. I adopted Marley about three months ago. He'd been abandoned and turned into the Twin Cities Poodle Rescue. Because he's so big, and has a few 'issues,' no one wanted him."

"What sort of issues?" Even her voice was softer as she talked about Marley. I kicked aside a McDonald's cup.

"He has separation anxiety. I can't leave him in my apartment alone for more than a few minutes. After that, he decides I'm never coming back and he goes ballistic, howling and bouncing off the door and chewing on the sofa. I tried crating him, but without someone with him, he destroyed the crate."

"Wow. Must be hard while you're working. Can't you leave him with friends?"

Randi gazed back at Marley. "Not many friends. My boss John has been very patient and lets me bring Marley to the office. And there have been a few weekends when I've had to be gone for work, so my next-door neighbor, who basically doesn't have a life and never leaves her apartment, has taken Marley for me. As long as he's with someone he knows, he's fine. Leave him alone with a stranger, and he goes berserk."

I reached back and began scratching the sleepy dog behind the ears, rubbing harder as he leaned into my touch. I also scanned the floor of the backseat for something I could use as a trash bag. "Why didn't you leave him with your neighbor this trip?"

"She's visiting her sister in Memphis."

"How have you managed these last few days? Do you leave him in the hotel during the day?"

"No, he'd destroy the place. But he's fine in the car. For some reason he just trusts that if he's in the car, I'll be coming back for him."

I stroked the soft ears spread out across the seat. "You could have told me, you know, instead of trying to keep him a secret."

There was that smile again, and that dimple, and the lurching of my stomach. Randi held my gaze for a second, then turned back to the road. "I didn't want you to think I was some softhearted animal lover."

"Instead of some hard-assed PI?"

Randi nodded.

"Well, don't worry. Now I think you're a hard-assed investigator *and* a softhearted animal lover." Randi flushed. "And I think it's really great that you've given Marley a home, especially considering his issues. Many people would have taken him back."

Randi didn't look at me. "Everyone has issues."

After we'd stopped a few times to eat and let Marley do his business, I finally got up the courage to start sorting the trash while Randi was with Marley in the pet area of the rest stop. I found a larger paper bag and began cramming in the stuff from under my feet. Then I hopped out of the car and reached for a wad of paper under my seat.

"You're very neat, aren't you?" Randi and Marley stood behind me.

I jumped, looking guiltily at the bag in my hand. "Sorry. It keeps the chaos away." I dug around for the last of what was stuck under my seat.

"Life is chaos. You're fighting a losing battle."

Stunned, I unfolded a swatch of black fabric to find a lace thong in my hand. We both stared at it, and I felt a middle school urge to giggle but tamped it down in time. "Yours?"

"Hardly," Randi said, then gently took the thong and dropped into my trash bag. "I'm sure she has another one."

Dying with curiosity, I had no choice but to march over to the waste bins and toss the bag. Now that she was watching, I wasn't going to tackle the backseat.

The drive passed quietly as I broke the silence now and then to talk about the dogs in my past, or to ask about the artist playing on Randi's iPod. The songs were all blues, which I knew nothing about. I wanted to ask her why blues, but that seemed too personal a question. I didn't understand my hesitation, since I'd already fished a fairly personal item from under my seat.

During our stops, I loved taking Marley off to do his business. He'd strain at the long leash, almost disappearing into the darkness beyond the rest area lights. By the time we pulled up to the Sheraton at the outskirts of Cincinnati, one of the few hotel chains Randi had found that allowed dogs, I'd become comfortable with our long silences, and I'd fallen in love with Marley. No risk giving your heart to a dog—they were much less likely to break it.

❖

The next morning Randi's route into downtown Cincinnati took us along the Ohio River. Five big white riverboats, their massive paddlewheels painted red and blue, were docked on the opposite shore. I'd never been on a riverboat, even though I'd lived a few miles from the Mississippi for ten years. What a leisurely day that would be, to just sit, sip wine, and watch life on the river banks. "Ever been on a riverboat?" I asked.

"No."

I resolved to put a riverboat ride on my to-do list when I had free time in my schedule. Perhaps when I was eighty.

Randi parked us in the ramp next to the Freeport Rare Book Collection, touched her forehead to Marley's, then stepped back and closed the door. "Later, big guy." Inside the library, she flipped her badge for the receptionist, then actually winked at me as the receptionist picked up the phone. "I love doing that," Randi whispered.

Eleanor Levinson was the most cooperative librarian we'd encountered to date, leading us immediately back to a cramped room with her pirate collection. "Please, look at anything you need. And when you're done here, I'll take you into the stacks."

"Oh, this is going to be fun," I said as I reached for the first box, which was full of movie posters in protective sleeves. She had them all: *Captain Blood, Against All Flags, The Black Swan, Double Crossbones.*

Randi opened a box filled with uncatalogued papers. "You're kidding, right? We don't have time to go through all this. We're looking for a map in a book."

I kept going, but after an hour of Randi sighing heavily, I determined nearly all of Eleanor's collection was movie memorabilia, and what real stuff might be there, like Shaw's letters, would take days to sort through. "Okay, you're right."

Eleanor took us back to the stacks. "It makes me just sick to think this Drummond is getting away with this. I'll send in a few aides to help you, if you'd like."

"Not necessary," Randi said. "One of us needs to examine each map."

"Understood. As I mentioned on the phone, the boxes from the Jamaican mission in Port Royal might prove interesting, since I believe a few of the artifacts might go back to the early eighteenth century. While my personal collection focuses on pirates, the library's acquisitions tend toward Catholic material from churches and missions."

"Tell me more," I said, stopping Randi's protest with a raised hand.

"One of our library's patrons inherited several boxes of material from a Catholic mission called Our Lady of the Blessed Hand and donated them. I've not spent much time with them yet, and nothing has been catalogued. The mission was founded by Father Daniel McLurin."

That name seemed oddly familiar. Had I run across it in my research on Captain Farris? "Blessed Hand?" I asked.

"Apparently the priest's hand had been cut off by a pirate, then miraculously restored the next morning."

"Don't you think we should focus on finding the map?" Randi asked.

"I might find something that will help us understand Tommy better. She spent a great deal of time in Jamaica, and that was where they said she'd been convicted and hanged. Get started without me. I'll join you in a few minutes."

"But the map—" I ignored the exasperated Randi and followed

Eleanor into an empty staff room. The pirate collection had been a dead end, but this might not be. Five minutes later the librarian wheeled in a metal cart carrying two white archive bins. "Please keep the items within this room, as I haven't catalogued them yet."

"Absolutely," I said, eager to be alone with any original material that had even a remote possibility of connecting to Farris.

After an hour and a half, I'd worked through the first box, finding ledgers of the mission's finances written in a cramped hand from 1750–1790. A few edicts from the pope. Articles from an 1810 *Port Royal Gazette*, and the personal journals of Father McLurin.

I skimmed through the first of the four journal volumes, struggling with the eighteenth-century English. Nothing but construction details about building the mission, and McLurin's observations on the people of Jamaica. Too bad I didn't have about three days to just sit there and read the journals, for the entries provided such a tantalizing peek into the West Indies.

Reluctantly, I put the journals aside and opened a thin leather book to the first page. *Ship's Log, the* Margaret, *July 1715–October 1715, Captain R. Brown.*

I stared at the scrawled words. Captain R. Brown again. Who *was* this guy? The ship's log was terse and bare bones, nothing like McLurin's rambling observations on life. I found heading, speed, weather conditions, distance traveled, and little else in each day's entry.

"I thought you were going to help," Randi said from the door so suddenly that I jumped.

"I'm sorry, but this material is just very interesting, and no one's looked at it yet. Who knows what could be in here?" I handed the log book to Randi. "In fact, here's your Captain R. Brown again."

Randi's low, appreciative whistle gave me a funny shiver. Steady, girl, steady.

"Who is this guy and why haven't you heard of him?" Randi began skimming the pages. "You knew the people in Farris's life, right? So if you don't have a clue, he's probably not connected to Farris."

"I need to go back through my files and check, but I've seen McLurin's name somewhere in my research. He might be the link that connects Captain R. Brown to Captain Tommy Farris." I didn't say it, but there was that weird coincidence of the six Brown books all spelling F-A-R-R-I-S.

"I don't see anything about Tommy in here." She placed it back onto the pile just as I opened a file of old letters. They were yellowed and brittle and needed to be archived properly. I skimmed each one, turning them carefully to look at the next one, then stopped at the third letter.

"This might be something. Here's a letter to McLurin from R. Brown. This guy shows up everywhere. *Dear Father McLurin, Accompanying this letter are six of my books which I send to you for safekeeping. My dear friend, I hope you are well and that the mission thrives.*" Could those books have been the ones we found in Chicago?

My cell rang. It was Michelle with an employee issue. Two aides were out sick and one had jury duty and when was I coming back? She also said the state legislature was about to cut the university funding, so our budget would be slashed as well and would she still have a job? I calmed Michelle down then asked her to search my Farris database for Daniel McLurin and call me back.

By the time I got off the phone, Randi had looked through my piles and replaced most of them in the boxes, so I gave up and followed her back out into the stacks. We spent another hour looking through books for the map, but found nothing. When we left, the librarian recommended we visit the New Penn Collection in Pittsburgh, as they had a huge collection of atlases. Keep going? Keep looking for the map? Randi and I just exchanged a glance, but neither of us said anything.

❖

We'd spent all day at the Freeport and were starving, so we stopped at a chain restaurant for dinner. Now that Randi's secret about Marley was out, she didn't seem as reluctant to spend time with me between libraries.

I couldn't keep my mind on the menu in my hands. "The timeline is bothering me." It was giving me a headache, in fact.

"What do you mean?"

"The Spanish fleet was attacked June 30 and the treasure stolen. Then the hurricane hit July 6, the day Avery Shaw said Tommy's ship sank. If those dates are true, and Tommy actually had the treasure, she wouldn't have had the chance to unload the treasure from her ship because she would have been days from any land."

"So you think the treasure never left the ship."

"The ship, with both its cargo and its captain, could be at the bottom of the sea somewhere in the Caribbean. Tommy wouldn't have had time to unload the cargo and make a map."

When the waitress appeared I ordered the taco salad and Randi ordered steak, then I waited until the young woman left us. "Have I taken us on some stupid wild good chase?"

Randi brushed back curling tendrils that had escaped from her braid. "What if Shaw was wrong? What if Tommy and her ship didn't sink?"

"I don't know how to verify that. We've been doing this for three days and have barely scratched the surface. Drummond, who obviously likes to think of himself as a pirate, could have hit other libraries by now. I don't know that it's worth it to drive to Pittsburgh." It might have been the PMS drearies, but doubt crept from my mind into my voice.

Randi leaned forward. "You said that no one on ExLibris or the other discussion lists has seen him since you reported your theft. He may have decided to cool it for a while."

"If Drummond's still out there, he's using a different name by now, different credentials, probably has even disguised his appearance." I threw up my hands. "And now that we know Farris might have gone down with her ship, the likelihood the map even exists seems very remote. Maybe we should go home. The best we can do is hope that you and your JLI colleagues can eventually track Drummond down."

Randi's voice was grim. "We're close. I can *feel* it. We *can't* give up now. We found the Captain Brown log. He must be connected to Farris. We just have to figure out how. Were they working together? Were they enemies? Were they running from each other? Looking for each other?"

The reversal of our positions surprised me. Reluctant at first, Randi was now all go, go, go, and I was losing faith in the whole idea. "We didn't have enough time to really examine the log in the library," I said, "so there's no way to tie R. Brown and Tommy together."

Randi reached into the pocket of her jacket and pulled out a slender book bound in soft leather. "That's why I decided to borrow the log for a few days."

My mouth dropped open. "You stole that," I sputtered.

"Borrowed. It's a library, right?" She flashed her most winning grin at me, but this time the dimple had no effect. "I asked myself, WWTD?"

"What?"

"What would Tommy do?"

Anger surged through me. "I can't believe you. You're using a woman who stole for a living as your moral guide? That's pathetic. Sometimes I think you're no better than Drummond."

She cocked her head. "Are we having our first fight?"

"First and last. We're taking the log book back tomorrow, and this trip is over." Maybe it was the recent thefts at my library, but Randi's actions really got my blood up.

"Tommy did what was necessary to survive, didn't she?"

"Yes, but we're not talking about our survival here, we're talking about our jobs. And now we're no better than Drummond. You can't just walk away with valuable, irreplaceable documents. And Eleanor trusted us."

Randi shook her head, thumbing through the log. "Captain R. Brown was sailing the West Indies in 1715. He might have met Tommy somewhere and noted it in his log. Look, you said every clue might help solve the puzzle of Tommy's death, right? There's something in Latin written inside the back cover of the log book: *Dum spiro, spero.* What if that's a clue?"

I sighed. "It's a very moving Latin phrase, but it won't change my mind. It means, *While I breathe, I hope.*"

Randi repeated the phrase. "I like that. It could be my motto. *And* it could be a clue."

"No, it's not. It's a sentence in Latin, nothing more. We can't keep going. We're done. There is no treasure map, and Drummond has gone underground, and you're taking things that don't belong to you. We take this log back tomorrow and go home."

"I think we should press on to that Pittsburgh library."

I glared at Randi. "Don't you even feel bad for stealing this? You're as bad as Tommy was, taking things that didn't belong to her—"

"She did that to survive, Emma. Not everyone is perfect like you. Sometimes people do the wrong thing for the right reason."

"Why didn't you just ask Eleanor if we could photocopy the log?"

Randi sat back, face ashen.

"Never even occurred to you, did it?" I was pleased to see, for the first time, a touch of embarrassment cross her face.

"No, I'm sorry to say, it didn't."

When Randi's phone binged, she glared at it with a snort of impatience. "I need to take this." She stood, pocketed the log with a glance at me, then started for the front door. "Yeah, what's up?"

First I called Cam, who was home recuperating and bored out of his skull, and quickly brought him up to speed.

"Emma, I don't like this, not one bit. A private investigator who steals? Who breaks into secure libraries? Are you sure you're really safe with this woman?"

I made a face. "Don't be silly. Of course I'm safe with her; I'm just upset with her."

"Well, maybe you won't think this is silly. I was sleeping this afternoon, and during my dream some of the details of my attack started coming back. The guy that passed me said, 'No treasure hunting for you. That silver is mine.' Then he cleaned my clock with a baseball bat."

I sat perfectly still. "You're saying the attack had something to do with my trip?"

"Exactly. This guy didn't want me along. Why is that?"

I described Benton, but Cam didn't think he matched the description of the man who'd beaten him. "I think I should fly out and join you."

"No, you have a broken wrist and bruised ribs. You're not going anywhere."

"Are you sure this woman can keep you safe?"

"Cam, I'm not in any danger. Stop being so dramatic. Now I have to go."

Randi still hadn't returned, so I called Michelle back.

"I was just going to call you," she said. "I finally had time to look through those few pages of the 1714 log book you had, and found this entry: *Sawkins and Billy see island again. D. McLurin and I don't. Ale must be bad. That's why the men be seeing things.*"

"Touchdown," I said. D. McLurin had been on Tommy Farris's ship in 1714.

"Does this help?"

"You're a doll, Michelle. Thanks." I hung up, suddenly excited again.

Randi returned and sank back into her seat, scowl darker than I'd seen. "Everything okay?" I asked.

"Don't want to talk about it." Randi drank nearly her entire glass of water, then practically slammed the glass down. "I'm sorry I didn't think to photocopy the book. Taking it was wrong. But let me look through the log tonight. Maybe I can find something that will convince you we need to keep going. We can't stop now."

I wondered at the tight desperation in her voice, but then my PDA beeped with e-mail. The return address was mappirate@yahoo.com. "Not again," I breathed, and opened the message.

> *Hi, Emma,*
>
> *Looking for me? You were right earlier—I don't have the map. But I'm still looking. God, what a great feeling to rip a map from a book. I like to think of it as cartographic liberation—let my maps go! I've liberated five more maps. Give up, little girl. I am going to find the Farris map first, and you'll never catch me.*
>
> *Kiss my ass,*
> *Edward Drummond*

I read the message out loud.

"Damn it," snapped Randi. "Let me see that." She read the message. "I need to forward this to my office. Maybe the FBI can track this one down." She keyed in an address, then forwarded the message. She handed my PDA back. "You still want to stop? It's about a five-hour drive to Pittsburgh."

I closed my eyes and pressed my palms against my forehead. Daniel McLurin sailing with Tommy Farris in 1741. Tommy Farris going down with her ship. Randi's illegal and disturbing methods. My own confusion. And then there was something else that I hadn't even voiced yet, the feeling that time had slowed down, as if I'd been gone for ten days, not two. I didn't know if it was being with Randi, or Marley, or just being away from the office, but the slow pace was intoxicating, and I didn't want that feeling to stop.

"We can keep going." I sat there, still unsure of what I felt. Maybe Cam was right. Below Randi's smooth voice and confident personality, was there an undercurrent of danger?

CHAPTER FIFTEEN

It was time to head for Pittsburgh. I'd never been there before, and looked forward to our next stop on this impromptu search. But we'd only reached the outskirts of Cincinnati, passing a chain of restaurants identical to every strip in every city, when something outside popped and Randi suddenly gripped the wheel, swearing softly as she struggled to control the car and move to the shoulder.

"What the hell?" she muttered.

"Flat tire, probably."

"Shit."

We both climbed out and considered the deflated tire. "Wow," Randi breathed.

I bent down and pointed to a small slice. "We must have run over something sharp." The same thing had happened to me just a month earlier.

"Crap," Randi muttered. "I let my AAA membership expire." She pulled out her cell phone, then looked around. "No service stations in sight. How the hell am I going to get this changed?"

I stared at her. "You're kidding me, right?"

"What?"

"We can change it ourselves."

"I...I've never changed a tire before."

That made me laugh, since I could tell from the way she moved there were muscles under her jacket.

"So you're a tough private eye who has a soft spot for dogs and is helpless around flat tires."

Randi flushed. "I wish you wouldn't put it that way."

I dug through the glove compartment until I found the manual, then tracked down the jack and handle. "Your spare tire is probably locked on. Do you have the key?"

Randi looked through her key ring. "Key?"

I dug deeper in the glove compartment and found two shiny keys, never used. "Here. Could you unlock the spare while I take off the flat?" Hiding my smile, I bent over the jack and placed it under the car. There was something endearing about a tough woman who couldn't change her own flat tire.

Randi hovered while I jacked up the front end. I might have grunted a bit for effect.

"You've obviously done this before," Randi said, her dark tendrils blowing in the warm evening breeze.

"A few times."

"Can you fix other stuff?" She stood over me as I loosened the lug nuts.

I loosened the last one, then looked up at Randi. "I guess. Doorknobs. Broken book bindings. Nothing big." Getty positively came unglued whenever the copier jammed, and always called me, sure I had some magic incantation that worked every time. "Stuff everybody can fix."

Randi didn't meet my eyes. "I can't fix anything."

"I don't believe that." I pulled off the flat and accepted the spare Randi rolled toward me.

"I have two left thumbs. I can't fix anything."

I slid the spare, which I was glad to see was fully inflated, onto the wheel. Marley hung his head out the open window, panting in encouragement. "I'll bet you're surprised a blond, doe-eyed femme can change a flat."

Randi had the grace to wince. "Crap. You heard that?"

I tightened the last lug nut and stood. "Yup."

"How *much* of that conversation did you hear?"

"Oh, enough. And since I'm so anal retentive, I remember every word." I wiped my hands on the towelette Randi had found in the glove compartment.

Randi pursed her lips, obviously a woman unused to apologies. "I'm sorry. That was rude and unprofessional of me." She cleared her throat. "Could we keep this tire business to ourselves?"

"I must confess, I don't know what to think about you. One minute you've pissed me off, then the next minute I think you're kind of cute."

"Cute?"

"Don't worry. I'm not going to make a pass at you or anything. It's just kind of cute that you come all unglued over a flat tire. Besides, this is potential blackmail material."

When Randi flashed that damned dimple, I felt like I was tumbling down onto a soft, warm bed. "Blackmailing a PI isn't really a good idea," she said.

"Neither is stealing from a library."

"Good point." She reached into her jacket and handed me the log book. "Here. You do what you want with this."

I stuck the log book in my briefcase, then while Randi wheeled the flat tire toward the back, I took advantage of the time to start cleaning the floor of the backseat, wondering if I might find a silk teddy or lacy bra.

I quickly filled another two bags as Randi struggled to get the tire locked back onto the frame. I knew I should help, but decided it'd be good for her.

Five minutes later we were both back in our seats and once again headed for Pittsburgh. Deep in worry I might not have tightened the lug nuts enough, I jerked when Randi reached over and touched my arm.

"Thank you for changing my tire."

I couldn't hold back any longer. "Cam thinks you're gay."

Randi looked over at me. "He's right."

"I'm not surprised. Cam's never wrong. Are you out at work?"

Randi nodded.

I hesitated. "In a relationship?"

Randi shook her head. "Not my thing."

"You're celibate?"

Randi threw back her head and let out the deepest chuckle I'd heard from her. "God, no. But I don't do relationships. They never work out, and falling in love is such a messy business."

"I agree, but my friend Maggie keeps trying to get me to find another girlfriend."

"How long has it been since Julia moved out? Eight months?"

My jaw dropped. "How did you know about her?"

Randi merged onto the freeway. "I'm an investigator, remember? I like to find out everything I can about the people I'm working with. I knew you were gay before I walked into your office that first day."

"That feels sort of invasive."

"Sorry."

"I'm not attracted to you." Holy crap, where had that come from? Suddenly I was warmer than a fully dressed woman in a sauna. And as soon as the sentence passed my lips, I knew it was a big honking lie. I *was* attracted to Randi Marx.

"Shit, woman, I didn't say you were."

"Woman? You're calling me 'woman' now? I don't think so." We glared at each other and my jaw worked as I struggled to calm down. Our second fight.

Randi's face shut down, and the cool, removed professional suddenly returned. "I apologize. I've let this conversation get off track, and it was unprofessional of me. Let's keep our conversations to business only."

In a huff, I began reading the log book, unsure if I was relieved or disappointed. I could usually read people well, but after a few days with Randi Marx, I still had no idea who this woman was. All I knew was that whenever Randi was around, I had to fight not to watch her move.

❖

We'd only driven an hour when Randi pulled off at Harrisburg, south of Colombus, and parked in front of a motel. "I'm sorry. I can't drive anymore."

"I could drive."

"It's not that. I've just got to get out of the car. Would you mind if we finished the drive to Pittsburgh tomorrow?"

Actually, I was sick of the SUV myself, so I readily agreed. As we passed the heavily chlorinated pool on the way to our side-by-side rooms, Randi looked with obvious longing toward the shimmering water, and I had a brainstorm. After I stashed my gear in my room, I visited the restaurant and asked to speak to the chef. A few minutes later, armed with a foil-wrapped package hidden in my backpack, and one hand behind my back, I knocked on Randi's door.

Randi had changed from her business suit into low-slung jeans and a tight-fitting green Henley. I struggled to keep my gaze where it belonged. "I was thinking that you might like some exercise. If you want to go swimming, I could watch Marley for you." The dog peered at me from behind Randi's legs.

Interest flared in her eyes. "I appreciate that. But even if Marley didn't go berserk with you, I don't have a suit."

I dangled the black Speedo in front of Randi. "I do. It's new. Never worn. It'll be a little big, but it shouldn't come off." By now Marley scented my hidden treat and pushed energetically at my thigh.

Randi stared at the suit, obviously tempted.

"Marley and I have ridden together long enough that he knows me. I'm happy to take care of him for you."

Exhaling loudly, Randi agreed. "But if he gets nervous, put him on the leash and come get me."

Randi stepped into her bathroom and changed while I rubbed Marley's ears, loving the sweet dog but also wondering how Randi managed to lead a normal life. She emerged in the suit and her jeans, and filled the suit out just fine. I gave Marley even more attention so I wouldn't stare.

Randi hesitated at the door. "Thanks for this. I'll be back in half an hour."

I nodded, then held Marley's collar. Once the door closed and Marley dashed for it, I dug out the foil-wrapped package. "Marley, Emma has a treat for you."

Of course he wolfed down the leftover beef in about seven seconds, which left me a mere twenty-nine minutes and fifty-three seconds in which to distract him. We played with his chewy toy, a thick blue ropelike thing that had been chewed into a mass of threads, but after five minutes he was bored with that. He began standing at the door, staring intently at the doorknob as if willing it to open and reveal Randi. Then a small whimper escaped those doggy lips.

Damn. He was heading for Ballistic Avenue. Desperate, I flung up my arms and said, "Poodle-noodle!"

Marley whipped around to stare.

"Noodle-doodle-poodle!" I don't know if it was my tone of voice, my outstretched arms, or the alliteration, but Marley popped straight up in the air and whirled in a circle. "Poodle-doodle-noodle!" I yelled again, and Marley leapt toward me, all wagging tail and pink tongue.

Every time I threw my arms wide and shouted our little code, he whirled in a circle. He became so excited he began leaping from bed to bed. Laughing, I finally made him stop and then straightened the bedspreads so Randi wouldn't think I'd been trying out her beds. Marley helped, so it took longer.

Exhausted, I threw the chew toy for him and he lay down happily to tear more of it into shreds. I lay down on one of the beds. Which one would Randi sleep in? The one nearer the window? Or nearer the bathroom? Could you tell anything about a person's personality by which bed she chose? Randi would choose the window bed, which was where I lay. I closed my eyes. In just a few hours, Randi would take off her clothes and put on…navy pajama top and bottom? Baggy athletic shorts and a T-shirt? A tank top and thong? Nothing?

Whoa. This was getting kinky. I hopped up and settled myself on the stuffed chair by the window.

When Randi returned, dripping wet with the white hotel towel draped around her hips, Marley and I were watching the news. "Wow," she said. "He's fine. How did you do that?"

I hopped up, unwilling to presume Randi wanted me to stay and chat. "I didn't want to mention it earlier, but I'm a dog whisperer."

"Bullshit," Randi said with another deep laugh that brought out that damned dimple. I reached for the nightstand behind me for support. Shit, shit, shit.

"Why?" I swallowed hard.

"Because I smelled gravy when I walked in here, and there's a wadded-up hunk of foil wrap in the waste basket. You bribed my boy."

I smiled as I slid past her and headed for the door. "Never," I said, deciding she didn't need to know about the poodle-noodle-doodle thing, and returned to my own room. I shut the door behind me and leaned back against it, wishing Randi had invited me to remain in her room a little longer. These last three days had stopped feeling like a burden, or a journey or a treasure hunt, and had suspiciously begun to feel like one long date. I hadn't spent this much time with anyone in a long time.

I liked it.

CHAPTER SIXTEEN

A weird edginess plagued me the next morning as we began our five-hour drive to Pittsburgh. I was a little confused by my constant awareness of Randi—when she moved, what she said, how she spoke, the little sighs that escaped for seemingly no reason. Add to that my anger at Drummond, frustration with Getty and our library funding, attraction to Captain Tommy, not to mention how I felt about the current Congress, the Taliban, global warming, and those subscription cards that continually fell from magazines, and I was a wreck. I was tired of reading the log book and tired of paging through library books thinking the next map might be the Farris map.

I found Captain R. Brown's log book slow going. Beside the weather reports and sextant readings, the captain would occasionally note a crew member who'd "taken the fever" or who'd been injured by a swinging boom, but otherwise there were no personal notes of any kind. The book was a total snoozer.

My mom called to ask if I'd picked strawberries yet, and if I wanted GeeGeeBee's famous strawberry pie recipe. "No time to pick, Mom," I said, "but thanks anyway." We talked about Dad's sore knee, and her first meeting as chair of the local library board, then hung up. Getty called with a few questions. Cam called to whine about his mother interfering with his life, and wished he could remember more about the attack.

Finally, after ten phone calls, Randi cleared her throat. "Any chance you could turn that damned phone off?"

"Ah, well." I looked at my phone. None of the calls had been emergencies. Nothing would fall apart if I turned the phone off for a few hours, so I shut off both phone and PDA, and went back to reading Captain Brown's log book.

"Anything interesting?" Randi asked after another hour on the road.

"Besides the ship's position and the weather, not much. So far I've found three mentions of R. Brown's ship sighting another ship, and all three times Brown changed course to avoid it." Every time Randi spoke to me, I felt charged and ready, as if something interesting was about to happen.

"Doesn't that sound like something a pirate would do?"

I closed the log book. "You think Brown was a pirate? Maybe he was trying to *avoid* a pirate." I skipped to the back of the log.

"You're one of those impatient people who want to know how the book ends?"

"I can't bear to read the same thing over and over again." I sighed. "Same old stuff back here."

Randi had been stiffer this morning, as if letting me see her in a swimsuit had violated some personal boundary or something. I missed those moments of easy camaraderie we'd shared, however short. That morning I'd looked out my hotel window and watched Randi tossing a Frisbee for Marley, and realized I'd never known someone so comfortable with animals and so uncomfortable with other humans.

But without Randi, I'd never have met Marley. He was a sweet, sweet dog and reminded me of Licorice, GeeGeeBee's black lab. I was going to miss Marley when our journey ended, and wondered briefly if I'd ever see him again. Maybe I should ask Randi for visitation rights. Three days on the road together, and already I wanted to coparent Marley.

"May I ask you a question?" Randi asked.

If I hadn't been wearing my seat belt, I might have fallen over. "Sure."

"If there really is a map, and we find it, and then we follow the map and find the treasure, who owns the treasure?"

"Well, I guess I hadn't thought much about that." That was a lie. Just last week I'd dreamt that I'd found the treasure and Tommy Farris with it, alive and sexy and ready to sail me around the world. "I don't know who would own it. Spain?"

"See, that's what really bugs me." I was thrilled to learn something bugged Randi Marx besides me. "Spain took over huge chunks of South America. They nearly killed off all the natives either by disease or through slavery. Even though they stole the silver from Peru, history keeps calling it the Spanish treasure."

"Good point. You think whoever finds the treasure should give it back to Peru?"

"Not to the government. To the people."

I nearly called her a radical, but her voice was so earnest I let it go. Randi was proving to be more complex, and more interesting, than I'd first thought. We discussed it for a while longer but stopped when we ended up going around in circles. Neither of us knew the answer.

After another hour, I turned on my phone, feeling a little guilty that Randi had convinced me to turn it off, and found fifteen messages. Crap. I turned my PDA on. There were too many work-related e-mails, but one was from Cam: *Feeling better since we talked. Remembering more of attack. Police artist drew this sketch. Keep your eyes peeled. I also remember him saying "The treasure belongs in the family."*

Weird. The guy was clearly connected to our hunt for the treasure map, but how? I scrolled down to the photo and yelped. "That's him! That's the guy I've seen, the one I thought was following me. The crew cut guy."

Randi looked over at the photo. "Ugly SOB."

I keyed in my reply to Cam. *What's his name? What's his story?*

Randi drummed her steering wheel. "This guy beats up Cam so he can't come along on the trip. That means three people want the map: Drummond because he collects maps and will likely sell it. Benton because he already has a buyer and stands to make a great deal of money, and our mystery crew cut guy, and who knows why he's involved."

❖

When we pulled into the Pittsburgh Sheraton, I checked my watch. Because it was Sunday, the library wouldn't be open. How were we going to spend the day—hanging out together like buddies, or each doing our own thing? Why hadn't I given this any thought?

"Now what?" I felt awkward, wishing we'd driven home. But then Marley stuck his wet nose against my neck and I reached for him. No, I wasn't ready to leave Marley yet.

Randi put the car in park but didn't shut it off. She seemed to be thinking, hesitating, but then turned toward me. "This may bore the hell out of you, but I'd like to check out some antique stores while we have the time."

My heart did the macarena and the hootchy-kootchy, whatever the hell that was, and the rumba and the foxtrot. "That might be fun," I said casually.

Randi punched something into her GPS, then nodded at the screen. "Excellent. We're going shopping."

Fifteen minutes later we pulled into a cozy older downtown neighborhood called the Strip District, lined with fresh produce markets, coffee shops, museums, *and* antique stores. My spirits lifted. "True confession," I said. "I *love* cruising through these stores."

Randi shut off the car and smiled shyly. "I do too." We strolled down one side of the street, then back up the other side. A spicy cloud spilled out a Thai restaurant and a saxophonist played jazz in the shade of a kitchen gadget store. Randi dropped a five-dollar bill into the man's case.

When we passed a narrow alley and stopped to pet a fat tabby cat, a man halfway down the alley suddenly whirled and ran in the opposite direction. I froze. "That's him. The guy with the crew cut from the airport!"

Randi sprinted after him and I followed, avoiding a stack of pallets and a smelly Dumpster. But when we reached the end, the alley spilled out into a busy street pulsing with energy from a street fair. Gasping for breath, I scanned the crowd, but didn't see him.

Disappointed, we walked back down the alley. Face grim, Randi opened her phone and called her boss, explaining that I'd seen the same man three times and giving a description. She hung up and jammed the phone back into its holder.

My heart still pounded from the chase. "It's not just a coincidence, is it?"

"No, it's not. But now that he knows you've seen him, he'll be gone, at least for today. And he'll be cagier when he follows us next." She shook her head. "Shit. Someone's been tailing us this entire trip."

I didn't say anything. Could it be that Randi was as distracted by me as I was by her?

"Okay, let's put that episode behind us and start with the largest store," Randi said, holding the door open for me, taking up enough of the doorway that I had to turn sideways, brushing against Randi's chest. I held my breath and felt my face blaze. Had she done that on purpose?

Struggling to focus, I scanned the store for a stack of boxes that might be puzzles, and spied a pile on an old black stove. "I'll meet you back here in fifteen minutes," I said, heading for the puzzles, nodding to the ancient woman behind the counter wearing too much lipstick and a baggy brown sweater.

"You break it, you buy it," the woman said flatly.

The store smelled musty and even the light seemed coated in dust. I quickly sorted through the stack, brushing off the dust to better see them. They were mostly bad landscapes by artists I didn't recognize.

"What are you looking for?"

I jumped at Randi's voice right behind me. "Old puzzles."

"I got that much."

"Puzzles of women, okay?"

"No surprise there."

"I like Edward Eggleston's paintings, but I only have the *Spanish Dancer*. I have a few Billy Devorss, and one Louis Berneker, *Dance of the Veils*."

"Hmm, sounds racy."

"It is. Three women wearing nothing but veils."

"Suddenly jigsaw puzzles don't sound boring."

"They're not boring. They're relaxing. GeeGeeBee and I used to spend hours working puzzles."

"Do you have a wish list? I'd be happy to keep an eye open for you, since I go through so many antique stores."

I stopped and stared at her. "Eggleston's *Treasure Princess*."

"What does it look like?"

"Sexy woman in pirate garb holding a sword in one hand and strings of jewels in the other. She's standing on a beach, with an open treasure chest beside her."

Randi nodded seriously. "I'll keep my eyes open for it."

I moved toward an alcove in the back of the store, expecting Randi to browse on her own. But when I stopped suddenly at a great puzzle, Randi plowed right into me. I lost my balance, flailed my arms, and fell against a rickety table. The table and books it held crashed to the ground.

"Whoa," Randi said, grabbing me and pulling me close against her chest. My heart pounded in my throat as I straightened and stepped out of her arms.

"What's going on back there?" came a harsh voice from the front of the store. "Did you break anything?"

"No, we're okay," I called shakily.

"I didn't mean *you*, for crying out loud. I meant did you break any of my merchandise?"

Randi chuckled softly. "I love old women. I want to be her some day."

"Mercy me," shrieked the proprietor, having finally reached the chaotic scene.

"I'm sorry. I fell against the table. I don't think anything is broken," I said. Randi and I righted the table, her strong hands brushing against mine.

"You break it, you buy it. That's posted right on the door. My lawyer said everyone agrees to this policy just by coming in the door." The store dragon watched for a few minutes, satisfied nothing ceramic or glass had broken, then returned to the front counter, grumbling under her breath.

My heart still pounded and I felt hot all over. Neither of us spoke as we worked. Had Randi felt the same thing I had? What was I supposed to do now? Why couldn't I see clearly what came next? My whole life I'd been able to see the wisest course of action, what I needed to say or do next, but my head was empty, all static and no sense. A full calendar with neat entries wouldn't help me here.

"Why don't we each browse separately?" I finally suggested.

Randi ducked her head in reply, then wandered down the main aisle. A few minutes later I heard a soft exclamation from Randi and found her in a dusty alcove toward the back of the store.

Randi's eyes gleamed in the dim light as she stared at a framed antique map on the wall, then carefully removed the map from the wall.

I didn't recognize the map, but it looked uninteresting. "You collect maps?"

Randi jerked around, mouth open. "Ah, no." She glared at the map in her hands, then sighed. "Okay, yes, I do."

"You look like I just accused you of drowning puppies or something. I collect puzzles, you collect maps. What's the big deal, and why didn't you tell me sooner?"

Randi wiped dust off the peeling gold frame. "I don't know."

Watching her, I saw again someone who didn't know how to change her own flat tire, and suddenly felt a rush of protectiveness. "I do," I said. "You didn't want me to think you were some weird, obsessed collector. You didn't want me to lump you and Drummond together."

Randi inhaled sharply, her eyes now unreadable. "Very perceptive."

"How did you get started collecting?" Randi shrugged but I clucked my tongue. "Oh, no you don't. C'mon, tell me."

Randi straightened a stack of books on a nearby table, then picked up an old hurricane lamp and brushed off the glass chimney. "My mom used to send me and my two brothers on scavenger hunts, her way of getting us out of her hair. She'd give us a list of stuff, like pine cones or pennies or milkweed pods, and the first one to find everything on the list got an ice cream sandwich."

"That's sounds wonderful."

She couldn't meet my eyes. "Well, Jack and Nick and I were very competitive about the whole thing, and after a while my mom's lists weren't challenging enough, so we started making lists for each other. The stuff was scary to get, like the lid to an Elvis cookie jar. The only Elvis cookie jar in the neighborhood was in Mrs. Valente's kitchen. Jack and Nick both tried to get in, but the woman wasn't very friendly. I pretended to skin my knee outside on her sidewalk, and rang her doorbell asking for a Band-Aid." Randi stopped, shaking her head. "Why am I telling you this?"

"Because I asked."

"But I've been trained to resist any technique designed to force information from me."

I leaned close and whispered in her ear, "Please, I really want to know." Too stunned at my own audaciousness to stop, as I moved back I let my hand slide lightly down Randi's arm.

Randi swallowed. "I got the Elvis lid, and our lists just got harder and harder, so we had to dig deeper and get more creative."

"Sounds like good skills for an investigator to develop."

"I suppose…"

"What?"

"Nothing. The three of us were competitive 24/7, that's all."

"Your childhood sounds intense."

Randi shrugged. "It helped me get this job, so it couldn't have been all bad. C'mon, let's get going."

Still thinking about Randi's childhood, I bought a puzzle; Randi bought the map and a small dusty book with a fraying green cover, *Myths and Superstitions at Sea*, by Martin Masterson.

Without discussing it, we moved easily into the adjacent coffeehouse and drank our coffee in silence as Randi read her superstitions book and I dug out my calendar to check the things I'd miss tomorrow. Soon the coffee went right through me.

When I returned from the bathroom, Randi had spun my Day-Timer around toward her and was casually turning the pages in a bold, invasive move that took my breath away. She wasn't really reading it, but just touching the pages, which made me more excited than if I'd found her looking through my underwear drawer and picking up something red and lacy of mine.

"Very neat," she said, running a finger along a line of something I'd written, her fingertips brushing the paper I'd touched. "Not much white space in this calendar."

The first time I tried to speak, nothing came out, so I cleared my throat. "No time for white space."

"I have a theory about busy people. Want to hear it?"

"No."

"Here it is. The reason you keep that calendar filled is so you won't have time to stop and realize how empty your life is."

I sputtered a bit, stunned at my desperation to prove her wrong. "And your life is so much better, I suppose."

Randi shook her head. "No, my life isn't that great. I work too much, have too few friends, have only one-night stands, and my most important conversations have been with my dog. But at least I'm not hiding from the truth behind a jam-packed schedule."

I should have been angry but was still so turned on by her looking through my calendar that the hair on my arms tingled. "I suppose it's difficult to find women only interested in one-night stands."

"Not at all," she said with such casualness my mind flashed to how hot it must be to pick up a different woman every night. But a steady diet of it? No thanks. I longed for something that would last.

Randi went back to her book, and I self-consciously closed up my calendar and put it away to read Captain Brown's log book for a while. At one point Randi shook her head at her book.

"What?" I asked.

"Centuries ago, sailors used to have some pretty strange ideas. And some of these myths? I'm guessing the sailors were high or something. Sometimes they'd see islands that weren't on the charts, but others on the same ships couldn't see those islands. One island they called Love Island could be seen only by those men with 'a lass on their minds.' Those men without lasses on their minds—the ugly, drunk, or married—didn't see the island."

"Weird," I said. I returned to Brown's log book, and while I didn't really care about myths of the sea, it reminded me of the Bermuda Triangle and the Grenada Triangle. Had Tommy held any stock in superstition, or was she more of a boots-on-the-deck sort of sailor, only believing in exactly what she could see, hear, smell, taste, or touch? And where did love fall into those categories? Had Tommy ever loved anyone?

Frustrated, I skipped ahead a few pages, since I couldn't take any more weather reports. "Holy crap! Whoa!" I bent over the book. "Listen to this. The August 5, 1715, entry says: *My crew all ask about Farris and the treasure, but I can't tell them the truth, so I tell them I don't know anything.*"

Randi leaned forward until our heads nearly touched over the book. "You just connected Tommy Farris and R. Brown," she murmured.

"It gets better. The August 28 entry includes this: *McLurin said I'd find her, but I haven't. McLurin's help was no help. What in damnation does Shakespeare have to do with my quest? Go to your bosom and knock? Yet I refuse to accept that she's gone forever, and the treasure with her. But I'm not giving up. Dum spiro, spero.*"

"How well do you know Shakespeare?"

"I could come up with a few lines from *Romeo and Juliet*, but only after a bottle of wine."

"Could I see the log?" Randi flipped through the pages and began scribbling coordinates down in her notebook. I watched, puzzled.

Finally Randi nodded at her notes. "R. Brown kept returning to this area of the Caribbean. Not the same coordinates, but the same area. Then he'd sail back to these coordinates, which I'm guessing is a port." Randi checked her notes. "I've only looked at a third of the entries, but he made that trip three times, each time returning to a slightly different location."

"Brown was looking for something, for a *her*."

We looked at each other. "He was either looking for a ship," I said.

"Or a woman."

"And he returned to port to either resupply the ship…"

"Or unload something off the ship…treasure?"

I got so excited I squeezed Randi's hand, and she didn't pull away. "This means something. We've found our first real clue."

We stared at our clasped hands, I jerked back, then stuck both hands in my jeans jacket.

Randi's watch beeped so loudly we both jumped. "Time to let Marley out."

Relieved, I hopped up. "Let me do it. I'm so excited about this I can't sit still."

Randi tossed me her keys. I merged into the Sunday afternoon foot traffic, then gratefully slipped down into the narrow parking lot tucked beside the building. A tan Buick sat halfway back in the slot across from Randi's SUV, idling. I peered closer and realized with a start that it was Benton. What the hell was he doing here? Had he followed us? Impossible!

Unsure if I should return to the café and get Randi, I stopped. But then a car door slammed and Lauren emerged from behind Randi's SUV with a leashed Marley trotting at her side. The woman froze when she saw me. Everything became clear. I'd interrupted something awful. Lauren and Benton were in the middle of kidnapping Marley, and I was too far away to stop it.

PART FIVE

THE SPANISH GALLEON, 1715

Drawn by the romance of the high seas, the drama of an ancient tragedy and the fever of treasure hunting, many will seek her gold, silver, and jewels…but maybe her hiding place will remain secret forever.

—Kenneth Mulder, *Piracy: Days of Long Ago*

Chapter Seventeen

Dawn came to the West Indies like a lantern slowly glowing hotter, melting the night's darkness into the sea. Once again Tommy Farris awoke after a cramped few hours' sleep in the longboat. She opened her eyes and heard sailors talking as the watch changed. What in blazes had she done last night? She'd kissed a woman full on the mouth and would've kept at it if she hadn't rolled from her hammock and fled the cabin. If not so damned upsetting, it might've been funny—Captain Tommy Farris, the Devil's Shadow, scourge of the West Indies, afraid to be alone with a mere woman named Rebekah. Tommy touched her lips and wondered how the pressure of Rebekah's lips on hers could feel as it did.

Tommy checked for nearby crew, then rolled herself from the boat, stifling a groan, and headed for the galley. If thoughts of Rebekah continued to torture her, Tommy'd lock her up in the brig. She couldn't lead this ship into battle if she didn't stop thinking of the curve of that woman's hip as she slept in her hammock. Damn that woman and her body.

The sun struggled to shine but gave up once a heavy blanket of clouds moved in. Tommy shivered in the cool breeze and watched Sawkins working mid-ship. Judging by the limp, the man seemed to be favoring his left knee, a sign that bad weather lurked nearby. The *Moon Shadow* had weathered dozens of storms and could take any pounding Poseidon delivered. But to stay with the other ships *and* battle the Spanish *and* take a galleon, even one as small as the *Maravillosa*, now that would be a feat.

Sawkins joined her. "Another storm's coming."

"I noticed. How long?"

He grimaced, then flexed his knee. "Day, mebbe two," Sawkins said, then shifted from foot to foot.

"Sawkins, you got something that needs saying?"

"I got me a bad feel about this one."

"Me too."

"I'm gonna die," Sawkins said.

"Christ Almighty, man, we're all gonna die sometime."

"No, ye know what I mean. How long we been at this?"

"Five years since I anchored us off Tortuga and dried you out."

"Captain, we be cheating death so many times I know she's keeping score. She's coming soon to collect on me gambling debts."

They watched the action on the deck below, and to a man, none of them had been three years on the *Moon Shadow*. Most had served under two years, thanks to scurvy, dysentery, shipboard accidents, falling overboard, being killed in battle, or put ashore for breaking the Articles. Sawkins sighed. "We've been watching hundreds of men walk these decks, then die or disappear, yet here the two of us are, still alive. Why's that?"

"Dumb luck." Tommy considered the horizon, a thin thread beckoning her. "Too bad you and me can't buy us a merchant ship and leave pirating behind."

"At least then the killin' would stop."

Tommy raised an eyebrow.

"Ye know we ain't out here for the killing. We're out here to live in the wide open, trying to keep ourselves fed." He inhaled deeply and Tommy swept her eyes across the choppy sea. No tenement buildings, no crowded London streets, no debtors' prison.

After a few minutes' silence, Sawkins leaned closer. "Captain?" Sawkins's voice dropped to a whisper.

"Aye?"

"I love the sea and never want to be anywhere else. But I was born on land and want me bones to rest on land after I'm gone."

"Sawkins, you're not going to die. We—"

"Cannon, musket, cutlass, a falling mast. Any manner of death's gonna be whizzing by me soon. Should I die, please don't be burying me at sea. Tow me behind the stern in a net if ye must and let the fishes feed, but plant my bones in the earth. Anywhere's fine."

"You're not—"

"Captain, please, I'm beggin' ye."

In their five years together, Sawkins had never—not once—asked for anything. Tommy sighed. "Should you be dying on this ship, I'll bury you on land. But Sawkins, if Davy Jones takes us—"

"I know. Nothing to be done if that happens." Sawkins touched his cap. "With your leave, think I'll go check on those pumps."

If the gray day and confusion over Rebekah hadn't brought Tommy lower than a teredo worm, Sawkins's talk of death certainly did the trick. But then Rebekah appeared on mid-deck to help Billy pick apart bits of old rope for oakum, and Tommy did her best not to stare. She failed, banishing all thoughts of death, Sawkins's or anyone else's, and instead marveled at Rebekah's kindness toward Billy, the curve of her neck as she bent over her work, and the mystery of those lips.

❖

They sailed west long enough that the Dolphin Islands appeared ahead. At the same time, several sails appeared on the northern horizon. Damn. Shaw had managed to find the rendezvous point on his own. In the wardroom Tommy and Sawkins discussed the best place to drop anchor as they neared the largest island, shaped like a kidney bean bending toward them. Sawkins recommended the southern tip, and Tommy agreed. After Sawkins left, the door to Tommy's cabin opened and Rebekah emerged. Tommy leapt from her chair and swept her gaze toward the mid-deck, hoping to make a quick escape.

"Tommy, have we arrived?"

"Yes." She pointed toward the chart on the table and gathered up her hat and sword.

"But where are we? I've not been following all the talk of islands and currents and hiding places."

Sighing, Tommy put her sword back down and flattened out the chart. "Up here's where we fished you out of the water, on the eastern part of the West Indies. We came south until we reached Carriacou, then headed west. You be sick most of that time. We now be here, to the east of the Dolphin Islands. The Spaniards'll either come between the Dolphins and the mainland or to the east of us heading straight up for Cuba."

Rebekah stood far too close to Tommy's side, smelling like sun and sweat and soap all at the same time. Tommy widened her nostrils and took it all in, wishing she could run her nose along Rebekah's neck for more. Instead, she rolled up the chart.

"You're like two people," Rebekah said suddenly.

"What?"

"You're two souls captured in the same body. One's strong and harsh and commands a fleet of three ships and over three hundred men. You keep them fed and clothed, and you do your best to make sure they don't kill each other. Yet I've heard the men talking. They worship you. You kill at will and without qualm."

Tommy jammed the chart into an empty cubbyhole.

"The other part of you is gentle and kind and wants no part of the killing. How do you live with both those two souls battling inside you?"

Tommy felt as if Rebekah had opened up a door in her chest and looked inside. How did she do that? She gazed into Rebekah's warm eyes and felt herself falling. "I've no choice."

"But you do. I know you feel deeply. You look at me with deep feelings, which makes my heart swell. Tommy, you and I—"

Tommy grabbed her hat and sword. "They need me out on deck. Look to your own job, as the sandglass will need turning soon." She brushed past Rebekah and fled the wardroom.

By nightfall all the ships had reached the tiny chain of islands, had tucked in behind the largest, and dropped anchor to wait for the Spanish fleet. The *Moon Shadow* bobbed on the gentle sea, as dark as the water because they dared not light lanterns and give themselves away. Rather than bump around belowdecks without light, the men snored softly on the deck, where sleeping was cooler.

The next day Tommy rode her men mercilessly, pushing them to clear the decks, batten everything down, sharpen their cutlasses, oil the guns, and repair rigging. The only way Tommy could keep her mind off the battle ahead was to give orders. She wasn't afraid but approached the battle with the same knowledge she did every time she began a chase—this might be the one that sent her to the bottom, or spilled her guts out onto a heaving deck. And now she had Rebekah to worry about. If anything happened to Tommy, Rebekah wouldn't be safe. Tommy had said as much to Sawkins, and he'd grunted, all the reassurance Tommy needed that he'd do his best to watch after the "wench."

Restless, Tommy hung over the railing, peering down at the water lapping against the hull. Rebekah's words yesterday had hit too close to the truth of it. Tommy had begun feeling like two people, and she hated it. The pirate in her wanted more treasure and more power and the thrill of the chase. The woman in her wanted to stop killing and settle down on a quiet island and spend her days sailing, fishing, exploring, and loving someone. The idea she'd even consider living on land, not the sea, stunned her. She'd always thought people who lived on land were weak and lazy and without adventure in their souls, but one could see the horizon as easily from the beach of an island as from the deck of a ship.

There was no place for that woman in the battle ahead. If Tommy were to survive, and ensure that her crew and Rebekah did as well, it'd have to be the pirate in her that prevailed. Tommy began to pace, aware again how small a ship actually was, a crowded wooden home for over one hundred men, hopefully filled with everything they needed to stay alive: water, food, weapons, and a fearless captain. She would be that captain, or the devil take her.

CHAPTER EIGHTEEN

Tommy was sure Coxon was bothering Rebekah, so she kept one eye on the man and told Sawkins and Hatley to do the same. Every time Tommy saw Rebekah, she'd look for Coxon. She itched to run her sword through the man, but she lacked both crime and victim, since Rebekah was unwilling to speak.

Four bells into the afternoon watch, a single sail approached from the south. All hands prepared to do battle until Billy, up in the crow's nest, yelled down it was the *Black Widow*.

All the captains ended up back on the *Sharktooth*. Tommy was relieved to see Calabria alive and in good health, despite what had to have been a hard, fast sail down to Puerto Bello to spy on the Spanish.

Shaw called on Weatherly, and the wiry man with no hair and few teeth fairly danced with glee. "That *Barcelona* be loaded to the gunwales with silver plate. We saw them loading some of the chests. The *Santa Maria* and her sister ship be carrying wine and supplies. That puny little galleon, *Maravillosa*, is packed with slaves. We watched the last of them being loaded and chained onto the deck. Then we hightailed it back here. The fleet was to put to sea yesterday, so it'll already be underway. They should be coming up along the coast by tomorrow. They only got five escorts—three frigates and two sloops."

"Galleons are slower than snot in winter," Shaw said, "so we don't have to worry about them. So it be our seven ships against the five escorts. Easy odds for us, right, Tommy?"

"Galleons can blast a hole in your hull as easy as a frigate or sloop."

"But they won't," Shaw snapped. "So this be the plan. We watch and wait. Weatherly, take the *Black Widow* over here." Shaw jabbed at his chart to the west of the Dolphins. "When you see them Spanish buggers coming up the coast, sail back and let us know. We'll let 'em pass, then sneak up behind 'em and attack."

Tommy listened as Shaw reviewed his plan, which was still crazy. A pirate who expected to live didn't just sail up to a Spanish fleet and start blasting away. You had to have some advantage to take over a ship, and with Shaw's plan, they'd have none. Tommy suggested they use longboats to sneak up on each ship at night, but Shaw pronounced this cowardly. She suggested using a fire ship, which Shaw said was a waste of a perfectly fine ship.

"You're set on this course of action?" Tommy asked. How could she escape this fool's plan without endangering her ship and her mates? "What if the fleet turns north before it reaches the Dolphins? I could send a ship to the east, then if the fleet sails north, we won't miss it."

Shaw shrugged. "Waste of a ship, but I don't have a problem with it."

Tommy looked at McLeod, who nodded smartly and said, "I'll be taking the *Windy Queen* out, then, but what if we miss the action? We'll be stuck out in the middle of the sea."

"You'll have a share, my friend," Shaw said. "All ships that follow me will share the plunder. We'll be filthy rich. What do the rest of ye say?" Shaw looked at each captain, including Tommy. Each of them nodded in turn. Tommy hesitated, feeling every eye upon her, then agreed.

The captains of both the *Black Widow* and the *Windy Queen* set sail well before dusk, one heading west, the other heading east. Tommy watched them go. If she was lucky, only one ship would return with news of the fleet. She and Shaw could pull off his ridiculous plan, she'd get her men out of this with their lives and a little coin, and it would all be over.

❖

Tommy hated waiting. She hated avoiding Rebekah. She hated worrying about all of it. Exhausted, Tommy sat at the table in her cabin, head resting on her arms. What was she to do? Would she follow Shaw's lead, take the *Barcelona* and ignore the *Maravillosa*? If she went for the *Maravillosa*, were her men following her to yet another useless prize?

Footsteps outside her open door. The scent of soap. Tommy didn't look up. "What have you eaten today?" Rebekah asked.

"Nothing." Tommy raised her head. "Not hungry."

"You need to eat."

"I'll eat when I'm hungry." They glared at each other.

Finally Rebekah folded her arms. "Your men had a bath day recently, but you didn't."

Tommy arched a brow. "You be expecting me to be bathing in my cabin in the middle of the bloody night?"

"No, but I'll wash and braid your hair. It's a mess."

Tommy protested, but Rebekah soon had a bucket of water partially heated by the galley fires, and dunked Tommy's head in it. Tommy closed her eyes and inhaled Rebekah's scent as Rebekah worked.

Rebekah rinsed out Tommy's hair, then moved her to the mast for support. Rebekah began braiding, tugging gently. "This is a braid my mother taught me." She paused. "Why do you have this streak of white?"

Tommy had been waiting for this question. "Because I do."

"Your hair reminds me of a wisp of smoke rising up through the night sky…or perhaps a shaft of moonlight cutting through the dark."

"Those words be too pretty to be describing my hair." Tommy grunted as Rebekah tugged harder.

"There's nothing wrong with that." She hesitated. "For years I heard other slaves whispering pretty words about their lovers, but the women's whispers were all about men."

Sweet Jesus. Tommy stepped away but was yanked back by her braid.

"I'm not done, so stay put. Tommy, you can run all you like, but something's happened between us. Why does my heart flip like a hotcake every time you look at me? What does that mean?"

Tommy's throat tightened, and she didn't trust herself to speak. She knew what she should say, that Rebekah's flipping insides meant nothing, but her mouth was too dry.

Rebekah sighed. "If I keep talking about this, you're going to run back out on deck again, aren't you?" She dropped the finished braid.

"For a brave woman you can be a coward, you know that? I'll sleep up on deck so you won't have to run away again."

Too tired to protest, and a little relieved, Tommy watched as Rebekah left, then she climbed into her hammock for a minute. Rebekah would be safe on deck as it was Hatley's watch. Tommy closed her eyes. What would happen if Rebekah were to return to their cabin—when had it switched from Tommy's cabin to *theirs*—and slowly approach Tommy? What if she were to bend down, gently turn Tommy's face toward hers, and kiss her again? What if Rebekah were to unbutton her dress, let it pool at her feet, then lie down beside Tommy? Tommy ground the palms of her hands against her forehead. If she didn't stop thinking these thoughts, one of these nights she might crawl into Rebekah's hammock and touch her in places that would shock them both.

It was either guilt or her own roiling emotions, but Tommy finally went in search of Rebekah. She strolled the deck, stepping over sleeping men, and found Rebekah sound asleep curled up in the deep longboat with a blanket. None of the men seemed to even know she was there. Tommy returned to her cabin and lay awake, wondering why she was so bloody disappointed.

CHAPTER NINETEEN

Tommy spent the day on deck reading in whatever shade she could find. The air was still and hot, as it often was before a tropical storm. The men were ready, the ship was ready. She took her watch, but of course no navigation readings were required since they were anchored in the island's bay. Rebekah was busy helping Cookie butcher the last of the chickens so Tommy hardly saw her. She felt uncertain if that was good or bad.

That night Tommy made sure Rebekah knew she was welcome to stay in the cabin, but the heat had grown so great that neither of them could bear it. Because the decks were littered with sleeping men who'd fled their quarters, Tommy helped Rebekah into one end of the longboat, and she took the other end. Even outside under the stars, sweat ran down Tommy's neck and back. She slept fitfully, coming awake at every bell.

Tommy was up four bells through morning watch, about six a.m. She left Rebekah, whose face was even more beautiful when she slept, if that was possible, and began pacing the quarterdeck. How long would they have to wait?

A cry went up from a nearby ship as the *Black Widow* rounded the end of the island and sailed toward them. So the fleet was approaching along the coast, as she'd hoped it wouldn't. The Spanish could easily lay in a trap along the coast. But then Billy yelled from the *Shadow*'s stern and Tommy followed his pointing finger. The *Windy Queen* was flying toward them under full sail from the east. Bugger all, what the devil did that mean? Were the Spaniards to the west, or to the east?

Within two bells all the captains, including the breathless McLeod and the equally excited Weatherly, stood in Shaw's wardroom. Tommy had left Hatley with instructions to keep his eye on Coxon and to make sure he didn't bother Rebekah. Sawkins was to make sure Coxon got no ideas about taking control of her ship while she was gone.

"The fleet's coming up the coast," Weatherly said. "Three of the galleons, including the *Barcelona*, and only three escorts. They'll be passing between these islands and the coast in two, mebbe three bells."

McLeod stepped forward. "Ten leagues east of here we saw the smaller galleon, the *Maravillosa*, and two sloop escorts. They be heading straight north, looks like for Cuba."

Chaos broke out as everyone talked at once, speculating on what to do. Finally Shaw knocked the butt of his pistol against the table and the chattering ceased. "There be no question what we do. The *Barcelona* carries the treasure, so bugger the *Maravillosa*. She's naught but a slaver. We give the Spanish bastards two bells to pass us, then we set sail and close the trap. Easy as slitting open a hog belly."

"But why do those three galleons only have three escorts?" Tommy asked. "What if this be a trap?"

"There ye go again with your womanly worries," Shaw said, laughing harshly. "The Spanish fleet has split into two, so the odds just got better for us."

Tommy's heart pounded so fiercely she feared the others would see it through her shirt. The *Maravillosa* was the ship to take. Finding Rebekah and saving her life was a coincidence Tommy couldn't ignore. Besides, her gut told her to ignore the *Barcelona* and go after the *Maravillosa*. Her gut had been wrong a few times, but not many. Had she fished Rebekah out of the sea to risk her life in a foolhardy chase that could end in disaster? No, she hadn't.

Tommy stepped forward and raised her hand. Shaw and the others fell silent. "I agreed to be part of this, and up until now I've been willing to go along with Shaw's plan. But I've changed my mind." She hadn't checked with her men, but if she could get her ship underway it would be heading toward a battle, which gave her complete control over the ship. To stand up to her then would be mutiny. It was underhanded but the only way to do what needed to be done. "The *Moon Shadow* be going east after the *Maravillosa*, and any others who want to join us be welcome to share the plunder."

Shaw pounded the table. "You bloody bitch! The plunder for that ship's nothing but slaves. And we need your ships to take the *Barcelona*. You can't back out."

"I be backing out and I don't care too much how you be liking it. That's the way of it, though, so you might as well give up yelling."

"I'll see ye in Hell before I'll let ye back out of this deal."

"I need to check with my men first," Stratton said, stepping forward, "but I trust Tommy's judgment. If my men say go west, we'll go with Shaw. If it's east, we'll go with Tommy."

"Me too," McLeod said. "I'll see what the men say."

Tommy's heart swelled and she nodded her thanks to her two friends.

"You cursed cowards! I'll fry the gizzard of any one who backs out and have it for supper." Shaw's face had gone white with fury, and spit flecked the front of his fine jacket.

"You can't be doing that," Tommy said calmly. "Each of us be making our own decisions. Stratton, McLeod, check with your men, then send word to me. The *Moon Shadow* sails northeast to cut off the *Maravillosa* in two bells." And with that she jammed on her hat and strode from the room before Shaw could draw a sword or threaten her with his pistols.

She put the men to work as soon as she returned, spreading the word that the Spanish fleet was passing and they were putting to sea to chase it down. She neglected to mention which ship they'd be chasing, however. With great energy the men dove into their tasks, and in record time the ship was ready to weigh anchor. She examined the charts in the privacy of the wardroom so no one would notice the part of the sea she was studying. She could hear Coxon bellowing in the gun room below as he whipped his boys into shape stacking cannonballs and greasing runners.

Sawkins tapped on her door once. "McLeod's here." Sawkins quietly let McLeod in so as not to rouse the interest of her men. Tommy's stomach plummeted at the grief on McLeod's face. "Captain, my men..." The young man could barely meet her eyes. "They be choosing to chase the *Barcelona*. They want to put in with Shaw."

Tommy kept her face calm. "It's not your fault, McLeod. I appreciate that you tried. Thanks for telling me yourself." They clasped hands as if they might never see each other again, and Tommy well knew that might be true. Cursing softly, McLeod saluted Tommy smartly, then left.

Sawkins appeared less than half a bell later to let Stratton in. "Captain." Stratton's eyes were red-rimmed, telling Tommy the whole story. "My bastard crew thinks Shaw'll bring them to the treasure, so my hands are tied. I must go with Shaw." A quick hug with Stratton crying on her shoulder, then Tommy stepped back and bade her man good luck and good sailing.

Tommy was so shaken her fleet was breaking up that she stood alone in the wardroom, unsure what to do next. Rebekah found Tommy there, a chart clutched in her hand.

"Tommy?" Rebekah put a hand on her arm. "The men are wondering why we haven't weighed anchor. The other ships have begun raising sail and moving south toward the end of the island."

Tommy held Rebekah's hand, desperate to understand her feelings for this woman and her need to pursue the *Maravillosa*. "Thank you," Tommy finally croaked out. "I'll be out shortly." Alone again, she composed herself, knowing what was to come next, then strode on deck and up onto the quarterdeck. She watched as the *Windy Queen* and the *Tiger Eye* fell in line behind Shaw's ships. Sadness filled her. The band of men that'd been her responsibility for years was breaking up. The chances that the three ships would sail together again were slim. However, an odd lightness mingled with her sadness. Now she only need worry about one hundred men instead of three hundred.

That was a start. If she wanted to change her life, this would be the moment for it. But she faced one more challenge, and that was Coxon.

With a look from her, Sawkins barked, "Weigh anchor," and the capstan below began to creak and moan as her men leaned into it, raising the anchor.

Tommy stood on the quarterdeck, relieved to feel the ship moving again after so many hours of bobbing like a bloody cork. "Men," she called, "we be going after a prize we can win, not one that'll lead to death. The fleet be breaking up. Shaw and the others are heading west to track down the *Barcelona*, a decrepit derelict supposedly carrying silver and being poorly guarded." The men stopped their work, some hanging from the riggings as they let down sails. "My gut tells me our path lies east, where another galleon, the *Maravillosa*, sails with only two escorts up to Cuba. She's a solid ship and will bring good coin. She's carrying some slaves, but who knows what else may be in the hold. Whatever it be, those of us on this ship be sharing it all." By now the men could see the *Moon Shadow* was heading northeast, the opposite direction as the rest of the fleet. "I be asking for your trust."

Coxon came thundering up from below, face red as he heard her words. "Trust? Stupid cunt!" he screamed. "We be going with Shaw and the others, not off on some wild chase."

Tommy drew herself up and looked down at the furious gunner. "We be underway toward battle. I'm running this ship and that won't change until the battle's over. You want to vote me out then, so be it. But for now, get your fat ass back down to your guns and look to your own job."

Coxon pulled his sword and waved it over his head. "Men, hear me! This bitch is taking us the wrong direction. We be taking over this ship." The crew looked nervously at each other. Which leader should they follow?

Tommy's sword nearly sang as she yanked it from the scabbard, the clear sound reaching every corner of the deck. "Mutiny be serious business. Think hard before taking me on."

"I'm not thinking another second," Coxon yelled, and he clambered up the short ladder to the quarterdeck.

Tommy raised her sword and the fight was on. Coxon was stronger but heavier on his feet. They slashed at each other, Tommy ducking and whirling to avoid the heavy blade, thinking ahead to her next move. She was aware Rebekah had come running from the wardroom and watched Tommy from below.

Tommy's arm soon tired from fending off Coxon's furious blows. With any other man she would have sliced him from neck to nuts, but with Rebekah watching she couldn't bring herself to do it. The damned gunner might win after all.

Tommy dropped and rolled to avoid Coxon's low slash, then she clattered down the ladder. She stood on the mid-deck, sword ready, and heard Rebekah's quiet voice as she stood in the shadows. "He meddled with me, Tommy."

That was all Tommy needed to hear. Nearly blind with fury, she attacked Coxon after he jumped off the ladder. The man was a powerful fighter but slow to recover. Within minutes he left himself open and Tommy thrust her sword into the man's belly. Coxon gaped at her, dropped his sword, clutched his belly, and bled to death on the mid-deck of her ship.

The dark blood pooling at her feet mesmerized Tommy. That could as easily have been Rebekah's blood, or her own. What the hell was she doing in this life? Rebekah had survived slavery because she had no choice, but Tommy had the choice to be a pirate. No one shackled her legs or beat her with a whip.

Standing there, Tommy felt her heart skip a beat. She was free of Coxon, free of Shaw, and freer from responsibility than she'd been for years. All that remained in front of her was to find the *Maravillosa,* free the slaves, and sell the ship so her men would have some cash. After that, an uncertain future stretched before her, but it could be a future free of the pirating life.

CHAPTER TWENTY

The death of Coxon affected Tommy's men as she'd hoped it would. None spoke of mutiny or even grumbled to each other. Instead, all hands worked quietly, efficiently, as if they were relieved the troublemaker was gone. Tommy said nothing to the shaken Rebekah while Sawkins and Hatley dumped the body overboard. A more respectful burial at sea was reserved for non-mutineers.

Suddenly Rebekah was at her side with a rag and was wiping the sword clean.

"Thank you," Tommy said, then sheathed the sword. Rebekah hadn't wanted her to kill Coxon, but then she gave her the reason she needed to do so. Would Tommy ever understand women? "Are you well?" Tommy asked. "When did Coxon—"

"The second day I was aboard. He tried again after that, but I was able to get away each time."

"The man was scum." With that, Tommy bounded up the ladder to her quarterdeck and took her place near the helm. "Look lively, men. Billy, you be earning not a pistol but a whole *cannon* if you spot the Spaniards before they spot us." The men laughed as Billy whooped and monkey-climbed his way to the peak of the sails. Tommy also asked Sawkins to lower the ship's flag and instead raise the Spanish one they'd stolen off a ship years earlier. The ship sailed all day and into the night without sighting the *Maravillosa* and her protection.

Early the next morning Tommy lay in her hammock, wide awake, as the ship rolled on high seas. Sawkins tapped lightly on the door then entered. "Beggin' your pardon, Captain, but Billy's seen sails."

"Coming." Tommy rolled from her hammock as Sawkins left. She reached for her coat, but Rebekah, who'd moved quiet as a cat, had already taken it off the hook. She had lost her haunted look from the night before.

"Let me help you," she said.

Tommy stood still as Rebekah strapped on her sword belt and jammed two pistols into their holders. Tommy hung onto the mast and widened her stance, but the seas still tossed her against Rebekah several times. "Sorry," she muttered, flustered at the softness of Rebekah's body.

Rebekah tightened Tommy's cutlass belt. "The seas are high. Will this hinder the chase?"

Rebekah's hand brushed against Tommy's breast when she tightened the pistol straps. Tommy struggled to find her voice. "Ah, yes and no. The Spanish ships will be struggling to stay together, so the *Maravillosa* will be more vulnerable. But we also be at a disadvantage in these winds, for we may drift too far downwind from our prize."

Rebekah helped Tommy on with her coat, then smoothed out the lapels. Tommy gazed down into those fathomless eyes and fought the urge to kiss her. What the devil was the matter with her?

"Tommy, if I'm killed or lost—"

Tommy stopped Rebekah with a finger to her lips. Gads, but they were soft. She had to get herself safely up on deck. "Bad luck to speak of this."

Rebekah nodded. "I wanted you to know that I don't fault you for keeping me aboard when you found me. These days with you have been the happiest—"

Tommy stopped her again. "You won't be dying. This ship's weathered many a storm and many a battle."

Rebekah blinked her impossibly long lashes. "I lacked the sense last night to say this…" They both grabbed the mast as the *Moon Shadow* slammed into a wave. "But I want you to know how…what I feel for you. I want to—"

"Sawkins needs me." Tommy grabbed her hat, jammed it on her head and fled. Jesus, Mary, and Joseph. Had Rebekah been on the verge of speaking out loud of this unnatural attraction? They could never speak of it, for should they do so, what would stop them from acting on it?

The tip of a wave sloshed over the railing as Tommy climbed

the ladder to the quarterdeck. The weather was wrong for this attack. Storms could be helpful, but from the looks of the sky and the howling of the wind, this would be more than a storm. A storm could scatter the ships, but a hurricane would sink them. She scanned the horizon to the northeast and saw the faint sight of Spanish sails. "Make all sails," she shouted. Her men scrambled up the rigging. She would need every sail to both catch up to the Spaniards and control the ship. The sounds of the *Moon Shadow*'s booms swinging, rigging clanking, and running feet set her heart racing. She was ready.

Tommy and Sawkins kept the *Moon Shadow* under full sail until the ships grew large enough she could see the Spanish flag flying. It was an old ruse, but with the *Moon Shadow* flying the Spanish colors, she'd be able to get a bit closer without alarming the galleon and her escort.

The gray day darkened to a frightening green as the fierce wind built. The seas grew higher as Tommy closed the distance. The weather had begun pulling the Spaniards' formation apart as surely as wind scattered seeds. Tommy peered through her spying glass and a cold shiver rippled up her spine. She might be as superstitious as her men to worry about this, but why did Sawkins have to raise the idea of death a few days ago?

By midafternoon watch, Tommy had moved the *Moon Shadow* directly behind the three Spanish ships, then lowered the lateen sails to slow her down. By now the Spaniards had caught on to her ruse and nearly flew ahead of her. Barrels and crates appeared overboard as the Spanish tried to lighten their ships.

The three ships were lined up one after the other ahead of Tommy—one first escort, then the second, then farthest away was the *Maravillosa*. Tommy would have to get past the escorts to take the galleon. She kept her ship in the wake of the nearest escort. Her men stood at each gun, and the rest of the crew waited, armed and ready to do battle. Rebekah stood aft by the ship's bell, ready to do her job no matter what. Tommy would send her below before the cannonballs began flying.

Hatley manned the helm. "Captain," he finally said after they'd been following the Spaniards for over three bells. "What we waiting for?"

"Hatley, you be too impatient." Tommy smiled at his grumbling. Then the second escort, either through wind or captain error, dropped back so the two escorts would soon be sailing parallel to each other. "There it is, Hatley. What we be waiting for." She shouted for another of the sails to be unfurled and the *Moon Shadow* leapt ahead. "Head for the gap between them," Tommy said.

"Mary, Jesus, and Joseph," Hatley said. "You mean to bring us between them? We'll be blasted out of the water." He moved the wheel accordingly. When the *Shadow* was within cannon range, at Tommy's nod Sawkins turned to the gun crews. "Fore guns, fire at will!" The front deck guns began blasting the two frigates, which only had guns pointing out their starboard and larboard hulls. The *Shadow* slid closer to the gap between the Spanish ships and the men began their horrendous shouts and threats as the faces of the Spanish crews became visible. The mizzenmast of the starboard escort crashed on the deck and fell overboard.

Tommy caught Rebekah's eye as the harsh cannon blasts echoed against the heavy sky. "Go back to the cabin," she shouted. "You be safer there."

Rebekah looked away, planting her feet and turning to watch the action. Tommy grimaced. The woman wouldn't be the first sailor pretending not to hear the order so he could disregard it.

Bloody hell.

The *Moon Shadow* continued to pound both Spanish frigates with the forward guns until three more masts fell and screams and cries and curses came from both ships. Smoke stung Tommy's nostrils, and her ears had begun ringing from cannon fire. Her ship's bow was nearly level with the ships' sterns, but still the Spaniards couldn't fire their cannon. Musket and pistol fire began raining down on the *Shadow*'s deck, but her men stopped it with return fire. They kept shooting until the Spaniards' masts were broken and their sails lay in shreds on the deck. Without the ability to control direction and speed in the powerful wind, the ships began drifting east. Tommy turned her ship into the wind and passed around the broken ships, which would soon be swamped and sunk by the waves unless the crews repaired the masts and regained control.

All that remained between Tommy and the *Maravillosa* was a

small stretch of sea. The winds dropped a bit, reducing the swells, but Rebekah still clung to the mast beside Tommy. "How can we possibly take a ship in this weather?"

"*Dum spiro, spero*," Tommy suddenly said, and grinned at Rebekah's pleased smile."Why are you still here? You fear storms."

"I must help if I can." Spray soaked Rebekah's dress and her wet cheeks shone like polished mahogany.

After Tommy barked out a few more orders, there was nothing left to do but let the wind, and her crew, close the gap. She inhaled deeply. "You asked about the white streak in my hair."

Rebekah clung to the mast as the ship pitched. "You want to speak of this now, in the middle of storm and battle?"

"The streak appeared at my scalp the day after I killed my first man." Rebekah waited. Tommy worked her jaw, unsure why she was choosing this moment, this place, and this woman to speak the words that had lain dormant within her for five years. "He be one of my crew, a bully like Coxon. He didn't like taking orders from a woman. He wanted to be captain."

"Yet the men had elected you."

"He grew more mutinous every day. Finally he challenged me once too often and I drew my sword." Tommy could still feel the surge of power and fury running through her that day. "I won. The next day my hair was streaked with white."

Tommy watched the activity on the *Maravillosa* as its captain realized a fight was imminent. The *Moon Shadow* leapt the waves like a dolphin and would soon overtake the heavy, slower *Maravillosa*, which rode low in the water burdened with its cargo of slaves.

Tommy's deck hummed with energy and excitement. "Coxon was my last killing. I'll do what's necessary to take this ship and get you and my men to safety, but then I be done with the killing."

"Tommy—"

"Bring her to starboard, Hatley," Tommy said. Then she grabbed Rebekah's arm. "Enough talk. We're all about to become targets, so you need to go below now or I'll drag you there myself. That's an order." Eyes blazing, Rebekah obeyed.

With a great deal of effort Hatley kept them on course and brought them up behind the yellow and red galleon. The tall ship was being tossed about mercilessly by the wind, but she remained afloat. In these seas Tommy couldn't unload the slaves onto the *Shadow*. She'd have to take command of the ship and sail her out of the storm herself.

They began firing on the Spanish galleon, many of their shots going wild in the turbulent sea. The ship refused to yield. In a reckless move, Tommy tacked the ship and brought her up nearly beside the galleon. Her men's bellows could be heard above the wind, and musket fire popped as the two ships traded fire.

Coming close alongside the *Maravillosa* in high seas was risky, but without this ship they'd have nothing to show for the last three hours, and Tommy's fleet would have broken apart for nothing. The crew of the *Moon Shadow* continued to fire at the Spanish crew, but the cowards had begun hiding behind the slaves chained to the deck. Roaring with anger, Tommy's men crowded the railing, hung from the rigging, and hurled fearful oaths as Hatley expertly brought the *Shadow* within a few feet of the *Maravillosa*.

With Tommy in the lead, grappling hooks, lines, and pirates leapt the gap above the black churning water and thundered onto the galleon. Sword drawn, Tommy landed with a grunt and stabbed the first Spaniard she met in the leg, not in the heart.

In less than a minute, Tommy fought her way across the gangway connecting the forecastle to the quarterdeck and pressed her sword against the captain's throat. The cry went up to surrender, and the ship was Tommy's.

The pirates confiscated every musket, pistol, and cutlass, rolling them into nets and lobbing them into the heaving deck of the *Shadow*.

Tommy forced the seven officers into the wardroom, which seemed to have been partitioned off into thirds, two of them locked. She turned to the officers. "You have but ten seconds to decide. Turn pirate or become my prisoner on the *Moon Shadow*."

"*Pirata*," cried five of the officers. The captain and the quartermaster both cursed violently to hear their men abandoning them.

"Smart boys," Tommy said. She held out her hand to the quartermaster. "Key for the deck chains or I'll carve your eyes out and toss you to the eels." The quartermaster reached with trembling hands for the keys at his waist. Tommy called out to four of her men. "Take these two officers back to the *Shadow* and lock 'em up." She turned to consider the five men remaining, unsure if they'd joined her out of fear or out of hatred for their own captain, which often happened. "You speak English?" One man raised his hand. "The rest of you, see to the ship. Repair any damage."

She whirled and ran right into Rebekah Brown. "Bloody hell! What the devil are you doing here?"

Rebekah was as drenched as the rest of them, but wore a Spaniard's bloody coat. "I'm here to help."

Cursing, Tommy thrust the keys into her hands. "Get the slaves unlocked and below deck. Find the other slaves below and unshackle them."

Tommy and the Spanish officers followed her out of the wardroom. The ships' hulls had begun grinding against one another, so they couldn't ride the waves in tandem much longer. She grabbed Hatley as they both held the mizzenmast for support. "We need to cut the *Shadow* free. Get back aboard her. You're her new captain."

"Captain of the *Shadow*?" Hatley whooped with joy.

"Head northeast. We'll meet at Sombero, where I'll let off the slaves and we'll split the booty."

"Aye, Captain." Hatley grinned, then thumped her soggy shoulder. "We did it, Tommy."

Tommy beamed. "That we did." She gripped Hatley's lapels. "Take care of my ship, you piss-faced dog, or I'll burn out your tongue."

Another grin and a saucy salute, and Hatley was climbing across to the *Moon Shadow*, shouting orders to cut the lines and raise the sails.

Tommy wiped the rain from her eyes and the salt water from her mouth. She had five Spanish officers, their crew of eighty men, Sawkins, Billy, Calabria, and twenty-five of her men.

They would have to scud their way north out of the storm using just the upper sails because the wave troughs were so deep there was no wind to fill the lower sails.

Sawkins barked orders in English and Spanish, and twenty sailors climbed the rigging to the highest point as the mast tips swung in dramatic arcs above the deck. Tommy clenched her fists to see Billy among them. Fool should have let the *Maravillosa* crew do it.

Rebekah and a handful of pirates unlocked the Negroes on deck and led them, slipping on blood and water, to the companionway. The poor bastards, nearly naked, shivered violently. When a sailor came to three Negroes shot dead during the battle, he looked up at Tommy and she nodded. They tossed the bodies overboard.

The two ships moved apart, and the *Shadow* soon disappeared in the storm. Tommy caught one glimpse of her when both ships crested a wave at the same time, but that was it. Would she ever see the *Shadow* again?

Tommy turned back to watch the helmsman, satisfied he knew what he was doing. Bow into the wave, perpendicular so the ship could ride it. Should the ship turn parallel to the wave, she'd keel over and sink to the bottom.

Twenty slaves still remained on deck, some bleeding from battle wounds, others bleeding at their ankles and wrists from being slammed around by the storm in chains. Tommy herded them down the companionway, where Rebekah stood at the bottom helping the freed slaves get out of the wind and rain, handing them each a ladle of brackish water from an open barrel.

Tommy looked around the lower deck, empty save for dozens of hammocks swinging wildly from every available beam. "Where be the rest of the slaves?"

Three of Tommy's men reported back to her. "There's hammocks everywhere, Captain, but no slaves. And the bow and stern compartments are locked up tight, as is most of the lower hold."

Tommy cursed. The galleon wasn't outfitted as a slave ship, with narrow berths stacked on top of each other, so the Spaniards had locked the slaves in the compartments, then had the crew sleep wherever they could string a hammock.

"Bastards," she muttered, leading the way to the forward compartment. "Find something to pry open these doors or bash 'em in."

One of the Spanish officers appeared at Tommy's elbow, hair plastered to his face, and introduced himself as Santos. He leaned close so only Tommy could hear. "I have key. But send your men above. If rabble learn what on this ship, we all dead."

Irritated, Tommy complied, allowing only Rebekah to remain. The man pointed to the lantern hanging by the door, so Tommy lit it while the officer unlocked the latch. Because no sound came from behind the door, Tommy feared all the Negroes were dead.

The door swung open with a deep creaking, and Santos stepped in, followed by Tommy and Rebekah. Tommy held up the lantern and tried to understand what she was seeing.

There were no slaves in the compartment, just chests and trunks and heavy burlap sacks stacked to the ceiling, packed well enough that the cargo barely shifted as the ship rolled wildly. "I don't understand," Rebekah said, holding on to the door for support.

"Sweet Jesus, I do," Tommy whispered, then opened the nearest chest. It was filled to the rim with silver bars. The next held gold coins, hastily minted and stamped with a Spanish crest. Tommy whirled on the Spaniard. "And the rest of the locked compartments?"

Santos smiled. "The same. I am hoping you'll remember my cooperation when it comes time to divide your plunder."

Tommy smacked her forehead. "What share of the fleet's treasure does *Maravillosa* hold?"

The Spaniard looked at her. "We carry the entire treasure."

"Bugger all," Tommy shouted. "And the *Barcelona*?"

"Slaves."

Rebekah gasped and Tommy winced. Shaw would foul himself at the news and hunt them down with a fierceness never seen in the West Indies.

"The *Barcelona* was the decoy," Santos said. "And we have more ships waiting along the coast to attack pirates. Everyone fell for the ruse except you."

Tommy shook her head. This couldn't be happening. She possessed the entire Spanish treasure. What in Hades' name was she supposed to do? She straightened. "How many of your men know?"

"The officers."

"That's why you chose to remain with us."

The man nodded, unashamed.

"Rebekah, if you would, bring Sawkins, Billy, and Calabria down here."

Minutes later the five of them stood inside the compartment. Neither Billy nor Sawkins nor Calabria could speak for a moment. Tommy let them take it in, then moved them back into the passageway. "We've a terrible choice to make. We possess the entire treasure. By rights it's ours since we split from Shaw. We could try approaching him and his ships, assuming he survived the ambush, and offer to share the plunder, but I fear Shaw will shoot us without listening. But if we don't be looking for him, once he learns we have the treasure he'll hunt us down."

Calabria snorted. "Shaw may not have survived the battle."

Tommy rested her hands on her hips. "The man's luck runs better than any of ours."

Sawkins kept looking back at the closed door. "So we sail west back to Shaw, or we run."

The passageway was silent but for the water splashing down the companionway, the planks creaking beneath them. "Either way, Shaw'll try to kill us," Calabria said.

They discussed the advantages and disadvantages of each, but Tommy knew in her heart if they sailed with the treasure directly to Shaw, he would exact his revenge for making him the fool. Plus, every ship in that small pirate fleet was now under Shaw's command, so it would be four ships against one. Everyone in those first meetings would remember Tommy Farris counseled to take the *Maravillosa*, not the *Barcelona*.

"Sawkins, be this ship sound?" Tommy asked.

"Aye, she be sound."

"Do we have enough crew to sail her?"

"We do."

She stared at the closed door, then smacked it with her palm. "Then we run."

❖

When the storm finally blew itself out and the sea calmed to a low boil, the *Maravillosa* had been tossed so far off course Tommy had no idea where she was, and couldn't find out unless the stars came out, so she staggered with exhaustion and a strange elation back to the captain's cabin on the upper deck.

The cabin was divided into thirds for storage of more silver and gold, but was still larger than the *Shadow*'s cabin. The cabin was also more ornate than the *Shadow*'s, with brass lanterns along the walls already lit by the Spanish steward, a most adaptable man. A wide table spread before the stern windows, a chest of drawers and wardrobe covered one wall, and a narrow bookshelf was tucked in behind the door. Tommy stopped and scanned the room frantically. There was only one bed, a real one with bedding, and judging by the lump under the covers, Rebekah was already in it.

Bloody hell. Bone tired, Tommy considered tucking herself into a corner of the floor, but the bed—the first real bed she'd seen in years—was too inviting. Rebekah was already asleep and that didn't need to change. Tommy rooted around in the captain's wardrobe and found dry shirt and trousers.

Once changed, Tommy sat carefully on the edge of the bed. This was, by rights, her bed now. She could ask Rebekah to leave. Surely there were other beds in the officers' quarters. But then Tommy became aware the cabin was chilly, so before she could ask herself what she was doing, she crawled under the blanket and fell asleep.

When she awoke the first time, it was dark and the sea calm. She felt the heat of someone in the bed with her and fought down panic until she realized it was Rebekah, in her sleep, clinging to Tommy's still-damp braid.

The second time Tommy awoke, Rebekah's hand was resting on Tommy's hip. Above them the night watch paced the quarterdeck, but otherwise, the treasure-filled rooms beside them were silent. Tommy froze when Rebekah slid her hand first up to Tommy's waist, then under her shirt. Unsure what to do, Tommy held her breath as Rebekah stroked the taut muscles over her ribs.

"What be you doing?"

Rebekah moved up closer behind Tommy. "I don't know."

Tommy rolled over to face Rebekah. "God help me, neither do I." She gently took Rebekah's face in her hands and kissed her. A force stronger than a hurricane welled up inside her and she felt as if she would burst. The only thing for it was to tug Rebekah's clothing aside and begin exploring her body in ways Tommy had never dreamed possible. And each time she touched Rebekah's skin, the woman responded with soft moans and gasps that nearly drove Tommy out of her mind with something she couldn't name.

When Rebekah lifted Tommy's shirt and roamed freely with her mouth, Tommy felt her own gasps rising like an advancing tide, higher and more powerful with each wave. Rebekah then slipped her hand down Tommy's trousers and she lost all sense of time and place and who she was. None of that mattered. Only skin and tongue and the shuddering waves mattered. Tommy lost count of the number of times they had to silence—with a hand or mouth—each other's surprised gasps and aching moans.

Tommy's heart pounded in the darkness at the things they did to one another, at the words Rebekah whispered in her ear as she climaxed yet again.

Finally exhaustion fell upon them like a sudden fog, and Tommy barely had the strength to reach down and pull the blanket up over their entwined bodies. Sweet Jesus, what had she done? Too tired to answer her own question, Tommy fell asleep.

PART SIX

THE TREASURE MAP

The doctor opened the seals with great care, and there fell out the map of an island, with latitude, longitude, soundings, names of hills and bays and inlets, and every particular that would be needed to bring a ship to safe anchor upon its shores.

—Robert Louis Stevenson, *Treasure Island*

Chapter Twenty-one

Ricardo Benton and Lauren Gilmore now obviously believed I'd never sell them the Farris map, so instead of making high-priced offers they were resorting to dognapping as a way to persuade me. My blood boiled at their cruel arrogance as I stood there on a Sunday afternoon in the small Pittsburgh parking lot, where Lauren Gilmore and I were still as statues. Would she dash for the car? Could I catch her? Only Marley moved, pulling at the leash clasped in both of Lauren's hands. Benton honked his horn, which was brilliant. Want to make a stealthy getaway when you're stealing a dog? By all means, blow your horn.

Damn. Too bad I couldn't wield my sarcasm as a weapon.

I gauged the distance. There was no way I could beat Lauren to the car. Once she and Marley were inside, there'd be nothing I could do short of throwing myself at the Buick.

Lauren began to run. Without thinking, I dropped down onto one knee, flung my arms wide and shouted, "Poodle-noodle-doodle!" Marley whirled at my voice and pulled straight for me.

"Marley, no!" Lauren yelled, trying to drag him back toward the car.

"Noodle-doodle-poodle!"

Marley yelped happily and dug his toes into the warm blacktop as I ran toward him. Lauren dragged him closer to the car, but he'd slowed her down enough that I had time to sprint the length of the small parking lot. Lauren was still struggling when I reached them and grabbed hold of the leash. Marley spun happily, then jumped up on me.

"Bitch," Lauren snarled. "Give him back."

Protective fury bubbled up in me so fiercely I wanted to punch her. Instead, I grabbed her hand and dug my fingernails into her flesh until she cursed and let go of the leash.

"I don't think," I managed to get out between gasps, "that Randi would appreciate you stealing her dog."

Lauren sniffed. "Whatever. We weren't going to hurt him." She looked down at Marley, then over at Benton. "At the same time you're giving Marley back to Randi, would you give her something else for me?"

"Look," I said, "I'm not your personal UPS—"

The hard slap took me by such surprise my head snapped around and I stumbled back.

"Tell her Lauren says hi." Lauren ran lightly over to the Buick and hopped in. I blinked my watering eyes clear in time to see Benton whip me the finger as he roared from the lot and turned into the rush of cars.

Marley danced beside me, happy to be out of the car and having no idea he'd almost gone with the wrong people. A little shaky, I walked back to the door of the café, where I stood until Randi looked up and saw us. I waved her outside and explained what had happened. Randi dropped to her knees and threw her arms around Marley. I waited for a minute as she murmured in his ear, then stood.

Then, eyes moist, Randi reached for me and gave me a tight, full-body hug that communicated her deep thanks. My highly sensitive body, a bit starved for touch, responded to her strong arms, her scent, her warm hair against my cheek, her hips bumping mine. Shit. Everything started throbbing so intensely finally I stepped back out of the hug, my senses on overload.

She stepped back as well. "I can't thank you enough," she kept saying as we dashed back inside to retrieve our bags, then back out before we could be scolded for bringing a dog inside.

I spied a wooden bench across the street, so when the traffic thinned out we ran across and sat down. "Lauren must have a key to your vehicle," I said.

"I forgot she never gave it back."

"I know how you can thank me," I said.

"Name it." Randi pulled Marley half onto her lap, which set his tail wagging furiously.

"After I got Marley, Lauren slapped me clear across the parking lot, a message I was to deliver to you, by the way."

I could see my reflection in Randi's shades as she stared at me. "You plan on delivering that message?"

"Not at the moment, no. But why the message?"

Randi opened the Tupperware that held Marley's lunch. Once the dog began happily crunching, Randi sighed. "Lauren and I were lovers for a while."

"Yeah, that had occurred to me."

"I actually got her the job with Benton."

"Good move."

Randi winced. "He wasn't always a bad guy. I worked with him on a number of map theft cases. He was our expert when John and I first started in this area. He helped me identify some of the recovered maps, and suggested people or libraries who might have owned them."

"What happened?"

Randi busied herself with packing up Marley's bowl. "Some maps on a case JLI was working went missing. The FBI brought Benton in for questioning, and he blamed me. He and I have been at each other's throats since."

"How did Benton know where we were?"

Randi shook her head. "That, I don't know. But we're sweeping my car before we drive another foot. Now I have a question for you. How did you get Marley to start running toward you? He barely knows you, and he's seen Lauren many times."

"If he saw her that much, it sounds like you had a relationship with her."

"No relationship. Lots of one nights. Unfortunately she didn't understand the difference."

I took a deep breath and told Randi about playing noodle-poodle-doodle with her dog. She bent over, elbows on her knees, as she listened. Then she looked at Marley. "I can't believe you fell for that." Marley panted happily, his long pink tongue sliding over his canines. "A beautiful, sexy woman calls out noodle-poodle-doodle and you run? *Toward* her?" But when she turned that grin and dimple toward me, I knew I'd been forgiven, and I felt as happy as Marley looked.

Back in the parking lot, Marley bobbed beside Randi as she

opened the door, and I bumped into her awkwardly as I stashed my puzzle on the floor behind my seat. I thought Randi would move out of the way, but she didn't. She stood there until I looked over at her. Standing so close to her was a bit overwhelming and dazzling and made thinking impossible. But thinking wasn't necessary when Randi slid her hands first up my arms, then higher until she held my face gently in her hands. Oh my God. She was going to kiss me. True confession: Some women's knees really do go all wobbly when they're kissed, and I'm one of them. I love sex, but I think I could go a long time without it if I were thoroughly kissed at least once a day. Sure enough, as my heart started playing this insane rock beat, Randi leaned forward and slowly, eyes half open, kissed me with a passion that would have staggered me if I'd not been so hungry for it.

Finally, Randi pulled back, but just barely. She brushed a lock of hair from my eyes. "That was for saving Marley."

I leaned in for another kiss, but Randi gently touched her finger to my lips. "But that was also the only time. It was unprofessional and we are wrong for each other on so many levels, so it ends here, before it starts."

My mouth would have dropped open if I hadn't clenched my teeth. My lips burned for another kiss, but I was too proud to beg. God, how could Randi kiss me like that, then back off? My body pulsed with need. It'd been eight months since Julia had decided she was straight, and if I didn't get laid I was going to embarrass myself. But instead of flinging Randi back against the car and ravaging her right there in the middle of this sweet Pittsburgh neighborhood, I just nodded, demoralized. Forget the one-night stands. I didn't even rate more than one kiss.

Randi moved on as if the kiss had never happened. A quick sweep of the SUV with some sort of beeping tool, and Randi found two tracers, one tucked inside the back bumper, the other inside the front bumper. She stared at the two little electronic devices in her hand. "These are two different makes, so I doubt Benton planted both of them."

We exchanged a glance, then I looked back down at the mysterious disk. "The man from the airport. We thought we saw him today in the alley."

Randi shook her head. "Damn. For a lesbian you have a lot of men interested in you."

We sat in the front seat of the SUV, watching the people of

Pittsburgh go about their Sunday afternoon. The thought that this trip could endanger Marley was too much for me, and judging by the frown on Randi's face, she felt the same. "It's time to head home, isn't it?" I said. "We aren't really finding anything, and we need to return the Brown log book, and as long as Lauren has a key, Marley's in danger."

Randi nodded. "I can't leave Marley alone in the car anymore."

"This was a long way to come to buy a jigsaw puzzle. I'm so sorry, Randi. It's been a wild goose chase. We've been on R. Brown's trail, not Tommy's. I'm giving up."

"I hate to say it, but I agree. I couldn't bear to have anything happen to Marley."

"It was crazy to think I'd solve everything. I'm not even upset about Drummond anymore. In fact, I think he's kind of pathetic."

"What do you mean?"

"He's a little weasel, hiding behind his e-mails. At least Benton's out there, doing something. It's funny, but I'm not as desperate to catch Drummond as I first was."

"JLI will catch him eventually, or the FBI will if the guy traffics across state lines."

I shrugged. "I know. But it hasn't been so bad. I got away from my office for a few days, shut off my cell phone, and spent time with… Marley. I'm almost grateful to Drummond."

Randi gave me a half-smile that sent a shock wave of heat through my body, but she said nothing.

CHAPTER TWENTY-TWO

To avoid babbling more on the drive back to Cincinnati and possibly asking Randi her underwear size or where she'd had her biggest orgasm and with whom, I asked her to stop at a bookstore at the edge of town. Back in the children's section I bought *Treasure Island*, by Robert Louis Stevenson, and *The True Confessions of Charlotte Doyle*, by Avi.

When we reached cruising speed on I-70, I opened *Treasure Island*. "Ever read this book?" I asked.

"I don't think so."

"Well, you're about to get an audiobook experience without the CD, or the trained actor reading the book."

"You're going to read to me?"

"Yup. *Part One: The Old Buccaneer. Chapter One: The Old Sea-dog at the 'Admiral Benbow.'* Here we go." The first paragraph was boring, which meant I might lose my listener, but the second one popped Randi to attention:

> *I remember him as if it were yesterday, as he came plodding to the inn door, his sea-chest following behind him in a handbarrow; a tall, strong, heavy nut-brown man; his tarry pigtail falling over the shoulders of his soiled blue coat; his hands ragged and scarred, with black, broken nails; and the sabre cut across one cheek, a dirty, livid white.*

God, I loved pirate stories. I read until my throat was dry and scratchy, then put the book down.

"You're stopping?"

"Gotta pace myself," I said, pleased she was enjoying the book. "Isn't it a great book?"

"My brothers must have read it when they were kids, but I don't remember reading it."

"That's the thing—it's not just a boys' book. You'll really like the Charlotte Doyle book, too."

The road hummed beneath the tires.

"There's something you should know about my brothers," Randi said.

"The banker and the podiatrist?"

Randi hesitated, looked at me, then back to the highway. "The reason Jack the banker never gets outside is because he's in a prison in New Jersey. Embezzling funds from his clients. Nick the podiatrist is still practicing, but he's in the middle of an insurance fraud investigation that will likely end up sending him to jail as well."

"Not the best track record in your family."

"Jack and Nick have always been looking for that big score, the biggest find, the best trophy."

I tried to read her face but couldn't. "They're still on a scavenger hunt," I said. "Like when you were kids."

Randi looked at me in amazement. "God, you're right. You're absolutely right."

"News flash: Anal librarian has rare insight into life."

She rewarded me with a smile and returned her attention to the driving.

An hour later we stopped at a rest area and Randi took Marley for a pee. When they returned, Randi scanned the car. "You've been cleaning again."

I handed her the small card I'd found under the back seat. There was a cute puppy on the front, and inside was a handwritten note: *With volunteers like you, we can't go wrong.* "So, what's this?"

Randi considered the note. "I'd wondered where that'd gone. You can toss it." I waited. "I walk dogs for the dog shelter near my house twice a week."

"Cool. What about this letter? *Dear Ms. Marx: Thanks for tracking down Rufus. He's paying now and we're doing fine.*"

"None of your business."

"I know that, but I've kissed you, loaned you my Speedo, and cleaned your car several times. I think we can make it my business."

"Sometimes women come to the firm needing help tracking down deadbeat dads."

"So you take those jobs?"

"They can't afford to pay, so I do it on the side."

"In exchange for what?"

"You think that's where I get my one-night stands?"

"Of course not! That would be—"

"Unethical. I do have some ethics, you know. Money isn't the only reason for doing something. Besides, I feel for these women. I know what it's like to want something but not be able to get it."

"What do you want but can't get?" I felt like a skilled interviewer sliding unnoticed into the mind of my subject, on the verge of discovering her inner secrets.

"End of interview," she said and turned on the music, which gave me too much time to think about how I'd fallen asleep last night thinking about Randi, and that in my dreams I drove her around my hometown on the Emma Boyd Grand Tour. I yearned to show her all my photos on my laptop and say, "This is me. Now you show me yours." I wanted to take her to Agate Beach on the north shore of Lake Superior. I wanted to curl up on a sofa with her and watch movies and eat popcorn from the same bowl. I wanted to take her dancing and know she'd dance all the slow ones with me.

This was insane. I'd told Maggie I didn't have time for even a fling, and yet I seemed to have skipped over the fling and was tottering on the abyss of something much deeper. But we'd only kissed once, and Randi had said "not again." Who the hell was she to set up all the rules?

My thoughts spun nowhere for an hour, then Randy shut off the CD player and asked me to read again, so I did.

But once we'd bypassed Columbus and were on the last stretch to Cincinnati, my voice wore out, so I stopped reading and screwed up my courage.

"You're a great kisser," I said.

The car swerved a fraction as Randi cut her eyes toward me. "Thanks."

"But there's room for improvement. I'd be happy to help you practice."

Randi's dimple appeared. "You're flirting."

"I'm shocked you'd say that."

"I'm shocked you'd do it. Let's stick to business, Emma. It'll be safer for both of us."

"Who says I want to be safe?" Why was Randi being so stubborn? Had the kiss been *only* to show gratitude for Marley's rescue? Seems to me a bouquet of flowers and a nice card could have sent the same message.

"Everything about you says you want to be safe. You're calm and warm and have such an open heart that if you aren't careful the wrong woman may crawl inside without your permission. Then what will you do?"

"How do you know what kind of woman is wrong or right for me?" I was trying to sound cool, but my words sounded huffy.

Randi's voice lowered just a touch. "Partly because of my job. Partly because I've spent the last four days with you. And here's what I know: if you *were* the one-night stand sort of woman, three nights ago I would have had you naked and in my bed."

I closed my gaping mouth so she wouldn't think her words had aroused me, which they totally had.

"But you don't need me," Randi continued. "You need someone more steady, more reliable, someone who keeps a neat calendar and a neat car and meets your ethical standards twenty-four hours a day and collects jigsaw puzzles."

I realized the instant she finished her sentence that Randi had just described exactly the type of person I *didn't* want. I didn't want a mirror image of myself, and that was what both Mari and Julia had been. I wanted someone totally different, someone who kept a messy SUV, put her dog before anyone else, was awkward in social situations but disarmingly open one-on-one, who collected old maps and liked rude elderly shopkeepers and sometimes broke the rules.

"Yeah, I guess you're right," I said. The last thing I was going to do was throw myself at the feet of a woman who wasn't interested.

So when we pulled into Cincinnati late, I said nothing but "good night" as I stumbled off to my room. At least Randi had Marley. I had no one.

CHAPTER TWENTY-THREE

We'd spent so much time in the car yesterday I almost couldn't drag myself out of bed. But the thought of seeing Randi for breakfast in the hotel restaurant was enough to get me into the shower and clean clothes. She was already in the crowded restaurant, looking incredible in black jeans and a white shirt open at the neck. Her glowing hair fell loose around her shoulders and practically screamed at me: *Run your fingers through me! Drape me across your naked body!*

Somehow I blocked out the hair's siren call and ate my omelet.

Cincinnati looked the same as it had two days ago. When we arrived at the Freeport Library and asked for Eleanor Levinson, we learned she'd left the building for a short break, leaving Kari in charge, a younger woman with dyed orange hair and an impossibly short skirt.

"Oh, yeah, I know who you are. Eleanor told us about this Drummond guy, and we've been watching for his name on the check-in sheet. But no one knows what he looks like. Could you send us a photo or something?"

I dug through my briefcase. "We have a security DVD that shows Drummond."

Kari grabbed my arm. "We *so* need to see that."

I looked at Randi and she nodded. Neither of us was in that much of a hurry to get home, since she had more work waiting, and I had budget woes.

Kari took us into Eleanor's office and she popped the DVD into the computer. We watched silently as Drummond inserted the dental floss, then tugged the page free.

"Bastard," I muttered. "I get angrier every time I watch this."

Kari replayed the DVD, then laughed. "I think the correct term is bitch, not bastard."

I stared at her and Randi froze. "What?"

"That's a woman disguised as a man."

I peered at the screen. "No way."

"I don't think so," Randi said.

"What are you two—lesbians or something? Don't you know anything about men—how men move, how they carry themselves? That's not a man. See how the weight's more in the hips than in the shoulders?"

Now both Randi and I were fixed in front of the screen.

"And the mustache is fake, totally. She's probably wearing dark contacts. And the hair color is too black, like it's been dyed, or is perhaps a wig. I'm in theater, so I notice details like that."

"But how could this be?" I sputtered.

"Easy to do. Women have disguised themselves as men for centuries." She motioned toward me. "She's about your size."

"Emma's too curvy to pass as a man," Randi said.

"I didn't say it *was* Emma," Kari said with a laugh. "But you're right. It would have to be someone with straighter lines, more severe."

I whirled on Randi. "Lauren's my height, only slimmer."

Randi's eyes shot open wide. "Lauren? No, absolutely not."

"Why? She's working with Benton. She might be doing it for him."

Randi shook her head. "No, not Lauren. She's arrogant and self-centered, and bends the rules a bit working with Benton, but I can't see her for this. Really."

I let it go, since Randi felt so strongly about this.

Kari copied the DVD and returned the original. "We'll show this to the rest of the staff. If you want to wait here in Eleanor's office until she comes back, I don't think she'd mind."

We waited until the door closed behind her, then I started laughing. "What are you two—lesbians or something?" Randi joined me and we chuckled together, which felt so right.

But I ruined the mood by pulling the log book from my case. "When Eleanor gets back, do you want to explain why we have this, or shall I?" I asked.

Randi squared her shoulders. "I will."

While we were waiting, I started reading it again.

"How can you keep plowing through all those boring entries?" Randi asked.

"Because I'm a research librarian, and that's what I do."

Randi lay her head back on the high-backed chair and closed her eyes. She looked tired.

The urge to take care of Randi nearly overwhelmed me. The woman had a number of weaknesses, and flat tires were just the beginning. She was tough but didn't have the ability to trust other people, to talk to them, to confide in them. It was like she was two people—hard on the outside and far too vulnerable on the inside. She must lead a terribly lonely life.

After thirty minutes of reading, my vision began to blur from the small handwriting, and I let my head nod a bit. I fought off exhaustion, but when I read a page without remembering a word, I forced myself to read it again. I sat up straighter and read it a third time. "Holy smokes," I breathed. "Randi, wake up."

Randi stretched her arms over her head, a sensuous move that set my pulse pounding. But that was nothing compared to what happened to my heart when I kept reading. I jumped up from the chair. "Holy crap. The handwriting's changed. Listen to this: *August 20, 1715. Captain Brown was gone this morning. One of the longboats is also gone, but we be leagues from land. He left this note: Angus, the* Margaret *is yours. Let the world know the truth: Captain R. Brown is dead. Captain Tommy Farris is dead. If you ever see Father McLurin of Port Royal, tell him he was right. Remember, priests have all the answers.*"

"That's weird," Randi said.

"Did Brown get so frustrated in his search that he set himself adrift in the sea to die?"

"Why not jump overboard and end it more quickly? Doesn't make any sense."

I reread the entry again. "This is another link between Tommy and Brown *and* McLurin. Priests have all the answers? Was Brown a religious man?"

"Brown sent six of his books to McLurin, which obviously became separated from the rest of McLurin's stuff since they're in two different libraries. But could Brown be referring to books when he talks about answers?"

I grabbed Randi's hand. "What if Brown's trying to tell someone that McLurin might have the answers in his books?"

Randi's face glowed with hope for the first time in days. "That's a really, really long shot, but at this point, I'll take it. Okay, let's review. You have a small section of the *Moon Shadow*'s 1714 log book, which told you that Danny McLurin was a pirate on Tommy's ship. Then at the Patterson Library in Chicago we find six sailing journey books, shelved together, owned by a Captain R. Brown. And I didn't want to say anything, but if you put the authors' names of those six books in a certain order they—"

"Spell FARRIS. I saw the same thing."

"Wow. Okay, then you find Father Daniel McLurin's journals here at the Freeport."

"Didn't I tell you this is how research works? Painstakingly slow and very small steps? McLurin and Brown both knew Farris. They might have even seen her map, or maybe she gave it to one of them, or hid it in one of those books."

"The place where the librarian kicked us out on our asses."

"Because you snuck us into the stacks."

Randi looked at her watch. "It's a six-hour drive back to Chicago, and it's ten a.m. now. If we leave now, we'll be there by four, well before it closes."

My heart raced and I forced myself to calm down. We had many hours of driving ahead of us. "Randi, the map *has* to be in one of those six books in Chicago. Tommy Farris made her map, gave it to R. Brown, and it's waiting for us back in Chicago. Let's go." We left an apologetic note for Eleanor and left the Brown log book on her desk. We no longer needed it.

CHAPTER TWENTY-FOUR

The trip passed in a blur of highways and gas stations. I finished reading *Treasure Island* to Randi and started on *The True Confessions of Charlotte Doyle*. We both loved the rollicking tale of a thirteen-year-old girl who went to sea against her family's wishes. This could have been Tommy's story. In the backseat Marley breathed heavily in his sleep, making little dreaming sounds and twitching his big paws as he chased something.

Somewhere around Fort Wayne, Indiana, I began fantasizing about kissing Randi again, and soon got so squirmy in my seat I couldn't bear it. I needed a distraction. "What do you think the map will look like? Maybe it'll be like those treasure maps in the movies, with a big red X right where we're supposed to dig."

Randi laughed weakly. "Life doesn't work that way."

"Well, then it'll be an ordinary map with invisible ink so we'll have to hold it up to the light or soak it in lemon juice."

"I doubt Captain Tommy ever read a Hardy Boys mystery or one of the Magic Treehouse books, so give up the sneaky angle."

I put my feet up on the dashboard to stretch out my back and give my legs and feet something to do other than rest on the floor. "But even if Tommy marked the spot with an X, that couldn't be very accurate since the maps of those days weren't necessarily very detailed, except for the coastline charts, which the sailors needed to avoid disaster."

Randi glared at my sandals on her dashboard, so I slipped them off and put my bare feet back up. Randi exhaled. "Given how messy your car is, I don't know why I can't put my feet on the dashboard," I snapped. We might have been longtime lovers snipping at each other from exhaustion.

Randi raised a hand. "Sorry, sitting for so long makes me cranky. As for location, they were using latitude and longitude by then, at least on land, so hopefully Tommy wrote down the exact location. If the sea's involved, however, she would have had to use dead reckoning, since they didn't have a reliable way to estimate longitude aboard ship. They would have used speed and time traveled to estimate longitude. Screw up and you could run into land, literally, much sooner than you'd expected."

"How did they measure speed?" I asked.

"Knots. They'd drop a log overboard with a knotted rope attached. They counted the knots that passed over the railing in thirty seconds, and that was the ship's speed. Six knots, eight knots, whatever."

"Jesus," I muttered. "It's a miracle anyone found their way anywhere. How do you know all this navigation stuff?"

"When I'm not collecting maps or working, I'm sailing."

I jammed my feet back into my sandals and tried to ignore my protesting bladder. The fewer times we stopped, the sooner we'd reach Chicago. "Let's find the map first. I'll be relieved when we do, so I can e-mail that scumbag and tell him we have it."

I'd become more relaxed about blurting things out, so at one point I did that. "You seem different than when this trip started."

"In what way?"

"You're a lot nicer than you let on."

Randi's smile was a bit sad. "I don't do well with first impressions."

"Why? What are you afraid people will see?"

"Are you going to start some sort of therapy session?"

"No, I find you fascinating."

She shook her head. "No, I'm complicated, and that's not good." She pursed her lips, then shot me a quick glance. "Do you know people who seem to be two different people—the person they present to the world, and the person they really are?"

"Yeah," I said. "You."

"Okay, maybe. But you know what I like about you? You *don't* feel that way. You're organized and calm on the outside, and you seem that way on the inside too."

I wasn't quite sure what to do with that. "Not always. Sometimes I want a life different than the one I have."

"That's normal—everyone wants that now and then. But what I'm talking about goes deeper. You feel…whole, like you're all together and complete and uncomplicated. That's very attractive."

Then why won't you kiss me again, my brain screamed, and I let the conversation end.

❖

By changing drivers and drinking coffee, we pulled into the Patterson parking lot by 4:30 p.m. My disheveled hair and Randi's bleary eyes screamed "really long road trip."

We stood at the foot of the library's entrance stairs. "My mouth feels like I've been kissing Marley," Randi said.

"My feet fell asleep hours ago," I replied, scratching my scalp.

The sun beat down hot on my head as cars whizzed by behind us. "How are we going to get back in there? If Brandt sees us, she'll call security."

Randi opened her cell phone. "We're going to need some help." She stepped away, talking in low tones. I watched the lovely back and strong shoulders as I strained to catch a word or two. The cell phone closed with a snap and Randi returned. "Let's step over here, behind these bushes. We shouldn't have to wait long."

Within five minutes, Charlotte Brandt, the pissed-off librarian from last week, hurried down the steps and headed away from them.

"Wow," I said.

Randi smiled. "John Lewis Investigations. We rock." She moved toward the stairs. "She'll be busy for about an hour, so that's all the time we have."

Randi took the steps two at a time, and I nearly jogged to catch up. We strode into the main library and headed straight for the elevator. At the third floor, we approached the Rare Book circulation desk and got the attention of the only worker there, a thin brunette with clear braces.

"Randi Marx, private investigator." She flipped her badge open, then snapped it shut so smartly I had to force back a smile. "I'm here with the assistant director of the Kline Library in Minneapolis. We're here to see Ms. Brandt. We need to examine several books in her collection."

The woman looked around her, as if what to do next might be written on a nearby teleprompter. "I'm sorry, but Ms. Brandt just left."

Randi scowled, an intimidating look. "We had an appointment. I need to see those books for a federal case I'm working on, and there's no time for delay."

"But...umm." The woman scanned the library but all other librarians were busy with patrons. "I should probably ask—"

"I know how to handle these books," I offered. I showed her my driver's license, my U of M card, and my Kline Library key card, wishing I had a little flippy holder like Randi's.

The woman hesitated, her throat and upper chest suddenly blotchy with distress.

"We need two wristbands from you, then we'll be out of here in twenty minutes," Randi said. "The Chicago PD will be very upset with Ms. Brandt if you deny us access. Don't make me call them."

Swallowing, the aide fished two bands from a drawer, activated them, then handed them over. Randi flashed the young woman her most winning look, and the woman smiled back, relieved she'd finally made a decision.

Neither of us could remember the exact shelf. "One of the books was Innisfree's *A Sailing Journey to the West Indies*," I said, "so look for that."

Fifteen minutes later Randi whooped. "Got it!"

By the time I reached her, Randi was already checking the inside cover for Brown's name. Her hands were shaking. "These are the six with Brown's name. C'mon." We wandered deeper into the stack room until we found a small wooden table.

I sat down, slid on the white gloves, then gently turned the first book upside down and lightly fluttered the pages.

Randi laughed. "What—you thought the map would be tucked in there, like those subscription cards?"

"You never know," I snapped then carefully paged through the book, "No maps."

"None in this one either."

I reminded myself to breathe and inhaled a few times to calm down. I'd never come this close to Captain Tommy before, not even with that brief section of her log. This map was part of Tommy and led to something that had been really important to her. All the books were about the same size, with thin covers, except for Basil Ringrose's *The Dangerous Voyage and Bold Attempts of Captain Bartholomew Sharp*, published in 1685. It was a little smaller and its padded cover was thicker than the others.

"Wait." I reached for the Ringrose. "The Francesco Rosselli map was printed in 1508 but then disappeared. Centuries later, when another book was being rebound, someone found that the Rosselli map had been used as filler under the book's cover."

Randi took the book, then pulled a polished brown Buck knife from her pocket.

"No," I said. "We can't harm the book. Shouldn't we call the FBI? Or wait for Brandt?"

Randi hesitated. "We're right here. We don't know if we're going to find anything, so I say we keep going. The FBI has nothing to do with the Farris map. They want Drummond."

I hesitated. What should we do? But like a predator scenting the blood of its prey, I decided we were too close to turn back now. Better to damage one book than to let Drummond damage dozens. When I nodded, Randi loosened the edge of the front endpaper with the knife. The over three-hundred-year-old glue gave up easily, and Randi released three sides, then bent back the paper. The edges of the cover were glued to the backing.

Bits of heavy paper clung to the edges of the cover as Randi cut the top edge free. She peered inside, then carefully reached in with two fingers. "Almost got it." Slowly, she worked out the opening a piece of folded paper approximately five inches by seven.

Randi inhaled deeply. "Okay, this is it."

"Careful. If this is what we're looking for, it's been creased for nearly three hundred years. It's not going to like being uncreased." I could feel the paper practically groaning as Randi unfolded it gently, first one fold, then another.

My heart thudded with excitement as I held down two corners and Randi pressed the other two sides, stopping briefly when the paper protested along one fold.

The printed map, obviously ripped from a book, showed the Caribbean Sea, the body of water surrounded by Jamaica and what was then Hispaniola to the north, the Leeward Islands to the east, and South America below. "This map could have come from any book," I said.

"I agree, but where it came from is no longer important," Randi whispered. "It's definitely been written on, looks like with pencil." She whistled softly. "Here." Along the bottom corner were the words, *This is my map. Let all who attempt to use it for ill be damned to hell for eternity. Captain T. Farris.*

Tommy Farris. Her map. Her handwriting. Joy and disbelief and triumph fought their way out of my tear ducts. We *found* it. Randi and I exchanged huge grins, then professionalism be damned, I reached over and hugged her. It was quick and platonic, but she didn't pull back. "I can't believe this," I said. Randi's hands shook as she held down the map.

Wiping my eyes, I pointed to a black *X* in the middle of the sea and chuckled. "Look, there's my *X* marks the spot. But it's not on land." We kept our voices down, afraid we'd bring a librarian, possibly Ms. Brandt, back into the stacks.

Next to the *X* was a small sketch. "What is that?" Randi asked. "A mountain? An island?"

Scribbled in the corner was Brown's motto: *Dum spiro, spero.*

Randi pointed to the opposite corner. "Here's the Shakespeare that Captain Brown must have been referring to: *Go to your bosom; Knock there and ask your heart what it doth know.*" She frowned. "How the hell is that supposed to help someone find the treasure?"

The last writing was a long string of letters, grouped together like words but spelling nothing. The letters began in one corner, snaked all around the edge of the map, then curled around the coast of South America when Tommy had obviously run out of room. Randi groaned. "This has to be a code." She cradled her head in her arms. "Shit."

"Hey, reality check. We found the Farris map. We've beaten Drummond. There's no reason for him to keep vandalizing libraries. We *won*, and you're acting like we lost."

Randi sat up with obvious effort, then waved wistfully at the map. "I have to admit, I was hoping it'd be that easy, that there'd be exact directions, like 'Go to the largest bay on the eastern shore of Barbados, pace off fifty paces inland, and start digging.'"

I pulled the map toward me. "We found the map. Isn't that enough?"

Randi's eyes gleamed. "How many buried treasures are there left with maps to find them? We've explored the hell out of this planet. There aren't many surprises left, but this is one of them."

I considered Randi. She'd spent five days with me trying to find the Farris map. For me, finding the treasure was less important than finding the map and stopping Drummond. But Randi obviously felt differently. "This X covers an area of probably hundreds of miles," I said. "There's no land out here, at least on the map, but Farris drew an island or a mountain. Is the X marking where the *Moon Shadow* went down? But Farris was going down with her ship. How could she have marked this map, then made sure it survived the shipwreck? We have a string of letters that need to be decoded. And we have a Shakespeare quote that gets all self-righteous about knowing your own heart. Basically, we have another puzzle on our hands."

Randi cocked her head, considering, then she reached for my hand and squeezed. "You're right. We look at what we have, look at what's missing, squint a bit, and imagine the pieces coming together." Suddenly energized, the confident Randi was back. "We can do this." She reached for my briefcase.

"Wait a minute," I said. "What are you doing?"

"I thought you'd have a manila folder we could use to store the map and keep it safe. I don't want to refold it."

The image of Randi Marx as two people—ethical and unethical—popped back into my head, and I gently took the map from her. "Randi, we found this map in a book owned by the Patterson. This map belongs to the Patterson. It's going nowhere."

Randi's jaw dropped. "You're fucking kidding me, right?"

"No, I'm not fucking kidding you. We found the map, but it doesn't belong to us."

"We tracked it down. We did all the legwork, the driving, the thinking. It's our map. We earned it."

My jaw went as rigid as Randi's face. "No, we didn't earn it. The map belongs to the Patterson." We stared at one another, both breathing heavily. What was she going to do—grab the map and run? Keep arguing with me? That'd be a total waste of time. "Oh look," I said lightly, "our third fight."

Randi leapt to her feet and paced up and down the nearest aisle for a minute, then she returned. "Could we at least photocopy the map?

Would that harm it? That way we could try to decode it. If there's really a treasure connected to the map, does the Patterson own that as well?"

I hated fighting with this woman. She looked wounded, as if I'd run her through with a sword. "I don't know about that. I just know we aren't taking this map."

"There was a photocopier behind the circulation desk. We still have time before Brandt comes back."

I gathered up the remaining books. With Randi by my side, holding the map gently between her gloved fingers, I reshelved the other books, but kept the Ringrose. Back in the main library, I flagged down the woman with the braces, and she escorted us behind the desk and over to the photocopier. I stood watching for Brandt while behind me Randi made two photocopies, one for me, and one for John Lewis Investigations.

"Done," she said.

"Good, because Brandt just walked in."

I squared my shoulders and led the way. "Charlotte? Emma Boyd from the Kline in Minneapolis. We were here last week looking through your books for the Farris treasure map."

Brandt frowned, then recognition dawned and she absolutely scowled. "I thought I'd made it clear you were no longer welcome here."

"Could we step into your office? We need to talk."

Brandt took in the curious stares of patrons and employees, then with a curt nod headed for her office.

"Since we were here four days ago, we learned that Farris's map was hidden in a book owned by R. Brown, a captain who sailed the Caribbean during 1715. We suspect Brown and Farris knew each other, and that Farris must have given the map to Brown to hide. We remembered that your library had six books owned by Brown, and this morning we opened the cover of one of them." I placed the book on her desk, ignoring her gasp. Before her sputtering could turn into words, I said, "We found this inside the front cover."

Randi lay the map on top of the book and Brandt fell silent.

"This is the Farris treasure map," I said. "As you can see, it's signed by Farris herself. It contains several written phrases, a notation of an island or mountain, and this string of letters, which might be a code for the treasure's location."

Brandt's ungloved fingers hovered at the edges of the map, but she didn't touch it. "This is real?" She looked up at me and I smiled. "Oh, my Lord. I'd read your article but didn't believe there were still treasure maps out there." When she looked up at me again, her eyes gleamed with excitement and I almost laughed. Everyone was a sucker for buried pirate treasure, even Charlotte Brandt.

"There's a Twin Cities map dealer, Ricardo Benton, who's willing to pay fifty thousand for the map. I could give you his number."

"No, never," Brandt said. "This is an historic find. We will build an exhibit around this. Pirates are very popular now. What a wonderful way to bring more people into our library." The woman's gaze grew misty as she began planning her exhibit, and I relaxed. While I was sad to let the map go after only thirty minutes, it'd be in good hands.

We excused ourselves and headed for the door, but I'm not even sure she noticed, having slipped on gloves and begun examining the map. Randi stopped in the doorway with one regretful glance back at the map, but she followed me out.

Too worked up to get back into the car, we retrieved Marley from the SUV and walked for a few blocks until we came to Grand Park, the long, narrow park stretching between Michigan Avenue and Lake Superior.

I bought Marley a cup of strawberry ice cream. My emotions bounced around inside me as wildly as the joyous Marley bounced at our sides. As long as he was with Randi, nothing else mattered. Why couldn't humans find that sort of contentment and be done with all the drive for excellence and self-improvement? Why not be content, like a dog?

We'd found the map and possessed it for less than an hour. But it would feel damned good to e-mail Drummond, or Lauren, and tell him, or her, "Kiss my ass." Soon my life would return to normal. Exercise class every Monday, Wednesday, and Friday at six a.m. Lunch in the Student Union food court with my friends. Working late. Tight schedule. Neat lines on a jam-packed calendar. No Marley. No dates, no sex, and worst of all, no kisses.

Walking beside me was the most complex woman I'd ever met, and she seemed to have melted all my insides and reshaped them into internal organs that hungered only for her. How did I feel about Randi?

Good God, could I be in love with her? How would I know? And if I was, how could something that happened that fast be real?

At one point we left the sidewalk and followed Marley as he explored a wooded area of the park. As he sniffed enthusiastically at the base of a tree, I took a deep breath and gently pushed Randi up against the tree. Then I lifted Randi's shades and tucked them up onto her head so I could see those eyes.

"What are you doing?" Randi asked. "I thought we agreed. It would be unprofessional—"

I moved in and silenced her with a kiss. Perhaps Randi needed to be thoroughly kissed as well. When she yielded to my kiss and we melted together, a delicious throbbing began between my legs.

But then Randi pulled away, taking me gently by the shoulders and holding me back. "Look, how many times do I have to tell you? I'm not the kind of woman you want to get messed up with. I'm the bad girl your mom would have warned you about if your mom had been warning you about women instead of men. I don't do relationships. I do encounters, hook-ups."

I opened my mouth but Randi shook her head. "Let me finish. I've made some really bad decisions in my life, and some of them have to do with Benton. I can't tell you everything, but not all my dealings with him have been entirely ethical. I'm not the person you think you know. And I will not—repeat, will not—risk hurting you. These last five days with you have been remarkable, and there's nothing I'd rather do than take you back to my apartment, undress you, and draw my own map all over your body."

My heart skipped a beat.

"But I can't, I won't. I've never wanted a woman so much, but at the same time known without a doubt that I can't act on that attraction. You'll only end up getting hurt, and that'd destroy me…maybe not right away, but over time, it would."

Randi felt like a mountain, unmovable. I didn't care. "Why don't you let me decide for myself what's right for me?"

Randi pulled me into a brief hug, whispering into my ear, "Because you don't know what I do." With that, she stepped back, whistled for Marley, and motioned toward the parking lot, which meant climbing into the SUV one last time and driving home.

❖

An hour into the trip Randi asked me to drive, which I agreed to gratefully. It'd give me something to do other than stare out the window and feel sorry for myself. Randi then began writing strings of letters in her notebook.

"Trying to break the code?"

"We'll probably need a computer, but Tommy might have used a simple transposition or substitution cipher."

I offered a legal pad from my briefcase, which she dug out and used. Soon she'd filled pages with odd columns of letters. She stopped and tapped the pad with her pen. "Tommy would have had to choose a keyword for the cipher. I've tried Moon Shadow, treasure, West Indies, pirate, *Dum spiro spero*, but none work."

We brainstormed a few more words gleaned from Tommy's life, and Randi made more letter charts, trying to explain how with a keyword you assigned a number to each letter, then wrote the message in columns under these numbers. Normally my brain would have loved the detail, but I didn't want detail. I didn't want little columns of mixed-up letters. I wanted Randi.

Finally Randi admitted defeat. "It's more complex than I can crack."

❖

When I pulled up to my house in Minneapolis it was nearly midnight. We stood on the sidewalk under the buzzing streetlight, suddenly awkward. She held out her hand as I leaned in for a hug, so she switched to a hug but I'd already switched to a handshake. We ended up doing a poor version of both, which was deeply, deeply unsatisfying.

I knelt beside Marley and buried my face in his neck, inhaling the smell of dog. Then I whispered in his ear, "Poodle-doodle-noodle." He whirled in a circle, tongue hanging out with joy. Too bad Marley's mom didn't find me as exciting.

"Thanks for your help," I finally said, stepping backward toward my door.

"Anytime," Randi replied, and she was gone. My five-day-long date was over.

Chapter Twenty-five

I walked into Getty's office at eight a.m, and the man was already in, had drunk three cups of coffee, and had been clutching his head so hard his combover was all out of whack. We didn't have the kind of relationship that would have allowed me to fix it, or even point it out, but it spoke to the mess we were in.

I sat down heavily. "Michelle e-mailed me last night. Here's what I know: the legislature cut the U's requested increase from thirty-five percent to zero percent."

Getty moaned.

"So not only do we have no budget increase, but there might be a cut from last year's figures. Any idea how much?"

Getty tossed me a sheet of paper. "Oh, no," I breathed. "We can't absorb that."

"We must not only cut next year's budget but start slashing at what's left of this year. You're back in time to help me do that."

"I found the Farris map."

"No kidding?" Getty perked up for a minute.

"But I found it inside a book at the Patterson, so it belongs to them."

"God damn it. We could have used the money. What could you have sold it for?"

"Fifty thousand."

We both sat there in silence, knowing I'd done the right thing, but still…fifty thousand dollars.

Getty handed me a stack of paper. "The Abbot and Jacobsen donations fell through. Here are the financial notes I've made. I need you to go through them, then come back with recommended cuts for this year. We have to cut our spending by forty percent."

Sickened, I slogged back to my desk. There was no way to do that without cutting staff. Some of the people I'd hired would have to go.

I spent the morning catching up, answering e-mails and phone calls, and wading through Getty's stack. It was hell, but thinking about Randi was a welcome distraction. Three times I reached for my cell to call her, then stopped. We'd completed our task. We'd found the map. True, there was still a code to break, but that wasn't my department. Also, Randi had made it clear she wasn't willing to move our relationship in the direction I wanted.

Instead of calling Randi, I typed up the e-mail I'd been planning in my head for hours. Was Drummond really Lauren Gilmore? It didn't matter when it came to what I had to say to him, or her. I read the e-mail one more time, the cursor poised over Send.

> To Edward Drummond:
>   Despite your taunts and threats, I've won. I've found the Farris map, so this ends now. We know what you look like. Whether you're a man or a woman makes no difference. Your disguises stink. Walk into any library in this country and the FBI will be all over your ass inside of three minutes.
>   All that's left is for you to turn yourself in and return the maps you've stolen.
>   Your worst nightmare,
>   Emma Boyd

I clicked the mouse, and the e-mail became bits of data flowing toward Edward Drummond's computer, wherever that was. Randi had assured me her agency, working with the FBI, was making progress in tracking him down, but why did it have to take so long? Now that the map was found, and lost again, all I needed was Drummond behind bars. Randi had said that last year another map thief had been given ten years for stealing maps, so I had reason to hope Drummond might suffer a similar fate.

I jumped when my office phone rang and I whirled around to check the caller ID. Damn. Another not-Randi call. I stuffed down my disappointment even though all my calls had been not-Randi calls. I dealt with the call, then returned to my daydreaming. God, it was hard to focus on work. I'd been away for five days, and in that time work had changed from my entire life to something irritating I wanted to escape.

I couldn't stop thinking about Randi and the map, and I still had no conclusive answer for what had happened to Tommy Farris. Did she drown? Was she hanged? I was saddened to think that this might be an unsolvable mystery. I started doodling on my calendar and ended up writing the Shakespeare quote. A quick check on Google yielded *Measure for Measure* as the source of the quote. Feeling a little guilty about skipping out of work, I walked across the bridge to the Walter Library and found a copy. Back at my desk I skimmed through the play, and while the play had duplicity and sex and love, I couldn't find anything that could explain its role on the map. It must have resonated with Tommy, which set my imagination aflame. Had Tommy been in love, or worse, figured out she was in love after it was too late?

God, I didn't want to stop working on this. The map hadn't resolved anything so I sent an e-mail to Eleanor Levinson, the librarian who'd found the Shaw letter, asking her if she'd had time to catalogue any more material in that pirate collection that might deal with Tommy.

Finally, at five p.m, I couldn't take it. I called Randi's cell, and she answered on the first ring.

"Emma."

"I'm…I'm calling to see how Marley is." Would Randi recognize the lie?

"That's sweet of you, but you're lying."

"Don't flatter yourself. I wanted to make sure he's adjusting to life off the road."

"Thanks."

"How does it feel to be back at work?"

"Fine. How's your job?"

"A mess thanks to budget cuts. I'm probably going to have to fire everyone later this week, including myself, but otherwise, things are cool."

"Glad to hear it. How many times have you read *Measure for Measure* today?"

I laughed. "How'd you know?"

"Because you're you. I've gone through it twice myself and can't find anything helpful."

"Any word from your codebreakers?"

"Not yet. The tech geeks are running it through every complex program they have, so it'll take a while."

I took a deep breath. "I've been thinking about you all day."

"I told you—we can't go there, Emma."

"Have you been thinking about me?"

"No."

"Liar."

Randi chuckled, and I closed my eyes to imagine that dimple. "Gotta go before you start reading my mind," Randi said.

"Too late. I know what you and I are doing in your imagination."

"Christ, Emma, stop," Randi whispered, and I shivered. I was not going to let this woman walk out of my life.

"Okay, but wouldn't you like to know what we're doing together in *my* imagination?"

Randi swore softly. I smiled and hung up.

❖

By the end of the next day, I had a plan and had given it a great deal of thought. I needed to share some news with Randi, so why not? I did a little investigating of my own and found her address. As I parked my car on the tree-lined street, my pulse pounded in my ears, but if I didn't do this now, I'd never screw up enough courage to do it again. I rang the buzzer for apartment 203. The building lobby was spotless, with a marble checkered floor and polished mirror walls.

"Yes?"

"Randi, it's me. Do you have time to talk?"

The pause was so long I was afraid she'd say no. "Sure, come on up."

Heart pounding, I stepped off the elevator to find Randi leaning in her open doorway wearing a fitted burgundy shirt and the low-slung jeans I loved.

"Hi."

"Hi," I said. "I…ah…had some news, and since I was in the neighborhood…" Was this the lamest, most obvious excuse ever? And wasn't she going to ask me in?

Marley poked his head out around Randi's legs and gave a happy yelp, so I knelt to hug the wriggling dog. "I've missed you, Marley." I ran my hands along his flank and across his shoulders. "I was having Marley withdrawal."

"C'mon in. I have some news too." As Randi closed the door behind us, I took a minute to absorb the apartment. Neat, clean, eclectic, but with the look of a person who was staying there, not really *living* there. Ivory carpeting, brown leather sofa with what looked like a Marley nest of plaid blankets at one end. Randi's apartment was much cleaner than her car.

Neighborhood lights twinkled through the wide sliding glass door, the bottom curve of the moon just visible from where I stood. Thanks to the brass wall lamps, the most dramatic feature in the apartment were the framed maps. I approached the nearest one. "This is La Florida, from Ortelius, sixteenth century?"

Randi nodded. "1584. It was one of the maps we recovered from my last case, but we couldn't trace the owner. The FBI had it appraised and I bought it."

I moved on to the next. "I don't recognize this one," I said, even though I knew exactly what it was. I thrilled at the charming embarrassment sliding across Randi's face. Standing here examining her maps felt almost as intimate as when Randi had slowly paged through my Day-Timer.

"Replica of the map used in the Humphrey Bogart movie *Treasure of the Sierra Madre*."

Chuckling, and emboldened, I began roaming the living room and dining room, examining each map. A small bookshelf held books on maps, sailing, and dogs. I stopped at the full rack of CDs by a Bose CD player. It took me a second to realize the CDs were arranged by type of music, but within those types, there didn't seem to be any sort of clear organization. My hand twitched. It would only take a few minutes to alphabetize them.

Randi let out a low, throaty laugh.

"What's so funny?"

"Whenever a beautiful, single woman comes to my apartment, she usually has only one thing on her mind. This might be the first time that one thing is reorganizing my CDs."

"Yes, well," I said, demonstrating my astonishing skill with snappy comebacks. I skittered over to the nearest map. "You have an amazing collection. Some of these must be quite valuable."

"I don't have many vices or hobbies." Randi offered me a beer, then moved us back to the living room where she sat down on the sofa. Before I could join her, Marley hopped up beside her, leaving the stuffed chair for me.

"What's your news?" I asked.

"We've ID'd your crew cut guy, the one who beat up Cam. Name's Roger Fletcher. No criminal record, award-winning insurance salesman, single, age forty-two, and hasn't been seen by family or coworkers for about a week."

"That's because he was following us."

"Yup. The Bureau will catch him, and then we'll ask him what he wants with you." She patted Marley. "So what's your news?"

"First, I have something for you." I reached into my backpack, then handed Randi one of the librarian action figures from my office. "I thought you might like one…to remind you of our map-finding trip."

Randi gave me an odd look, then placed the action figure on the end table between us, next to *Myths and Superstitions of the Sea.* "Thank you. Now what's your news?"

"Remember Eleanor in Cincinnati with the pirate database? She e-mailed me this afternoon. I'd asked her if she had anything more catalogued, and she did. Apparently Shaw wrote to Mommy quite often, and Eleanor discovered another letter." I sipped my beer, suddenly shy, and wished we were on the road again. Travel made us comfortable; it made us colleagues, and gave us a reason to spend time together. "This is another letter from Shaw to Mother Shaw. It's written *before* the other letter."

June 25, 1715.

Dearest Mother,

My life's hell. We can't find any prizes. If there are any, Tommy's already taken 'em. But my fortunes are soon to change. I got a plan, and Tommy's men made her agree with it. Just one problem. Coxon told me about that Rebekah Brown, the slave Tommy fished from the sea.

I stopped reading, waiting for Randi to react. She slapped her forehead. "Holy crap. Rebekah Brown. Captain R. Brown was a woman. We're talking about two women here, not just Tommy. Was Rebekah a pirate?"

"Don't know," I said. "Here's the rest."

That Brown bitch hates me on account of me throwing her overboard. Coxon say there be something unnatural between Tommy and that black witch. I know Tommy. She's randy as a man. It's disgusting, the thought of her and that slave.

Randi smiled broadly. "So Tommy was not only stealing silver, but she might have been stealing women's hearts as well."

"At least Rebekah Brown's. But how did they end up on different ships, and both captains? And while Tommy never made an effort to hide her sex, it sounds like Rebekah passed as a man."

"Rebekah Brown." Randi grabbed the legal pad and pen on her coffee table. "What if Rebekah Brown is the keyword?" She worked quietly for five minutes, trying both Rebecca and Rebekah, then threw down her pad. "No, wrong again. No words, just letters with no meaning."

I watched Randi. What did I feel for this woman? Simple lust? Or had I let her climb into my open heart? "What about something like 'I love Rebekah,' or 'I love Rebekah Brown.'"

"You don't give up, do you?"

"Puzzles. Me. Anal librarian."

"You're not, and I'm sorry I ever said that. You're thorough and determined and make me want to be that way too." She picked up the pad again.

She scribbled for awhile, muttering to herself. "Okay, groups of five didn't work. I'll try seven." I watched, fascinated, as she organized the letters in different columns, hoping the jumble of letters would start forming words that either ran down the columns or across them.

Randi suddenly sat up straight. "Wait, I've got words here, actual words. Oh my God." I jumped up and squeezed onto the sofa between Randi and Marley, who'd picked up on Randi's excitement and stood wagging his tail so hard the sofa bounced. He stuck his nose in my ear.

"I transposed the columns twice, then started writing down the string." I looked over Randi's shoulder as she began inserting slashes through what she had so far. FROMNTIPCARRIACOURUN became *From N tip Carriacou run.*

"Keep going," I said, eager to help but a little distracted by Randi's hip next to mine.

She must have been distracted as well because she stood and paced the room as she finished decoding the string. "Oh my God," she said again, eyes shining, hair tumbling around her face, mouth open in amazement. "I did it." She held up a hand before I could stand. "Wait. Let me double-check." She flipped to a new page, wrote out the message again, then ripped off the sheet and handed it to me, triumphant.

I felt like a kid on a treasure hunt as I read the message: *From N tip of Carriacou run W down N twelve fifty-two seventeen at three knots for one bell.* "I get the first part, the northern tip of Carriacou, but the rest?"

"Northern hemisphere, twelve degrees fifty-two minutes, seventeen seconds has to be the latitude. Run W down that latitude means to sail west along that latitude. And remember, they couldn't easily measure longitude then, so speed and time traveled was the closest they could come to describing a location. Tommy's saying that we start out at the northern tip of Carriacou, which must be at the latitude in the message, then we sail west at three knots for thirty minutes. The treasure, whatever it is, must be there."

I reached for a heavy atlas on the lower shelf of the coffee table. Together we pored over the two-page spread of the Caribbean. Carriacou was on the eastern edge, a small island north of Grenada. "But Tommy put the *X* in the middle of the sea on her map, instead of near Carriacou."

"That way no one could use the map without cracking the code, which we did."

"But there isn't an island at this location on the map."

"Perhaps the island's too small for this atlas. We need navigational charts." She brought over her laptop and began searching. She found a chart, but there was nothing along that latitude. Randi leapt to her feet and paced. "There has to be an island there, or a sunken ship." She stopped. "Let's go find it together."

"What?"

"Forget our jobs, take Marley, and run away. No one will have to know where we've gone. We'll disappear into the Caribbean. We'll live on savings and look for the island."

I stared at Randi. "You're serious."

"Dead serious. Let's go. Now. We have the coordinates. We can drive to Miami, charter a boat, and sail to Carriacou."

"I can run an inflatable dinghy, but I don't know the first thing about sailing."

"I do. I can't change a tire, but I can sail a boat with my eyes closed. That was something *good* my brothers taught me. We can do this. It's every person's dream to chuck it all and live on a tropical island somewhere."

My practicality moved in and sat right down on my excitement. "What would we eat? If we found the island, it may not be inhabitable. What if there's no treasure? My savings would run out very quickly."

Randi pulled me to my feet. "We don't need to worry about any of that now. We'll figure it out as we go."

I reached out and stroked Randi's flushed cheek. "I'd love to go on an adventure with you. And if I had to choose between the life I'm living and a life on some deserted island with you, I'd choose you. But I think I can have both my life *and* you."

Randi passed a hand over her eyes. "If only it were that simple." She shrugged, then stepped back. "Forget I suggested it. Stupid idea. Of course you can't abandon your life." She smiled weakly. "Besides, I've made it perfectly clear I'm all wrong for you."

"Yes, you have." I suddenly knew I wasn't leaving this apartment without at least trying one more time to get what I wanted from her.

"I'll see you out," Randi said.

"Fine." I waited until we were in the narrow hallway just inside the front door, softly lit by two wall sconces, then I pushed her gently up against the wall and pinned her hands behind her back.

Randi shook her head, but didn't pull her hands free. "Emma, you'll only get hurt. Please."

Holding Randi's wrists with one hand, possible only because

Randi didn't struggle, I used my other hand to unbutton Randi's shirt. She inhaled sharply and I tightened my grip on her wrists. Adrenaline and fear and lust surged through me.

"You've got to stop."

I pulsed with strength to feel Randi trembling beneath me. "You don't have any assault issues in your past, do you? That would make my restraining you uncomfortable?"

"No," Randi whispered. "But we can't. I'm not—"

"Shut up," I whispered into her ear, then brushed my lips across her cheek. When I barely touched her lips with my own, Randi moaned and arched her back. "I don't like the rules you've come up with for us," I said. "You break rules all the time, so now it's my turn." Randi nearly melted my socks when she yielded to my kiss, responding with a hunger that made me weak.

In one quick move I slid Randi's shirt off her shoulders and used the sleeves to keep her arms pinned helplessly behind her. Both of us were breathing hard now and Randi's eyes had darkened. She wasn't wearing a bra.

I ran my tongue lightly along one collarbone, then circled the sensitive hollow at the base of Randi's throat. She dropped her head back. I did the same with the other collarbone, and when I ran my tongue up along the side of one naked breast, I fully expected Randi to continue her feeble protests.

But she only said, "You've got exactly twenty minutes to cut that out, and then I'm calling the cops."

Thrilled, I chuckled against Randi's neck. "You keep telling me how bad you are for me."

"God, it's so true."

"I don't believe you."

"Let me go and I'll prove it." Randi nuzzled my ear. "God help me, but we're both going to regret this in the morning."

"Oh, I doubt that." I loosened my grip on Randi's shirt and was suddenly pinned against the opposite wall, my own shirt now being expertly unbuttoned. I didn't know if this was a one-night stand or not, but at this point I didn't care. "Bedroom?" I murmured.

"Too far away," Randi said, and we slid to the floor where she tugged off my shorts and I peeled her jeans down to reveal smooth thighs and perfect calves. After days of sitting beside this woman, I couldn't believe she was actually kissing me. When our tongues met I pulsed with need, and our hands slid around and between and then into each other's bodies. There, on the carpeting, we both came hard and fast.

We made it as far as the sofa before we did it again. By the time we reached the bedroom, Randi had picked up on my rhythms so expertly she tormented me for the longest time before leading me to the edge of the cliff, pushing me over, then catching me at the bottom. She held me tightly when all my tension and need and desire streamed in hot tears down my cheeks. Then I pushed her back onto the bed and took possession of her body with my mouth.

We barely spoke, which was perfect, since words were unnecessary. Randi had been so sure I would regret sex with her, but after a few hours the only thing I regretted was waiting so long to seduce her.

❖

Sometime in the middle of the night, Randi's cell phone rang and I snapped awake, delighted to find my naked limbs entwined with Randi's. "I'd better get this," Randi whispered, gently extricating herself. The sight of Randi's naked body glowing in the faint moonlight took my breath away.

I stretched on the cool sheets, arching my back and marveling at how my body felt. It had *never* felt like this with anyone else before, yet I struggled with the idea that a rational woman like me would fall so hard, and so fast, for a woman I'd known less than two weeks. It wasn't possible, not for me. But how else to explain the incredible feelings bubbling around inside me, like laughter flying around looking for a way to burst free?

I stretched again, and when my hands fell below the bottom edge of the quilted headboard, my fingers grazed something hard and plastic. I gave a tug, heard the rip of Velcro, and pulled a remote from behind the headboard. That was clever. You never had to search for the remote on your night stand or in the bed. Just reach back and stick it to the headboard. But where was the TV? I didn't remember seeing one as we'd fallen onto the bed. On the other hand, I'd been focused on Randi's body at the time.

Randi's voice was muffled down the hall, but I heard, "Fuck," then, "I owe you one."

Within minutes Randi slipped back into bed. "I have to work a stakeout in an hour."

"Should I leave?"

Randi gently took the remote from me and stuck it back up behind the headboard. "Not yet," she said, and we made love with such intensity we were both breathless. We lay there afterward, limp, chests heaving, then Randi rolled onto my steaming body. "Much as I hate to say this, *now* you can leave."

After slowly dressing while we kissed body parts, then undressing again to kiss more parts, then dressing again, I was finally clothed and out the door. I floated down the stairs, and drove home in a haze of orgasms and kisses and Randi Marx.

PART SEVEN

THE STORM, 1715

Love lives in sealed bottles of regret.

—Seán O'Faoláin

Chapter Twenty-six

Tommy loved sleeping aboard a ship, probably because the sea constantly rocked her, something she doubted her mother ever did. Born of the unwed Eliza Hack and Jacob Farris during a tumultuous storm that battered the western coast of Devon in 1690, Tommy'd been struggling for calm ever since.

As usual, Tommy woke before the sun had even thought of sailing above the horizon. She lay there, eyes closed, wondering at herself. What was this feeling inside her? She felt light as the beach foam skittering ahead of a breaking wave, yet her body felt heavy, as if her flesh had become an oak rooted in the planks of the hull. She sighed, wondering if this was what happiness felt like.

Tommy's eyes shot open. Rebekah Brown, hair tousled and clothing alarmingly absent, stirred in Tommy's arms. A hot flush shot up Tommy's chest and neck. Lord God Almighty. What had she done?

All happiness fled as memory returned. She'd taken her pleasure of a woman. While Tommy had certainly killed and tortured her share of men, she feared rotting in hell for lying with a woman. Tommy extricated her arms and legs from the slumbering woman, lips pressed together to hold back a groan, then climbed out of bed clutching her clothes like armor to her chest.

As she yanked on her trousers and tucked in her shirt, hot shame beat through her veins. This could never happen again. The thrill of the chase and the joy of the treasure must have weakened her natural inclinations and defenses. Didn't she always choose a man upon each prize they took? Even on prizes with women prisoners, she'd never considered taking a woman. Yet she'd taken Rebekah in this manner. She wouldn't do it again.

When Rebekah rolled over in her sleep, the thin blanket fell away from her naked chest. "Bloody hell," Tommy muttered. She cooled her face with a splash of water from the basin, then angrily wiped it off with her sleeve.

No sun would show its face today, for angry black-green clouds swirled overhead. The water's color so closely matched the dark sky that the horizon was nearly invisible. When she stepped out on deck, Tommy realized they'd be sailing blind for another day, with only her compass to guide them.

Sawkins sat on the top rung of the ladder, glum.

"Any sign of the *Shadow*?" she asked.

He shook his head. "Nothing."

Tommy hugged herself for warmth, determined not to miss the heat of Rebekah's body. "Hatley could have been blown farther north, and be heading to Sombrero."

"Ye know the hardest part of all this?"

They exchanged glances and he nodded. They were of like mind. When their men on the *Tiger Eye* and *Windy Queen* heard of the treasure on the *Maravillosa*, and the ship gone, the men might think Tommy had planned from the start to take sole possession of the treasure.

Tommy resisted the urge to turn the ship around and tack her way back toward the Dolphins. But what if, by the time she reached them, Shaw knew the truth of the treasure and had turned McLeod and Stratton against her? Then it would be six ships against Tommy's galleon. Those six ships could have crippled the galleon without sinking her, and Tommy, Rebekah, Sawkins, Billy, and all others aboard would be tortured for sport, then tossed overboard.

For the first time, Tommy took a moment to examine the Spanish galleon she now commanded. She loved the gangway that allowed her to walk the center length of the ship without having to scoot down the ladder, cross the mid-deck, and climb another ladder. Then from the quarterdeck she could climb another ladder to the poop deck, and do the same at the fore of the ship as well. The rigging was overburdened with lateen tops and topgallants, but she could change it. Although the ship sailed sluggishly, slowed down by barnacles on the hull, there was no time for careening. And the treasure slowed them down as well.

"Mr. Sawkins, we need to lighten our load. The deck was awash far too much in the storm, and it's a miracle we weren't sunk. Then let's meet in the wardroom."

The tiny part of the wardroom not filled with treasure was lined with cubbies containing charts, which Tommy eyed greedily. Her navigational charts had to be stolen from ships she captured, which meant she had huge gaps in the areas mapped. There were entire islands she had to avoid for lack of accurate charts of shoals and other dangers.

She checked the labels, then pulled out the chart she needed and spread it over the table, suddenly aware that Rebekah was on the other side of the wall. Still abed. Possibly still naked.

Sawkins arrived and held a lantern above them while Tommy studied the chart. "With the storm, I can't take a reading, but given our speed and last night's storm at our back, we must be somewhere in the middle here, south of Hispaniola. We'll run south of Puerto Rico, then sail up into Sombrero on the ocean side. We'll deposit the slaves with supplies, meet up with Hatley and the *Moon Shadow*, then travel down to St. Bartholomew to let off any Spanish crew that wants off. We'll need to unload treasure with each group since we still be top-heavy. With this upper wardroom filled with treasure, the ship bobs like a child's wooden boat."

She moved her finger from the Leewards down along the eastern edge of the West Indies, past Carriacou and Grenada. "Weren't we in this area when you and Billy saw that uncharted island?"

Sawkins nodded.

"Did you really see something, or was your head just full of ale?"

"No, the island be there. Why?"

"It might be the best place to hide the treasure. Then we can decide what to do with it." The cabin door unlatched and Rebekah stepped out, dressed now, and wearing the wool coat she'd taken off the Spaniard. She'd pulled her hair back into a bun, but her cheeks flushed upon seeing Tommy.

Tommy's tongue stuck to the roof of her mouth.

"Good morning, Mr. Sawkins." Rebekah's voice was husky.

"Ma'am." The sailor tapped his forehead in respect, as if Rebekah were a fine lady.

Tommy avoided Rebekah all that day, then climbed into an empty hammock on a lower deck to sleep between her watches.

The next morning another tropical storm hit, and for three days Tommy barely slept. Compass readings told her they were bearing east, but how far east were they? With the storm at her back, she might sail right into one of the Leewards and kill them all.

The sun came out on Tommy's sixth day on the *Maravillosa*. She quickly took readings with her quadrant and determined the storms had pushed them within leagues of Sombrero Island.

Four bells later they reached the island and ferried slaves and material to the island in longboats. The slaves had boarded the *Maravillosa* in Puerto Bello in shackles, but were leaving the ship as free men. Tommy sent along barrels of water, meat, and hardtack. Although her men protested, Tommy also sent ashore four chests of treasure. The Spaniards had mined the silver using the backs of slaves; it was only right that some of the treasure be given to slaves.

When one man protested too vigorously, Tommy pulled out her cutlass and slammed the blade into the railing, knowing Billy would have to sharpen it yet again. "I'll hear no more. The ship's top-heavy and some of the treasure must go. I be captain of this ship, and until the ship is free and clear of danger from Shaw and his ships, I be in command." She met the eyes of every man within earshot, and each lowered his gaze first. Satisfied, she dismissed the lot of them, and once the Negroes were ashore, set sail for the next stop.

At one point Tommy spied Rebekah heading toward her, so she scampered down the nearest companionway and worked her way through the labyrinth of stores, hammocks, and men to reach the stern and return to the quarterdeck. She'd evaded Rebekah for days and discovered nearly every hiding spot on the huge galleon.

By midafternoon they'd reached St. Bartholomew, where they put ashore most of the Spaniards, save the officers and twenty Spaniards willing to turn pirate. Tommy had offered the officers one and a half shares, the sailors each one share. They unloaded more supplies and treasure chests onto the island.

Tommy was better satisfied with the riding of the ship, but still worried she might be sluggish in flight. After they'd left the ocean behind and sailed back into the sea between the Leewards and St.

Christopher, Tommy felt grateful they'd seen no other ships save a few fishing boats, but worry over the *Moon Shadow* ate at her. Then the wind died with the day and the *Maravillosa*'s sails hung limp as a dead fish. Tommy and Sawkins returned to the charts. She decided to deliver the treasure to Sawkins's island, then return to Sombrero in hopes that Hatley and the *Moon Shadow* would be there waiting.

"Tomorrow, God willing, the wind will return and we'll sail south," she said, trying to recall the coordinates in the *Shadow*'s logbook for the night they'd first sailed past Sawkins's island. "In two days we should be close."

The door to the captain's cabin opened. Rebekah stood in the doorway, face impassive. "Captain, may I speak with you a moment?"

Tommy looked down at the chart, flustered. "Busy."

Sawkins rolled up the chart, the bastard, and popped it into a cubby. "Not anymore, Captain. Nothing to be done till daylight. I'll knock on ye door for morning watch."

"I won't be in—she's—"

"Good night, Captain." Sawkins gave Tommy an odd look, then excused himself.

Tommy could see no way out other than outright rudeness, and given what she'd done to Rebekah, she owed her more than that.

Rebekah slammed the door behind them and Tommy jumped.

"You've been avoiding me. Why?"

"Large ship to run. Don't have time for tea and crumpets every afternoon." Tommy jammed her fists into her coat pockets.

"You don't wish to speak of what passed between us?"

Tommy felt her eyes widen. "Speak of it? Curse it, no. Can't speak of it. Can't do it ever again. Best to just forget it."

"Forget it?"

Tommy had never been frightened by a woman before, but she took a step back. "Yes, what we did together was wrong. Very wrong."

Fast as lightning Rebekah's mood changed and her eyes filled with tears. Tommy felt a panic rising in her chest. One lantern flickered weakly in the cabin and the covers of the bed had been turned back. Tommy's heart thumped in her ears. By thunder, she'd command this woman to step aside.

"But it isn't wrong," Rebekah said. "Why did God hurl me into the middle of the sea if not to be saved by you? Why were you drawn to the *Maravillosa*'s figurehead? I feel a strong sentiment for you that I have never felt before."

Tommy fought the rising panic. "No, don't say that. You can't feel anything for me because I'm not a man, and what we did together was wrong."

"What we did together was beautiful."

Tommy shook her head to clear it. "No, you—" She stopped, unable to explain the shame of touching a woman the way she had. "You be female. I be female."

"Both women, both beautiful," Rebekah whispered.

"I must leave."

"Let me show you what you couldn't see in the dark that night." Tommy's protest was only half finished when Rebekah unbuttoned her dress and let it slide to the planks. "You saw some of this when I was ill, but I'm well now." Tommy began to sweat. This was no figurehead, but a soft, warm woman. She jerked when Rebekah took her hand and placed it on her bare breast.

"Look at your hand on my skin. Is this not beautiful?"

Tommy shivered.

"And your other hand down here." Tommy gasped when Rebekah put Tommy's hand between her legs. "I've missed you," Rebekah whispered, her lips brushing Tommy's cheek, her breasts pressing against her.

Tommy closed her eyes, then took a deep breath, something that always helped her think more clearly. She wouldn't yield to these temptations. She was stronger than that. She opened her eyes.

But then with a low growl, Tommy scooped Rebekah into her arms and carried her to the bed. Cursing, she unbuckled her belts and flung off her coat. Tommy was as powerless to resist Rebekah as the sea was powerless to resist the tides.

She latched her door and blew out the lantern. If God couldn't see, perhaps it wouldn't be a sin.

CHAPTER TWENTY-SEVEN

For the next two days Tommy and Rebekah sinned every moment they could retreat to the cabin and latch the door. Tommy was weak from wanting Rebekah and had given up trying to understand why.

The third morning Tommy sprang from the bed at Sawkins's soft knock. Afraid to look behind her at the tempting sight, she dressed quickly and joined Sawkins in the dark passageway.

"Wind's picking up," Sawkins said, "and my knee hurts like a creaking capstan."

"Another storm."

"Can't say when, but it's gonna be a big one."

Tommy accepted a mug of cold cider from the Spanish steward, then sprinted up the ladder for her watch. She roamed the ship, examining the rigging and guns to ensure their soundness. The work also kept her mind off her raging weaknesses. She had never understood lust before, since her own needs had always been tended to when convenient and ignored when it wasn't. Yet what burned in her now was entirely different and filled Tommy with despair at her horrific lack of control. These last few days spent touching Rebekah had not slaked her need but only flamed it higher.

"Great guns, a sail!"

At Billy's voice, Tommy craned her neck but couldn't see him through the billowing sails overhead. She scanned the horizon then saw a flash of white to their stern. She climbed up the rigging and looked again. Yes, there it was. She shouted for her spying glass. Could it be the *Moon Shadow*? The Royal Navy?

She hooked an arm around the ropes and examined the ship through her glass. Damn that man's eye. "It's Shaw," she yelled to Sawkins as she climbed down. "Helm a-starboard. Hands to braces! Hands aloft!"

Within seconds every yardarm had sailors draped over it, their bare toes clinging to the rigging as they let out every sail on the ship.

The *Maravillosa* leapt ahead, but as Tommy scrutinized the distance between the two ships, she realized with a sinking heart the *Sharktooth* was gaining, not falling behind. And he wasn't alone. She counted his three other ships, and there, coming up behind, was the *Moon Shadow*. Hatley had either been turned or killed. She knew Hatley; he'd been with her for years. The only way the *Moon Shadow* could be convinced to run Tommy down were if Hatley was dead.

Anger surged through her. It was bad enough Shaw'd killed her friend, but he was using her own ship to chase her down. The *Windy Queen* and *Tiger Eye* weren't in the fleet, so either they'd been lost in the battle, lost in the storm, or Shaw couldn't control them, which meant at least Stratton and McLeod were still alive.

"Calabria!"

"Captain?" The Spaniard raced for her.

"Find this ship's gunner. Save five balls for each cannon, then throw the rest into the sea to lighten the ship." She motioned to the nearest Spanish officer. "Start tossing barrels over—water, grog, food. If we don't lose this bastard we'll have no need for food." She continued listing material that could be dumped over. Extra masts, torn sails awaiting repair. The gun ports banged open on the deck beneath her and cannonballs splashed down with dull thunks.

She climbed back into the rigging and cupped her hands. "Billy! Do we pull ahead?"

The wind blew away his words, but his shaking head and look of fear spoke clearly enough.

"Essex, get down to Calabria. Tell him to dump every other cannon overboard."

"Aye, Captain."

Tommy wracked her brain. What else could they toss? The treasure? But if she was to get out of pirating, she needed the shares to be as large as possible. She considered the trail of debris scattered in *Maravillosa*'s wake, then looked forward, where gray-green clouds seemed to be galloping toward them. Sawkins appeared, limp forgotten. "The pumps be working, so we're dumping water from the bilge."

"Not too much. This ship's unstable as it is."

"I know, but Captain, we're at top speed now."

Tommy considered the ship, a stirring sight under full sail. "If we can't outrun Shaw, then we'd best slow him down. Prepare to lower all four longboats."

"The boats, Captain?"

"With two chests of silver in each, and a flag run up a pole so Shaw'll be sure to see each boat."

Sawkins grinned. "You think the shark will take the bait?"

"Countin' on it."

"Hard to port! Look lively, men." Tommy tacked the *Maravillosa* back and forth to spread out the boats so it'd take the *Sharktooth* more time to recover them. Within an hour all four boats were lowered and released to bob off on their own journeys.

Any crew not actively working sails or pumps gathered astern or climbed to the yardarms for a better look. The only sounds were the wind, the hull cutting through waves, and the creaking of pumps being worked below.

Tommy peered through her glass, tense as a pup sailor high up a mast, then she let out a whoop, which her crew echoed. The *Sharktooth* was turning to port to pursue the first boat. The lightened *Maravillosa*, pulled by current and pushed by the shifting wind, leapt ahead until the sails of Shaw's fleet were dots on the horizon.

Tommy consulted her chart, rolling it out on the stateroom floor since the table had been thrown overboard. She'd seen Carriacou ahead, with its distinctive humps, so it'd soon be time to turn west for that mysterious island.

Only now, crouched alone in the muggy wardroom, did Tommy admit to the stab of fear she'd felt upon seeing Shaw's sails. Her fear had not been for herself, but for Rebekah.

❖

When it finally hit at dusk, the storm was more ferocious than any Tommy had seen. The crew—Spaniards and pirates alike—worked like dogs to batten things down and take in the sails before a sudden gust could roll the ship.

Tommy watched the ugly shapes in the shifting clouds overhead. Cold rain pelted her face, but she would not take cover. She stood near the helmsman, and as the waves swelled well above twenty feet, it often took the strength of both to manage the helm. In these high seas, muscles went rigid after thirty minutes fighting the wheel, but without the rudder to keep them perpendicular to the waves, they were dead pirates. On Tommy's orders, two more men stood by to relieve them.

Sawkins sent men below to man the pumps, but two pumps broke under the strain. The sea successfully fought its way into the *Maravillosa*—through the oakum jammed between the planks of her hull and down the gangways from arching waves that fell with heavy slaps. The men formed a bucket brigade and began bailing out the hold.

As Tommy clung to the helm, another wave crashed down and swept two men overboard. Tommy growled in rage at the sky. Then with a startling crack high overhead, the top half of the foremast snapped off and crashed to the deck, sending screaming men scattering. They returned quickly to free the handful of men trapped in the pile of rigging.

The *Maravillosa* rode up each twenty foot swell, then raced down the other side, but she was holding together. Tommy couldn't ask for more, but had she been taking the *Shadow* through this storm, she'd have had no worries. Through the rain, now blowing almost horizontally, she saw Rebekah at the end of the bucket brigade and felt a stab of pride at her courage. She wasn't a sailor, but she threw herself into any job that needed doing.

When the *Maravillosa* began riding the next wave, something felt wrong under Tommy's feet. The ship dragged, so full of water she couldn't keep her bow up. Tommy's heart leapt into her throat when she realized they wouldn't ride the next wave, but instead plow right through it.

"Hang on!" she screamed, just before the bowsprit pierced the wave and took the *Maravillosa* straight into a ten-foot wall of water. The ship dipped, then forced her way back up through the wave. Water rolled over the ship, sweeping Rebekah across the deck and tossing her over the opposite side.

"No! Rebekah!" Tommy jumped down onto the slippery deck, fell, then scrambled for the gunwale. She grabbed the railing and threw one leg over the side but was yanked off her feet by a hand at her coat. She kicked and fought, screaming Rebekah's name, broke free and flung a leg up onto the rail but was pulled back again.

"Billy, grab her arm!" Sawkins yelled as they dragged her backward.

"Rebekah!" Tommy screamed as she fought, but Sawkins and Billy slammed her against the mizzenmast and held her there.

"Essex!" Sawkins yelled over the wind. "Cut that piece of mast free and toss it to the black wench."

"I have to save her. Let me go!" Sawkins and Billy pinned her with their bodies and she couldn't break free. "Let me go, let me go!"

Moving quickly, Essex cut the rigging from the broken mast and sent the log flying.

Tommy shook the water from her face, straining to see. She choked on her fear as the mast splashed near Rebekah and she paddled to it. Then the wave crested and Rebekah was swept out of sight.

Crazed, Tommy cursed and fought until Sawkins put his mouth at Tommy's ear. "Naught more can be done for the girl. I seen the island. She be paddling that way. She'll make it."

"I have to save her," Tommy yelled.

"Tommy," Sawkins whispered in her ear. "Ye have to save yer ship." He bent her arm back so painfully that she gasped, and through her pain she heard his words. He was right. Tommy sagged in his arms for a second, then she straightened, wiping her streaming face.

Dear God. Rebekah. Tommy didn't see any island. She'd never be able to rescue Rebekah in these seas, even if she still had a boat. A sob escaped, but when Sawkins gripped her arm, she pulled herself together.

She'd lost Rebekah. Now it would take everything she had not to lose the ship, and all aboard her.

PART EIGHT

THE SECRET

Where secrecy or mystery begins, vice or roguery is not far off.

—Samuel Johnson

CHAPTER TWENTY-EIGHT

I lived in the most beautiful city in the world. Minneapolis was all blue skies and towering trees and scented flower gardens and happy people. The birds sang directly to me as I parked my car and walked through campus. I couldn't stop smiling, even though I knew the sight would alarm the other people sharing the sidewalk with me. I didn't care. The impatiens in the flower bed outside Blegen Hall were so incredibly red, and even the stella d'oros, those short daylilies that so many people planted ten years ago that they struck me as weeds—even these glowed like yellow stars.

The lawn outside the Conrad Kline Library was no longer a tedious green but an amazing blend of shapes and shades, each blade a miniature work of art. I resisted the impulse to lie down on my stomach for a closer look because such things weren't done in Minnesota.

I chuckled softly as I entered the library, feeling almost high. Michelle raised the eyebrow I knew she would, but thankfully didn't comment as I floated up to her desk. I didn't want to talk with anyone about this yet. I wanted to keep quiet for days until I grew so heavy with the secret I couldn't stand it.

"You have a few messages here," Michelle said, handing me a pile of slips. "The only one I don't recognize is a Mary Gerritson. She wants you to call her back."

Nodding, I drifted into my lovely office. With its rich blue carpeting and handsome wallpaper, it no longer seemed the prison it'd become after returning from my journey.

I didn't return my messages, but instead tried to focus on the stack of employee evaluations on my desk. That didn't work, so I ended up at my window, feeling Randi's breath against my wrists and recalling her stunned look when I had, and I quote here, "taken her somewhere she'd never been before." Imagine that. I decided the joy of sex had less to do with orgasms and more to do with the vulnerability that came from letting someone else touch your body.

My intercom buzzed at ten. ""Emma, it's that Mary Gerritson again."

I pushed the speaker button. "I'll call her back later." Why ruin my morning with someone else's problems? I returned to the window, wondering what Randi was doing now on her stakeout, if she was having the same problems concentrating.

I joined the Lunch Bunch just before noon and hugged Cam long and hard. He looked like hell, but the doctor said everything was healing well. "I'm so glad you're okay," he said. "I've been worried about you."

"No need to worry. I'm fine. I'm just glad you're doing better." I explained what I'd learned about Roger Fletcher, the man who'd attacked Cam.

"But how did Fletcher know Cam was going on the trip with you?" Maggie asked.

I'd already worked that out. "The jerk was sitting right here in the Union, at the next table, and heard the whole thing. He'd been watching me even then. We still don't know why, but it's likely connected to the Farris map."

"Where is he now?" Jason asked.

"Missing." We all took a minute to look around the Food Court. No Roger Fletcher.

I started eating, pleased I'd disguised my joy over Randi, when Maggie suddenly narrowed her eyes. "You're smiling at your sandwich. Lord have mercy on us all. Our librarian got laid."

Jason choked on his burrito. "How can you tell that? How can women always see that?"

I actually enjoyed the hot blush spreading up my neck. Okay, maybe I didn't want to keep the secret as long as I'd thought. "Maggie, you're a busybody and a snoop."

"Uh-huh, you got that right. Was it your sexy private eye?"

The table hooted as my blush deepened, but I didn't mind. I

refused to give details, so I had to bear the good-natured ribbing for the entire lunch hour.

I strolled back to the library, then headed up to Getty's office for our meeting. He'd had a few hours to look over my budget cut recommendations. As I trudged up the stairs, the weight of my job settled over me like a cement coat. Even without the budget cuts, my job felt so much harder and less enjoyable since I'd been back, and that had nothing to do with wanting to be with Randi all the time. This was why taking a vacation was a bad idea. When you came back, you instantly lost all sense of rest and a slower pace of life and were suddenly thrust back into a life that moved too fast. I began to hate the calendar in my arms.

"Emma, please sit." Getty's upper lip was moist, and he had dark circles under his eyes.

"What do you think of my cuts?"

He smoothed his five strands of hair over his head. "We have to do more. We need to cut the staff in half."

My mouth dropped open. "But…how will we run? How—"

"We have no choice. Michelle has to go."

Now my chin ended up in my lap. "Marcus, we'll cut hours. We'll stop replacing computers."

"I've looked at all those options. You're going to have to do your job, and Michelle's." I walked down the stairs to my office in a daze. My life was on overload as it was. There was no way I could possibly do Michelle's job. She ran the circulation desk. She coordinated the interlibrary requests. She did about a thousand things for me every day.

I stopped in the stairwell and leaned against the cold wall. Within the space of twenty-four hours, how could one part of my life go so right and another part go so wrong? After a short attack of self-pity, I recovered and kept going.

As I approached my office, and Michelle's desk, I tried to arrange my face to hide my shock, but wasn't sure I was successful. Luckily, Michelle didn't notice anything wrong. "There's someone from John Lewis Investigations in your office."

Okay, I'll admit it. My heart did an Olympic-style twirl around the uneven parallel bars. Randi.

But no. A tall black man with kind eyes and a salt-and-pepper beard introduced himself as John Lewis, head of John Lewis Investigations. He flashed the same badge that Randi had, and I recognized him from a photo in Getty's office.

"Oh, yes. JLI." I put my job pressures out of my mind for the moment and shook John Lewis's hand energetically. "It's so nice to finally meet you. Randi speaks very highly of you. Please, sit down."

He did, looking oddly uncomfortable. Lewis cleared his throat, then pressed his lips together, obviously in some sort of pain. "Ms. Boyd, I really don't know how to make this easier, so I'm just going to say it. I've just learned that Randi has been under investigation by the FBI for the last two weeks."

"The FBI? Why?"

"She worked a number of map theft cases for JLI and became swept up in that world. Some maps in her care mysteriously disappeared. Others showed up on the open market." Lewis looked me in the eye. "Randi's one of my best investigators, and I consider her a friend, but it seems her passion for collecting maps has obviously crossed the line into obsession. The FBI believes she's been selling stolen maps."

I said nothing, my brain whirling around without actually going anywhere.

"Ms. Boyd, there have been a number of library thefts reported in the last few months, but the libraries have all done so quietly, requesting that the FBI keep a close hold on the information to avoid damaging their reputations. We've been working with a number of these libraries in conjunction with the FBI." Lewis checked a page in a small notebook like the one Randi used. "We've determined that one person has used four aliases to gain access to rare books and remove valuable maps with dental floss."

I nodded. "That's what Drummond used."

"The aliases are Woodes Rogers, Grace O'Malley, Bartholomew Roberts, and"—Lewis looked up—"and Edward Drummond."

"Clever. Those are all names of pirates."

"Based on security tapes, handwriting analysis and DNA taken from the page stubs, we believe the person successfully carrying off these four aliases is a woman."

Again, I nodded. "Thanks to another librarian watching our security DVD of Drummond, Randi and I also believe Drummond might be a woman. I suspect Lauren Gilmore, Benton's assistant. Randi didn't tell you because she's trying to protect her." My emotions were already in such a turmoil I could barely identify any of them, but a tiny stab of jealousy pricked me.

Lewis put down his notebook and placed both hands on his knees, as if to shore himself up. "Ms. Boyd, it wasn't Lauren Gilmore. The FBI brought both her and Benton in for questioning this morning, and while they'd been after the map, Lauren wasn't the one. Edward Drummond had agreed to sell the map, when he found it, to Benton. But here's the hard part." Lewis exhaled slowly. "The FBI believes, and I agree, that the map thief you know as Edward Drummond is really Randi Marx."

I moved my jaw, but nothing came out.

"I know this comes as a shock to you." Lewis's voice held a touch of pain. "None of us want to believe this of Randi, but it's true. When Marcus Getty called and asked my company to investigate your thefts, I assigned Randi without knowing of her obsession with the Farris map."

My mouth was so dry my lips stuck to my teeth. My head began to pound.

"Ms. Boyd, someone from my firm has been watching Randi's apartment for a few days, and he reported you left this morning at approximately one thirty a.m."

I suddenly felt so hot I feared I'd pass out. "Why isn't the FBI asking me these questions?"

"They will. But because I care about Randi, I'm trying to stay a step ahead of the FBI. Randi left approximately thirty minutes after you did, but my man lost her. Do you know where Randi is, or where she might have gone?"

I drank half of the bottle of water on my desk, then wiped my mouth. This could not be happening. "She told me she was on some sort of stakeout."

"I'm afraid there was no stakeout." Lewis leaned forward. "I want to get her help, Emma. I'm not out for blood here. I can't help her if I can't find her. We might be able to make some sort of deal with the FBI, but not unless I find her."

Anger began burning a hole in my heart. "Let's go to her apartment."

"I don't think that's a good—"

"Please." I needed to return to that apartment. Could last night have been just a dream? Dazed, I followed Lewis out to a waiting black sedan. I felt nothing. After I fastened my seat belt, I moved my fingers across my leg and still felt nothing, as if I were watching someone else touch my leg. I watched the city outside my window, seeing everything and recognizing nothing. Randi was Drummond? Impossible...and totally possible.

Lewis continued, even though I didn't want to hear anymore. "It was Lauren who helped Randi develop her disguises, then Randi broke off all ties with Lauren and Benton. But when Lauren sensed the FBI closing in, she called Randi late last night and tipped her off. She said she couldn't bear the thought of Randi in prison."

That should have hurt, but it didn't. My whole body felt thick and heavy, as if my bones had turned to concrete. When we arrived, I followed Lewis into the building, past the building manager who buzzed us in after Lewis flashed his badge, then up the stairs to 203. Two men in JLI jackets stood waiting for us. My heart pounded so furiously I thought I might scream. Was Randi inside? Did I want her to be?

Lewis knocked. "Randi, it's John." Obviously, he thought she might have returned.

No response. He knocked again.

Another apartment door opened and a fortysomething woman wearing round black-rimmed glasses peeked out. "You there. Are you Emma Boyd?"

Stunned, I could only nod.

The woman disappeared, then reappeared with a paper bag and a leashed Marley, who bounded toward me. "I'm Mary Gerritson. Thanks *so* much for returning my messages." She thrust the bag and leash into my hands. "She said I was supposed to get Marley to you, and I done that now. Don't really like dogs, although Marley's okay."

Lewis was at my side. "When did Randi leave Marley with you?"

"Middle of the night. Rudest thing I ever heard, waking your neighbor up at one thirty in the morning all sudden like."

Lewis swore softly. "Randi's left for good."

"I have a key. She gave it to me to help with Marley. I don't really like dogs, you know."

Lewis used the key to unlock Randi's door and we all stepped inside to escape Mary Gerritson's indignation. I released Marley, who ran with obvious relief to his nest on the sofa. He didn't lay down but instead sat upright, watching the strange men moving through his home.

I checked the end table. Both the librarian action figure and *Myths and Superstitions of the Sea* were gone. I collapsed onto the sofa. Randi had left every single map in her collection hanging on the walls. What did that mean?

"See anything missing?" Lewis asked.

"No." The action figure was personal, and suddenly too painful to even think about. In fact, when I returned to my office, I was going to throw mine away. Marley and I leaned into each other as Lewis and the others took photos, then began knocking on the walls, which made Marley jump, ears held out far from his head. I stroked his back and tried to reassure him it'd be all right. Could a dog tell if you were lying?

Confusion turned my insides into a mini cyclone. What should I do? I rested my cheek on the top of Marley's head. "Mr. Lewis?"

"Yes?" The man was at my side in about two steps.

"Is there a TV in the bedroom, or an MP3 player, or anything else that would use a remote?"

He returned one minute later. "None of the above."

I sighed, then stood, feeling drunk-tired, as if I hadn't slept in weeks. "Then there's a remote you need to know about."

The bedding was rumpled and soft, just as when I'd left it. I could still smell Randi's soap, faint but present. Nearly overwhelmed with images from the night before, I knelt on the bed, then reached behind the headboard and pulled off the remote. "I…I found this last night."

John Lewis kindly said nothing but just examined the remote.

"Let's try the remote in here." Two men were in Randi's large walk-in closet.

Lewis stepped inside the closet and clicked the remote. The entire closet wall swung open like a door, the clothes rustling on their hangers. Behind the original wall was another closet, with clothes and a dresser. Men's suits, women's dresses, four wigs, a flannel-covered board with moustaches and sideburns, and a make-up mirror. An artist's black portfolio leaned against the dresser, tagged with an orange sticky note that said, "Conrad Kline Library."

I gasped and looked over Lewis's shoulder as he opened it. "Those are the maps Drummond—" I stopped. "The maps Drummond stole from our library."

"Here's a note," said one of the men as he squeezed into the closet. He handed a white business envelope to Lewis. My head hurt when I saw *For Emma* written on it.

Lewis looked at me. "We're going to have to turn this all over to the FBI, but you may read it first." He sliced it open and handed me a letter.

I backed up until I reached the bed Randi and I had shared just hours ago, then sat. Hands trembling, I unfolded the two sheets and blinked rapidly.

Dear Emma,

I can't even begin to imagine what you're feeling at this moment, but the fact that you're reading this letter means John found the closet, my disguises, and your maps.

I have no defense to offer that wouldn't sound pathetic. I can't explain why my need to acquire maps is so strong that I'll steal to get them. You once said you thought my childhood was too competitive, but I'm not going to blame my early years for my weaknesses as an adult. I started collecting maps, and got so hooked I wanted to own the best maps and the most maps I could.

The Farris map consumed me more than all the others— the idea of a female pirate and what her life must have been like…the idea of all that treasure still hidden somewhere… the idea of going on the mother of all treasure hunts…the idea of finding the treasure and returning it to Peru.

For a brief shining moment I imagined we could go on that hunt together, and you'd never have to know of my past. But that proved to be utter fantasy. I suspect that my friend John (Hi, John, Happy Birthday, by the way) is fast closing in on the truth.

As for the rest of it, I'm so sorry that in a weak, selfish moment I let you in. I've been struggling since I met you to protect you from the truth, and from me. I'd succeeded until tonight. I wanted just one thing in my life to feel right, and it did…we did. I'm not sorry it happened, because remembering it will be all that I'll have of you. I'm sorry I hurt you.

For days I've been torn between two lives—the one I created when I became Drummond, and the one I wanted when I met you. The two can't exist together. For the first time in my life I've met a woman I want to spend more than one night with, a woman who takes my breath away every time she enters the room. Yet because of my stupidity, one night is all I can have. I know this is the last thing you want to hear, Emma Boyd, and I'm really, really sorry to say this now instead of last night, but I've fallen in love with you.

I stopped reading and cursed violently. John Lewis watched me, but said nothing.

My punishment is that I'll fall asleep every night alone, knowing the woman I love hates me. I can't stop now, Emma. I've lost so much in my search for this treasure, including you, and since the way back to my real life has been blocked by all I've done, I have no choice but to move forward.

I can't ask for your forgiveness. I can't ask you to understand. All I can ask—and do ask—is that you take good care of Marley. He doesn't deserve to suffer for my transgressions, and I know you love him well enough to make him happy. I can think of no better home for him than you. If John or the FBI track me down and I end up in prison, Marley will still need a home, so he's yours, no matter what happens.

Randi

No "best wishes." No "take care" or "hasta luego," "see you soon," or "sincerely." I handed the letter back to Lewis, then just sat there. All the lust, respect, curiosity, warmth, attraction, and yes, love, I'd felt for Randi Marx was escaping my body in a toxic purge. Replacing those emotions was a thick, empty darkness, a heaviness I couldn't name.

Lewis folded the letter and looked at me. "I'm sorry you were dragged into this. Do you have *any* idea where Randi has gone?"

Did Randi expect me to keep my mouth shut? What would happen if I gave John the information we'd decoded the night before? I stood, on fire. Whatever happened, it was Randi's responsibility. My job was to tell the truth. "If you want to find Randi, get yourself down to the Caribbean, over by Grenada. From the northern tip of Carriacou, which is at N twelve degrees, fifty-two minutes, seventeen seconds, run west at three knots for one bell." While John and the others hit their cells and began barking instructions, I returned to the living room and kissed Marley on his head. I would take good care of him.

But as I considered the framed maps around the apartment, all the shock and confusion of the last ninety minutes fell away and anger surged through me. I'd fallen in love with a fucking pirate. Well, fuck it. I'd fall out of love with that pirate. That shouldn't be too hard. Then I'd fan the flames of my newest passion—revenge—and hunt down Randi Marx.

PART NINE

THE HANGING, 1715

Faith is to believe what you do not see.

—St. Augustine

Chapter Twenty-nine

The raging West Indies storm was bad enough it could swallow ships whole and never spit them out. Within minutes of losing Rebekah over the side of the *Maravillosa*, Tommy watched helplessly as three more men were swept away. Enraged at her losses, Tommy ordered all men below, save the men at the helm. It now took three men to keep the ship heading into the waves, and three more clung to the railing ready to relieve them.

Tommy let the men continue their bucket brigade up from below, not because they were making a difference, but because staying busy kept the fear at bay. She surveyed what was left of the *Maravillosa* and knew she must face the truth. The Spanish galleon was not up to this fight.

She slid to the nearest hatch, digging her nails into the sodden edge of the opening. "Abandon ship!" she hollered down to the crew. The dozens of faces peering up at her flashed white in the lightning. "Grab a barrel or float, empty a chest. Grab anything that floats and abandon ship!"

Men passed the word and sailors swarmed up on deck. Tommy's heart stuck in her throat, for she knew the chances of surviving these seas clinging to a piece of wood were small, and if the storm didn't abate, or if another ship didn't pass by, anyone surviving a sinking would not live much beyond it.

"Abandon ship!" she yelled down another hatch. The men at the helm remained there, understanding they had to stay at their post until all others were off or everyone *would* die. Tommy dragged bits of broken mast up for each man at the tiller to cling to when he jumped.

"Help! Help!" A man's voice came from the bowsprit, so Tommy worked her way forward. One of her men had jumped over but had become tangled in the rigging under the bowsprit.

"Fool," Tommy muttered, but she pulled out her dagger and crawled out along the slippery, narrow beam, cutting off the rigging as she went. She had to stop twice and cling to the sprit as it and the figurehead below her plowed through another wave, but gasping and cursing, she'd almost succeeded in freeing the man when a scream rose from behind her.

"The rudder! We lost the bloody rudder!"

Tommy looked over her shoulder. The men spun the wheel frantically, but the ship wasn't responding. No rudder meant no hope.

With her last burst of strength, Tommy cut the rigging so the man dangling below her had some chance of escaping. Then from her spot at the very bow of the ship, she felt the entire *Maravillosa* swing around behind her, now parallel to the next deadly wave swelling beneath her.

She had failed to save Rebekah. She had failed to save the ship. Sawkins would have a watery grave after all.

She closed her eyes, heard the screams of her men as the ship began its death roll. The bowsprit snapped off and Tommy, still clinging to it, plunged into the sea.

❖

Time became meaningless in the darkness of the storm as Tommy clung to the bowsprit. For hours she paddled to keep herself perpendicular to each wave, but now and then gave up. She might have slept as she rode up a wave, then woke up for the ride down. Now and then she'd yell out in case one of her men floated nearby, but she heard no sound save the wailing of the wind. No cries for help, no men's voices, nothing. Being at the bow of the ship had saved Tommy because the bowsprit broke free before the ship rolled. The *Maravillosa* would have sunk so fast it was likely no one aboard, or in the water next to the ship, had survived.

She could no longer feel her arms and legs, yet somehow she stayed afloat. Delirious with exhaustion, at one point she imagined she'd meet Rebekah just over the next wave but felt a crushing despair at the crest to realize she was still all alone in the middle of a vast, angry sea. But then the waves diminished, the rain stopped, and Tommy relaxed, her face pressed against the wet wood, her legs floating in the water. Now that she no longer had to battle the storm, only one thought echoed through her mind: Rebekah was gone.

❖

When she awoke, the sea was calm, the sky blue, and the clothes on her back were dry and stiff with salt. Wincing, she pushed herself upright, dangling her legs down in the water, and looked around. No *Maravillosa*, no mysterious island. She thought she saw the peaks of an island to the east, possibly Carriacou, but the haze on the horizon always tricked the sight.

Tommy wiped her salty lips, desperate for a mug of ale or even a glass of brackish water. Something to drink, anything. Why in God's name was she still alive? Grief nearly tumbled her off the log. Rebekah was dead. And her men...Sawkins, Billy, Calabria. Tommy curled up in pain, resting her forehead on the bowsprit.

That was when she realized she rode the base of the bowsprit, complete with the ship's figurehead. The carved woman was as clear-eyed and defiant as the first time Tommy had seen her. Suddenly Tommy didn't feel quite so alone.

She began paddling east, resting on the figurehead's chest every thirty minutes or so. The loss of the silver meant nothing to her. The loss of her friends would ache for the rest of her life, which she measured in hours, not years. Had the storm been her punishment for lying with a woman? For fleeing from Shaw instead of standing up to him?

She paddled for hours, not from a desire to live, but for something to do. She lay face down on the bowsprit when darkness fell and somehow managed to stay on during the night. The next morning her paddling was the only sound in her head, broken by the occasional kerplunk from a jumping fish. Her breathing became so loud she didn't hear the ship until the first shout.

The words were French, then repeated in Dutch, then English. With effort, Tommy raised her head.

"Ahoy there!" came the call. "We save you."

A Dutch merchant ship approached from the north. Tommy waved weakly. Broken English, then shouting, then a longboat lowered and

Tommy was lifted into the boat and given fresh water, which had never, ever felt so wonderful sliding down her throat.

Moments later the men handed her up onto the ship. The human shapes were blurry around her, but there was no mistaking when the sailors standing over her were pushed aside by four women in wide, stiff skirts that swept over Tommy's legs and arms. The widest woman threw up her hands, clucking like a hen in her strange language, then barked orders in a high voice that resulted in Tommy being lifted and carried toward the officers' cabins.

Tommy spoke no Dutch, so she couldn't protest. Instead, she rolled her head to the side and watched as the merchant ship left the figurehead drifting alone on the sea.

Chapter Thirty

The captain's wife, the hefty woman with the high voice, adopted Tommy. Lotte had the sailors put Tommy on one of two narrow bunks in an officer's cabin, the other bunk being used by another woman. Lotte fed Tommy a bowl of tasty soup, washed the dirt and salt from her face, and used sign language and emphatic Dutch to try to get Tommy to change out of her salt-encrusted clothes into a brown gingham dress.

Able to stand now, Tommy had backed away, hands raised in horror. But she accepted the bunk and slept for two days. The morning of the third day, her skin itched so badly she thought she would go mad. Lotte knew a little English, so when Tommy asked if the captain had an extra pair of trousers, the woman giggled, then offered the dress again.

Tommy took it. She turned her back on Lotte, undressed, wiped the salt from her skin with a wet rag, then slid the layers of fabric over her head. Lotte buttoned the dress up the back, making happy sounds. The bodice was too large, the sleeves too tight, but the captain's wife acted as if she had a new doll, and Tommy let her. What difference did it make? Rebekah was dead. Sawkins and Billy were dead. Who cared if Tommy Farris wore a brown gingham dress?

Living on the Dutch merchant ship was sheer torture. Tommy wanted to sit on deck and remember those she had lost, but the four women—Lotte, her sister, and their two cousins—wouldn't let her. Day after day Lotte forced her to rise, dress, and join them in the wardroom where the women knitted. When the sister had offered a pair of needles and a skein of yarn to Tommy, she nearly began to cry. This wasn't the life she wanted, but neither was pirating.

Tommy watched the women working and listened to their voices, wondering about her attraction to Rebekah. She'd thought it'd been because she'd been starved for female companionship, and that it'd had nothing to do with Rebekah herself.

But as Tommy sat in the stuffy room, hour after hour, longing to be up on deck in command of the ship, she realized she'd been wrong. Female companionship wasn't what she'd needed, for after a few short days with these women, Tommy was ready to throw herself overboard. The women were all young, and Tommy supposed a man would consider them attractive, but she didn't find herself mesmerized by them as she'd been with Rebekah. She didn't yearn to sit near any of them. She didn't feel her breath catch in her throat when any of them smiled at her.

All she wanted was Rebekah. Stunned at her tears, Tommy wiped them away impatiently. The other women noticed, but only exchanged glances with each other.

The fourth day, after Lotte must have decided Tommy was strong enough, the captain sat her down and in halting English, asked her how she'd come to be drifting on a log in the eastern West Indies.

Tommy sighed. The truth would be unacceptable. "I was on a ship with my family when a storm swept me overboard."

He gazed at her with hard eyes, then nodded to her braid. "You'd be wise to cut your hair. I've heard talk of a fearful woman pirate with long black hair. It'd be a shame for you to be mistaken for her."

Tommy stared at him dully, then nodded. Without her own clothes, her pistols, and her cutlass, she apparently appeared so docile and domestic the thought never entered his head she might be that pirate. She thanked him for his concern but had no intention of cutting her hair.

After she'd been Lotte's dress-up doll for a week, at the end of a very long afternoon the captain appeared in the wardroom to announce they'd be taking on a pilot the next morning to sail them into Port Royal, Jamaica. Once they docked, the captain said with a small bow to Tommy, he and Lotte would help her find her family.

At his kind words, his wife looked up at him and her mouth grew softer, her eyes brighter, and she radiated something so powerful a lump formed in Tommy's throat. She saw in that woman's face what she had felt each time Rebekah had entered a room, or spoken to her, or touched her.

"Sweet Jesus," Tommy whispered. Could it be? Tommy Farris, the Devil's Shadow, in love? Tommy swallowed hard. She was in love with Rebekah Brown. The woman was dead, and Tommy was still in love with her. Tommy closed her eyes. Dear God. She'd wasted all that time, and Rebekah had gone to her watery grave thinking Tommy didn't want to acknowledge their feelings for one another.

Tommy put a hand over her pained heart and bent over her lap. How cruel she had been. How blind. She'd been too proud, or ignorant, to admit she'd fallen in love with a woman.

She sat back up and watched the women chattering. This was to be her punishment for her pride, for not finding a way to rescue Rebekah, for not finding a way to save her ship. A sick dullness spread through her. She sank into a melancholy that did not abate, no matter how hard Lotte tried to cheer her up by rebraiding her hair, then coiling it and pinning it to her head. She'd lost something she'd never find again.

The next morning the pilot came aboard, and Lotte dragged Tommy out on deck to watch the approach to Port Royal. Out of habit, Tommy watched the pilot's route into port, always a good idea if one needed to leave the port quickly, and without an official pilot. The women were excited, but a sick dread settled in Tommy's gut. As a pirate she'd learned to avoid major ports and keep to small coastal towns that were unguarded, so she hadn't set foot in Port Royal since she'd started pirating over five years ago.

The pilot knew the harbor well and brought them safely to the pier. Tommy had no idea what she would do next, and she didn't actually care. After she walked down the gangplank and stood on the dock, Lotte bustled up behind her and took her arm, steering them behind the captain as he began greeting men on the crowded pier.

Tommy's heart beat faster when they passed each group of men. Her blasted dress still felt foreign, but it offered some anonymity, and her hair was pinned up and covered by a ridiculous frilly cap. She averted her eyes from each group, instead gazing upon the ships.

Tommy stopped so suddenly Lotte lost her hold on Tommy's arm. The *Moon Shadow* lay at anchor just beyond the dock. Her ship! But she'd seen it in Shaw's fleet as he'd chased her. The ship's hull had been painted black and obviously renamed, since *Margaret* was now painted across the flat stern. She found the energy to stop a man they passed. "Pardon me, sir, but who be the captain of the *Margaret*?"

"Captain Fletcher, newly arrived in the West Indies," the man said.

Fletcher? Who the bloody hell was that? She whirled around to search the faces of the men on the dock behind her but recognized no one. In the press of crowds, a goat broke loose from its tether and a man chasing it nearly knocked Tommy over. Her cap fell off and her braid swung wildly. She grabbed the end and began stuffing it down the front of her dress, but it was too late.

A voice rose faintly above the noisy pier. "Call the guards! That woman there—she's Tommy Farris! She's that bloody pirate!"

Lotte's mouth formed a perfectly round *O* as Tommy clutched her hand. "Thank you for saving my life." Then Tommy dashed down the dock, turning a few times to see her accuser, but she recognized no one in the crowd of men chasing her.

The chase was over before it began, since the men thundering behind her drove her straight into the arms of the soldiers waiting at the end of the pier. Three guards grabbed her arms and held her firmly as she struggled to pull away. If she could only jump off the dock, she might lose them.

The voice came from behind her again. "I thank you, gentlemen, for your assistance. This pirate stole my ship, and I've just now recovered it. She's a vicious, evil scoundrel, and despite this dress, she's scarcely a woman at all."

Tommy twisted and bucked in the soldiers' grip. "Shaw, you thieving bastard. That's my ship." She heard no answer as the soldiers dragged her off the dock and up the hill to the stockade. Shaw didn't have the bulk of the silver—none of them did—but it burned to think he now claimed her beloved ship as his own. There was no doubt now that she must add poor Hatley to her list of dead crew.

All the fight drained out of Tommy as the soldiers announced they'd caught the Devil's Shadow. A British officer smirked as the soldiers threw her at his feet. She didn't even struggle as he stepped on her braid, forcing her cheek onto the hot stone. She'd been too selfish to return Rebekah's love, so she deserved whatever came next.

And for a pirate caught by the British, she knew exactly what that was.

CHAPTER THIRTY-ONE

The rock walls of the prison cell were gray with mold, which Tommy could smell more than see, since the only light came from a tiny square window high up on one wall. A man moaned in the cell next to her, but Tommy felt no fear. This was what she and Sawkins had always known: a pirate's short life ended one of three ways—at the bottom of the sea, at the tip of a cutlass, or at the end of a rope. Sawkins lay entombed in the *Maravillosa*, and she would soon be swinging in the breeze, dead of a broken neck.

Voices reached her from the hallway. "Father, I'm not supposed to let anyone see the prisoner."

"I'll only be a minute, my son. Stay nearby if you must. I merely need to confirm the prisoner's identity for the governor."

Soft lantern light swung into view and the guard unlocked the cell door. "Call me when you're ready, Father," the guard said, stepping back and closing the door behind the priest.

Tommy remained on her bench, waiting for the priest to join her as he held the lantern before him.

"Bit of a cock-up, eh, Tommy?"

"You could say that, McLurin."

"That's Father McLurin, my dear."

Tommy shrugged.

He sat next to her and lowered his voice. "I could lose my mission, and my life, if I'm found out, but there's no way I'm going to sit back and watch you hang."

She tipped her head toward him. "The governor has Captain Tommy Farris in a prison cell. He'll hold a trial, I'll be found guilty and hanged by my neck until dead. I be notorious enough that perhaps I'll be put in the cage to rot for all to see."

"No, Tommy, no." McLurin's whisper dropped even lower. "Here's what we'll do. First, I'll bring you new clothes. You look ridiculous in that dress."

"Not as ridiculous as I feel."

"In a few nights, there's to be a large celebration. I'll find a way to distract your guards and break you out before a trial can even be held."

Tommy considered her friend, his face drawn and sad in the warm lantern glow. "Sawkins, Billy, Calabria, Hatley...all dead."

"Damnation," McLurin muttered. "All the more reason to keep you alive. Once you're free—"

Tommy held up her hand. "I don't want to be seeming ungrateful, for I appreciate the risk you're willing to take, but I be going nowhere."

McLurin frowned. "I don't understand."

Tommy sighed, unsure she could explain it. "I've been a pirate for many years, and I've killed or tortured a fair number of people."

McLurin snorted. "Not all that many. You frightened more than you killed or tortured. But what of it?"

"I'm belonging in this prison, and at the end of a rope."

McLurin let loose a string of curses rarely uttered by men of God, then jabbed his forefinger in her face. "You belong at sea, in command of a ship."

She could have forgiven herself for all she'd ever done because she'd done it to survive, but to reject Rebekah because of who she was, now that was more than her heart could bear. "I deserve to die," she said. "There'll be no prison break."

McLurin banged the back of his head gently against the wall. "But this is something I can do. So many people have problems I can't help them with. Praying is what I'm supposed to do, but what good is that? Praying doesn't take away the pain. I have a parishioner, Mrs. Wingate, who's slowly, painfully dying. She keeps begging me to end her life but I can't do that. Her husband can't stand to watch her pain, so he drinks all night down at the docks. I can't do anything to help her. I have another parishioner who's lost his mind and thinks everyone is trying to kill him. I can't help him either. But I *can* help you."

"No."

"Is it true you have the treasure? Shaw will track you down and torture the location from you. Let me get you out before that happens."

"No. The treasure's at the bottom of the sea and will never be recovered, by Shaw or anyone else. It be lost to us all." She hugged herself. "I could use a coat or blanket, for this cell is dank, but that's all the help I will accept from you."

"Tommy, you can't be—"

"Heave your anchor and get underway, McLurin. Back to your post."

"Damn you for a bloody fool," McLurin snapped. Shaking his head, the pirate-turned-priest called for the guard, then the two men left her in semidarkness again. She'd meant every word she'd said. No one deserved to hang more than Tommy Farris.

CHAPTER THIRTY-TWO

The next footsteps marching down the passageway fell heavier than McLurin's. Tommy straightened, praying it was no one she knew, since this dress continued to humiliate her. The guard was accompanied by a man dressed like a gentleman, which Shaw had never been, even before he turned pirate.

"Thank you, guard. Please leave us now."

Tommy stood. "Wait, guard, don't you want to be letting this man into my cell so we can talk more clearly?"

Shaw waved the guard away, then turned to face her. "Believe me, you bilge-sucking cunt, you best keep those bars between us so I don't kill you."

When Tommy grinned her most feral grin, Shaw took a step back. "You'd be dead before your fat ass made it all the way into this cell." She grabbed the cold metal bars and rattled them in fury. "What the hell did you do to Hatley?"

"Bugger him. I'm the one asking the questions. You're gonna hang, Farris, make no mistake about that." Shaw's white shirt gleamed in the dim light and Tommy clawed through the bars to smear it with her grime, but he hopped back in time.

"I see you wasted no time in using the treasure I threw overboard," she snarled. "You'll never convince people you be a legitimate merchant. If I tell people who you really are, Shaw, you'll swing with me."

"They'll never believe the words of a pirate desperate to save her own skin. So here's the bargain. You tell me where the treasure is, and I'll see to it that McLeod and Stratton, those yeller bastards, get their shares."

"They made it through the battle?"

Shaw shrugged. "Guess I could throw you a few tidbits. Yeah, they did. We took the *Barcelona*, discovered her cargo, then tortured the captain until he confessed the treasure was on that stupid little galleon you'd been panting after, just like you pant after that slave whore."

Tommy struggled to control her fury. As long as Shaw stood out of her reach, her only weapon was her tongue. "And Stratton and McLeod?"

"The next day the scum and both their ships were gone. But I'll find 'em and give 'em their shares."

"Bollocks, Shaw. You'll find them and murder them." She inhaled deeply, forcing herself to calm down. "The treasure's lost, Shaw. The *Maravillosa* sank. As far as I know, I be the only survivor. She be at the bottom of the sea, filled to the rail with a treasure none will ever see again."

"Lying whore."

Tommy pressed her lips together.

"Okay, I'll change the deal. Tell me where it sank, and I'll talk to the magistrate. No hanging, just prison."

Why would she want to remain alive? Each day would remind her of the woman she'd lost. Tommy smiled. "I wouldn't tell you where the treasure was if you were the last man alive. I'd sooner have my eyes dug out and my nails ripped off and my guts unraveled than tell you one more friggin' word about the treasure."

Shaw howled in frustration. "You'll be sorry you didn't deal with me." Shaw whirled, but then turned back, suddenly pleading and begging with her to reveal where the ship went down. She turned her back on him and sat down against the far wall, eyes closed. Soon the asshole gave up and left, cursing her name in a steady stream as he walked the passageway.

The trial was held two days later. Tommy sat shackled at the front of the courtroom while the judge in a white powdered wig stood and thundered the list of Tommy's crimes. She could argue with none of them.

She had no doubt she'd be found guilty, but the last nail in the coffin was pounded in by the only witness, a pompous captain named Jeremiah Fletcher, who was the weevil-brained bastard Shaw hidden under the mustache and beard. He told an elaborate tale of how Tommy had stolen his ship last year and killed his men.

That was enough for the judge, who proclaimed Tommy guilty of piracy and murder. The sentence was death by hanging, to be carried out in the morning.

❖

Tommy shivered in the clammy cell, numb. Nearly everyone she cared about was dead, so it was fitting she join them. She just wished she could banish this fear quaking her bones. Was it a fear of death? A fear of being alone? She pulled the blanket McLurin had given her tight up under her chin and closed her eyes.

Father McLurin woke her up with a gentle shake. "Tommy, I'm here to give you absolution."

Tommy sat up but kept the blanket wrapped around her. Would she ever be warm again? Perhaps in Hell. "Absolution?" She looked to make sure the guard had left. "You be a pirate. Be that legal? Does the pope know?"

McLurin smiled sadly. "Retired pirate, and I'm all the town has right now. The other priests are too old or too dead." The faux priest sat down next to her, his black book on his lap. "I've been sent to hear your confession, should you be ready to release your soul from its burden of guilt."

What guilt? The guilt of all the men she'd killed, or the guilt over Rebekah? Tommy briefly considered telling McLurin about Rebekah. She opened her mouth, then closed it again.

McLurin patted her knee. "Come, my child, confess."

"Damn your eyes," Tommy muttered, and McLurin laughed.

"I know, I make a terrible priest. But people do confess amazing things when they're about to die, things I'm not supposed to repeat." His eyes twinkled in the dim light from the window. "They tell me about women, about cheating, about their dreams and nightmares. One old man spent his last breaths telling me of an island that no one else could see but him. He went on and on about this beautiful island until I nearly smothered him myself."

Tommy snickered. "Sawkins and Billy did the same thing last year, and this year they got drunk and be seeing it again. They were so sure it was there they even had me believing it. The night my ship sank, Sawkins saw it again."

Silence settled over them until McLurin sighed. "Sawkins and

Billy. Now there were two mighty fine sailors. And the poor sots were head over heels for you, I'm afraid."

"Billy was, I know. Sawkins was my friend."

"He loved you something fierce."

"To the devil with you for lying."

"Not about this. One was too old for you, and the other too young, and both knew you'd never have 'em, but they loved you anyway." Tommy didn't know what to say. "And it was odd. The dying old man loved his wife but was afraid she didn't love him because she wouldn't admit to seeing the island. He kept quoting Shakespeare. What was it? 'Go to your bosom; Knock there and ask your heart what it doth know.'"

Tommy straightened. Sawkins and Billy loved her, and they saw an island. At the height of the storm, Sawkins said Rebekah was paddling for the island, so Rebekah must have seen it too. All three loved her, yet she hadn't, knowingly, returned that love. *Ask your heart what it doth know.*

No, this couldn't be, could it? Had Sawkins been right, that there really was an island, and Rebekah had been heading straight for it? She'd sailed the West Indies long enough to have witnessed any number of strange occurrences.

Tommy jumped to her feet, startling McLurin. Could Rebekah still be alive, stranded on that island? And more importantly, would Tommy be able to find the island, and see it? "I'm needing a map of the West Indies."

McLurin opened the black book, flipping through the pages.

"The Bible has a map of the West Indies?"

McLurin grinned. "This is a copy of Dampier's book. Thanks for recommending it, by the way. I was going to sit here reading while you thought about your sins. Here's a map."

Tommy bent over the book. "Did the old man say where he saw the island?"

McLurin's finger went to the eastern edge of the sea. "Somewhere around here, along these islands. But there's no island out here on the map."

Hope started the blood racing through Tommy's body. "That's where we were sailing all three times Sawkins saw the island." She looked him in the eye. "I be changing my mind. I want to escape."

McLurin stared at her for a full five seconds. "By Satan's bones," he snapped. "Last week you were just someone in a jail cell, but now you're a convicted criminal. Do you know what would happen to me?"

Tommy waited.

"Blast my eyes," he muttered then looked up and laughed. "I hate you for this, but I'm so glad the Tommy Farris I know is back. I'll free you tonight. Don't go anywhere." They both laughed at that, and McLurin left.

While she waited, Tommy paced and paced, her terror so great she often had to lean against the wall, imagining it to be the *Moon Shadow*'s bulkhead, and remind herself to breathe. If there was any chance Rebekah were still alive, and Tommy couldn't reach her, but instead died at the end of a noose… Tommy yanked on her braid until it hurt.

Hours passed and still McLurin didn't return. Tommy sat on her bench, gripping her knees. She had to get out. She had to. Still McLurin didn't come.

She stretched out on the bench and rested, eyes closed, until she slept. The next time she opened her eyes, thin daylight lightened the far wall. Tommy fought against the despair rising in her, and sat up. She inhaled slowly to steady herself, then with each inhalation and exhalation, she listened to Rebekah's voice: *Dum spiro, spero.* While I breathe, I hope.

A door clattered open at the end of the hallway, and Tommy stood. Was it McLurin, or was it the guard?

If it was McLurin, Tommy would escape this cell, deal with Shaw, reclaim the *Moon Shadow*, then sail for the eastern edge of the West Indies. She'd find that island and Rebekah would be there, alive and well, waiting for her. Tommy would fall to her knees, beg Rebekah's forgiveness for not having the courage to love her. Rebekah would lift her up, take her in her arms, and never let go.

But if it was to be the guards coming to lead her up onto the scaffolding she knew was just outside, she would go to her death holding her head high. For a shining moment in her hard life, she'd known what it was to love and to be loved. Neither Shaw nor the hangman's noose could take that from her.

As footsteps approached, Tommy approached the bars of her cell. *Dum spiro, spero. Dum spiro, spero.*

PART TEN

THE PUZZLE

Puzzles can be solved…but a mystery offers no such comfort.

—Gregory Treverton

Chapter Thirty-three

The odd thing about a heavy workload is that when it's doubled, you just put your head down, and like oxen hitched to a plow, you pull and pull to get through the day. I'd become an ox, pulling myself through every day at the Kline Library. We cut our hours, laid off staff, cut cleaning staff and computer updates and even intracampus mail. Over the next two months I must have lost five pounds running mail to the different buildings.

The sad part was the books. We didn't have the staff to keep up with the backlog of treasures being donated as the relatives of elderly people cleaned out attics and bookshelves and donated. Much of what came in was of little value, or beyond rescue, but some of it was priceless. Yet all of it sat in boxes, uncatalogued and uncared for, and soon our storerooms looked like the St. Louis Chapman Library's rooms. I soon became inured to boxes overflowing with books being piled everywhere…along the hallway, into the staff break room, bathroom, and along the edges of all our offices. We finally had to start throwing them away for lack of space.

I know everyone was hit hard by the budget cuts. The athletic department had to cut almost all intramural sports. But our books? They were a piece of the past we couldn't recover once they were gone. It broke my heart, but since it had already been broken two months before, I didn't really feel much of anything. I called my parents like a dutiful child, but told them nothing. Sometimes I cried bitter tears at night and missed my GeeGeeBee more than ever. I could have talked to her and told her everything and she would have made me fresh cookies and helped me forget.

I worked like a robot, moving through the day, talking to people, eating, keeping myself alive. I often slept on a padded bench in the reading room. I knew I appeared perfectly normal to everyone else because I checked my appearance in the mirror several times a day. The face staring back at me was calm, impassive, and a bit cold around the eyes. I couldn't see on my face what I felt inside.

Inside, I went from raging pain and anger to hopelessness, and then to feeling nothing. Those days I'd spent with Randi, talking about Drummond, looking for the map so "he" wouldn't find it first, and here Drummond had been right by my side the whole fucking time. Randi had probably e-mailed me as Drummond while sitting beside me in a restaurant, or in a library.

A sick wave of heat passed through me when I remembered our night together. What kind of monster could live such separate lives? Had it been easy for Randi to lie to me? It must have been, for she'd done it so well. I'd never had *any* inkling that Randi had it within her to conduct Drummond's massive stealing campaign, or that she'd be devious enough to actually maintain and use so many different identities.

The FBI had checked out the location Randi had come up with, but had found nothing, just open water. They'd doubled the speed from three knots to six, doubled the time from thirty minutes to an hour, and still nothing. None of the aliases Randi had developed had been used to leave the country, so Lewis suspected she had another set of fake IDs he didn't know about. Two severe men from the FBI spent hours grilling me about Randi, but all I could tell them was what I'd already told John Lewis.

The FBI guys called me once a week for a month, but then their interest in the case faded as they struggled with their own budget cuts, and more serious cases like murder and kidnapping. At least Randi hadn't hurt anyone physically, if you didn't count my broken heart, which no longer beat normally but just sort of coughed along like an old Buick with a bad muffler.

Only one thing these last two months had gone right. I grabbed a stack of books and took them to the circulation desk where Marley sat on his wide stool, watching the action with great interest. When Claire brought out a book from the back stacks for a patron, Marley wagged his pom pom tail and went into action. He picked up a new security wristband from the pile in front of him, ran it across the monitor set into the counter until it beeped, then sat back down, eyes bright with pride.

Claire traded him a dog biscuit for the wristband, and all involved were content. Then Claire put the wristband on the patron and escorted him into the reading room. At the same time we'd cut staff and cleaning and everything else, we installed a security system. Luckily the company had been willing to extend credit.

Marley had started out as a dutiful behind-the-desk mascot, but once Sam, Claire, and the others taught him his job, the dog couldn't wait to come to work. I told myself it was because Marley loved all the activity, not because he scanned the face of every person who passed him, hoping to see one particular face.

"Claire, was that a whole biscuit?"

"Sorry, I forgot." She gave Marley a hug. "There's just more of you to love, right?"

I scowled. "About ten pounds more, thanks to those dog biscuits." I opened the dog gate and snapped on Marley's leash. "Let's go work off some of your salary, Security Dog."

We'd just started across the bridge to the East Bank when someone called my name. I didn't need to turn around to know it was Maggie. Sighing, I pulled Marley to a stop. Maggie caught up with us, gasping for breath, her short hair plastered to her forehead.

"Shit, girl, don't ever make me run like that again. I'm gonna have them put on my gravestone that you were the cause of my heart attack. Is this the guy who's been taking up all your time?"

I introduced Marley, who jumped up on Maggie, licked her chin, then dropped down and stuck his nose in her crotch. She laughed good-naturedly.

"We can't go into the student union because of Marley, but we can sit and talk, and that's what we're gonna do, girl." She hauled me back off the bridge and toward a small plaza with a scattering of black iron tables. Massive potted trees sprinkled cooling shade across the table Maggie chose. Bikers streamed by, obediently following the bike lanes and arrows, moving so fast it made me dizzy. "You don't answer my calls or my e-mails. Cam says you're doing the same thing to him. Frankly, I'm sick of it. Spill it, and I mean now."

I sighed, rubbed Marley behind his ears in just the right spot to make him moan softly and lean toward me. I didn't want to talk about it. Why relive it? I shook my head, opened my mouth, and suddenly spilled it.

Fifteen minutes later Maggie took my hand and gently squeezed. "Well, that's one I haven't heard before. You're pissed at Randi, right?"

I laughed without feeling it. "Pissed isn't the word. If she were standing right here in front of me and I was armed with a weapon, I think I'd use it."

Maggie narrowed her eyes. "Really."

"Really." Two skateboarders rattled down the ramp behind us. That was what I wanted to do—skate away from my life.

"But it sounds as if Randi tried to warn you every step of the way, saying she was bad for you, and you didn't know the whole story, and that you'd regret everything. Yet you kept pushing."

I stiffened. "Wait a minute. You think I'm to blame?"

"Just asking a question, honey. Why didn't you stop when she warned you off?"

"Because I couldn't!"

"Aren't you the woman who's in control?"

"Yes, but—"

"Yet you go and fall head over heels in love with a woman who comes right out and warns you about herself."

"I shouldn't have let it happen. I shouldn't have been so weak."

"Honey, love just happens. Our poor, lonely hearts don't know if a person is honest or dependable or picks up his or her socks. Our hearts only know that person touches something inside us, that the person makes us feel bigger than who we are, more complete, happier, and less alone in the world. Love's a good thing, Emma, not a bad thing."

My insides clenched. "It's a bad thing when you fall for the wrong person."

"Who's to say someone is wrong or right? People are made up of good and bad, and you can't fall in love with parts of a person. You fall in love with the whole person and have to take the good with the bad. Love just is, okay?"

Now that Marley had fallen asleep at my feet, I slipped off my sandal and ran a toe along Marley's back. His fur was so soft. "You think I should forgive her."

"No, honey, I think you should forgive yourself. And you should stop blaming Randi. You went after her like a bitch dog in heat, girl, and you had an incredible night. I'm guessing for the first time in your life, you know what it feels like to really love someone. Isn't that a good thing?"

I swallowed hard and wiped my eyes, surprised and embarrassed. "Not if you're never going to see that person again, or if you do, you hope to see them behind bars."

"That's really what you want?"

"More than anything." Actually, my feelings for Randi were so mixed up I still felt nauseous when I thought of her, but imagining Randi behind bars helped focus my emotions so I didn't feel so confused. "But we can't find her. I'm frustrated and feel helpless."

Maggie gathered up her shoulder bag. "You need a project, girl, something outside of work to get your mind off Randi. Isn't there something else you want to worry about?"

I stood, clucking softly for Marley to wake up. "I still don't know what happened to the pirate. Tommy Farris could have been hanged or she could have died at sea, and that continues to eat at me. I feel as if someone began telling me a bedtime story, got almost to the end, then patted me on the head and turned out the light. Not knowing how the story ends keeps me up at night."

Maggie hugged me. "So find out. You're a research whiz. Finish that bedtime story, and find out if it has a happy ending or a sad one. At least then you'll know. Gotta go now."

Marley and I strolled back to the library, my mind whirling with Maggie's suggestion. Yes, that was what I needed: a project. Randi had been, for obvious reasons, only interested in the map, but I could find out what had happened to Captain Thomasina Farris. I had no time for something like that, but it was my life and I had to take a least a little part of it back. Of course, every minute I spent researching the pirate Tommy Farris was a minute I'd spend thinking about the other pirate in my life.

CHAPTER THIRTY-FOUR

I carved out a few minutes every day to work on my new project and made a list of everything I knew about Tommy Farris.

- Her ship was the *Moon Shadow*
- Her crew included Ezekiel Sawkins, Billy Flood, Daniel McLurin, and Miguel Calabria
- She was part of a pirate gang that attacked the Spanish silver fleet, and the *Maravillosa* disappeared after the attack
- The *Moon Shadow* disappeared around that same time
- Tommy was arrested in Port Royal on July 15, 1715
- Or Tommy drowned when her ship went down on July 6, 1715
- Shaw hated Tommy
- Tommy might have been in love with Rebekah Brown
- Rebekah Brown dressed as a man and sailed the West Indies looking for someone, or something.
- Tommy made a map to something that appears to be a few miles off the western coast of Carriacou. That map could be a treasure, a place, or a person.

Randi's boss John Lewis and I talked once a week. He worked hard to keep me in the loop, reporting leads, like the man who thought he'd seen Randi in Jamaica, but that had proved to be a dead end. Talking to John was a weird way to stay connected to Randi and keep my anger fresh. It did occur to me to wonder, in the middle of a horrible day or at night when I couldn't sleep, what my life would have been like if I'd taken Randi up on her suggestion to run away to the Caribbean. We'd have been together, I wouldn't have been stuck in this hellish job, and I'd never have found out Randi had been stealing maps as Drummond.

One Friday I took sick leave and flew to Cincinnati to visit Eleanor Levinsen, the librarian who collected pirate material, leaving Marley with Claire, who agreed to stay with him 24/7. Eleanor was once again gracious and helpful, even though we'd temporarily stolen the Brown log book from her. Of that, she said nothing, but just took me back to the same pirate storeroom, then wheeled in the same four boxes of material I'd looked through before. "I still haven't had time to catalogue these yet."

Without Randi there to bug me about spending time away from the map search—of course she'd been hell-bent on the map, since she was Drummond—I spent many glorious hours burrowing through the librarian's collection of pirate material, and read all of Shaw's letters. But the only mentions of Tommy were in rants about how she'd stolen from him, and his family would avenge this evil deed. Shaw exhorted his mother to let all his brothers know Farris had stolen from them all, because he'd been planning to share the silver with his entire family. Yeah, right. But the letters were worded so earnestly that I could see the family growing to hate Tommy as much as Shaw did.

Then I attacked the McLurin materials, making a list of the items to help Eleanor. The work was tedious. I looked at every item that had been connected in any way to Danny McLurin, and at the bottom of one box found the four thin journals he'd kept. I hadn't spent much time reading them before, but since Randi wasn't here nagging about the map, I leaned back, propped my feet up on another chair, and began reading.

Early in the first journal, McLurin wrote about "starting my mission with monies graciously donated by my dear friend TF." That little tidbit kept me glued to the journals for the next six hours, taking breaks only to pee and stuff a candy bar in my mouth.

But I didn't find anything directly relating to Tommy until the last page of the last journal, and a small, yellowed envelope fell out. I picked up the fragile paper between my gloved fingers and noted with amazement that while it was addressed to Father McLurin, it had never been opened, for the wax seal hadn't been broken. There was no return address.

I worried my lip. What to do, what to do. I should really show the envelope to Eleanor and let her decide if we should open it. But as I turned the envelope over, the seal moved, so dried out it'd separated from the envelope. A person could open and read the contents without ruining the seal.

I pressed the opposite edges of the envelope together—and oh, look at that—the letter fell out. I might as well read it. Gently, I opened the folded sheets. I brought the letter closer to read the fine, spidery handwriting, then exclaimed when I realized who'd written it. The signature at the bottom of the second page confirmed it. But the date? How could that be? Still, joy buoyed me up and I thought I might float away. Instead, in the employee workroom I carefully photocopied the letter, then returned it to the envelope and the box from which it came.

There was one more item I hadn't yet looked at, a long, flat Moroccan inlay box, so I undid the thin clasp and opened the box. What rested inside set my heart pounding so loudly I was sure Eleanor would come running. "Holy mother of God," I breathed. "This doesn't belong in a library." Now that I'd found the letter in McLurin's journal, I knew where the contents of the Moroccan box belonged. But it would sound too crazy if I tried to explain it to the librarian. If I'd been Eleanor and someone had come to me with a story about pirates and treasure and maps and needing to take the contents of this box back where they belonged, I'd think the person was crazy.

I stared at the box. I needed to return the contents to their rightful owner. Taking it was wrong, but it hadn't yet been catalogued and no one would miss it. This box had no value to anyone. Sometimes rules needed to be broken. For Tommy's sake, and hers alone, I'd break this rule. I stuffed the box into my backpack, cursing Randi the whole time. Would I have ever done something like this before knowing her?

I now had nearly every piece to the puzzle that was Tommy Farris's life. I knew what had happened. I knew *when* it had happened. All I needed to know was where. Only the map could yield that, but it hadn't…at least not yet.

Chapter Thirty-five

Back at work the next week, I burned with the desire to solve the mystery of the map. I called John and bugged him. "Are you sure your people checked the right coordinates? Could they have gotten them wrong?"

"Sorry, Emma. Even when following the decoded message in a sailboat traveling at three knots for thirty minutes, they found nothing. They also did a search by air, but no islands."

After another tense meeting with Getty to discuss how to continue cutting costs that had already been cut in half, I stomped back to my desk. God, I'd come to hate my boss, my job, my fuckin' life. And then I found my desk piled high with the day's mail. At least Marley was content to curl up on the fleece dog bed in the corner while I sorted through the mess. The last was a large manila envelope. I squinted at the foreign stamps. Grenada.

I shuddered. No, don't be ridiculous.

The cancellation was smeared, but I hadn't misread it: Grenada. And the address was in Randi's handwriting.

I dropped the envelope. I picked it back up. I dropped it again. Shit. I picked it up again and shook it, surprised at a slight rattle. Hmmm. Either what was inside had broken or had been in pieces to start with. Finally I ripped open the end and pulled out a quart-size Ziploc bag.

Puzzle pieces. Brilliant.

I called John Lewis. "John, it's Emma. I think Randi wants us to put a puzzle together."

"Finally. I knew she'd break eventually. I'll be there in twenty minutes."

A shiver of excitement passed down my arms. While I waited, I imagined the final confrontation with Randi. She would be handcuffed, head hanging in shame. I would ask for five minutes alone with her, during which I would cut her to shreds with my words. Or I'd kiss her until she passed out. Damn it. I wished I'd known that falling out of love with a pirate was so hard.

John Lewis finally arrived. I'd spent so much time with him, he felt like an old friend. He sighed. "Okay," he said, "open 'er up."

I dumped out what amounted to about three fistfuls of pieces and began sorting through them. "Sky, sky, vegetation…hmm, water?"

"What's on the back?"

I flipped a piece over. "Writing, probably an ultra fine black Sharpie." I clenched my teeth. The last thing I wanted to read was some gloating note from Randi. I started putting the puzzle together, motioning for John to pull up his chair and help.

"Let's start with the edges first to see what we have." I began pulling out sky pieces with straight edges.

"You sleeping any better?" John asked as he found a match for the piece in his hand.

"Doctor gave me some sleeping pills." I lined up five pieces of edge. All the pieces were cut into odd shapes, not like modern puzzles. My pulse quickened. The pieces were old and dry. We talked about nothing in particular until I found a home for the last piece and sat back. "Well, we seem to have the entire right side of a smallish puzzle, perhaps twelve by eighteen inches. In the background there's sky, then part of an open trunk, two bags sitting next to the trunk, then sand. This seems to be the left side of a person, probably a woman, with her arm up, dripping with jewels." I stopped. "Hmm."

"Let's see the back."

I broke the puzzle into two pieces and turned them over. "You reconnect them."

"Don't you want to read this?"

"God, no. I have no intention of reading it, ever."

"It starts 'Dear Emma.'"

"Tough. Not interested."

He scanned it quietly. "Nothing here about location, but there are many intriguing partial lines, like 'finally found the treasure and…'" He shook his head. "This note won't make sense until we have the whole puzzle, which I'm assuming Randi will provide. The handwriting is very dense—must be a long note."

I flipped the pieces over again and stared at the puzzle. "This looks vaguely familiar. Wait a minute!" I swore, reached for my laptop, and Googled Edward Eggleston's *Treasure Princess*. A tiny spark of excitement flamed inside, but I tamped it down immediately. "This might be an old puzzle I've been looking for."

"Sounds like Randi. She wouldn't send you a note on just any old puzzle." We compared the image on my screen with the puzzle. "This slice of red is her shorts, then this is her thigh, and then her boots topped with red leather."

Yes, it had to be *Treasure Princess*. Now I had three reasons to make sure Randi ended up in jail. One was for stealing my library's maps. Two was for breaking my heart. Three was for defacing the back of a very rare puzzle with a goddamned Sharpie.

CHAPTER THIRTY-SIX

The second bag of puzzle pieces came two days later, and John and I played out a repeat of the first bag. After piecing together this bag, we now had the left third of the puzzle, showing sky, a small masted ship, and two men carrying a trunk through the surf. John read the back of the new section. "Our Randi is one clever girl. She says—"

"I don't want to hear it. We'll finish this puzzle, and if she's given away any clues about where she might be, you'll go find her."

John motioned to the puzzle. "From this note so far, telling us exactly where she is seems to be the whole point."

I snorted and put the puzzle on top of my file cabinet. Out of sight, out of mind.

Every day I waited anxiously for the mail. One, two, three days— nothing. I hated Randi for tormenting me like this. The only kind of torment I wanted from Randi was—No, not that. I flushed at the memory of a naked Randi Marx moaning desperately beneath me, then squeezed my eyes shut. I so didn't need this shit.

I began to wonder if Randi was having second thoughts about disclosing her location, but then a third envelope came and I paced my office waiting for John.

"Okay," he said, striding in. "Let's see if she's going to finish this today."

I spilled out the pieces, and it didn't take us long to construct a fetching woman with the face of an angel in a white blouse and red shorts, cutlass strapped to her side. John handed me the last piece. "Here, you do it."

Struggling with a mix of emotions I couldn't even begin to identify, I finished the puzzle, then flipped it over for John to read while I stared out my window.

"This is the smartest thing Randi's done in months." He rotated the puzzle back toward me. "You need to read this."

"No."

"Emma, read it."

"I don't care if she's turning herself in or—"

"Read it." Easygoing John disappeared, and the private investigator took his place.

Exhaling loudly, I looked down.

Dear Emma,

It's taken me weeks, but I found the treasure referred to on Tommy's map. I should feel ecstatic and satisfied, but I feel neither.

It wasn't worth it, Emma. I see that now. My true quest ended the day I met you. You're what I needed in my life. You were my treasure, and I couldn't even see that.

My jaw tightened. Too late. Too fuckin' late.

Because you're not here, there's no reason to remain where I am, so I'm ready to turn myself in. I've committed a crime—a number of them actually—and must pay the price. At least I'll be in the same country, and hopefully the same state, so we'll be breathing the same air. Sounds pathetic, I know, but that's how desperate I am for you. I'm sure you hate me, so I won't be some sort of weirdo who keeps writing you letters from prison, but my life made sense for the first time in years when I was with you. I'm going to hang on to that, and start from there.

But first, I want you to see what I've found, so here's what needs to happen. You and John fly to Grenada, catch a boat to Carriacou, and meet me at these GPS coordinates. N 12.52.17, -61.51.14. Here's yet another reason to hate me: In my apartment just after I broke the code, I altered the information in case you didn't want to go with me, or reported me to John or the FBI. I also altered the Farris map itself before photocopying it at the library. I wanted to be the only one to find the island.

Bring Marley—he should be fine in his crate as long as you stay with him. I suspect you'll need him—he's the only one who can lead you to me. And remember Shakespeare's line. That's the key.

Love,
Randi

PS. I'm serious. You must bring Marley or you likely won't find me.

P.S.S. Don't talk to anyone but John, and keep your eyes open for a three-masted sailboat called Shaw's Revenge. *It's been hanging around the island.*

Steam poured out my ears. "She gave me the wrong coordinates from the beginning. No wonder the FBI couldn't find anything." I cursed in my head, ashamed and embarrassed and madder than hell.

John checked his notebook. "I think these GPS coordinates are much farther west than the location you gave us two months ago."

I keyed them into a Web site and pressed Enter. "Fifteen miles off Carriacou. No way could Tommy have reached that spot sailing at three knots for thirty minutes. Randi messed with the speed and time."

John shrugged. "What the hell. Let's follow the lead. The company will pay for this, since we stopped charging the library the day Randi disappeared. I think, though, that we'll have to leave Marley at home, no matter what Randi says. Maybe she's just lonely for him. But traveling that far, to a foreign country, with a dog?"

We discussed all our options, and I did some online research. "The best flight," I said, "is an American Airlines flight that leaves Minneapolis at six a.m., flies to Chicago, then to San Juan, Puerto Rico. After an afternoon layover, there's a flight to Grenada. That's as close as we can get to Carriacou."

John threw up his hands. "I hired Randi, I trusted her, I assigned her to this case. I want to help her and at the same time I want to protect the reputation of my firm. If it gets around that JLI investigators are crooked, well, there goes my business." John picked up his phone. "I'm going to charter a plane. Let's just get this done." He rubbed his eyes.

"Sometimes I wish Randi hadn't been my favorite employee. Let's go bring her in."

The next morning, bleary-eyed but keyed up, I arrived at the small charter airport at eight a.m. with Marley and his kennel. John met us at the front gate, and he was accompanied by two very large men who didn't smile and were painfully polite, calling me "ma'am" as they helped us find a trolley for Marley's kennel.

"So," I asked John, "are these Spy Guys coming with us?"

John smiled, a wide grin that was hard to resist. "That they are."

"You don't think Randi's dangerous, do you?" I sneaked another look at the two silent mountains.

"No, but things will go more smoothly if Rick and Mike are along."

Chartering a private jet was definitely the way to go, but I shuddered to think what it cost John. With twenty seats but only four of us and a dog, we had plenty of room, although the ceiling was low and I felt as if we were flying inside a cigar. Marley rested happily in his crate next to me, and when the attendant wasn't fussing over us with drinks and snacks, I let Marley run up and down the short aisle, trusting his training to keep him from messing.

Midafternoon we stopped in San Juan to refuel. One of the Spy Guys wheeled Marley's crate across the tarmac and I let him out on a leash. We spent an hour in the shade of a small tree at the front of the airport, and I couldn't believe I was actually here, in the Caribbean, just where I'd hoped the Republican National Committee would send me for converting Mari and Julia, yet I hadn't converted any women to heterosexuality for months. I had fallen in love with a thief, but other than that...

I lay back on the spiky grass and watched the sky as a warm breeze ruffled my shirt and puffed Marley's ears out like wings. Even the clouds here looked tropical, lighter, more exotic. And the air smelled hot with exotic scents I couldn't identify. I didn't travel much, but when I did, I marveled that the air smelled and tasted so different.

After a short flight over startling blue water, we landed in St. George's, Grenada. The officials in their pressed white uniforms huddled over the vet certificate I'd gotten from a veterinarian friend who'd come over and examined Marley late the night before, but eventually they accepted it.

The Spy Guys showed up with a black SUV and drove us through the soft dusk to a modest white house that rented rooms. I was so tired all I could do was feed Marley, then collapse. As I lay on the lumpy futon, Marley snoring happily at my side, it felt almost like an adventure, not like a manhunt. The filmy curtains, bright yellow and orange, billowed into my room like a woman's sheer dress.

The next morning we awoke to the sensory assault called Grenada. Noisy traffic. Men whizzing by on very old bicycles. Women selling from stands in the central market under red striped umbrellas—fruit, guava jelly, coconuts, flowers. Nutmeg was everywhere. "We make one-third de world's nutmeg," the minibus driver shouted over his noisy engine. Instead of cabs, people moved around in minibuses with names. Ours was called *Hang On*, and the man meant it. I wished I could have wandered through the market looking for treasures, much as Randi and I had wandered through the antique stores in Pittsburgh.

Hang On finally ended his brief tour by bringing us to the docks. "I help you find boat to Carriacou. My uncle, he has de best boat in de world."

The uncle's cargo boat was loaded down with crates covered in tarps, but there was room for the four of us to stagger on board with our luggage and Marley. I watched Marley closely as the pilot gunned the engine and took us out into the sea. Did dogs get seasick?

We sat on a tarp along the side, close enough that mist from the boat's spray settled on my upturned face. God, this felt good.

When the boat began to buck some major waves, I caught the pilot's eye. "Waves kick like de mule, no?" The sun-wrinkled man smiled, his lower teeth missing. "We going over underwater volcano."

John and I exchanged alarmed glances. Holy smokes.

We finally motored into the port of Hillsborough, a neat, low set of buildings with dozens of moored sailboats, the only real town on Carriacou. We boarded yet another minibus and were taken to a long row of narrow metal buildings. John explained these dorm rooms were originally meant for marine biologists, but now served as a hotel. The thin wooden walls and flat, creaking metal roofs were unlike those of any hotel in which I'd stayed, but the early garage sale decor was oddly charming. After a lunch of chicken and turtle soup, John looked at his watch. "Rick and Mike are chartering a boat for us. Let's walk down to the docks."

My heart began thudding loudly in my ears. We were close to finding Randi, and I was possibly close to solving the mystery of Tommy Farris's life and death. I tugged on Marley's leash, which had become necessary with all the chickens running around the island, then shifted my backpack. Everything I needed was in the pack.

On our brisk walk we passed ambling donkeys in the street and front yards planted with corn. When we reached the marina, I walked Marley up and down one pier, marveling at the money that must be floating at each mooring. Sleek three-masted sailboats with pristine sail covers, wide yachts with cabins that towered over the dock. One whole section, however, was nothing but small fishing boats that had shed their paint long ago, with the occasional sailboat with faded mahogany trim and a battered U.S. flag flying from the mast.

Despite our reason for being here, I soaked up the sun, the smells of fish and saltwater and diesel fuel, and the musical language spoken all around me. A breeze off the water felt good against my bare arms.

John called from the far pier. When I reached them, John helped me into the trawler, a sturdy boat with dirty white sides and a large deckhouse. Marley leapt down into the boat as if he'd been born to it, then began barking at the Spy Guys, already on board, as if he'd never seen them before.

"Marley, quiet. Matthew has agreed to take us out," John said.

I shook the shy man's rough hand, taking in his baggy pants and John Lennon T-shirt. "We'll be having de most pleasant voyage, missy, don't you worry."

As John gave Matthew the coordinates, I stowed my backpack, then settled against a blue cushion. My pulse quickened when the powerful engines beneath my feet rumbled and coughed. This was it. An hour boat ride, and this would all be over. With Randi Marx behind bars, perhaps I could get on with my life, hellish as it was. A few days ago Maggie had called and said she'd invited a new woman at work to join the lunch bunch, and Maggie was *sure* the woman played for my team, and that I would *totally* fall for her.

I whistled Marley to my side. There would be no more falling for anyone. In fact, background checks, fingerprints, and lie detector tests were all part of my new dating kit. And thanks to my job, I wouldn't have the chance to use that kit until I retired.

The water was calm, so the boat leveled off and practically flew over the sea. I kept one eye on the dog. While Marley hadn't thrown up on earlier legs of the trip, he could always surprise me.

In less than an hour, the pilot throttled back, and I stepped out the back of the deckhouse, Marley at my heels. The low blue hills of Carriacou skimmed the horizon to the east, but the rest held nothing but sea. "Why are we stopping?"

John frowned. "Because we're here."

To the west, a three-masted sailboat floated. When I stared, the guy reading in the bow raised his bottle of beer. Was this *Shaw's Revenge*? I nodded politely, then scanned the horizon again. Nothing but the sailboat. "Damn it, she sent us on some stupid wild goose chase."

"That's not Randi's style, Emma. She's always tried to stay as close to the truth as possible. You know that. C'mon." We climbed a ladder to stand on the deckhouse for a better view. I shaded my eyes and squinted against the blinding sparkles dancing across the water. Other than a slight mist hanging over the water ahead, there was nothing. John and Matthew rechecked the GPS coordinates. We were floating at the exact coordinates Randi had sent us.

"Shit," I muttered. "Where did we go wrong?"

We climbed back down to the main deck, and for a second time checked John's notebook, checked the photocopy of the *Treasure Princess* puzzle back, and conferred with Matthew. There was no doubt.

I dropped down onto a bench, and Marley leapt up next to me. But then he froze, his gaze fixed on the horizon to the north. "Nothing there, big boy."

Marley's tail began wagging, a wave moving up his spine until all of him trembled. He threw back his head and howled. "Marley, what's wrong?"

Marley raced up and down the boat, then back up onto the bench.

"What's he so excited about?" John asked.

"I don't know. He's acting really weird. Marley, come. Come!"

But the dog had worked himself into such a frenzy he wasn't listening. When he ran past me I grabbed for his collar but missed. He raced back and forth three more times and now everyone on the boat lunged for him. Mike got his fingers on the collar but Marley pulled away. Then he leapt onto the bench, barked once, and launched himself over the side of the boat.

"Marley!" I screamed. I reached out, but he'd already landed with a dramatic splash. Marley began to swim, snorting and shaking his head. He was an awkward swimmer, head held delicately above the water, paws splashing more than swimming. "Marley, come back!" The dog kept swimming toward nothing but sea. When the low mist seemed to reach out for him, I went cold with panic.

"Let me go after him," I cried. "This boat has a Zodiac and I know how to run it."

But the taller spy guy was already in the gray inflatable dinghy pulling on the starter. The other guy climbed in and I untied the line and pushed them off. But when John and I returned to the gunwale, my heart sank like a rock. "Where did he go?" The calm sea shone like glass, but Marley was gone.

I clutched at my chest, moaning. This could not be happening to me. What had I done? Why had I brought him along? The men in the Zodiac circled for nearly thirty minutes, but it was obvious their search was futile. Marley had not been a strong swimmer, and had sunk beneath the waves. The mist stretched over the water like a menacing animal.

I curled up in a ball near the stern, waving off John when he tried to comfort me. I didn't deserve any comfort. I hadn't cried when Randi had left, but Marley's death was too much, so I just let go and lost myself in the horror of it all until I could barely breathe.

I'd lost Marley.

CHAPTER THIRTY-SEVEN

Back on Carriacou, we took a van to the hotel. I'd taken the end room, which had a window looking out on the beach, and John had settled into the room next door to me. Rick and Mike each had a room in the next row of buildings. My room also had a small patio of what must have once been concrete, but was now mostly grass and sand.

At dinner I picked at the fish on my plate. Now I'd lost two loves in just over two months. I excused myself and walked back to the little motel on the beach. As the sun set, sending romantic ribbons of orange rippling toward shore, I couldn't bear being there, gazing out at the soft colors dancing across the water. It hurt too much. Marley was gone, and I had no idea how to find Randi. I'd never be able to learn Tommy's fate. Why had that been so important in the first place? Maggie might say I'd been looking for something in my life and thought I could find it in Tommy's, but that made no sense because Randi was the pirate, not me. Maybe I had focused on Tommy's life so I wouldn't have time to look so closely at my own.

To shut my mind up, I sought distraction by ambling down the dirt street, nodding to an elderly woman passing on the back of a donkey, and watched some boys playing baseball in an empty lot. Shouts rang out ahead, which concerned me a bit, but I stopped to join the small group that had formed around two men in odd costumes shouting at each other. I could barely understand their thick accents, but the words sounded like Shakespeare. The appreciative audience laughed and clapped when one man seemed to forget his lines, so the other bashed him with a cloth bat. I began to pick up more words, and recognized a sentence I'd just read days ago. It was *Measure for Measure*. The wait wasn't long for the line I wanted to hear: *Go to your bosom. Knock there and ask your heart what it doth know.*

When the men ended the play and hugged, laughing with delight, I turned shyly toward the woman who'd been standing beside me.

The question must have already been in my eyes, for the woman laughed. "De be practicing for de Shakespeare Mas next year. We be doing dis for years, ever since a plantation owner started his slaves reciting Shakespeare."

"I'm surprised they were doing *Measure for Measure*. It's not a well-known play."

"Dey do all de plays, but weeks ago de woman ask for dis play and de men not know it, so de learn, and dis is der first try." She laughed, then shouted to one of the men shrugging off his costume. "Dey need more practice, no?"

Could Randi have been the woman who'd requested the play? Was she here, on Carriacou? Had she meant we were to find her on Carriacou? And even worse, how would she feel to learn Marley was gone?

I couldn't sleep, tossing on the saggy mattress until two a.m., when I finally got up and switched on the flimsy floor lamp. Waves lapped quietly out my window as I sat on the floor and spread out all I'd brought with me. The short section of Captain Tommy's ship log. Captain R. Brown's log. Copies of McLurin's journals. Shaw's letters. The Moroccan inlay box. The notes Randi had made from Captain Tommy's map.

The Farris map had three elements: the letters Randi had decoded to be a set of coordinates that led nowhere. The Latin phrase about breathing and hope. And the Shakespeare line, which now had come alive thanks to this afternoon.

What the hell. I had nothing left to lose, so maybe I would knock on my heart, invite it out for coffee, and see what it had to say. I sat there, quietly, waiting, but since I'd shut down so completely these last two months, my emotions were stiffer than a door hinge gone rusty.

You still love Randi.

"No, I don't," I said to the empty room, cast in dark shadow by the single lamp.

Yes, you do.

"No, I don't. She lied. She stole from me. She ran away from me."

You still love her.

Damn it.

I dropped my head back against the wall and missed Marley's warm breath on my neck, the way he'd work his muzzle under my arm until I'd pet him. Why had Randi insisted I bring Marley? All he'd done was drown himself. For months now I'd envied Marley's ability to love without question, to accept without judgment. Dogs didn't question or analyze love—they just felt it. On the other hand, I'd been fighting it because my head refused to accept what my heart already knew. I was still in love with Randi Marx. Shit. I didn't know how to stop. She haunted my dreams and followed me through every step of the day, not like a black cloud overhead, but like a secret treasure tucked inside my heart. Damn.

I suddenly felt as if I'd begun rolling down a hill, picking up speed but unsure of where, or when, I'd end up. I thought about what life on the *Moon Shadow* must have been like. Tommy would have been fierce and powerful and terrible, a woman young Billy might have fallen for. Sawkins would have been older, wiser, but seemed to have stuck with Tommy right up to the end. What an impossible situation that would have been for those men—to love Tommy without any hope that she might love them back, especially after Rebekah appeared.

I froze. *Ask your heart what it doth know.* What if Billy and Sawkins shared an impossible love for Tommy, and accepted it? What if Tommy finally accepted she'd fallen in love with a woman? They accepted their love rather than fought against it.

Billy and Sawkins could see an island. Marley had seen something out there, something John and I couldn't see. Then I remembered the book Randi had bought at the antique store in Pittsburgh. *Myths and Superstitions of the Sea.* Randi had read to me of islands that some could see and others couldn't. Jason's Grenada Triangle.

My hands began to sweat. This was an impossible idea. What if only those people, or dogs, whose head and hearts were aligned could see this island? Was this that silly Love Island?

Could it be that simple? That freaky? Accept your love and see the island? Now that I'd admitted I still loved Randi, what might I see at those same coordinates? I still wanted nothing to do with her, despite that love, but I had to see this thing through. I checked my watch. It would be dawn in a few hours. I packed everything up, changed into clean clothes, and headed for the docks.

Maybe Marley wasn't dead after all.

PART ELEVEN

THE HUNT

Not all treasure is silver and gold, mate.

—Captain Jack Sparrow

Everything lost is meant to be found.

—Lara Croft, tomb raider

Chapter Thirty-eight

I hurried down the main street of Carriacou, passing a few men sleeping on front porches, a dog chewing on something dead, and a fisherman heading for his boat. Before looking for Matthew, I jogged up and down each pier, but didn't see *Shaw's Revenge*. Was that good news or bad? I had no idea.

Matthew's boat was docked in Slip 8, and judging by the soft snoring drifting from the cabin, he was on board. "Excuse me? Hello? Matthew?" It was rude to board without permission, so I knocked awkwardly on the boat's hull and called again. Finally a mussed and groggy Matthew stuck his head out the deckhouse.

"Matthew, it's me, Emma, from yesterday. I need you to take me back out there."

"Where is Mr. John? Should we not wait for him and de other men?"

When I climbed on board, the boat rocked gently. "I'll explain when we get there." I handed him $200, unsure how much John had paid for the trip, but it must have been enough, for Matthew shook off the last of his dream and went into action.

At five a.m. the ride was considerably cooler, so I pulled my jacket tighter but didn't go below, afraid I'd miss the island. Behind us the eastern horizon was bluish white, but we were zooming into the dark blue haze still blanketing the west. Matthew's running lights were beautiful spots of color in the dawn, as were hundreds of lights dotting the horizon—either inhabited islands or boats that had dropped anchor for the night.

I strained to see a dark shape ahead, but I saw nothing save the increased light tipping the waves with silver. Damn. I should have been able to see it by now. Randi, I love you, even though you're a pirate and a scoundrel and a thief.

Still nothing. Perhaps it wouldn't work because I was angry and wanted nothing to do with Randi, but admitting my love was as far as I was willing to go.

Matthew throttled back, then shrugged at my puzzled look. "Dis is de same place." The boat bobbed in the mild sea.

I breathed deeply and closed my eyes, and remembered those days in the car with Randi, wanting her, loving the sound of her voice, the energy she sent shooting my way with every glance. I missed the way Randi had made me feel special. I missed the sense that the rest of the world had fallen away and it was just the two of us. God, I missed that. I missed the way Randi would roll her eyes at my teasing and totally ignore my sarcasm. I missed the feel of Randi's arms around me.

I opened my eyes, turned to the north, and nearly choked on my tongue. A gigantic island towered right in front of us, not more than one hundred yards from the boat. "Oh, my God." It was huge. How could I have missed it before? Jagged peaks rose up from a thick forest, and a waterfall plummeted down one of the cliffs. The sun crested the horizon, bathing the mountains' east slopes in gold, throwing the west slopes into warm shadow. Seagulls scolded overhead, and the surf crashed gently up onto a sandy beach.

The beach. There they were. Randi stood in the water up to her knees, perfectly still, watching me. Marley chased a tern farther down the beach, splashing happily through the surf.

I wanted to run around like a wild Marley, but instead I retrieved my backpack. "Matthew, I'm going to borrow your Zodiac. Please return to these coordinates with John Lewis six hours from now." I figured we'd need that much time to finish this treasure hunt.

"But, missy, dat's crazy. De dog disappeared, and you will too."

"No, I checked the weather this morning—no storms today. I'll be fine." I hopped into the rubber boat. "But tell John *no* earlier than six hours from now, or he may not find me."

Matthew tugged at his T-shirt. "De man no gonna like dis."

"Six hours." I snapped the outboard motor to life and freed the line. Heart pounding, I steered the little craft away from Matthew and toward the gentle mist surrounding the island.

"Lady, come back! Lady, where you go? I can't believe dis. Now she gone too."

I forgot Matthew as I focused on closing the distance to the island. I rode the last wave in, then shut the motor off and raised it. The shallow water was surprisingly cool as I pulled the boat up onto the sand.

"Marley!" The dog threw himself at me and I buried my face in his curly coat, determined not to cry.

By the time I stood up, Randi had reached me, glowing with happiness. I'd seen the island, and we both knew what that meant. We stopped five feet apart. Randi's pulse beat at her throat, thrumming as fast as my own. It took all of my strength not to reach for her waist and pull her close until nothing separated us. Tan, muscled, she looked good. She'd cut her hair short, and the soft, tousled auburn curls had been lightened by the sun. Her shorts and tight tank top were clean. A machete hung from a belt slung around her hips. She didn't look like a woman on the run. I drank my fill. When I nearly forgot why I'd come, I dug my nails into my palms to help me remember. Stay under control, girl. Don't lose it. The two of you had one night together.

"Welcome to the Grenada Triangle," Randi said.

"No kidding." I'd forgotten everything I'd planned to say to her. Randi held out her wrists. "I'm your prisoner."

"Put your hands down. I didn't bring cuffs."

"Unfortunate," Randi said softly, and the suggestiveness in her voice was enough to set me off.

I stepped closer. "Remember that message from Lauren I never delivered?"

Randi closed her eyes and I slapped her. "That was from Lauren," I said. "Now open your eyes."

When she did, I slapped her again. "And that's from me." Slapping Randi didn't feel as good as I thought it would.

Randi ran a finger along her lip. "Guess I deserved both of those."

I glared at her. "I came here without John because I need to follow up on my research about this island. He'll be here in a few hours to take you back to the U.S."

Randi's face didn't change, but still shone with happiness, and her eyes gleamed with unshed tears. I faltered. Good Lord, was Randi going to cry? "We both know why I was able to see this island," I snapped, "but…that's it, okay? You and I *aren't* going to happen. It's not what I want or why I'm here."

Blinking furiously, Randi nodded. "Of course, I understand." She swallowed. "It's just that I'm overwhelmed you're here. After yesterday, I'd given up all hope. It means so much to me…that you can see this island."

I gazed up at the nearest peak. "This is pretty freaky, you know. An island that comes and goes with a person's emotional state. It makes no sense."

"I know." Randi wiped her eyes quickly, then waved her arms around. "The Bermuda Triangle doesn't make sense, but it exists nonetheless, so why not this island? Welcome to Captain Tommy's treasure, her secret island. You were right. The Farris map did lead to a place." Randi suddenly didn't seem to know what to do with her hands, and my heart skipped erratically to see Randi so unsure of herself.

"Are you sure there's no silver?"

"I've spent the last month climbing all over this island, searching caves along the shore, hacking paths through the forest, and I never found any treasure chests or markings that said 'dig here.'" She shrugged. "I'm not as disappointed as I thought I'd be, maybe because the island itself is so incredible. That's why I wanted you and John to come. I needed to share it with someone before I…turned myself in."

"You understand that nothing's changed, right? You're still going to prison."

She nodded. "That's okay. I'm ready to do the time. That you…" Her voice faded so low the surf nearly drowned her out. "That you love me, at least enough to see this island, that's all I need." Our eyes locked, and when Randi began blinking again I fought the ridiculous urge to comfort her. "It took me a while to find the island. I was angry at myself and angry you hadn't agreed to come with me before you found out the truth. So I crisscrossed these waters for days, just like Captain Brown had done."

"How did you finally find the island?"

"I just started coming out here and drifting. I stopped trying to find the treasure, and just thought about you and Marley." She swallowed then quickly recovered. "Well, if John's right behind you, how about a quick tour? I could start by showing you the sheltered grove where I've pitched my tent. I haven't found much evidence that anyone ever lived here, so I suspect that even if Tommy found the island, she didn't actually spend any time here."

I bit back a smile. "Really?"

"Yeah, I've been thinking about Tommy and feeling bad she died so young."

I smiled and swung my pack off my shoulder. "Well, we might as well get started." I retrieved a manila envelope, undid the red string, then pulled out a piece of paper. "Let's sit down for a minute. This is a photocopy of a page from McLurin's journal. I returned to Cincinnati and went through everything." We dropped down in the shade of a coconut tree and I handed Randi the journal entry.

Port Royal, July 19, 1715.

Today I buried a dear friend. She was a strong woman, able to withstand pain and face death with courage and grace. I nearly called off the hanging yesterday because I was so unsure of what I'd done, but I didn't, since this was what she wanted.

Mrs. Wingate is no longer in pain. I may burn in hell, but I don't care. She put on Tommy's brown gingham dress, I attached Tommy's braid to her cap, then before the guards came, I put the black hood over Mrs. Wingate's head. I apologized that she wouldn't be able to see during her last minutes of life, but she said the fabric was thin, and that I was a lovely man.

As the guards marched her to the scaffolding, the braid served as evidence Tommy Farris was about to be hanged. I held my breath, worried someone would notice how bent and frail the prisoner was, but I suppose everyone assumed the pirate was penitent and feared death. Mercifully, the end came swiftly for Mrs. Wingate, and her pain was over. I took possession of her body before anyone could remove the hood. Her family and husband were told she had died in her sleep. We laid her to rest this afternoon.

As for my other friend, she knows nothing of what I've

done. It took me all night to arrange things, but early the morning of the hanging, I bribed the guard, cut off her braid (despite her protests) rubbed charcoal into her white streak, then gave her trousers, shirt, and jacket. I blessed her, kissed both her cheeks, then watched as she slipped away into the dark streets of Port Royal.

Randi whistled when she'd finished the letter. "Wow. I didn't see this coming."

"Me either."

Randi handed the letter back. "So Tommy Farris wasn't hanged in Port Royal. But what does that have to do with the island?"

I savored the moment. "While you've been focused on the map and this island, I've been researching—Farris, McLurin, and Brown. Why this island exists, and works the way it does, is a mystery, and we'll probably never know the truth about it. But the Farris map and what it leads to? That's a puzzle, and I have almost all the pieces now."

"But I already told you. There's nothing here but trees and sand and water and my tent and my boat moored in a small cove on the western side of the island."

I considered our position. "We're on the south end of the island, right?"

"Yes, it's sort of shaped like a *J*, and we're at the bottom."

"Are there any rock outcroppings, about fifteen to twenty feet high, that rise up from the western beach?"

Randi played with her ear lobe. "Well, yes, but—"

"You want to stand here arguing the whole time, or do you want to finish this treasure hunt?" I loved the puzzled look. Damn, it felt good. Too bad I didn't have a badge I could flip: Emma Boyd, Reference Librarian.

"Okay, I'll show you the outcroppings." Some of Randi's spark returned, along with color in her delicate cheekbones.

I checked my watch. "We only have five and a half hours now, so let's get going." Randi whistled for Marley, then led us off the beach and into a thick forest.

It took nearly an hour to walk the narrow path through the forest. We only stopped once so Randi could point out three graves, marked only with large rocks for headstones. "There was writing on the rocks at one time, but I can't read it. Most of it has worn off." I stood for a moment, sadness lapping at my heart, wishing I knew who was buried there.

I shook off the sadness, knowing more was ahead. I followed Randi out onto another beach, the inside curve of the *J*, then stopped at the sight of two sailboats moored offshore. One was the massive three-masted one I'd seen yesterday.

Randi followed my pointing finger. "Well, that's new."

"You don't have two boats, do you?"

Randi shook her head. "We have company, and it's the *Shaw's Revenge*. I don't know who sails her, but the bastard must have finally seen the island. Stay sharp. I don't know what this guy wants, but he's been hanging around Carriacou for weeks."

After walking a short stretch of beach, Randi pointed toward three small cliffs. "There they are."

My heart thudded in my ears. Were the letters I'd read correct? Would I find what I sought? "There, the middle cliff. We need to get to its base."

Mystified, Randi used her machete to hack a path through the vines and close-growing bushes. "Want to tell me *why* we need this cliff?"

"In a minute." I yanked aside the vines. "Here we are." I scanned the rock face, most of it hidden by foliage, then felt my way around the cliff's curve. "Here!" Oh my God. It was real. The letter had led me right here. I ran my hands over the small indentations in the rock, natural ledges and holes just large enough for a toe. I grabbed the vines, tugged to make sure they'd hold, then began climbing the rock using the toe holds.

"Well, this is unexpected," Randi breathed.

At the top I flung my leg up and crawled onto the ledge. "Okay, I'm up."

Randi must have been part monkey, for she scaled the rock face in half the time. "Hey, there's a little cave back here." She looked back down at the ground. "Marley, you stay. I'm right here."

"Don't go in the cave yet," I said. What if the letter was wrong? If so, the treasure hunt would end right here. I sat down on the warm ledge so Marley could see our legs, and retrieved another paper from my backpack. "Stuck into one of McLurin's journals was an envelope, unopened. But then the seal broke so I read it. The letter had arrived after McLurin's death, so someone had just stuck the letter in a journal and forgotten it." I handed the photocopies to Randi.

Randi read the dated. "November 15, 1755. But that was forty years after Tommy disappeared."

I nodded. God, this was delicious. "Read."

> *To my old friend, Father Danny McLurin,*
>
> *I'm never forgetting the debt I owe you, and it's time for me to pay up. There be two parts to my payment. The first is to tell you what happened after you gave me a second chance and freed me. I didn't melt into the crowd and become an honest sailor before the mast as you suggested. Instead, I found the* Moon Shadow *at the docks, now called the* Margaret, *and that scoundrel Shaw, or should I say "Jeremiah Fletcher." He put up a fight, but couldn't hold out against me, since I was needing my ship for the most important quest of my life, and Shaw was the only thing that stood in my way. I could have run him through but I didn't. Rebekah doesn't like me to kill people. Instead I marked my initials on his back with my sword, and dumped him overboard. He probably lives since he's too mean to die.*
>
> *I donned men's clothing, wrapped my chest, took over Shaw's crew, and called myself Captain R. Brown, then began my journey.*

"Wait," Randi said. "Captain R. Brown was really Tommy Farris?"

"Yes. Once I had this letter, I compared the handwriting to the Brown log book, and it was the same."

I continued.

> *What did I seek? I sought the most precious thing in my life that I'd lost weeks earlier. Her name's Rebekah Brown and she's the love of my life. I'm sorry if that shocks you as a man of the cloth, but I'm thinking you'll recover. It certainly shocked my bones. Rebekah'd fallen overboard and made her way to a mysterious island, and lived there on fruit, fish, and*

*fresh water from the streams as she waited for me. I sailed a
grid until I finally found the island, and found my love.*

*This island west of Carriacou is too mysterious for me
to understand, probably for you as well, but it's where we've
been living for the last forty years. We sail into Carriacou
or Grenada for supplies every few years, but otherwise we
be feeding ourselves, exploring the islands, and caring for
each other.*

There's more news. My ship, the Maravillosa, *heavy
with silver and men, went down just off the western shore of
the island, but instead of sinking to the bottom of the ocean,
she sunk in but four fathoms of water. A shelf surrounds the
island, and caught the ship as it sank. It took me years, but
I managed to bring most of it up, basket by basket, and hide
it on the island.*

*I also brought up and laid Sawkins, Billy, and Calabria
to rest.*

I was stunned to see Randi wiping away a tear. "Those would be
the graves in the woods I found," she said.

"You have a soft spot for dogs, can't change your own tire, *and*
you cry?"

Randi blew her nose. "It's been known to happen now and then."
I shook my head. "Okay, well, there's more."

*I'm wanting you to have some of the treasure. After
many years here, I made a map, and hid it in one of my books,
then sent it and five other books to you years ago. I hope you
still have them. I realize you didn't know who R. Brown was,
but the authors' names should have given you the clue you
needed. The map's in one of those books.*

*I'm writing to you now because we're at the end.
Rebekah's unwell, and no doctor in the eastern West Indies
has been able to help her. I, too, am sick with a stomach
ailment, and my grief at the thought of losing my Rebekah
cuts just as deep.*

*When you find the map, and the island, look for the
middle rock outcropping among three on the western shore,*

one with rock steps, a ledge, and a cave. There'll you'll find us and everything you'll be needing to finish your quest. Rebekah and I've spent many hours of our life together on this small cliff, watching the world revolve around the island. When my Rebekah dies, or perhaps just before, I'll bring her up there and won't leave her. I haven't left her once in thirty years, and I'm not about to start now.

So, dear friend, I hope you're well. I've inquired after you along the islands over the years, and am told you still run the mission. You and I might be the only two pirates who escaped with our lives.

With much affection,
"Captain R. Brown"

Randi sniffed a few times, then blew her nose. "I'm just so glad Tommy and Rebekah found each other...twice. They fell in love, were separated, then found each other again."

My groin tightened at the look Randi gave me. "We aren't Tommy and Rebekah."

"I know that."

We sat there, watching a line of brown pelicans skim less than a foot above the waves. The last one plunged into the surf and rose with a fish in its generous beak. Frothy white waves broke in irregular patterns near shore, and a handful of sailboats spiked the horizon.

"How were Tommy and Rebekah able to leave the island if she didn't have a ship?" Randi asked.

"I suppose she salvaged enough from the *Maravillosa* to cobble together something to get them to Carriacou, where they could have used some of the treasure to buy a real boat."

"You've thought this through, haven't you?"

I shrugged. Of course. I always thought things through.

"I'm trying to prepare myself for what we're going to find in the cave," Randi said.

I switched on my flashlight, feeling like a well-prepared Girl Scout, then took a deep breath. "I know this is a lot to throw at you. I've had a few weeks to prepare myself, and I'm still not sure *I'm* ready. Let's go."

"Marley, stay, boy. I'll be right back."

The cave was too low for comfortable walking, so we dropped to our hands and knees. Ten feet in, my beam found them.

Two skeletons lay side by side, the flesh and clothing gone, leaving nothing but bone.

"Jesus," Randi said.

I rocked back on my haunches, too stunned to breathe as sadness and joy collided. I finally moistened my dry lips. "Thomasina Farris and Rebekah Brown."

The cave floor was dry and sandy, and I sat back and leaned against the wall, suddenly weak. My eyes were beginning to adjust to the dim light, so I switched the flashlight off.

Daylight reached back far enough to illuminate a few planes of both skulls, and a hip bone. Neither of us could tear our eyes from the remains of two women in love, who'd been at rest in this cave for over two hundred and fifty years.

"So Tommy brought Rebekah up here, then lay down to die beside her." Randi's low voice bounced off the back of the little cave, and she looked down, but not before I saw another tear glistening in the dim light.

"It's sad, I know."

Marley began to whine.

"That's not why I'm crying. It's because I know exactly how she felt." Randi suddenly rose to a crouch and went outside onto the ledge. I followed, and we dangled our legs off the edge and watched the world revolve around the island as Marley paced, now quiet.

"Thank you," Randi finally said. "I'm glad to know their love story had a happy ending, even in death."

"I brought something I found in McLurin's effects. Eleanor had dug into some other donations that hadn't been catalogued yet and found another box." I reached into the pack for the Moroccan box. When I opened the lid Randi covered her mouth in shock.

"Tommy's?" Randi finally choked out.

A single braid, thick as a rope and black as night but shot through with strands of white, lay coiled in the box. I caressed the still-soft hair. "McLurin kept it. He might have been a little in love with her himself. I don't know. Or maybe he thought she'd want it back someday."

"Jesus." Randi stroked the braid. "This is almost too much to absorb in one day."

I bumped her shoulder, smiling. "Hang on, we're not done yet."

We returned to the skeletons, where I lay the box next to the taller body. Then, flashlight on, I began reaching under the shorter skeleton.

"Hey, don't disturb them," Randi cried. Marley now barked frantically at the base of the cliff.

As gently as possible, I shifted the weightless bones until my fingers found the oilcloth. Carefully I lifted out the package. "There was one more piece of information in Tommy's letter, the one McLurin never read and no one at the mission cared enough to open."

Inside the heavy cloth was a stack of thin leather books. I handed all but the last book to Randi. "These are Tommy's journals, which fill in the details of their lives here." I flipped to the last page of the last journal and read to myself. Yup, there it was. The location I needed. The last piece of the puzzle. I closed the slender journal. "One more step, then we'll be ready to meet John."

"Emma, you are the most astonishing person I've ever met."

To Marley's relief, we climbed back down the short cliff, then both gazed back up the cliff face. We pulled the vines back over the steps until they disappeared into the foliage. Tommy and Rebekah shouldn't be disturbed again. This would always be their ledge, and their island.

CHAPTER THIRTY-NINE

As we walked, I was overwhelmed with happiness for Tommy. She gave up the pirate life *and* got the girl. How often did that happen? And I'd done what I'd come for—to discover the pieces to the puzzle of Tommy's life. Anything that happened next was icing on the cake.

Once we'd crashed our way back to the beach, I brushed off my arms and legs, then enjoyed the welcoming breeze that had been absent in the brush. "Okay, now we need a small cove on the eastern shore of the island, one that has lots of big boulders scattered along the beach."

Randi nodded. "I know that cove, but it's a long walk north. We'd make better time if we walked back to your Zodiac and used that."

"All right. Let's go." I started back along our original path.

Marley ran on ahead, and I tried not to feel Randi's eyes watching me as she followed. When Marley disappeared ahead, then began barking frantically, I looked over my shoulder at Randi.

"He's been barking at anything that moves since he arrived," Randi said. But then she suddenly cursed and her eyes widened.

I turned around to find a tall man standing directly in the path. He wore a red polo shirt, a navy windbreaker, rumpled khaki pants and docksiders without socks. He smiled and waved, and I began to return the smile until I realized the man's hair was reddish blond and no longer a crew cut. But I recognized the face now. This was the man who'd beaten up Cam, who'd followed me. Randi came up and stood beside me. "Roger Fletcher," Randi said. "What the fuck are you doing with my dog?"

That was when Marley came from behind Fletcher, clipped to a leash in Fletcher's hand.

My mouth went dry. "I'll bet you're one of those sailors who orders all his clothing with his boat's name embroidered on it."

The man chuckled, then moved aside his windbreaker. *Shaw's Revenge* was stitched in blue. "Very perceptive. And thanks to your dog barking a while ago, I was able to find you fairly quickly. Aren't dogs great? Now, shall we save us all a bundle of time and just get right to it? Where's the treasure?"

"What treasure?" Randi asked.

Fletcher smiled without meaning it. "Cute. I mean what you call Tommy Farris's treasure, but what was really Avery Shaw's treasure."

I jammed fists onto my hips. "Says who?"

"Says every generation of Shaws since Avery. He made sure all his relatives knew of Farris's theft, and the story's been handed down since then."

"Shaw and Farris were both pirates, and they were stealing from the Spanish fleet."

Fletcher shook his head sadly. "Not true. Avery Shaw was an honorable man who'd earned a shipload of silver by transporting goods on his merchant ship. After Farris stole his silver, Shaw struggled to go on, but he ended up with so many debts he lost his ship. To get a fresh start he changed his name to Fletcher. Each generation since has been told of the Shaw in our blood. When I was doing research on my ancestor and that cursed Farris bitch, I read your article in the *Library Journal* about the Farris map. I realized it might really exist and not just be part of the family myth. Here was my chance to right the wrong done to my family all those generations ago."

"I'm afraid your story has gotten twisted in the telling over the generations," I said. "Tommy and Shaw were stealing the silver together and something went wrong. Shaw made up that story because Tommy got the silver and he didn't. Didn't you ever read *Pirates I Have Known?*"

"Of course."

"It's clear in there that Fletcher, obviously your ancestor, hated Tommy beyond reason. The man was wacko."

"That's bullshit."

"How did you find this island?" Randi said suddenly. "You've been shadowing me for weeks."

The man smiled sweetly. "That I have been. You sold your photocopy of the Farris map to Benton, and I bought it from him. I sweated that damned code for weeks but couldn't break it. I finally decided you'd altered something before selling the map to Benton. So I just came down to Grenada and started asking questions. I caught up with you in Carriacou. But I couldn't find the island, even after following you out here day after day. Not until that dog yesterday did I get it. All I did was think about my last dog, and the island popped into view. Freaked me out for a second, but I recovered. So let's get to the fun part of this day."

My heart sank—my actions had brought Fletcher straight to the island.

"And what part is that?" Randi asked.

Fletcher reached into his pocket, pulled out a gun, and pointed it at Marley's head. I flung out my arm to hold Randi back. "I don't want to use this gun," Fletcher said, "but I will, so take me to the treasure."

Randi shook her head. "There isn't any treasure. The treasure is the island."

"I heard you two talking. Emma here said you had something else to find. I'm guessing it's the treasure, and I'm happy to come along."

I couldn't take my eyes off Marley's happy face only inches away from the gun. "I don't know where it is."

Fletcher made a sad face. "That's a shame. But just to show you what a nice guy I am, I'm going to give you the chance to save this dog's life."

Randi cursed but stayed where she was.

"Emma, here's how you save the mutt's life. I'm going to ask you again to take me to the treasure. You'll pretend you don't know, so I'll blow the big pup's head off. Then you'll be shocked but will still plead ignorance. So then I'll put the gun up against your butch's head and threaten to pull the trigger. You'll suddenly remember where the treasure is, but the dog will have died for nothing."

"She's not very butch." I was so terrified I felt like giggling hysterically. This couldn't be happening.

"What?" Randi snapped.

"Well, you're not. You can't change your own tire. How butch is that?" I had to distract the man. How could he possibly shoot Marley? I was sick and tired of people using an innocent dog.

"Ladies, we can certainly debate this on the way, but don't you think we'd better get going?" He waved the gun at Marley's head.

I held up both hands. "We need to get to a cove on the eastern side of the island. We were heading back for our Zodiac."

Fletcher nodded. "You go get it. Ms. Marx and the dog will remain here with me. Then we'll use both your Zodiac and mine to visit this cove."

"But—"

"All I have to do is tie you two to a tree and leave. You'll die here and no one will ever know. Maybe you'd better cooperate."

I carefully moved past Fletcher, then began running through the forest. I reached the south beach sweating and out of breath and startled a flock of seagulls when I raced for the Zodiac. It took me about thirty minutes bouncing through the waves to get around to the beach where Fletcher and his hostages waited in his Zodiac. Because Randi knew where the cove was, she rode in Fletcher's boat and took the lead. As I followed, my mind raced. How could I get the gun away from him? There was no way he was letting us leave the island.

Chapter Forty

Even before Fletcher's Zodiac slowed down, I could see where we were headed. The cove was easy to recognize. A sharp cliff towered overhead, and below great chunks of it lay scattered across the beach, a giant's discarded marbles. The tides had created impressive sand craters around each boulder.

Fletcher beached his boat expertly and Randi jumped out to help me drag mine up out of the water. "There's a cave entrance behind those two boulders," Randi said, "and the tide's just started coming back in so it's safe to be inside for an hour or so. But I've been over that entire cave. There's a deep pool surrounded by a narrow ledge, but that's it."

I didn't look at Fletcher. "That must be it," I said.

Randi showed me the cave entrance and we stepped inside, Fletcher and Marley right behind us. Daylight filtered into the cavern, which was about fifteen feet high and oval-shaped, about thirty feet from end to end. The cave smelled of dead fish and rotting seaweed.

I shone my flashlight against the far wall.

"What are you looking for?" Fletcher asked.

"An *X* carved into the rock."

"You're kidding," Fletcher said.

"No, I'm not."

The *X* appeared on the glistening rock on my second sweep of the cave. It was small and irregular, as if the carver had struggled with the dense rock, but it was still an *X*.

Fletcher whooped, sending out an echo. "Now what?"

I shrugged off my backpack and slipped off my sandals. The cool sand under my feet was wet but firm. "I go for a swim."

Fletcher frowned. "Why?"

"Because the treasure, if it's here, is in the next cave over, which you can only reach by swimming underwater."

Randi looked at the pool, then back at me, doubt evident in her posture. Even Fletcher looked confused. "I don't get it," he said.

I sat down, then slid into the cool pool, treading water. "Below that X is a tunnel to another cavern." The water was too dark below to see the tunnel, but I trusted it was there.

"A tunnel? Underwater? Well, shit. I can't swim." Fletcher started pointing his gun at Marley, then Randi. "How will I know what you find? You could come back and say there was nothing there, and I'd never know." He jerked Marley closer to him and the dog growled. "I might just shoot the dog now so you'll know I'm serious."

"I can't swim either," Randi said.

"What?" I said.

"Well, I can swim, but I...I can't put my face in the water. I can't open my eyes. And I'm a little claustrophobic."

I threw up my hands and let them splash into the water. "Soft on dogs, can't change a tire, cry, *and* can't put your face in the water?"

Randi turned to Fletcher. "If Emma can get me into the cave and back in one piece, then she can do the same thing with you. So you can get in there and see for yourself."

Fletcher considered her idea. "I still think you'll take me more seriously if I shoot the dog."

I didn't say it, but we were surrounded by rock. Unless he had great aim, the bullet could ricochet right into him. Or he could hit Marley with the first bullet.

"Randi, come on," I urged. "Tommy's journal says the tunnel's just two feet below the surface at low tide, and it's only about three feet long."

"Marx, quit your whining and go with her. If you don't come back, I'm shooting the dog. So don't go off on some long cave exploration."

Randi looked at me, then turned to Fletcher. "You want us to leave you here, alone, with Marley?"

I ground my teeth at Fletcher's rough laugh. "I don't see too many headlines that read 'Man killed by poodle.'"

Randi and I exchanged a quick glance. What would Marley do? Randi slid into the water, wincing at the coolness. "He gets a little nervous when I leave."

"I'll sing him a lullaby. Now get going."

Randi paddled over to me, her face white, her brown eyes dark with fear. "Emma," she whispered. "I'm not sure I can do this. Did I mention I'm a little claustrophobic?"

Despite the danger, Randi's fears were sort of endearing. The big, bad private investigator and map thief was a bundle of insecurities just like everyone else on the planet. "You'll be fine."

"I can't do this," Randi whispered.

"Well, okay, Randi-With-An-I. This might be too much for someone like you."

"Screw you," she snapped.

"You wish."

"I need to plug my nose."

"Then use your other hand to shine the flashlight for me."

"Oh, damn, I can't believe I'm doing this." We swam over to the X.

"Okay, I'll come around behind you and put my arm around your waist." I gently held Randi against me, remembering the pose from my high school Red Cross water rescue class. "Okay? Now you'll kick along with me. We'll go down and in three kicks we'll be through." Randi was shivering so I tightened my grip. "You'll be okay. I won't let go." I was likely going to die before this was over, but I was going to be proud of how I died. "Deep breaths. We go on three. One, two, three."

We dove together. Thank God I could see the tunnel almost immediately. As I kicked us through it, I wanted to laugh out loud. I was being held at gunpoint on a deserted tropical island diving into a secret cave to find a long lost treasure. Talk about a Librarian Action Figure.

The tunnel was shorter than three feet, really just a hole in the rock. I kicked upward and we surfaced almost immediately. Randi coughed and spat as I held her afloat, then I directed the flashlight to the nearest ledge and we scrambled up out of the water. Unlike the first cave, this one was pitched in total darkness and the air was chilly. Randi coughed and spat beside me.

Marley began his panicked barking. "You okay?" I asked.

"That was more like ten feet," Randi sputtered. "I didn't think I'd make it."

I gave her shoulder a squeeze. "Big baby." I flashed the light around. Nothing but rock. Shit. If the treasure wasn't here, I had no idea where it was. Marley's barking bounced back and forth, as if he were running along the narrow ledge.

Randi groaned. "There's nothing here."

Fletcher began yelling at Marley to shut the fuck up or he'd shoot.

"Crap," Randi muttered. "Marley's going ballistic. Fletcher may just shoot him to shut him up."

The sound of a gunshot cracked through the water and without a second's hesitation, Randi took a huge breath and dove. I was right behind her.

"Don't shoot him!" Randi screamed as we surfaced. Marley was running like a crazy animal around the entrance and Fletcher was trying to get a bead on the zigzagging dog.

I climbed from the pool. "Don't shoot. We're back." Randi flung herself between the gun and Marley, grabbing the dog's collar and talking him down.

"I hate barking dogs. Did I mention that?" Fletcher's eyes were wide. He recovered, then waved us together with his gun. "Okay, Plan B."

"What's Plan B?" I asked.

"Obviously there's another cave and it's not far, since you came back so quickly. So here's Plan B. I tie you both up, then I kick my way into the cave. If your weenie butch can do it, so can I."

Randi's eyes narrowed.

Fletcher pointed the gun at me. "Emma, be a good girl and get the rope out of my dinghy. If you're gone longer than two minutes I'll shoot her."

I returned quickly and Fletcher slammed us together, back to back, and tied our hands. Then he walked us forward along the narrowest part of the ledge. "Sit."

We stood on a ledge maybe eighteen inches wide. "We'll fall in," I said. Cursing, he held me until Randi had sunk to her knees, then he lowered me as well onto the slippery rock. Randi and I leaned against the cave wall. There was no way we could stand without falling in.

Fletcher put down his gun and took off his shoes. "You ladies better hope there's something in that cave."

"Why?" Randi said. "If it's empty, maybe we just have the wrong cave." We reached for each other's hands.

"If it's the wrong cave, then you have no idea where the right one is, so there's no longer any reason to keep you around. I can search for the cave myself."

Fletcher walked past Marley and moved toward the *X* on the wall. "I can do this. I just gotta kick and I'll get right through."

My heart thudded dully in my ears and Randi's hands felt as clammy as mine. When Fletcher found out there was nothing in that cave, we were dead. "He called me 'weenie butch,'" Randi murmured.

"You're not."

"I know, but I hate labels." Randi raised her voice. "You'll need the flashlight, asshole."

Fletcher snapped his fingers and turned back, carefully working his way along the narrow ledge. Just as he squeezed past Marley, cursing the "damned dog," Randi shouted, "Poodle-zoodle-foodle!"

Marley leapt up and whirled in a circle, knocking Fletcher off his feet. He fell feet first into the pool, hitting his head on the rocky edge with a sickening crunch. Unconscious, Fletcher sank from sight.

I struggled against the rope. "We need to get him out." But he'd tied us so well that struggling only tightened the knots. We each put a foot out and tried pushing against each other, but my foot slipped and I nearly dumped us both into the pool.

"Stop," Randi said. "If we fall in tied like this, we're screwed."

"I don't suppose Marley knows how to untie knots?"

Randi pulled at the rope. "No."

Trying not to panic, I leaned back against Randi. "When will the tide come in?"

"It'll start rising in about thirty minutes. It'll rise to about half the height of this cave."

"Not good."

"Do you have a knife in your shoe?"

"I'm a librarian, not Indiana Jones. I do have a knife in my backpack, but it's back there by the entrance, twenty feet away. Might as well be twenty miles."

"Marley, pick it up," Randi said. "C'mon, boy, pick it up." Marley trotted over to the sandy part of the cave, picked up the extra rope Fletcher'd left, and after picking his way carefully along the ledge, he dropped it at Randi's feet. "Good boy. Now go back and pick it up." Marley cocked his head, then backed up, nosed around until he found the flashlight, and dropped that at Randi's feet. It rolled into the pool with a soft splash.

"Third time's a charm," I whispered, relieved I had a second flashlight in my pack.

"Marley, pick it up. Go on, Marley. Pick it up."

There was nothing else for the dog to retrieve but the pack. He dragged it along beneath him until I snagged it with my foot. Using our feet, backs, and teeth, we managed to position the pack between us. "How'd you get Marley to do that?"

"I'm not without dog skills myself, you know. He leaves toys all over the apartment, so I taught him to just keep picking them up until the floor's clean." She pulled out the knife and began sawing at the rope.

"Zoodle-foodle?"

"Please. It's humiliating." She cut us free and we both slid into the water. When I began the side stroke, I hit something with my foot and yelped.

"Fletcher's body," Randi said. "Don't look."

"Jesus." I splashed to the far side of the pool and hoisted myself up onto the wider ledge while Randi paddled over to Fletcher. The man's eyes were open and vacant.

Randi towed Fletcher's body to me, near the cave's entrance, and we pulled him out of the water. My stomach flipped to see the dent, barely bleeding, in the man's head.

Now both breathing heavily, we stood over the body. Marley sniffed the dead man's hand. "Can't say that I'm sorry," Randi said softly.

"No, me neither." I hugged Marley. "You saved us, Cutie Bug."

"Cutie Bug? You call my eighty-pound dog Cutie Bug?"

"*Your* dog?" I said in my librarian voice, and reality came crashing back for both of us. I checked my watch. "We're running out of time. I'm going back into the other cave."

Randi threw up her hands. "What for? There's nothing there.

Besides, the tide's going to turn soon. We need to go back and meet John, then bring him back here for Fletcher's body."

"I trust Tommy Farris. If she said the treasure would be there, that's where it is. Are you coming or not?"

She stared at me for a minute, then attached the rope to Marley's collar and wrapped it around the base of a boulder near the cave's entrance. "Stay, Marley. We'll be right back. I don't want you doing a Fletcher into the pool."

Back in the water, Randi swam up close to me.

"You still need me to hold you?" I asked. "But you shot through that tunnel all by yourself when Marley was threatened."

"No time to panic then. Now I have plenty of time."

Sighing, I wrapped an arm around Randi's waist.

"I should probably tell you," Randi said softly, teeth chattering, "that if you accidentally touch my breasts or any other part of me, that's okay."

I chuckled into the back of Randi's wet head. "One, two, three."

The cave looked just as empty the second time, but we climbed up onto a shallow ledge, then followed the slope up to higher ground. I walked all around the pool shining the flashlight against the walls. Marley barked and barked as if he'd been left for dead. At least there was no one there to shoot him.

I shifted the beam when a small shape caught my eye. "Look at this." Small, round, flat. I rubbed the sand off on my shirt then whooped. It was a gold coin. Randi's eyes widened. Together we began searching the ledge and followed a trail of coins to a bend in the wall. I poked my head around and shone the light into another branch of the cave. "Mother of God." A mountain of what must have once been hundreds of wooden chests towered above me. The chests had disintegrated into mush, and their contents spilled down the sides of the pile like sand.

Stunned, we slid through the narrow opening and approached the nearest pile. The coins were crusted with minerals but Randi scraped one clean with her knife. "Stamped with a Spanish crest." Our eyes met in the dim light. "Emma, you found Tommy's treasure."

Giddy with success, I dug deeper into the pile. There were silver and gold bars, each bearing the same stamp. Some jewelry and gold trinkets were mixed in, but it was mostly bars and coins. I let the coins fall through my fingers, enjoying the satisfying tinkling as they landed on the pile.

Randi snorted. "You were so right. I was totally focused on the map, and you kept trying to convince me we had to broaden and deepen our search. Jesus, Emma, if you hadn't done that while I was searching all over this island like an idiot for over a month, we'd never have known the truth about any of this."

That felt so good I almost asked her to repeat it. "We were both right. The Farris map led to a place, and a person, and a pirate's treasure." I filled my pocket with a handful of coins.

"Are those to show John?"

"I'm not sure yet. Speaking of John, we're out of time. We have to head back." I watched as Randi returned the coins in her hand to the pile. "There's enough here that you could certainly take a few."

Randi shook her head. "Where I'm going, these coins won't do me much good. And besides, I don't need a souvenir. I'm *never* going to forget a minute of this day."

Back in the water, Randi insisted on being held again so she could close her eyes, even if the tunnel was just a hole. I suspected it was an excuse to get close to me, but I did it anyway.

A few minutes later the three of us walked through the rising tide now rushing into the mouth of the first cave, out into the sunlight, squinting against the brightness. Randi recovered first, flinging her arms wide and twirling around and around until she fell over, laughing. "You found it. You found the greatest pirate treasure ever." She got to her feet. "What's going to happen to it?" She dropped to her knees and hugged Marley. "Who has jurisdiction? This is one freak of an island. Who owns it? Carriacou? Grenada? Peru? Do you think they'll give the treasure back to Peru? Some of those people are so goddamn poor."

As I watched Randi babble and cavort like a teenager, my head and heart both realized in the same instant that Randi Marx didn't belong in prison.

She belonged on this island.

Chapter Forty-one

As we walked toward the Zodiac, I couldn't stop staring at Randi. She looked lighter than the airy foam the waves pushed gently up onto the beach.

"What?" Randi said. "You're staring." Even her voice sounded different.

"You look and sound different. Why?"

Randi stopped walking, then bent over, hands on her knees. When Randi straightened again, her eyes glistened. "It's as if I've been released from a dark prison. I don't feel obsessed about maps, about Farris, about anything anymore. I'm not even upset that I'm going back to face the music. No jail can be as controlling as my need to keep looking for that damned map. It wasn't even the treasure I was interested in, really, but it was the searching that gripped me."

"It was the ultimate scavenger hunt, one you went on without your brothers."

"But I was still competing against them," Randi said, raking back her wet hair. "Now enough analyzing. John's going to beat us to the rendezvous point and wonder what's happened to you. Hang on." We hopped in, then Randi gunned the Zodiac and took us from the cove out into the choppier water. The sea spray felt almost hot against my wet skin, and the sun was already baking my clothes dry. I felt plump and sleepy with pleasure. Not only had I found the treasure, but I'd held Randi close to me for a few seconds.

With just a few minutes to spare, Randi beached the Zodiac on the southern shore of the island. "I need to get my duffel bag from my tent." She flashed me a wide grin, complete with dimple. "Better come along to make sure I don't make a run for it."

I followed Randi into the woods. "What about your sailboat?"

"I won't need it where I'm going. I'll leave it here in case someone finds themselves marooned on the island."

As we hurried back to the beach the distant sound of a powerboat reached us. By the time we got to the Zodiac, the same powerboat that had delivered me that morning bobbed a few hundred yards from the island. Randi pushed the Zodiac out into the water. "All aboard."

But I just stood there, staring out at the boat, then back at the mountains behind me.

"Emma, as far as John knows you've drowned or drifted away. Until you get past that mist, he can't see you." Randi waved me toward the boat. "C'mon."

I stared at Randi. Why was I hesitating? Could I really be contemplating this? I had a life and a job and I couldn't tell the world to just go screw itself.

"Emma, we have to go. I don't want John to worry about you."

I shook my head slowly, then backed up beyond the tideline until I was on the dry, higher sand. "I'm not ready."

"Ready for what?" Randi helped Marley into the boat. "Look, leaving this island is hard enough. Dragging it out might kill me. Let's just get it over with."

I didn't move. John stood in the bow of the fishing boat, which bobbed just beyond the low mist.

"Emma, if you want justice for what I did, then you have to get into this boat."

Was I going to be a good little girl and return to my crappy job and my lonely house? Or was I going to do something radical and off the wall and unexpected, and then go from there? I laughed. "No. Come up here with me for a second." What had Randi said when she'd tried to get me to search for the treasure—we'd figure it out as we went along?

"Unbelievable," Randi muttered as she beached the boat again and Marley hopped out. Randi joined me up the beach, where the view of John and the boat was better. The boat circled the area, but every time it seemed to be heading for the island, an invisible force pushed it off course. The boat circled for a few minutes, then John sank onto the nearest bench, head in his hands, and motioned to the pilot.

We watched the boat grow smaller. Randi jammed her fists on

her hips. "I'm so damned confused right now, I have no idea what to think."

"Can we send a letter to John? I want him to know we're both okay."

"I sail over to Carricaou or down to Grenada every week or so."

"Good. Walk with me."

"Do you want to sail back to Carriacou on my boat? Are you letting me go? I don't appreciate being jerked around like this."

At one point a few arching palm trees created a small pocket of shade on the beach, and I sat down there, gasping at the coolness against my thighs. Randi joined me.

I gazed out at the horizon. "At first, all I wanted to do was catch Edward Drummond and put him behind bars. I wanted revenge for what 'he' had done to my books." I didn't look at Randi. "Then for the last eight weeks, I've hated you with a passion I didn't know I could feel, and I wanted revenge for what you'd done to me."

"Emma—"

I held up my hand. "I'm not used to feeling such intense emotions, and I'm feeling all worn out. I don't know how I feel anymore, about anything. But these last six hours something has shifted, and I'm not even sure how I feel about that either. But sticking you in some prison isn't going to make me happy. I don't think I'd get much pleasure from that sort of revenge." I exhaled loudly. "You're a pirate, you know. A fucking pirate. You saw something that you wanted, that wasn't yours, that belonged to someone else, and you took it. Maps *and* hearts." Randi dropped her head. "But I think you stole those things not out of maliciousness, but because of an obsession, because of a need to keep playing the scavenger hunt to beat your brothers."

"For what it's worth, I'm done with pirating. I'm hanging up my cutlass, beaching my ship and trying to figure out what my life will look like next. There'll be no more dead cats in my life."

"What?"

Randi smiled so widely the dimple went deep. "I've been thinking about this the whole time I've been on this island, and I've decided my life went very wrong because of a dead cat."

I dug my finger through the sand. "Spill it."

"Remember those scavenger lists my brothers and I used to make for each other? One day I saw a dead black and white cat on the street near our house, so I put that on my list for my brothers to find. But instead of bringing the dead cat I'd seen, Jack brought a dead orange cat, and it was still warm."

My eyes widened. "He killed a cat just for your scavenger hunt?" Randi nodded.

"That's awful. Some people will go too far to get what they want."

"Sadly, I took the opposite lesson from the dead cat. I learned from my brothers that you can *never* take things too far, that you should to do *whatever* was necessary to win. That's why one's in jail, one's heading there, and I'm here."

We watched as soft waves lapped at our heels and slid up under our calves. The water tickled the backs of my knees, and I didn't know what to say. No wonder she'd been so driven.

"Speaking of which, Emma, why *are* we here?" Randi ran a hand through her hair.

"You deserve a second chance. You aren't a bad person, you just did bad things."

"I appreciate that, but I still don't get why *you're* here. Why not go back to your life and leave me on the island?"

I'd been struggling with that very question as we sat there, and suddenly straightened up and started to laugh. Of course. Oh, my God. I flung myself back on the sand and kept chuckling. Randi stared at me as if I might be losing it. I was laughing so hard she had to help me sit back up.

"Enough laughing."

I wiped my eyes. "While you've been leading a dead cat life, I've been leading a girdle life."

"What?"

"GeeGeeBee always wore a girdle. I could see it under her dresses, and she looked nice. Then I noticed she wore the girdle under her polyester slacks, which made sense. But once, at a picnic when she was wearing jeans, I saw her adjusting the girdle. She was wearing it under jeans. Then one spring on my way home from college I dropped in without telling her, and she was ready for bed, wearing her nightgown. As I hugged her, my hand brushed against her hip and I remember shrieking 'You're not wearing that girdle to bed, are you?'

"'Emma,' she said, 'I don't dare let my body out of the girdle for longer than it takes to bathe because it won't fit back in. You gotta keep the flab under control or it'll spread out and be so happy it won't fit back into the girdle.'"

"Was she serious?"

"I think so, and that's what's happened to me. I took that trip with you, slowed down, let my life expand outside my damned Day-Timer. And now it won't fit back in. I can't make it. I don't want to." My heart pounded faster than Marley's feet as he dashed up and down the beach after seagulls. I didn't know what I wanted next, but I knew I didn't want to go back to my life. "I want something different," I said.

"And by different, you mean here, on this island, with me? But how would that work?"

"I'll call Cam and have him pack up my stuff and sell my house. He can do the same thing for you, and sell any of those maps on your walls that you actually purchased."

"I purchased all of them, but—" She held up her hand. "I'd feel better if the money went to your library. I defaced your books."

Emma nodded. "You certainly did. Fair enough. The library could use the money." When she wasn't stealing, Randi could be a generous woman. "We'll bury Fletcher's body. We'll find a way to earn a living down here. We don't need much. And we have all of Tommy's journals to read. We could write a book about Tommy and Rebekah. We have a treasure we need to return to the indigent people of Peru."

"You'd help me with that?"

"As long we don't use any of it."

Randi stood. "But I stole things. And I stole them from *you*. I shouldn't be allowed to get away with that, even if I give the library money. I hate people who think they can buy their way out of trouble."

I climbed to my feet and took Randi's face in my hands so tenderly I thought she was going to start crying again. "Your punishment has three parts. The first is to donate your map sale proceeds."

"The maps will bring about two hundred thousand dollars."

I smiled, pleased that Getty's job had just gotten easier. "Second, you live here, on this island, with me."

Randi swallowed. "Dear God, anything but that."

I laughed, then kissed her softly. "And third, you'll be the one diving into the cave and recovering the treasure."

Randi's eyes popped. "Shit." But she recovered and pulled me close, reaching for my ass.

Laughing lightly, I pulled back. "Not so fast, Captain Kidd. I'm not quite ready for that."

Randi returned my grin, then leaned forward. I knew exactly what she was going to say because it was floating through my head as well.

"While I breathe, I hope," we both said, and I slipped my hand into hers.

❖

Tommy paddled the longboat with such urgency that it surged through the water, sleek as a fish, toward the island rising up out of the mist ahead. When the boat scraped sand, Tommy thought land had never sounded so sweet. She leapt from the boat, leaving it to roll with the shallow surf, and ran up the beach.

She and Rebekah met at the tideline, eyes shining, chests heaving, then without hesitation Tommy drew Rebekah into her arms and kissed away their time apart.

When Rebekah pulled back to breathe, she touched Tommy's head where the braid once hung. "You've been through much to find me."

Tommy touched Rebekah's shirt, which couldn't hide her thinness. "As you've been through much waiting for me."

"While I breathe, I hope," they both said, smiling shyly.

Then Rebekah held out her hand. "Come, let me show you our island." Tommy grasped the waiting hand and they set off down the beach.

About the Author

Friend is the author of six children's books, including *The Perfect Nest*, illustrated by John Manders, and was awarded the 2007 Loft/McKnight Artist Fellowship in Children's Literature. Her memoir, *Hit by a Farm: How I Learned to Stop Worrying and Love the Barn*, won a 2007 Goldie, and was a finalist for both a 2007 Lambda Literary Award and the Judy Grahn Award. *The Spanish Pearl* and *The Crown of Valencia* both won 2008 Goldies. Her nonfiction book, *The Compassionate Carnivore: Or, How to Keep Animals Happy, Save Old MacDonald's Farm, Reduce Your Hoofprint, and Still Eat Meat*, was released by Da Capo in May, 2008. She's at work on another nonfiction book, but hopes to return to fiction soon.

Friend raises sheep in southeastern Minnesota with her partner of twenty-five years. Learn more about her books and her Farm Tales blog at www.catherinefriend.com.

Books Available From Bold Strokes Books

Green Eyed Monster by Gill McKnight. Mickey Rapowski believes her former boss has cheated her out of a small fortune, so she kidnaps the girlfriend and demands compensation—just a straightforward abduction that goes so wrong when Mickey falls for her captive. (978-1-60282-042-5)

Blind Faith by Diane and Jacob Anderson-Minshall. When private investigator Yoshi Yakamota and the Blind Eye Detective Agency are hired to find a woman's missing sister, the assignment seems fairly mundane—but in the detective business, the ordinary can quickly become deadly. (978-1-60282-041-8)

A Pirate's Heart by Catherine Friend. When rare book librarian Emma Boyd searches for a long-lost treasure map, she learns the hard way that pirates still exist in today's world—some modern pirates steal maps, others steal hearts. (978-1-60282-040-1)

Trails Merge by Rachel Spangler. Parker Riley escapes the high-powered world of politics to Campbell Carson's ski resort—and their mutual attraction produces anything but smooth running. (978-1-60282-039-5)

Dreams of Bali by C. J. Harte. Madison Barnes worships work, power, and success, and she's never allowed anyone to interfere—that is, until she runs into Karlie Henderson Stockard. Eclipse EBook (978-1-60282-070-8)

The Limits of Justice by John Morgan Wilson. Benjamin Justice and reporter Alexandra Templeton search for a killer in a mysterious compound in the remote California desert. (978-1-60282-060-9)

Designed for Love by Erin Dutton. Jillian Sealy and Wil Johnson don't much like each other, but they do have to work together—and what they desire most is not what either of them had planned. (978-1-60282-038-8)

Shots Fired by MJ Williamz. Kyla and Echo seem to have the perfect relationship and the perfect life until someone shoots at Kyla—and Echo is the most likely suspect. (978-1-60282-035-7)

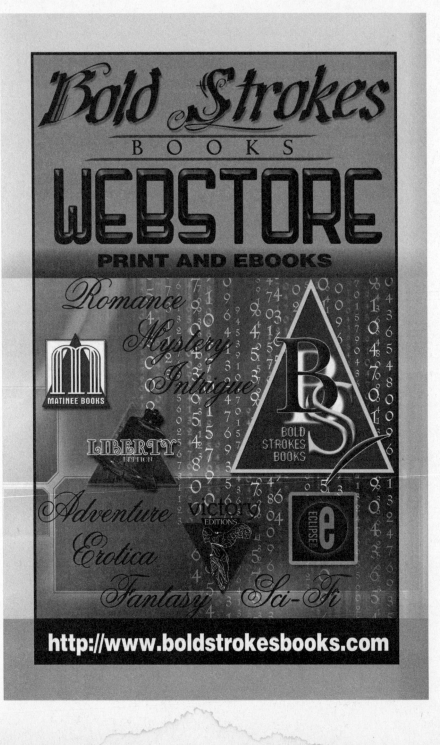